FORD MADOX FORD

Parade's End

VOLUME II

No More Parades

A Novel

Edited by Joseph Wiesenfarth

CARCANET

No More Parades was first published in Great Britain in 1925 by
Duckworth & Co.

This edition first published in Great Britain in 2011 by
Carcanet Press Limited
Alliance House
Cross Street
Manchester M2 7AQ

ISBN 978 1 84777 013 4 (*No More Parades*)
ISBN 978 1 84777 021 9 (*Parade's End* volumes I–IV)

The publisher acknowledges financial assistance from Arts Council England

Supported by
**ARTS COUNCIL
ENGLAND**

Typeset by XL Publishing Services, Tiverton
Printed and bound in England by SRP Ltd, Exeter

CONTENTS

ACKNOWLEDGEMENTS

This edition of the second novel of *Parade's End* is indebted to the unstinting care given both to it and to me by the editors of the other volumes of the tetralogy. Max Saunders (editor of *Some Do Not . . .*) and I have been discussing Ford Madox Ford, from near and afar, since we met in the mid-1980s at what is now the Carl A. Kroch Library of Cornell University. He was then at work on his definitive biography of Ford and I on Ford's friendship, personal and literary, with James Joyce. We have discussed and argued amiably over every aspect of this new critical edition of *Parade's End* generally, and of *No More Parades* particularly. His constant attention to the latter's textual annotation and its informational notes have kept us in almost daily contact as it reached completion. His contribution to it has been such that his name could easily stand next to mine on its title page.

Sara Haslam (editor of *A Man Could Stand Up –*) has directed my attention as editor of Ford's *England and the English* (Carcanet, 2003) to social matters, to passages in others of Ford's books than this one, and to textual niceties that escaped my eye. Paul Skinner (editor of *Last Post*) has given particular attention to the two longest chapters of *No More Parades* (the second chapters of Parts II and III), noting textual nuances that I missed and, as the editor of Ford's *No Enemy* (Carcanet, 2002), pointing me to military matters that improved my strategy and tactics in editing this volume. To put it in a sentence, there might have been *an* edition of *No More Parades* without my three colleagues' help, but there would not have been *this* edition of it without their help.

Finally, on the personal side, Max Saunders, Sara Haslam and Paul Skinner have literally been my eyes through weeks given to cataract surgery and my support through the sudden death of my brother – Charles J. Wiesenfarth, a meticulous craftsman with a love of precision in work and words – for whom there are no more parades but to whom this edition of Ford's novel is dedicated.

LIST OF ILLUSTRATIONS

LIST OF SHORT TITLES

Mightier	*Mightier Than the Sword* (London: Allen & Unwin, 1938)
Mister Bosphorus	*Mister Bosphorus and the Muses or a Short History of Poetry in Britain. Variety Entertainment in Four Acts… with Harlequinade, Transformation Scene, Cinematograph Effects, and Many Other Novelties, as well as Old and Tried Favourites* (London: Duckworth, 1923)
Nightingale	*It Was the Nightingale* (1933), ed. John Coyle (Manchester: Carcanet, 2007)
On Heaven	*On Heaven and Poems Written on Active Service*, The Bodley Head (London: John Lane, 1918)
Panel	*The Panel: A Sheer Comedy* (London: Constable, 1912)
People	*The Spirit of the People* (London: Alston Rivers, 1907)
Pound/Ford	*Pound/Ford: the Story of a Literary Friendship: the Correspondence between Ezra Pound and Ford Madox Ford and Their Writings About Each Other*, ed. Brita Lindberg-Seyersted (London: Faber & Faber, 1982)
Provence	*Provence from Minstrels to Machine* (1935), ed. John Coyle (Manchester: Carcanet, 2007)
Reader	*The Ford Madox Ford Reader*, with Foreword by Graham Greene, ed. Sondra J. Stang (Manchester: Carcanet, 1986)
Return	*Return to Yesterday* (1931), ed. Bill Hutchings (Manchester: Carcanet, 1999)
When Blood	*When Blood is Their Argument* (London: Hodder & Stoughton, 1915)

LIST OF MILITARY TERMS
AND ABBREVIATIONS

128s: See **A.F.B.**

A.C.I.: Army Council Instructions: the Army Council had command of the Army, and issued Orders and Instructions; the latter were more concerned with organisation, training, and logistics.

Ack emma: phonetic alphabet for a.m. (ante meridiem)

A.C.P.: Army Command Pay

Adjutant: officer whose business is to assist the superior officers by receiving and communicating orders, conducting correspondence, and the like (*OED 2 Mil.*).

A.F.B.: Army Form followed by B and a number; thus A.F.B. 128. These were called 'attestation papers' and certified the identity of a soldier, who was always to carry a copy. A duplicate copy was kept on file.

A.P.M.: Assistant Provost Marshal; one who assists a Provost Marshal, who is the head of military police in a camp or in a unit on active service and charged with the preservation of order.

A.S.C.: Army Service Corps

Bandy chair: not a chair but a seat formed by two people linking hands, crossed at the wrist; Cockney slang for a Banbury chair according to *A Penguin Dictionary of Historical Slang*.

Batman: attendant or orderly who performs a variety of tasks for the officer to whom he is assigned.

B.E.F.: British Expeditionary Force, i.e. the British army sent to France.

Casual battalion: battalion that troops pass through on their way from one station to another; a military entity that facilitates such movements of troops.

C.B.D.: Cavalry Base Depot

C.C.S.: Casualty Clearing Station

Clasp: military decoration: a bar or slip of silver fixed transversely upon the ribbon from which a medal is suspended (e.g. D.S.O with clasp); the medal being given for the whole campaign, the clasps bear the names of those significant operations in it at which the wearer was present (*OED* 6.).

Colour-sergeant (also colour-serjeant): army sergeant whose special duty is to attend the regimental colours (a flag, ensign, or standard of a regiment) in the field (*OED*).

D.C.M.: District Court-Martial

Draft: group of soldiers drawn from a larger body of men for a specific strategic or tactical purpose.

D.S.O.: Distinguished Service Order; military decoration awarded for exceptional service during combat in time of war.

Fatigues: the extra-professional duties of a soldier (*OED* 3.a.)

Flea-bag: a soldier's sleeping bag (*OED* flea 6.a.)

Garrison: body of soldiers stationed in a fortress or other place for purposes of defence, etc. (*OED* 4.†a.)

G.C.B.: Grand Commander of the Bath

G.M.P.: Garrison Military Police

G.O.C.I.C.: General Officer Commanding-in-Chief

G.S.: General Service

G.S.O.: General Staff Officer

H.E.: high explosive

H.Q.: headquarters

I.B.D.: Infantry Base Depot

Indent: to make a requisition *on* or *upon* a person *for* a thing (*OED* v.5.intr.)

K.C.M.G.: Knight Commander of St Michael and St George

Kitchener battalion: named for General Herbert Horatio Kitchener who, as Secretary of State for War during H. H. Asquith's term as Prime Minister, recruited an all-volunteer force called the New Army by way of a poster picturing him saying, in effect, Kitchener 'wants YOU / JOIN YOUR COUNTRY'S ARMY!' This New Army had no limitations on its deployment and hence, it was hoped, would provide overwhelming power against German forces.

L. of C.: lines of communication

M.C.: Military Cross; decoration awarded to men of any rank – though, at first, captain or below – who showed exemplary gallantry during battle.

Mess: each of the several parties into which a regiment or ship's company is systematically divided, the members of each party taking their meals together (*OED* 4.b.).

Militia battalion: army unit composed of ordinary citizens called up for duty as auxiliary forces rather than one composed of professional soldiers.

Mills bomb: type of hand grenade, serrated on the outside to form shrapnel on explosion, invented by Sir William Mills, 1856–1932 (*OED*).

M.O.: Medical Officer

N.C.O.: Non-Commissioned Officer; enlisted member of the armed forces, including the ranks of sergeant and corporal, who is a link between commissioned officers and the ordinary soldier.

No Man's Land: space between hostile trenches that neither warring side owned but where many on both sides died trying to capture the trench opposite.

O.C.: Officer Commanding

Parade: assembling or mustering of troops for inspection or display; especially a muster of troops that takes place regularly at set hours, or at extraordinary times to hear orders read, as a preparation for a march, or any other special purpose (*OED* 2.a.).

P.B.: permanent base

Pip emma: phonetic alphabet for p.m. (post meridiem)

P.M.: Provost Marshal. See **A.P.M.**

Quarter: short form for Quartermaster, whose duty it is to provide quarters for soldiers, to lay out a camp, and to provide ammunition, rations, and supplies of various kinds.

R.A.S.C.: Royal Army Service Corps; perhaps an anachronism since the R.A.S.C. was not formed until 1918.

R.E.B.D.: Royal Engineers Base Depot

Red Caps: nickname for Garrison Military Police, who have a scarlet flash on their caps.

R.G.A.: Royal Garrison Artillery

R.S.M.: Regimental Sergeant Major

R.T.O.: Railway Transport Officer

Soldier's Small Book: AB-50 (Army Book-50) was a 32-page book that each soldier was required to carry for purposes of identification and notation, e.g., for making out a will.

V.A.D.: Volunteer Aid Detachment

W.A.A.C.: Women's Auxiliary Army Corps, established in 1917; duties included cooking, catering, storekeeping, clerical work, maintaining motor vehicles, and a variety of other such non-combat tasks.

Warrant officer: one appointed by an official certificate who is intermediate in rank between the commissioned and non-commissioned officers (*OED*).

"THE FINEST NOVEL OF THE YEAR"

NO MORE PARADES

By

FORD MADOX FORD

Unanimous Agreement of

The New York Times:	"The most distinguished novel of the period."
The New York Herald Tribune: (Isabel Paterson)	"Far and away the finest novel of the year."
The New York Evening Post:	"On my list of the ten best novels of 1925."
The New York Sun:	"An extraordinary work."
The Philadelphia Public Ledger:	"Vigorous and pungent with life."
Louis Bromfield (Author of "Possession")	"As great as anything produced in English during the past twenty years."

(See inside flap for ot   )

INTRODUCTION

> Just as every human face differs, if just by the
> hair's breadth turn of a nostril, from every
> other human face, so every human life differs if
> only by a little dimple on the stream of it.[1]

All Rouen is divided into three parts in *No More Parades*. Part I
belongs to Christopher Tietjens; Part II to Sylvia Tietjens; and
Part III to General Lord Edward Campion. The first part finds
Tietjens at work; the second finds Sylvia at play; and the third
finds Campion sitting in judgment on them both. The subject of
all three parts is sex and death, madness and parade.[2]

The three-part structure of *No More Parades*, the second novel
of the *Parade's End* tetralogy, shows Ford's debt to Joseph Conrad,
who died on 3 August 1924. In that very month, Ford set to work
on *Joseph Conrad: A Personal Remembrance*,[3] which he finished
on 5 October 1924. He began writing *No More Parades* on 31
October 1924. The influence of the biography on the novel is
obvious. Ford makes clear in his metafictional memoir of Conrad
the individual strengths they each brought to their collaboration
on three novels: *The Inheritors* (1901), *Romance* (1903), and *The
Nature of a Crime* (1909/1924).[4] 'The writer', Ford says of himself,
'probably knew more about words, but Conrad had certainly an
infinitely greater hold over the architectonics of the novel, over

---

1 Ford Madox Ford, 'Epilogue', in Ford Madox Ford, *War Prose*, ed. Max Saunders (Manchester: Carcanet, 1999), 63.
2 Madness and parade were discussed at length by Ambrose Gordon in *The Invisible Tent: The War Novels of Ford Madox Ford* (Austin, TX: University of Texas Press, 1964), 100–18.
3 Ford Madox Ford, *Joseph Conrad: A Personal Remembrance* (London: Duckworth, 1924).
4 See Joseph Wiesenfarth, 'Ford's *Joseph Conrad: A Personal Remembrance* as Metafiction: Or, How Conrad Became an Elizabethan Poet', *Renascence*, 53.1 (2000), 43–60, for the way that Ford wrote his memoir as a novel about writing *Romance* with Conrad.

the way a story should be built up so that its interest progresses and grows up to the last word.'[5] And as the typescript of *No More Parades* shows, it took Ford a long time to get to a satisfying last word – so long a time that it had to wait for the proofs to appear.[6]

In the broad discussion of the methods he and Conrad agreed upon in writing novels, Ford insists that their strategy was 'Above All To Make You See', which is the title of the third part of *Joseph Conrad: A Personal Remembrance*. And one tactic to put a reader on the spot of the action is to tell the story in conversations. The genius of these, as he and Conrad agreed, was 'that no speech of one character should ever answer the speech that goes before it'.[7] This is so because as one person speaks, the other invariably preoccupies himself with his own thoughts on a subject unrelated to the one under discussion. For instance, although General Campion needs to pass judgment on Tietjens, he puts himself at one remove from him by sending Colonel Levin to speak for him, being too taken up with running an army to do so himself. When Levin speaks to Tietjens on matters related to Sylvia, Tietjens is offended and becomes preoccupied with the proper way to tell the colonel that he is an 'ass' without getting himself court-martialled. Thus we have many conversations that move along the action of the novel at the same time as developing nuances in the characters conversing, as we see their thoughts and feelings to be completely at odds with the matter at hand. The cogency of the three-part architectonic structure of *No More Parades*, and the marital and sexual problems whose constant discussion interferes with the various military problems of the moment, remind us that there was less than a month between Ford's finishing *Joseph Conrad: A Personal Remembrance* and his beginning to write *No More Parades*. The integration between the methodology outlined at length in the one book and the rendering of plot and incident in the other was not lost on the reviewers of *No More Parades*. Though they may not have made an explicit connection between the two books, they saw bril-

---

5 *Joseph Conrad* 169.
6 This is clearly an inference on my part because we do not have the proofs. But Ford crossed out the last word (indeed, crossed out the last seven lines) of the novel in his typescript. Consequently he had to add the last two sentences in the proofs.
7 *Joseph Conrad* 188.

liance in Ford's vividly rendering – in his making us see – his subject. And the reviewers' enthusiasm for the novel helped produce sales that exceeded its predecessor, *Some Do Not ....* [8] Indeed, for many readers *No More Parades* became their introduction to the tetralogy as a whole.

What Ford was able to do with this overall structure by dramatising the thoughts and feelings of the three main characters and those attached to or dependent upon them – with their 'interminable worry, frustration, and degeneracy'[9] – is give us 'the first mature, unbiased statement of a clear and comprehensive vision of the World War'.[10] He produced 'a novel of great distinction',[11] a novel that is 'an amazingly good, an heroic book'[12] and 'far and away the finest novel of the year'.[13] Louis Bromfield went further – and also further back – calling it 'As great as anything produced in English during the past 25 years'.[14] 'As an intellectual feat, the book has few peers', said *Time* magazine, adding that 'consummate art has converted a mountain of material into a story taut as a humming wire, though the spiritual current conducted has terrific voltage'.[15] Like these, most reviews of *No More Parades* were appreciative and laudatory. Indeed, one described it as 'probably the most highly praised novel of the year'.[16] Ford was seen as giving 'an amazing impression of war', and 'those first hundred pages easily surpass in truth, brilliance and subtlety

8 Although David Dow Harvey, *Ford Madox Ford 1873–1939: A Bibliography of Works and Criticism* (Princeton, NJ: Princeton University Press, 1962), records only one printing in England by Duckworth in 1925, there were five printings by A. & C. Boni in the United States in 1925–6 and an additional printing by Grosset & Dunop, 'by arrangement with A. & C. Boni' (n.d. but probably 1927).

9 Edward A. Weeks, *Atlantic*, CXXXVII (May 1926), 16; review of *No More Parades* excerpted in Harvey, *Bibliography* 363, #500.

10 John W. Crawford, *New York Times* (8 Nov. 1925), 9; excerpted in Harvey, *Bibliography* 361, #485.

11 Unsigned review, *The Independent*, CXV (5 Dec. 1925), 650; excerpted in Harvey, *Bibliography* 361, #488.

12 P.J.M. *Manchester Guardian* (9 Oct. 1925), 9; excerpted in Harvey, *Bibliography* 359, #478.

13 Isabel Paterson, *New York Herald Tribune* (22 Nov. 1925), 3–4; excerpted in Harvey, *Bibliography* 361, #486.

14 Bromfield, quoted in *Time* magazine (22 Feb. 1926). Not in Harvey's *Bibliography*. See http://www.time.com/time/magazine/article/0,9171,721682-1,00.html, accessed 4 February 2007.

15 *Time* magazine (22 Feb. 1926).

16 Mary Colum, *Saturday Review of Literature*, II (30 Jan. 1926), 523; excerpted in Harvey, *Bibliography* 362, #494.

everything else that has yet been written in English about the physical circumstances and moral atmosphere of the war'.[17] 'Mr. Ford has carried the traditional technique of the novel to a point not remote from absolute perfection.'[18] 'It is an astonishing method, and astonishingly effective.'[19] 'Only one writer, James Joyce, knows as much about the technique of writing English as Ford or is able to write perfectly in as many different manners.' Consequently, 'there is writing in this book to make the judicious weep – with envy'.[20] 'This is the work of a genius'; therefore, 'when most war books are forgotten "No More Parades" will survive'[21] because it is 'vivid and brilliant, and startlingly outspoken [...] a superlatively fine thing [...] written [...] with a strength which compels one's admiration'.[22] Combined with *Some Do Not ...*, its predecessor, *No More Parades* is 'already an achievement of the order of Marcel Proust's "Remembrance of Things Past"'.[23]

Ford does not give us Combray as Proust did or Swann's falling in and out of love with Odette. He gives us Tietjens' complex social and emotional attachments, first introduced in *Some Do Not ...*, in snatches of memory that set his love for Valentine Wannop against Sylvia Tietjens' hatred of him, ironically for saving her reputation from ruin. A midnight ride with Valentine contrasts vividly with Sylvia's beating a bulldog to death because it reminds her of Tietjens. As Combray disappears for Swann, London disappears for Tietjens, with death replacing love on the frozen fields of war. And what better place for every kind and variety of language than an army, with its Welsh subalterns discussing their cows and their wives, a Scots officer gone mad

17 Unsigned review, *The Observer* (11 Oct. 1925), 4; excerpted in Harvey, *Bibliography* 360, #481.
18 Lloyd Morris, 'Skimming the Cream from Six Months' Fiction', *New York Times Book Review* (6 Dec. 1925), 2; excerpted in Harvey, *Bibliography* 361, #490.
19 Gerald Gould, *Daily News* (28 Sept. 1925), 4; excerpted in Harvey, *Bibliography* 358, #472.
20 Burton Rascoe, 'Contemporary Reminiscences', *Arts and Decoration*, XXIV (Feb. 1926), 57; excerpted in Harvey, *Bibliography* 362, #495.
21 H. C. Harwood, *The Outlook*, LVI (3 Oct. 1925), 230; cited in Harvey, *Bibliography* 359, #477.
22 Ralph Strauss, *Bystander*, LXXXVII (14 Oct. 1925), 168; cited in Harvey, *Bibliography* 360, #482.
23 John W. Crawford, *New York Times* (8 Nov. 1925), 9; excerpted in Harvey, *Bibliography* 361, #495.

with the noise of war and his wife's infidelity, Tietjens' attempting to set down his relations with his wife as a military communiqué, and later, in A Man Could Stand Up –, his composing a proposal to Valentine Wannop for her to live with him in the style of a military order.[24] Then there is the overwhelming variety of military abbreviations and acronyms that give the impression of schoolboys learning their A-B-Cs, contrasted with a healthy degree of profanity among the troops that in turn squares off against officers skirmishing with each other as one writes a sonnet in English and the other translates it into Latin. And, of course, there is the expected smattering of French and German spiced with an unexpected dollop of Lancashire to confuse the minds and imaginations of even well-educated men.

This extraordinarily well-received novel opens with Captain Christopher Tietjens, ably helped by Sergeant-Major Cowley, trying to move a draft of 2,994 Canadian troops up the line from the Rouen base camp to the trenches. His efforts are blocked by having orders given and then countermanded; by having inadequate supplies for these troops from a quartermaster who profits by holding them back; by a French railway strike meant to prevent the withdrawal of British troops from the front; and by the interference of the British Garrison Police, who constantly harass the Canadian volunteers whom they wilfully take for conscripts. In addition, Campion has assigned to Tietjens' staff the shell-shocked and intermittently mad, though highly decorated, Captain McKechnie,[25] a classical scholar and proud of it. He has just returned from divorce-leave without getting a divorce. All this while Tietjens' hut is being shelled by the Germans, whose shrapnel kills O Nine Morgan. He bleeds to death in Tietjens' arms – Morgan, a Welsh soldier whom Tiet-

---

24 'Well, then, he ought to write her a letter. He ought to say: "This is to tell you that I propose to live with you as soon as this show is over. You will be prepared immediately on cessation of active hostilities to put yourself at my disposal: please. Signed, 'Xtopher Tietjens, Acting O.C. 9th Glams'."' A Man Could Stand Up – II.vi.

25 The character of McKechnie is undoubtedly drawn from that of another Scotsman whom Ford encountered at Red Cross Hospital II in Rouen and whom he describes in 'I Revisit the Riviera': 'Diagonally opposite me was a Black Watch second lieutenant—about twenty, wild-eyed, black-haired. A shell-shock case. He talked with the vainglory and madness of the Highland chieftain that he was, continuously all day. Towards ten at night he would pretend to sleep' (War Prose 64).

jens has denied leave to settle matters with his unfaithful wife in Pontardulais because he would have been beaten to death by her lover, Red Evans Williams, a prize-fighter. Morgan's marital troubles as well as McKechnie's trigger Tietjens' brooding on his own as he recalls his 'excruciatingly unfaithful' wife. She is out and about making trouble for him, after spending some time in a convent, where he 'imagined Sylvia, coiled up on a convent bed. . . . Hating . . . Her certainly glorious hair all round her. . . . Hating . . . Slowly and coldly . . . Like the head of a snake when you examined it. . . .' The result is that military work that urgently needs to be carried out is interfered with by forces both personal and impersonal. There is sex and death, madness and mayhem constantly to contend with. It is all 'intense dejection: endless muddles: endless follies: endless villainies'. There are, at the moment, for Tietjens, no more parades.

Nothing that happens here was in any way foreign to Ford. He had enlisted in the army at the age of forty-one in July 1915 and was assigned to the Welch Regiment (Special Reserve) as a second lieutenant. He was sent to Rouen, attached to the 9th battalion,[26] and then stationed with 'battalion transport, near Bécourt Wood, just behind the front line near Albert', in late July of 1916, during the Battle of the Somme. There he was blown up by a German shell, lost his memory for three weeks, and could not remember his name for the better part of two days. In hospital he saw a soldier die '*very* hard, blood pouring thro' [his] bandages'. Ford himself, like McKechnie, suffered debilitating shell-shock, which lasted long after he was discharged in January 1919, if H. G. Wells is to be believed: 'The pre-war F.M.H. was tortuous but understandable, the post-war F.M.H. was incurably *crazy*.'[27] Ford was nonetheless sent to the Ypres Salient in late August 1916, where, among other things, he did not get on with his Commanding Officer. But he was unable to obtain a transfer to a staff job, working with an intelligence unit, because his German ancestry was deemed an obstacle to such a position. Consequently, he was on the scene of the two bloodiest actions of the Great War.

26 Saunders, Introduction, *War Prose* 3.
27 Max Saunders, *Ford Madox Ford: A Dual Life*, 2 vols (Oxford: Oxford University Press, 1996), II, 2, 3, 31.

Ford (on the right) with fellow officers of the Welch regiment.
Courtesy of the Carl A. Kroch Library, Cornell University, Ithaca,
New York

Prior to his enlistment, Ford had separated from his wife, Elsie
Martindale, and had been living with Violet Hunt. She proved
to be, in part, an adequate model for Sylvia, being as sexually
ravenous towards him as she was antagonistic, writing in her diary
for 21 August 1917, 'I hit him & then took him to bed.'[28] If Violet
did not visit Ford at the Front, she made herself present there by
sending her novel, *Their Lives*, for him to write a preface, which
he did under the pseudonym 'Miles Ignotus'.[29] In the last novel
of the tetralogy, *Last Post*, Sylvia does in fact invade Tietjens' and
Valentine's country house in an attempt to disrupt their union.[30]
In addition, while living with Stella Bowen and writing *No More
Parades*, Ford had an affair with Jean Rhys, who dramatised it in
her particularly vindictive novel *Quartet*.[31] Put briefly, Ford knew
enough of sex and death, madness and mayhem to give us the
three different parts of *No More Parades* with the authenticity of
life itself. What Sylvia and Campion do, then, can surprise no
one who is aware of Ford's pre-war life, of his service in the British
Expeditionary Force in France and Belgium, and of his complicated love affairs after his demobilisation in January 1919.

Sylvia Tietjens appears on the scene in Part II of *No More
Parades*. She comes to France without passport and papers,
convinced that the war is a schoolboys' game played in order to
seduce and rape women. Her supposed purpose is to have Christopher sign a document, which in fact requires no signature, that
gives her the legal right to live at Groby, his estate, and makes
their son Michael successor to it. But the real purpose of her
extraordinary adventure is to seduce the husband whom she has
not slept with for five years: 'By God, if that beast does not give

---

28 Robert and Marie Secor, *The Return of the Good Soldier: Ford Madox Ford and Violet
    Hunt's 1917 Diary*, English Literary Studies No. 30 (Victoria, BC: University of
    Victoria, 1983), 73.
29 On Ford and Hunt's love (and hate) affair, see Joseph Wiesenfarth, *Ford Madox Ford
    and the Regiment of Women: Violet Hunt, Jean Rhys, Stella Bowen, Janice Biala* (Madison,
    WI: University of Wisconsin Press, 2005), 30–60.
30 Violet Hunt invaded Ford's and Stella Bowen's country house in Bedham in the
    autumn of 1920 when Stella was pregnant with her daughter Julie. Hunt also hired
    some locals to send reports to her about Ford and Bowen's life together. Her intrusion
    on them there clearly inspired Sylvia's intrusion on Tietjens in Rouen and on Tiet-
    jens and Valentine in *Last Post*. See Saunders, *Dual Life* II 101–2, 249–50;
    Wiesenfarth, *Regiment* 59–60.
31 On the Ford–Rhys affair, see Wiesenfarth, *Regiment* 61–89.

in to me tonight he never *shall* see Michael again.' But Tietjens' interest in Sylvia evaporated entirely with her disappearance into a convent of Premonstratensian nuns near Birkenhead. His mind and heart have now settled on Valentine Wannop, who had agreed to be his lover at the end of *Some Do Not . . .* although he has never even kissed her. Sylvia nevertheless contrives to get Tietjens to her bedroom at the same time that a former lover and an aspiring seducer appear there, only to have Tietjens forcibly eject them, which brings about his arrest.

This leaves matters in the hands of General Campion in Part III. He has to determine whether Tietjens is guilty of manhandling superior officers without cause and whether he is also guilty of a handful of other accusations that have been made against him as the action of the novel unfolds. Not insignificantly, in the three days that the novel covers, Parts I and II are set in the dead of night and deal with troop movements and shellings as well as with seduction and rape. Part III is set in the morning light; it deals with clarification and inspection. Having satisfied himself of the baselessness of charges against Tietjens, Campion puts Tietjens' cook-houses on parade: 'a mustering of troops for inspection and display'.[32] In an epiphanic moment, Tietjens sees the pomp and circumstance of this parade as a funeral.

All of which is to say that both Mars and Eros make demands on Christopher Tietjens in *No More Parades*. The army requires him to feed, shelter, and transport a draft of Canadian troops. His wife requires him to settle their marital and family affairs. The problems that beset him in attending to these matters are so many that he is unable to get to bed for two nights running and fears for his sanity. 'The martial and the marital: sex and violence' threaten his body and mind.[33] At his weakest moment Tietjens is forced to deal with the importunities of the God of War and the God of Love together, when his godfather, General Officer Commanding-in-Chief Lord Edward Campion, questions him about his marriage and announces his promotion to a post that entails 'certain death'. This deadly posting as second-in-command of Colonel Partridge's regiment in the 6th battalion of

---

32 Parade (*OED* 2.a.)
33 Saunders, Introduction, *War Prose* 19.

General Perry, commanding the 16th section, comes about
because Tietjens has made his life an insoluble riddle to
Campion: Tietjens cannot join the general's staff because that
would smack of nepotism; he cannot join the 9th French Army
because a confidential report, prepared by Sylvia's former lover,
Colonel Drake, accuses him of being a French spy; he cannot be
sent to the 19th Division of the Fourth Army because Lord
Beichan, a meddling newspaper mogul, has placed Second-
Lieutenant Hotchkiss in charge of hardening horses for combat.
Tietjens despises both men and their works: 'In their hearts these
people are crass cowards walking in darkness.'[34] But he cannot
stay where he is, doing the splendid job he is doing, because he
has physically attacked General O'Hara of the Garrison Police,
throwing him out of Sylvia's bedroom at three in the morning.
Campion tells Tietjens that 'all the extraordinary rows you've got
into ... block me everywhere'. And because Tietjens, no more
than Campion, cannot find a way away from death, the general's
order becomes Tietjens' riddle: How can one be 'promoted' to
'certain death'? It reminds us of the question Sergeant-Major
Cowley poses twice in the novel: '"Do you know the only time
the King must salute a private soldier and the private takes no
notice? ... When 'e's dead...."'

Tietjens falls victim to Campion's riddle of promotion to
death because he has not solved a riddle of his own: 'For it's insoluble. It's the whole problem of the relations of the sexes.'[35] This
problem is personalised for Tietjens in his inability to determine
'the paternity of his child': to determine whether he or Drake is
the father of Sylvia's son, Michael. Moreover, no one in the novel
has solved the problem of 'the relations of the sexes', but Tietjens is the one who pays the price for their failure because,
presumably, in being a Christ-bearer (a Christopher) he must
fulfil the words spoken about Jesus: 'They used to say: "He saved
others, himself he could not save."' Sylvia, who speaks these
words, enumerates the 'others' whom Tietjens has saved: '"He
helped virtuous Scotch students, and broken-down gentry....

---

34 'Preparedness', in *War Prose* 72.
35 Ford was not proficient at solving this riddle either. He was said to have been involved
   romantically with eighteen women and, perhaps, with eleven of them sexually. See
   Wiesenfarth, *Regiment* 97.

And women taken in adultery...."' Sylvia alludes to Tietjens'
saving of Vincent Macmaster, Mrs Wannop, and Edith Ethel
Duchemin in *Some Do Not* .... And *No More Parades* shows him
continuing such activities. He saves the Canadian volunteers
arrested by O'Hara's military police; he saves Cowley from lone-
liness by celebrating his promotion to lieutenant with him; he
saves Colonel Levin's betrothal party from disaster by promising
'the disagreeable duchess' at Lady Sachse's, bargain-priced coal
for her hot houses; he saves Sylvia from ignominy by refusing
Campion's offer of a court-martial to clear his own name by
soiling his wife's reputation. Campion sums up Tietjens' abilities
clearly when he praises him: "'He's got a positive genius for
getting all sort of things out of the most beastly muddles.... Why
he's even been useful to me.'" The other side of it is that Tietjens
has got a "'positive genius for getting into the most disgusting
messes"'. To Campion "'Christopher is a regular Dreyfus.'" Sylvia
makes a similar claim. She tells Cowley of Tietjens that "'They
used to call him Old Sol at school.... But there's one question
of Solomon's he could not answer.... the one about the way of
a man with ... Oh, a Maid! Ask him what happened before the
dawn ninety-six – no ninety-eight days ago...."' Ninety-eight
days previously at dawn Christopher had heard Sylvia direct a
taxi driver to Paddington Station, where she was to take the train
to Birkenhead and enter a convent.

The word *Paddington* echoes through *No More Parades*. It is the
keynote of Tietjens' freedom. He interprets it as Sylvia's giving
him leave to love Valentine Wannop. But Sylvia has changed
her mind and is on the scene again; consequently, *Paddington*
becomes Tietjens' riddle. What does it mean?

But he *had* noticed the word Paddington.... Ninety-eight
days before.... She had counted every day since.... She had
got that much information.... She had said *Paddington*
outside the house at dawn and he had taken it as a farewell. He
had ... He had imagined himself free to do what he liked with
the girl.... Well, he wasn't.... That was why he was white
about the gills....

Tietjens sees that Sylvia has contrived to make a scene 'before

the Tommies of his own unit. . . . It was a game. What game? . . .
What then was the game? He could not believe that she could be
capable of vulgarity except with a purpose.' Her game is his seduction. But as Tietjens tells Campion, Sylvia has been too artful in
her attempt: she has pulled one shower-bath string too many and
given him a deadly dousing. Playing bedroom games with Major
Perowne and General O'Hara sends her husband 'up the line' and
out of her reach. *Paddington* proves a fatal word. It forces him to
save her, but himself he cannot save.

Failure to solve the riddle entails 'certain death' because of
Tietjens' bad health. If he is not killed in the line, his lungs – 'all
charred up and gone'[36] – are certain to give way, and even if they
don't he suspects that his mind will. So *No More Parades* is a
death-haunted novel. It begins with a death and ends with a
funeral. O Nine Morgan is hit by shrapnel and dies in Tietjens'
hut; in fact, in his arms, bleeding his life away on Tietjens' best
tunic. Tietjens is obsessed by O Nine Morgan's death throughout
the novel. It recurs to him so insistently that he fears that he has
a 'complex'; indeed, he fears for the balance of his mind. And
Morgan's death spreads out beyond itself to encompass the deaths
of many others when, in a lyrical passage, Tietjens meditates on
the spectacle of loss:

> at the thought of the man as he was alive and of him now, dead,
> an immense blackness descended all over Tietjens. He said to
> himself: *I am very tired.* Yet he was not ashamed. . . . It was the
> blackness that descends on you when you think of your
> dead. . . . It comes, at any time, over the brightness of sunlight,
> in the grey of evening, in the grey of the dawn, at mess, on
> parade; it comes at the thought of one man or at the thought
> of half a battalion that you have seen, stretched out, under
> sheeting, the noses making little pimples; or not stretched out,
> lying face downwards, half buried. Or at the thought of dead
> that you have never seen dead at all. . . . Suddenly the light
> goes out. . . . In this case it was because of one fellow, a dirty

36 Ford's words in a letter of 19 December 1916 to Joseph Conrad about his own lungs
in *Letters of Ford Madox Ford*, ed. Richard M. Ludwig (Princeton: Princeton University Press, 1965), 79; the ampersand in the original quotation has here been changed
to 'and'.

enough man, not even very willing, not in the least endearing,
certainly contemplating desertion.... But your dead ... *yours*
... your own. As if joined to your own identity by a black
cord.... [37]

What Tietjens experiences here is what moved Ford to write that
'every human life differs if only by a little dimple on the stream
of it' and moved him further to quote Ecclesiasticus in the
epigraph of the novel:[38] 'For two things my heart is grieved: A
man of war that suffereth from poverty and men of intelligence
that are counted as refuse.' The 'man of war' here is Captain Tietjens himself, who is impoverished by his wife Sylvia: 'she had
drawn all the balance of his banking account except for a
shilling'. And as one of the 'men of intelligence' mentioned by
Sirach, he is counted as refuse by his commanding officer,
General Campion: 'he is unsound. He's too brilliant.' At the same
time that they treat him as they do, Tietjens values a man of intelligence in McKechnie, mad as at times he may be, and men of
war in Sergeant-Major Cowley and the 2,994 soldiers whom he
has under his command. Indeed, the entire novel is a complex
dramatisation of its epigraph. And insofar as Tietjens is treated
as refuse, he becomes nothing more than what Ford termed 'the
stuff to fill graveyards'.[39]

Moreover, insofar as Tietjens' 'certain death' is foreseen in his
posting to the line, the last parade in the book is appropriately a
funeral; indeed, his funeral. The Tory gentleman, the Anglican
saint, must now perish at the front. That persona must die and
be buried if Tietjens is to rise again. He cannot come back as an
eighteenth-century landholder but must come back as a twentieth-
century working man. That, however, strikes Tietjens as

37 Ford wrote about his own experience of mass death in 'Arms and the Mind/War and
    the Mind', saying: 'And there is no emotion so terrific and so overwhelming as the
    feeling that comes over you when your own men are dead. It is a feeling of anger ...
    an anger ... a deep anger! It shakes you like a force that is beyond all other forces in
    the world: unimaginable, irresistible....' (*War Prose* 41).
38 Ford attributes the epigraph to Proverbs (his title page reads 'Prov. II vii' after the
    quotation), but the quotation is from the Book of Sirach (Ecclesiasticus) 26:28, which
    is 'modelled in great part on Proverbs' according to Alexander A. Di Lella, O.F.M. in
    Bruce M. Metzger and Michael D. Coogan, eds, *The Oxford Guide to the Bible* (Oxford:
    Oxford University Press, 1993), 697.
39 *Thus to Revisit* (London: Chapman & Hall, 1921), 203.

reprehensible. 'Reprehensible! . . . He snorted! If you don't obey the rules of your club you get hoofed out, and that's that!'[40] To be reprehensible is to cast off an outmoded code of conduct and to take command of one's self and live. *Reprehensible* is the saving word. What *Paddington* is to *No More Parades*, *Reprehensible* is to *A Man Could Stand Up –*. The former is death-dealing; the latter is life-giving. 'He was going to write to Valentine Wannop: "Hold yourself at my disposal. Please. Signed . . ." Reprehensible!'[41] But before he can do that there must first be a death of a kind and a funeral of a kind. These begin with the inspection of the cook-houses in which Campion is described as a godhead, Sergeant-Cook Case as his high priest, and the cook-houses themselves as a cathedral. There is an insistence in the novel that soon there will be no more parades at all, civilian or military. This last parade, Tietjens' burlesque funeral, follows upon Campion's rejection of Tietjens' insistence that a gentleman must keep up the parade of his wife's honour, even if she is a sadistic whore, by not divorcing her: '"no man that one could speak to would ever think of divorcing any woman"'. Campion dismisses out of hand this parade as rubbish: '"then there had better be no more parades. . . . Why *don't* you divorce?"' Campion sees that Tietjens' parade of Sylvia's honour has contributed to his inability to solve the riddles that cost him his life.

But, in fact, Tietjens, as *A Man Could Stand Up –* will show us, does not die; but he does go directly to hell in *No More Parades*:

> *Es ist nicht zu ertragen; es ist das dasz uns verloren hat* . . . words in German, of utter despair, meaning: It is unbearable: it is that that has ruined us. . . . The mud! . . . He had heard those words, standing amidst volcano craters of mud, among ravines, monstrosities of slime, cliffs and distances, all of slime [. . .] and the slime moved [. . .] The moving slime was German deserters. . . . You could not see them: the leader of them—an officer!—had his glasses so thick with mud that you could not see the colour of his eyes, and his half-dozen decorations were like the beginnings of swallows' nests, his beard like stalac-

tites. . . . Of the other men you could only see the eyes—extraordinarily vivid: mostly blue like the sky! [. . .] In advanced
pockets of mud, in dreadful solitude amongst those ravines . . .
suspended in eternity, at the last day of the world. And it had
horribly shocked him to hear again the German language a
rather soft voice, a little suety, like an obscene whisper. . . . the
voice obviously of the damned; hell could hold nothing
curious for those poor beasts. . . . His French guide had said
sardonically: *On dirait l'Inferno de Dante!*

This infernal vision of what Tietjens is to go to contrasts radically
with the supernal vision of what he has come from.

Tietjens had walked in the sunlight down the lines, past the
hut with the evergreen climbing rose, in the sunlight, thinking
in an interval, good-humouredly about his official religion:
about the Almighty as, on a colossal scale, the great English
Landowner, benevolently awful, a colossal duke who never left
his study and was thus invisible, but knowing all about the
estate down to the last hind at the home farm and the last oak;
Christ, an almost too benevolent Land-Steward, son of the
Owner, knowing all about the estate down to the last child at
the porter's lodge, apt to be got round by the more detrimental
tenants; the Third Person of the Trinity, the spirit of the estate,
the Game as it were, as distinct from the players of the game;
the atmosphere of the estate, that of the interior of Winchester
Cathedral just after a Handel anthem has been finished, a
perpetual Sunday, with, probably, a little cricket for the young
men. Like Yorkshire of a Saturday afternoon; if you looked
down on the whole broad county you would not see a single
village green without its white flannels. That was why Yorkshire always leads the averages. . . . Probably by the time you
got to heaven you would be so worn out by work on this planet
that you would accept the English Sunday, for ever, with
extreme relief!

Heaven and hell: the country estate and the battlefield: the
cricket pitch and the trenches. Heaven is gone and hell is here.
The contradiction inherent in the heaven of the one – especially

since country estates have fallen into the hands of the Macmasters and the Beichans and will fall into the hands of the De Bray Papes in *Last Post* – has bred the hell of the other. Now there is only one more parade to attend. That is the inspection of the cook-houses when the godhead – 'Major-General Lord Edward Campion, V.C., K.C.M.G., tantivy tum, tum, etcetera'[42] – descends to officiate at Tietjens' funeral:

> The general tapped with the heel of his crop on the locker-panel labelled PEPPER: the top, right-hand locker-panel. He said to the tubular, global-eyed white figure beside it: 'Open that, will you, my man? . . .'
>
> To Tietjens this was like the sudden bursting out of the regimental quick-step, as after a funeral with military honours the band and drums march away, back to barracks.

After his funeral Tietjens is transported to the trenches for burial, and *A Man Could Stand Up* – begins. And he is buried there in mud by an exploding shell, but rises from it to take command of himself and his battalion and become admirably . . . *reprehensible*: 'Reprehensible! He said. For God's sake *let* us be reprehensible! And have done with it!'[43] Once that choice is made, clearly, for Christopher Tietjens, there are no more parades.

42 *A Man Could Stand Up* – III.i.
43 *A Man Could Stand Up* – II.vi.

A NOTE ON THIS EDITION
OF *PARADE'S END*

This edition takes as its copy-text the British first editions of the four novels. It is not a critical edition of the manuscripts, nor is it a variorum edition comparing the different editions exhaustively. The available manuscripts and other pre-publication materials have been studied and taken into account, and have informed any emendations, all of which are recorded in the textual notes.

The British first editions were the first publication of the complete texts for at least the first three volumes. The case of *Last Post* is more complicated, and is discussed by Paul Skinner in that volume; but in short, if the British edition was not the first published, the US edition was so close in date as to make them effectively simultaneous (especially in terms of Ford's involvement), so there is no case for not using the British text there too, whereas there are strong reasons in favour of using it for the sake of consistency (with the publisher's practices, and habits of British as opposed to American usage).

Complete manuscripts have survived for all four volumes. That for *Some Do Not* ... is an autograph, the other three are typescripts. All four have autograph corrections and revisions in Ford's hand, as well as deletions (which there is no reason to believe are not also authorial). The typescripts also have typed corrections and revisions. As Ford inscribed two of them to say the typing was his own, there is no reason to think these typed second thoughts were not also his. The manuscripts also all have various forms of compositor's mark-up, confirming what Ford inscribed on the last two, that the UK editions were set from them.

Our edition is primarily intended for general readers and

students of Ford. Recording every minor change from manuscript to first book edition would be of interest to only a small number of textual scholars, who would need to consult the original manuscripts themselves. However, many of the revisions and deletions are highly illuminating about Ford's method of composition, and the changes of conception of the novels. While we have normally followed his decisions in our text, we have annotated the changes we judge to be significant (and of course such selection implies editorial judgement) in the textual notes.

There is only a limited amount of other pre-publication material, perhaps as a result of Duckworth & Co. suffering fires in 1929 and 1950, and being bombed in 1942. There are some pages of an episode originally intended as the ending of *Some Do Not . . .* but later recast for *No More Parades*, and some pages omitted from *Last Post*. Unlike the other volumes, *Last Post* also underwent widespread revisions differentiating the first UK and US editions. Corrected proofs of the first chapter only of *Some Do Not . . .* were discovered in a batch of materials from Ford's *transatlantic review*. An uncorrected proof copy of *A Man Could Stand Up* – has also been studied. There are comparably patchy examples of previous partial publication of two of the volumes. Part I of *Some Do Not . . .* was serialised in the *transatlantic review*, of which at most only the first four and a half chapters preceded the Duckworth edition. More significant is the part of the first chapter of *No More Parades* which appeared in the *Contact Collection of Contemporary Writers* in 1925, with surprising differences from the book versions. All of this material has been studied closely, and informs our editing of the Duckworth texts. But – not least because of its fragmentary nature – it didn't warrant variorum treatment.

The only comparable editing of Ford's work as we have prepared this edition has been Martin Stannard's admirable Norton edition of *The Good Soldier*. Stannard took the interesting decision to use the text of the British first edition, but emend the punctuation throughout to follow that of the manuscript. He makes a convincing case for the punctuation being an editorial imposition, and that even if Ford tacitly assented to it (assuming he had a choice), it alters the nature of his manuscript. A similar argument could be made about *Parade's End* too. Ford's punctuation is certainly distinctive: much lighter than in the published

versions, and with an eccentrically variable number of suspension dots (between three and eight). However, there seem to us
four major reasons for retaining the Duckworth punctuation in
the case of *Parade's End*:

1) The paucity of pre-publication material. The existence of
an autograph manuscript for *Some Do Not* ... as opposed to
typescripts for the other three raises the question of whether
there might not have existed a typescript for *Some Do Not* ...
or autographs for the others. Ford inscribed the typescripts of
A Man Could Stand Up – and *Last Post* to say the typing was
his own (though there is some evidence of dictation in both).
The typescript of *No More Parades* has a label attached saying
'M.S. The property of / F. M. Ford'; although there is nothing
that says the typing is his own, the typing errors make it
unlikely that it was the work of a professional typist, and we
have no reason to believe Ford didn't also type this novel. So
we assume for these three volumes that the punctuation in the
typescripts was his (and not imposed by another typist), and,
including his autograph corrections, would represent his final
thoughts before receiving the proofs. However, without full
surviving corrected proofs of any volume it is impossible to be
certain which of the numerous changes were or were not
authorial. (Janice Biala told Arthur Mizener that 'Ford did his
real revisions on the proofs – and only the publishers have
those. The page proofs in Julies' [*sic*] and my possession are the
English ones – no American publisher had those that I know
of.'[44] However, no page proofs for any of the four novels are
among her or Ford's daughter Julia Loewe's papers now at
Cornell, nor does the Biala estate hold any.)

2) Ford was an older, more experienced author in 1924–8 than
in 1915. Though arguably he would have known even before
the war how his editors were likely to regularise his punctuation, and had already published with John Lane, the first
publisher of *The Good Soldier*, nevertheless by 1924 he

44 Biala to Arthur Mizener, 29 May 1964, Carl A. Kroch Library, Cornell University;
quoted with the kind permission of the estate of Janice Biala and Cornell University.

certainly knew Duckworth's house style (Duckworth had published another novel, *The Marsden Case*, the previous year). More tellingly, perhaps, Ford's cordial relations with Duckworth would surely have made it possible to voice any concern, which his correspondence does not record his having done.

3) On the evidence of the errors that remained uncorrected in the first editions, the single chapter proofs for *Some Do Not...*, and Ford's comments in his letters on the speed at which he had to correct proofs, he does not appear to have been very thorough in his proofreading. Janice Biala commented apropos *Parade's End*:

> Ford was the worst proof reader on earth and knew it. Most of the time, the proofs were corrected in an atmosphere of [...] nervous exhaustion & exaperation [sic] with the publisher who after dallying around for months, would suddenly need the corrected proofs 2 hours after their arrival at the house etc, etc, you know.[45]

At the least, he was more concerned with style than with punctuation.

4) Such questions may be revisited should further pre-publication material be discovered. In the meantime, we took the decision to retain the first edition text as our copy-text, rather than conflate manuscript and published texts, on the grounds that this was the form in which the novels went through several impressions and editions in the UK and the US during Ford's lifetime, and in which they were read by his contemporaries and (bar some minor changes) have continued to be read until now.

The emendations this edition has made to the copy-text fall into two categories:

---

45 Biala to Arthur Mizener, 29 May 1964, Carl A. Kroch Library, Cornell University; quoted with the kind permission of the estate of Janice Biala and Cornell University.

1) The majority of cases are errors that were not corrected at proof stage. With compositors' errors the manuscripts provide the authority for the emendations, sometimes also supported by previous publication where available. We have corrected any of Ford's rare spelling and punctuation errors which were replicated in the UK text (the UK and US editors didn't always spot the same errors). We have also very occasionally emended factual and historical details where we are confident that the error is not part of the texture of the fiction. All such emendations of the UK text, whether substantive or accidental, are noted in the textual endnotes.

2) The other cases are where the manuscript and copy-text vary; where there is no self-evident error, but the editors judge the manuscript better reflects authorial intention. Such judgements are of course debatable. We have only made such emendations to the UK text when they are supported by evidence from the partial pre-publications (as in the case of expletives); or when they make better sense in context; or (in a very small number of cases) when the change between manuscript and UK loses a degree of specificity Ford elsewhere is careful to attain. Otherwise, where a manuscript reading differs from the published version, we have recorded it (if significant), but not restored it, on the grounds that Ford at least tacitly assented to the change in proof, and may indeed have made it himself – a possibility that can't be ruled out in the absence of the evidence of corrected proofs.

Our edition differs from previous ones in four main respects. First, it offers a thoroughly edited text of the series for the first time, one more reliable than any published previously. The location of one of the manuscripts, that of *No More Parades*, was unknown to Ford's bibliographer David Harvey. It was brought to the attention of Joseph Wiesenfarth (who edits it for this edition) among Hemingway's papers in the John Fitzgerald Kennedy Library (Columbia Point, Boston, Massachusetts). Its rediscovery finally made a critical edition of the entire tetralogy possible. Besides the corrections and emendations described above, the editors have made the decision to restore the expletives that are frequent in the typescript of *No More Parades*, set at the Front, but which were replaced with dashes in the UK and US book editions. While this decision may be a controversial one, we believe it is justified by the previous publication of part of *No More Parades* in Paris, in which Ford determined that the expletives should stand as accurately representing the way that soldiers talk. In *A Man Could Stand Up* – the expletives are censored with dashes in the TS, which, while it may suggest Ford's internalising of the publisher's decisions from one volume to the next, may also reflect the officers' self-censorship, so there they have been allowed to stand.[46]

Second, it presents each novel separately. They were published separately, and reprinted separately, during Ford's lifetime. The volumes had been increasingly successful. He planned an omnibus edition, and in 1930 proposed the title *Parade's End* for it (though possibly without the apostrophe).[47] But the Depression intervened and prevented this sensible strategy for consolidating his reputation. After Ford's death, and another world war, Penguin reissued the four novels as separate paperbacks.

The first omnibus edition was produced in 1950 by Knopf. This edition, based on the US first editions, has been reprinted exactly in almost all subsequent omnibus editions (by Vintage, Penguin, and Carcanet; the exception is the new Everyman edition, for which the text was reset, but again using the US edition texts). Thus the tetralogy is familiar to the majority of its readers, on

---

46 If the decision to censor the expletives in *No More Parades* is what led Ford to use euphemistic dashes in the typescript of *A Man Could Stand Up* –, that of *Last Post* complicates the story, containing two instances of 'bloody' and two instances of 'b—y'.

47 Ford wrote to his agent: 'I do not like the title *Tietjens Saga* – because in the first place "Tietjens" is a name difficult for purchasers to pronounce and booksellers would almost inevitably persuade readers that they mean the Forsyte Saga with great damage to my sales. I recognize the value of Messrs Duckworth's publicity and see no reason why they should not get the advantage of it by using those words as a subtitle beneath another general title, which I am inclined to suggest should be *Parades End* so that Messrs Duckworth could advertise it as PARADES END [TIETJENS' SAGA]'. Ford to Eric Pinker, 17 Aug. 1930: *Letters* 197. However, the copy at Cornell is Janice Biala's transcription of Ford's original. The reply from Pinkers is signed 'Barton' (20 Aug. 1930: Cornell), who says they have spoken to Messrs Duckworth who agree with Ford's suggested title; but he quotes it back as 'Parade's End' with the apostrophe (suggesting Biala's transcription may have omitted it), then gives the subtitle as the 'Tietjen's Saga' (casting his marksmanship with the apostrophe equally in doubt). These uncertainties make it even less advisable than it would anyway have been to alter the title by which the series has been known for sixty years.

both sides of the Atlantic, through texts based on the US editions. There were two exceptions in the 1960s. When Graham Greene edited the Bodley Head Ford Madox Ford in 1963, he included *Some Do Not ...* as volume 3, and *No More Parades* and *A Man Could Stand Up* – together as volume 4, choosing to exclude *Last Post*. This text is thus not only incomplete but also varies extensively from the first editions. Some of the variants are simply errors. Others are clearly editorial attempts to clarify obscurities or to 'correct' usage, sometimes to emend corruptions in the first edition, but clearly without knowledge of the manuscript. While it is an intriguing possibility that some of the emendations may have been Greene's, they are distractions from what Ford actually wrote. Arthur Mizener edited *Parade's End* for Signet Classics in 1964, combining the first two books in one volume, and the last two in another. Both these editions used the UK texts. Thus readers outside the US have not had a text of the complete work based on the UK text for over sixty years; those in the US, for forty-five years. Our edition restores the UK text, which has significant differences in each volume, and especially in the case of *Last Post* – for which even the title differed in the US editions, acquiring a definite article. This restoration of the UK text is the third innovation here.

With the exception of paperback reissues of the Bodley Head texts by Sphere in 1969 (again excluding *Last Post*), the volumes have not been available separately since 1948. While there is no doubt Ford intended the books as a sequence (there *is* some doubt about how many volumes he projected, as the introduction to *Last Post* discusses), the original UK editions appeared at intervals of more than a year. They were read separately, with many readers beginning with the later volumes. Like any writer of novel sequences, Ford was careful to ensure that each book was intelligible alone. Moreover, there are marked differences between each of the novels. Though all tell the story of the same group of characters, each focuses on a different selection of people. The locations and times are also different. In addition, and more strikingly, the styles and techniques develop and alter from novel to novel. Returning the novels to their original separate publication enables these differences to be more clearly visible.

Parade's End in its entirety is a massive work. Omnibus editions

of it are too large to be able to accommodate extra material. A
further advantage of separate publication is to allow room for the
annotations the series now needs. This is the fourth advantage of
our edition. Though *Parade's End* isn't as difficult or obscure a
text as *Ulysses* or *The Waste Land*, it is dense with period references, literary allusions, and military terminology unfamiliar to
readers a century later. This edition is the first to annotate these
difficulties. One feature revealed by the annotations to *Some Do
Not . . .* is how steeped it is in the literary culture of Englishness.
One might not have expected Ford, the apostle of Flaubert and
Turgenev and international literary experiment, to refer so
frequently to R. S. Surtees, Rudyard Kipling, George Borrow,
Gilbert White, and even George Herbert. While some of these
recur in the later volumes, the density of reference to them here,
alongside Pre-Raphaelites and the obligatory Shakespearean
allusions, show Ford thinking himself back, from the perspective
of post-war France, into the pre-war English literary world.[48]

To keep the pages of text as uncluttered as possible, we have
normally restricted footnotes to information rather than inter-
pretation, annotating obscurities that are not easily traceable in
standard reference works. English words have only been glossed
if they are misleadingly ambiguous, or if they cannot be found in
the *Concise Oxford Dictionary*, in which case the *Oxford English
Dictionary* (or occasionally Partridge's *Dictionary of Slang*) has
been used. *Parade's End* is, like Ford's account of *The Good Soldier*,
an 'intricate tangle of references and cross-references'.[49] We have
annotated references to works by other writers, as well as relevant
biographical references that are not covered in the introductions.
We have also included cross-references to Ford's other works
where they shed light on *Parade's End*. To avoid duplication, we
have restricted cross-references to other volumes of the tetralogy
to those to preceding volumes. These are given by Part- and
chapter-number: i.e. 'I.iv' for Part I, chapter IV. We have,
however, generally not noted the wealth of cross-references
within the individual volumes.

---

48 See *Ford Madox Ford and Englishness*, ed. Dennis Brown and Jenny Plastow, International Ford Madox Ford Studies, 6 (Amsterdam and New York: Rodopi, 2006).
49 'Dedicatory Letter to Stella Ford', *The Good Soldier*, ed. Martin Stannard (New York
   and London: W. W. Norton & Company, 1995), 5.

Works cited in the footnotes are given a full citation on first appearance. Subsequent citations of often-cited works are by short titles, and a list of these is provided at the beginning of the volume. A key to the conventions used in the textual endnotes appears on p. 249.

Tietjens said:

"He still sends money to his sister."

The general said:

"I can't understand why he doesn't marry the doxy/... He went absent over her when he was colour-sergeant and was reduced to the ranks... Twenty years ago that must be.... Yes, I'll see your cook-houses. I bet you I catch you out."

Tietjens said:

"I respectfully bet that if you do I find an excuse..."

They moved towards the door side by side. The general tapped Tietjens on the shoulder with the horn handle of his crop.

"I wanted to ask you something before we go...", he said. "You know everything..." He said: "By the bye... With your health... I'm bound to say it's alarmed me... you can be in hospital in ten days after you reach your battalion..."

Tietjens said:

"Oh I can last two months of it, sir. I know myself..."

The general said:

"I'm damned sorry... But... Damn it it sounds a callous thing to say we must take the rough with the smooth. We're both soldiers, you and I. *If one does what one likes one must take what one gets for it.*

Tietjens said:

"I wish you would not worry, sir. I've figured it out very careful I shall last two months. The German offensive cannot begin before the 17th of March. They have to re-train their men to use the rifle It'll be me for Blighty before then. After quite a quiet time. Besides you will *a we shall* have the single command by the middle of February...
The Germans will make their great break through in March."
The general said; his jaw fallen down.

A NOTE ON THE TEXT OF
NO MORE PARADES AND THE
HISTORY OF ITS COMPOSITION

Description of the Typescript

A typescript of *No More Parades*, with Ford's handwritten corrections, is housed in the Hemingway Collection at the John Fitzgerald Kennedy Library in Boston, Massachusetts. Hemingway edited the *transatlantic review* while Ford was away in the United States for some months in 1924. Ford may have presented this corrected typescript as a token of his appreciation to his co-editor.

According to Ford's numbering of them there are 294 leaves of typescript from the half-title page to the second-last sentence of the novel (the last sentence does not appear in the typescript). The actual number of leaves is 322, if one excludes the cover in the count. The difference in numbering can be accounted for by Ford's inserting leaves as A, B, C without changing page numbers. After leaf 8, for instance, appear leaves 8A, 8B, 8C, 8D, 8E, 8F, and 8G before we get to a leaf numbered 9. In another instance we have a single leaf numbered 23–24 (evidently because the original leaf 22 was removed; the original leaf 23 renumbered as 22; and the original leaf 24 redesignated 23–24). This kind of re-numbering occurs occasionally throughout the typescript, but is particularly notable in the first and the last chapters, which gave Ford the most trouble in getting them precisely the way he wanted them to read. Instances of such numbering practices account for the discrepancy between Ford's page-count and the actual number of leaves in the typescript.

Unlike the other two *Parade's End* typescripts, that for *No More Parades* does not bear Ford's inscription stating that it was the version used by the publisher to set the novel. However, the compositor's mark-up (detailing font sizes, removing many of Ford's capitalisations and expletives, and so on) throughout show that this must have been the case, and that any subsequent revisions between the typescript and first edition must have been made on the proofs.

I was not able to look through the original typescript in the Hemingway Collection; indeed, touching the typescript itself was prohibited. But I was permitted to have a photocopy of it made, and I have used that in establishing this critical edition of *No More Parades*. Very few, if any, passages were unreadable as a result of my not having access to the original typescript.

Kept with the typescript of *No More Parades* is an odd item that Ford may have sent with it to Hemingway. This is an advertisement for a Fairview Mausoleum that was printed in *The New York World* and reads: 'Let Those Whom You Love Repose in Sunshine'.[50] The subtitle continues the pitch even more extravagantly: '*Think! Will you let your loved ones moulder in the grave, or will you give them the imperial eternal entombment of the world's greatest leaders—of a Lincoln or a Grant?*' Across the top of this full-page advertisement, just above a particularly melodramatic drawing, are written these words, which appear to be in Ford's hand: 'Prepare for the Resurrection'. This may have been Ford's way of dealing with a novel about a war in which both he and Hemingway fought and were wounded, but in which millions of others died and were buried in unmarked graves. If so, it would be an ironic comment on a novel that is itself filled with irony.

Biographical Context and History of Composition

Shortly before Ford began writing *No More Parades*, he and Stella Bowen left Boulevard Arago on Paris's Left Bank, where he had finished *Some Do Not . . . .* Money was tight. Thomas Seltzer, his American publisher, had not paid Ford for that novel or for copies of the *transatlantic review*, which his firm was distributing in the United States. The *review* was already in financial difficulties,

50 This issue of *The World* is dated 4 May 1925. The advertisement is on p. 7.

and Ford and Bowen were subsidising it themselves. They took a 'poky little flat'[51] in Rue Denfert-Rochereau in Montparnasse before moving on to a more spacious studio-flat in Rue Notre Dame des Champs. Meanwhile they were entertaining friends at the *Bal du Printemps*, just behind the Pantheon, a *bal musette*: 'a little café where there is an accordion player, sometimes with cymbals tied between his knees and bells upon his ankles, sitting above the dance floor on a raised seat or gallery'.[52] It was a simple café that doubled as a working-class dance hall. Though usually closed on Fridays, Ford got the owner to open it for them, so that he and Bowen could hold weekly parties there in the evening.

They also sought out a place more suitable to their life as artists as well as their life as parents. Esther Julia, their daughter, born on 29 November 1920, was now four years old. At the suggestion of Gertrude Stein, they hit upon Guermantes, a tiny village about an hour by train from Paris. There they found 'an old stone labourer's cottage with four rooms and a small orchard, to let for five hundred francs a year. We took it as a kind of insurance against complete homelessness', Bowen remarked.[53] They installed Julie there with Madame Annie, 'a lively little widow of forty with a formidable temper', to look after her.[54] They moved between the village and Paris, spending weekends at Guermantes and then longer stretches when the summer was over. It was as remote as 'the centre of the bogs of Ireland', according to Ford;[55] but in 'pleasant country of an insignificant sort', and 'not far from Paris and just this side of the devastated zone'.[56] It was at Guermantes that much of the writing of *No More Parades* was done.

Although Ford had been trying to find further American backing for the *transatlantic review*, he had to abandon it after December 1924. His tribute to Conrad, published in the September issue, caused a controversy when Jessie, Conrad's widow, wrote to the *Times Literary Supplement* contesting Ford's

51 Stella Bowen, *Drawn from Life* (London: Collins, [1941]), 125.
52 Bowen, *Drawn from Life* 129.
53 Bowen, *Drawn from Life* 123.
54 Bowen, *Drawn from Life* 122.
55 *Ford Madox Ford Reader*, with Foreword by Graham Greene, ed. Sondra J. Stang (Manchester: Carcanet, 1986), 488.
56 Ford to Scott-James, 3 Feb. 1925; *Letters* 165–6.

account of his and Conrad's collaboration. The loss of the *transatlantic* and the dispute about his fictional memoir *Joseph Conrad: A Personal Remembrance* weighed upon Ford. In addition, sickness contributed to the sombre atmosphere. On Christmas Eve he told Sisley Huddleston that they had 'been rather under the clouds of a house full of grippe & coughs for nearly a month', but were 'making efforts to celebrate Xtmas with a tree for Esther Julia, rather lastminuteish'.[57] It was in these hectic times that Jean Rhys came onto the scene to complicate further this already complicated state of affairs.[58]

Rhys arrived about the time that Ford began *No More Parades* in October 1924,[59] introduced to him by Mrs Pearl Adam, a journalist and writer, who sought to relieve Rhys's penury by having Ford publish some of her stories or find a publisher for them. He did both and apparently fell in love with her too, she becoming his mistress all too quickly. On 28 December 1924 Rhys's Dutch husband, Jean Lenglet, was arrested for embezzling and sent to Paris's Santé prison for six weeks before his trial. Rhys was poor, ill, and desperate; possessed, Bowen wrote, of 'nothing but a cardboard suit-case and the astonishing manuscript' of 'an unpublishably sordid novel of great sensitiveness and persuasiveness'.[60] This had been called 'Suzy Tells' by Mrs Adam, but Ford renamed it 'Triple Sec'. The later and more astonishing novel that Rhys published after her falling-out with Ford was *Postures*, retitled as *Quartet*. It severely damaged his reputation since he appears in it as H. J. Heidler, a heartless seducer and faithless husband of a compliant wife.

In the 1970s Rhys recalled that the second time she met Ford and Stella they invited her to live with them. When Lenglet was tried on 10 February 1925 and sentenced to eight months' imprisonment, Rhys was already with them. Ford wrote to his agent William Aspenwall Bradley on 25 January 1925 that 'Miss Rhys

---

57 Ford to Huddleston, 24 Dec. 1924 (Harry Ransom Memorial Library, Austin, Texas); quoted in Saunders, *Dual Life* II 281.

58 On the Ford–Rhys affair, see Wiesenfarth, *Regiment* 61–89.

59 Carole Angier, Rhys's biographer, estimates that Ford 'met Jean in the autumn, probably in October; at the end of that month he began *No More Parades*'. *Jean Rhys: Life and Work* (Boston: Little, Brown, 1990), 131.

60 Bowen, *Drawn from Life* 166.

is here but has been too ill to do anything about that ms'. Stella was also ill and Ford was doing all the cooking and housework; nevertheless, he continued to write *No More Parades* and offered 'to send the mss along in chunks' to Bradley.[61] Whereas Ford was ready to deal directly with Duckworth, he wanted Bradley to handle the American rights with Seltzer, whom he refused to talk to.

At the end of the dedicatory letter to William Bird, the UK edition gives the dates for the writing of *No More Parades* as 'PARIS, 31 *October*, '24—GUERMANTES, 25 *May*, '25'. However, the end of the same letter in the typescript gives a different ending date: '25 March, '25'. This date was when he told his friend Jeanne Foster that he had corrected the last draft and sent it to the publisher.[62] The 25 May date is thus likely to be when he had the novel back to correct in proofs; probably the first set, the unpaginated 'slip proofs', since, as he wrote to Bradley from Paris almost a month later:

I left the page proofs of No More Parades on [*sic*] you yesterday evening [...]

I think it is really quite a good book which is a relief to me, for it seemed to me to be appalling in slip proofs and I have been going about in a state of deep depression. But in page proof it really seems to be something heavy and gloomy and big. So I may yet knock spots off Mr. Dostoevski, though that secret ambition of mine should be kept between ourselves.[63]

---

61 *Reader* 487–8.
62 Ford to Foster, 26 Mar. 1925, written from 16 rue Denfert-Rochereau; 'A Portrait of Ford Madox Ford: Unpublished Letters from the Ford–Foster Friendship', ed. Janis and Richard Londraville, *English Literature in Transition*, 33:2 (Feb. 1990), 180–207 (189–90). The cover of the TS gives a third date for completion: '25/4/25'. Either this or the 25 March date would have made it possible for Ford to give a copy of the typescript to Hemingway with the lugubrious advertisement from *The World* in a timely fashion. Of course, Ford could have given him the TS any time after the compositor had finished with it and sent the page from the newspaper along with it or sent it at another time altogether.
63 Letter of 21 June 1925, *Reader* 489. The 'slip proofs' (also known as 'galley proofs') were the unpaginated first proofs taken from the galleys (trays the type was set in) onto long slips of paper; major revisions could be made at this stage without causing the work to be repaginated. Once any such revisions were incorporated the text was divided into pages for the page proofs. That Ford made changes in the proofs is particularly evident in III.ii where a significant number of passages that were not deleted in the typescript were deleted in the first edition, as the textual notes show.

Fortunately for Ford, the reviewers of *No More Parades* agreed
with him. Edwin Muir was reminded of Prince Myshkin and
Nastasya in Dostoyevsky's *The Idiot*.[64] Others compared the
novel's brilliance to the genius of Joyce and Proust.[65] The physical hardship and emotional turmoil that surrounded the writing
of *No More Parades*, therefore, did not prove detrimental to – and
may finally even have contributed to – its success.

No More Parades was first published by Duckworth in the UK
in late September 1925; and then by A. and C. Boni in the US
in late November of the same year.[66] It was the only volume of
Parade's End to be translated during Ford's lifetime. A Russian
version (which there is no record of Ford knowing about)
appeared in 1928 as *Parad litzemeriya* (literally 'A Parade of
Hypocrisy'). It was translated into French as *Finis, les parades* in
1933.[67]

The Nature of the Revisions

When editing the text of *No More Parades* from the typescript,
using the first British edition as copy-text,[68] a variety of problems
emerges. Simply paging through the typescript, two things are
dramatically apparent. First, Ford deleted many passages after he
wrote them; second, he inserted additions that range from a word
or two here and there to pages of closely handwritten paragraphs
that are often difficult to read. For example, he cut nine sections
out of I.i, amounting to some seventy-five lines or two-and-a-half
double-spaced typewritten pages. And he inserted one section of

64 Edwin Muir, *The Nation and Athenaeum*, 38 (31 Oct. 1925), 186; excerpted in Harvey,
    Bibliography 360, #483.
65 See Introduction to this volume.
66 The first review of UK in Harvey's *Bibliography* is dated 28 September; the first review
    of US, 22 November (64–5). Edwin Muir mentioned the book as 'a remarkable work'
    in the *Nation* (New York), 121 (18 Nov. 1925), 577. But as this was in a review titled
    'British Books: Autumn', he was presumably using the UK edition, which he had
    reviewed fully in the *Nation and Athenaeum*, 38 (31 Oct. 1925), 186. The closeness of
    US to UK, and the two-month gap between the two, makes it probable that US was
    set from UK.
67 Прад лицемерия, trans. K. Zhikharevoy (Leningrad: Proboy, 1928). *Finis, les parades*,
    trans. Fernande Bogatyreff and Georges Pillement (Paris: Librairie de la Revue
    Française, 1933).
68 Ford Madox Ford, *No More Parades* (London: Duckworth, 1925).

one-and-a-half handwritten pages that, if typed, would at least equal the deletions. The manuscripts of all four volumes of *Parade's End* bear traces of such revisions, of different kinds (including a variant ending for *Some Do Not . . .* ; a possible substitution of a later draft of a large part of *A Man Could Stand Up –*; and an entire deleted extended scene in *Last Post*). But arguably in the heavily revised first and last chapters of *No More Parades* Ford's process of rewriting is most visible, and the revisions among the most intensive. There are both typed and autograph additions to the typescript, indicating changes made at different stages. The autograph insertions are more numerous and more substantial, and are often complete sentences, or clauses added to the ends of sentences to give them that 'final tap' that Ford said had been Conrad's main contribution to their early collaborative novel *The Inheritors*.[69] They frequently end with exclamation marks, giving the passage a final flourish as well. Some of the most memorable passages of *No More Parades* were the result of such revisions, as, for example, in the case of Tietjens' haunting memories of the death of O Nine Morgan at the beginning and end of I.iv. All the significant deletions and insertions are recorded in the endnotes, but some instances that especially illuminate his creative process are described here.

Ford once remarked that he and Conrad would, on occasion, close their eyes and randomly strike out lines of the book they were working on. He concluded that this practice, indiscriminate as it was, invariably improved the telling of the tale. There is, however, nothing blind or haphazard about the deletions he made in *No More Parades*. Each crossing-out either eliminates a passage that might seem repetitive or eliminates details that delay the march of events. Sometimes the deletions do both simultaneously. For instance, the first chapter finds Captain Tietjens in a hut close to the front line with Captain McKechnie (misnamed Mackenzie until I.iii),[70] who has been sent to Tietjens for him to

---

69 *Joseph Conrad* 136. The typed insertions (presumably made as instantaneous afterthoughts while Ford was typing the first draft) are generally slighter; usually a word or a few words, and only occasionally a whole line. Only the longer or more significant of these have been recorded.

70 'The hut was unreasonably warm: He had invited Mackenzie—whose real name turned out to be McKechnie, James Grant McKechnie—to occupy the other end of it.'

monitor because McKechnie has gone mad as a result of an aborted divorce-proceeding in England and the horrific noise of battle that he has just returned to in France. The first British edition has Tietjens saying to McKechnie:

> "Look here, pull yourself together. Are you mad? Stark, staring? ... Or only just play-acting?"
> The man suddenly sank down on the bully-beef case that served for a chair. He stammered a question as to what— what—what Tietjens meant.
> "If you let yourself go," Tietjens said, "you may let yourself go a tidy sight farther than you want to."
> "You're not a mad doctor," the other said. "It's no good your trying to come it over me."

Ford cut nineteen lines out of the typescript version of this passage. They dilated on two different kinds of madness, one of which manages to include bizarre references to the 'Emperors of China and Queen Victoria' in its exposition. The nineteen lines amplified the problem of madness but did nothing to move things along as speedily as necessary given that German bombs are exploding around them. Later when McKechnie returns to the 'mad doctor' accusation and Tietjens answers him, Ford deletes another five lines. No need for him to deny his psychiatric credentials twice. This is just one set of instances of the way that some of the deletions work.

A significant handwritten addition to the typescript in I.i is inserted to substantiate Ford's sense that soldiers always fight on two fronts simultaneously.[71] The insertion takes the reader from the actual war where shrapnel is flying about to the war at home that can make soldiers mad with worry. As Ford notes in his dedicatory letter, he is writing about 'mostly emotional struggles— since as a rule for every twenty minutes of actual fighting you were alone with your emotions, which being English, you did not express, for at least a month!' To complicate Tietjens' worries,

71 See TS 12a and 12b (both autograph manuscript), which became UK 22–5 from 'Tietjens laughed' to 'as a whore'. See especially UK 22, last paragraph ('Tietjens laughed') to the end of the first sentence on the top of UK 23: 'at a distance'. The remainder goes on to show Sylvia's antics and how they occupy Tietjens' mind and feelings.

Ford's additions to the text show him vividly imagining Sylvia's transgressions by dramatically indicating her glittering social life, her brazen infidelities, and her matchless cunning. These vivid recollections and the worry they bring just about drive Tietjens mad until Sergeant-Major Cowley interrupts his thoughts with a call to immediate duties. Having just seen McKechnie as crazed, we now see why Tietjens should be going crazy too. But duty refuses him the leisure to do so. That is why McKechnie, his senior officer, isn't in command and Tietjens is.

There are no substantive deletions or insertions in I.ii, but I.iii is a different story. There Ford has Tietjens reviewing his marriage to Sylvia, which requires some summaries of scenes from *Some Do Not . . . .* Writing this chapter involved Ford adding and deleting passages. Typescript leaves 78a, 78b, 78c, 78d, and 78E comprise Tietjens' determined effort to give an exact account of his life with Sylvia by writing it as 'a report for use of garrison headquarters' on 'the history of himself in his relationship with his wife . . . and to Miss Wannop, of course'. The only significant deletion in this segment comes on 78d–78E when Tietjens decides 'He was no writer and this writing gave no sort of psychological pointers.' The long deleted passage of twenty-three lines recapitulates his principles, his argument with Sylvia, his meeting Valentine in St James' Park, and his making an assignation with her for that evening. Like the report itself, it provides no psychological insight and delays the process of more efficiently reviewing the reasons for Sylvia's visit to Rouen. The major deletions in this chapter are there for the same reason – they are of elements that would otherwise delay the action with details, such as trying to determine who did or did not say 'So long' before Tietjens left for France. These deletions, comprising some 128 lines, amount to just about five pages in a chapter of some twenty-seven leaves. In other words, Ford cuts about the same amount of material as he adds to the typescript on the lettered leaves that follow the one numbered 78.

The only other chapter of *No More Parades* that is replete with deletions and insertions is III.ii, the last chapter of the novel. This is so thickly lined with stricken passages and inserted handwritten additions that, for an editor, it is like dealing with barbed wire and occasional explosions (of Ford's sudden insights). It contains some 200 deleted lines as well as another 100 or so lines that were neither deleted from the typescript nor printed in the Duckworth first edition. That means that the equivalent of nearly eleven typescript pages of the sixty-four leaves do not appear in the first edition. In addition, among that total of sixty-four leaves there are seven handwritten leaves of insertions, which is by far the largest number in any chapter of the typescript.

The problem that Ford was having with this last chapter is that Campion has to find a way to deal with Tietjens after Tietjens has ejected Major Perowne and General O'Hara from Sylvia's hotel bedroom in Rouen, having at that time threatened to have O'Hara, the head of Garrison Police, arrested if he did not leave. Campion as commanding officer of the garrison feels that he must act to restore order. But he is also Tietjens' godfather, committed by Tietjens' deceased mother, whom Campion adored, to watching over her son. Because of the trouble that Sylvia has stirred up in Rouen, because of the lies that she has told previously about her husband, because her one-time lover, Colonel Drake, has also spread lies about Tietjens being a French spy, because a man named Ruggles spread libellous rumors that Tietjens sold Sylvia for sex and wasted his fortune on women, because Tietjens has defied Lord Beichan in refusing to 'harden' horses, and because Tietjens has constantly defended the Canadian volunteers under his command against O'Hara's police, Campion feels that Tietjens must leave the Rouen base and go elsewhere. The places where Tietjens might go are exhaustively canvassed and rejected one by one. Campion's logical conclusion is that the only place he can send Tietjens is 'up the line' and back to his battalion. This he pronounces a 'promotion', but it is more nearly a death sentence.

Ford's constant tinkering with the text of this chapter, then, deals with both Campion and Tietjens being caught in this trap of events. Their thoughts, their feelings, their differing individual senses of honour, their deceptions and their lies have constantly to be articulated, refined, and presented in a believable way. That Ford left passages in the typescript that do not appear in the first edition means further changes were made in the proofs (none of which have survived), almost certainly by Ford. That he crossed out the last sentences of the typescript and added a final sentence to the proofs shows how intent he was to get the ending precisely right. That he did get it precisely right is suggested by the way *A Man Could Stand Up* – begins with Valentine Wannop telling Miss Wanostrocht that her leaving the 'Great Public School (Girls')' "is, you know, rather more my funeral than yours'". *No More Parades* ends with what can be considered Tietjens' funeral. This new couple to be, then, have both died to the thoroughly corrupt and hypocritical world that brought about the war that comes to an end of sorts on Armistice Day, the day *A Man Could Stand Up* – begins. They are both born again that day to a life of singularly shocking integrity.

Further Changes during Duckworth's Editing

Deletions and additions are one thing; an author's style and his publisher's style are another. One need not compare more than a few pages of Duckworth's printed text with Ford's typescript to see the difference. They have a glaringly different sense of capitalisation, and the publisher has much greater faith in the efficacy of commas than the author. Some spellings were routinely converted into the house style. Where Ford uses 'shewed', Duckworth emends it to 'showed'. Duckworth is also certain that its editor can spell better than its author. Having published extensively with Duckworth previously, Ford knew that alterations in these matters were inevitable. Consequently, he simply turned his mind to the things I have indicated in his deletions and additions. But there are significant discrepancies in what Ford wrote and what Duckworth published. These are deliberate changes in transcription, if not errors.

Duckworth seemed wary of naming places that could in any way offend anyone in the place named. Thus we read in the printed text:

There was a quartermaster in a west country cathedral city who'd got more D.S.O.'s and combatant medals than anyone on active service in France, from the sea to P[é]ronne, or wherever our lines ended. His achievement was to have robbed almost every wretched Tommie in the Western Command of several weeks' separation allowance ... for the good of the taxpayer, of course.

Ford had named this 'west country cathedral city' – the circumlocution is not the author's, but the editor's – writing: 'There was a quartermaster in Shrewsbury...' God forbid that Duckworth should offend and lose a reader in Shrewsbury! One sees the deletion of proper names frequently. When Sylvia comes to visit and torment Tietjens in Rouen, Duckworth allows only one mention of the city when the typescript has several. Lord Beichan (whose name Ford altered from Breighan, which he repeatedly crossed through, writing Beichan above it) was a Welsh peer: specifically a Jewish peer from Caernarvon who owns a newspaper. Tietjens refers to him as 'the Carnarvon Israelite newspaper proprietor peer' (I.iv), which Duckworth changes to 'the newspaper proprietor peer'. Tietjens despises Beichan because he wants to put military horses into a 'hardening' regime and has had a Lieutenant Hotchkiss appointed to carry out this plan. Tietjens, who knows more about horses than either Beichan or Hotchkiss, simply will not allow this to be done because it sickens and kills the horses. Duckworth seems willing to put up with Tietjens' anger at Lord Beichan and Hotchkiss, but not with his anger at a Welsh peer from a specific town who is Jewish and owns a newspaper. In a word, where Ford wants to be specific, Duckworth wants to be general. Whereas Ford seems willing to offend specific constituents, Duckworth is not. An interest in sales trumps the colour of the text. This becomes glaringly evident in the proliferation of dashes that we constantly meet as we read.

Expletives

The censorship laws presented a problem to any novelist wanting to give verisimilitude to a rendering of soldiers' language.[72] As St John Ervine wrote of Frederic Manning's *Her Privates We* (1930):

---

72 J. H. Willis, Jr, describes 'a growing number of serious works of fiction that tested and protested the limits of acceptable language in the Anglo-American literary communities patrolled by repressive vice societies citing outdated obscenity laws': 'The Censored Language of War: Richard Aldington's Death of a Hero and Three Other War Novels of 1929', *Twentieth Century Literature*, 45:4 (winter, 1999), 467–87.

'His soldiers speak as soldiers did speak. His men go into action and die, as men did go into action and die, with oaths on their lips and blasphemies on their tongues.'[73] And as the war books boom reached its crescendo, many writers expressed their awareness of the issue. R. H. Mottram's method was either to use dashes ('d——d'; 'b——') or to draw attention to the censoring more self-consciously by writing 'Blank me' or 'Aren't there any blank orderlies on these dashed trains?'[74] Ford's friend Richard Aldington told his editor in 1928 that he was writing all the swear words into *Death of a Hero*, but that they could be taken out later to avoid prosecution.[75] Ford appears to have tolerated Duckworth doing the same thing when he wrote *No More Parades* three years earlier, but we have no documentation to attest to it. We only have the dashes in UK to suggest his submitting to it. The British and American expatriates in Paris were perhaps especially aware of this linguistic flux that the war had begun and that its fiction was continuing through the 1920s. Archibald Lyall, in his book *It isn't done; or, the future of taboo among the British islanders*, observed that 'in 1927 Mr Robert Graves referred to two of the most strictly tabooed words as "x–ing" and "y–ing". By 1929 he had progressed to "b–ing" and "f–ing".' He went on to note that Frederic Manning's *The Middle Parts of Fortune* (published anonymously at first as by 'Private 19022') did print the words in full, but this edition (of 1929) was sold only to subscribers and never appeared in that form in bookshops.[76]

It is scarcely surprising, then, that Duckworth played it safe, censoring words that might risk offending readers or incurring prosecution. The result of such squeamishness is that the conversation of soldiers is peppered with dashes. Thus we get this exchange between two Welsh soldiers:

73 Ervine, 'Do Our Publishers Really Know their Job', *Daily Express*, 30 Jan. 1930, 6. Cited by Andrew Frayn, 'Writing Disenchantment: The Development of First World War Prose, 1918–1930' (unpublished PhD thesis, University of Manchester, 2008).
74 Mottram, *The Spanish Farm Trilogy 1914–1918* (London: Chatto & Windus, 1927), 282, 761, 490, 382.
75 Richard Aldington to E. L. Skinner of Allen & Unwin, 17 Nov. 1928: University of Reading.
76 Lyall, *It isn't done* (London: Kegan Paul, Trench and Trubner, 1930), 51–2. The expurgated version of Manning's book was published in 1930 as *Her Privates We*. The first edition of Lawrence's *Lady Chatterley's Lover*, also from this crucial period, had to be published in Florence, and would not be published in the UK until 1960.

"Lost the ——, they 'ave," the runner from Rhondda made his voice startlingly heard [. . .]

"No reason," his mate from Pontardulais rather whined in his sing-song, "why the bleedin' searchlights, surely to goodness, should light us up for all the —— 'Un planes to see."

Ford had written this: 'Lost the *buggers*, they 'ave.' [. . .] 'why the bleedin' searchlights, surely to goodness, should light us up for all the *fuckin'* 'Un planes to see.'

Or there is this: "For God's sake, sergeant-major, stop these —
—. I'm too —— drunk to halt them. . . ." Ford wrote: "For God's sake, sergeant-major, stop these buggers. I'm too bloody drunk to halt them. . . ." And so it goes on throughout the entire novel.

Such profanity is what we would expect in the trenches and its use sustains the realism of the moment. But wherever these words appear they are replaced by a dash. It's hard to imagine why 'bloody' isn't permitted to soldiers, since it was permitted to Eliza Doolittle in Bernard Shaw's *Pygmalion* the year before the war began.[77] We know that Ford countenanced such strong language appearing in a published text because he used it in a somewhat shorter version of this chapter that had appeared previously in the *Contact Collection of Contemporary Writers* in 1925.[78] Consequently, the profanity has been restored in this edition to replace dashes without a textual note to indicate each instance.

There are significant differences in the first chapter of *No More Parades* as it appears in the *Contact Collection* as against how it appears in the first British edition. For instance, changes of single words are numberless. More dramatically, what appears on pages 19–25 in the British first edition (a discussion of McKechnie's madness and Tietjens' competence to deal with it and a description of Sylvia's beauty, her hatred of Tietjens, and her social appearances) does not appear in the *Contact Collection*. And pages 30–35 of the British first edition (Tietjens' conversation

77 E. S. Turner, *Dear Old Blighty* (London: Michael Joseph 1980), 16, refers to 'the succinct comment popularized that summer [1914] in Shaw's *Pygmalion*, "not bloody likely"'.
78 *Contact Collection of Contemporary Writers*, ed. Robert McAlmon (Paris: Contact Editions, 1925), 57–74.

with McKechnie about the depredations of the War Office in London and of the quartermaster in Rouen) are also omitted in the *Contact Collection*, as is any mention of McKechnie as a Latin scholar.

The *Contact Collection* was published in June 1925, at least three months ahead of UK.[79] However, it is impossible to determine whether it represents an earlier draft of the opening, or a revised version of the typescript. We don't know when it was drafted, or when submitted. If it was written before the typescript, it would date from before the end of October 1924, and be likely to have been submitted in late 1924 (which is relatively early given the publication date, though not impossible). However, there is no compelling indication in the typescript of any insertion of a revised version of the early part of the novel.[80] This suggests either that the *Contact* fragment was not an earlier version, or that, if it were, Ford immediately rewrote the first chapter before continuing with the typescript. In that case he would surely have wanted to submit the revised opening instead, which there would have been plenty of time to do. Indeed, since we now know that Ford completed the typescript in March, there would still have been time to resubmit the revised opening for *Contact*. If, as these arguments suggest, the *Contact* fragment was cut and revised from the typescript (whether taken from a carbon of the typescript, or a retyped version of it), without a manuscript or proofs for it we don't know whether the cuts (or even the revisions) were authorial or were made by the volume's editor, Robert McAlmon. Either way, the two publication processes appear to have been running in parallel (possibly with Ford correcting the proofs differently for each version). The crucial point is that the *Contact* version included the expletives, in the same month that Ford returned the final proofs for UK which (almost certainly) replaced them with dashes. In the typescript the expletives have

---

79 See Donald Gallup, *Ezra Pound: A Bibliography* (Charlottesville, VA: University Press of Virginia, 1983), 148.

80 The last page of I.i is numbered 30; the first page of I.ii has no typed number; the second page was numbered 31; which was then altered by hand to 31A when the unnumbered page was given the number 31. But as Ford had missed numbers from the first pages of four chapters in the MS of *Some Do Not . . .*, this omission is unlikely to signify a break in the composition.

been crossed out, and replaced with what is clearly the compositor's mark-up for the dashes rather than Ford's revision. Thus, though he appears to have acquiesced in Duckworth's practice, and perhaps accepted their commercial wisdom, the *Contact Collection* demonstrates that he could take a very different view of the question.

Aside from the house's style trumping the author's style, there are errors in transcription by the compositor of UK that further compromise the soundness of the text. For instance, Ford develops a motif of horses in *Parade's End*. There is in *Some Do Not ...* a serious incident in which General Campion, a notoriously bad driver, runs his motor-car into a horse and cart carrying Tietjens and Valentine Wannop. In a war in which motorised vehicles were insufficient in number, horses were an important element of transport. And Sylvia Tietjens, notable on horseback, is always turned out elegantly on her mount. As Tietjens thinks about her in the passage that Ford added in longhand to the first chapter of *No More Parades*, he recalls her vividly in the Duckworth edition in this way: 'She appeared before him so extraordinarily bright and clear in the brown darkness that he shuddered: very tall, very fair, extraordinarily fit and clean even. Thoroughbred!' 'Clean even' is distractingly absurd as well as unidiomatic (as if there might be something remarkable in a woman as well turned-out as Sylvia having taken a bath). What Ford wrote was 'clean run', which describes a perfectly elegant horse. Clearly, Sylvia here is such a mare, so to speak, as the word 'Thoroughbred!' in a sentence all its own makes clear. This small mistake in transcription disrupts the imagery of the moment and interferes with a motif of the novel as a whole.[81] Although they do not survive – or at least have not been found – we know that Ford read two sets of proofs for *No More Parades*. But that such a

---

81 In I.iii.79 Ford has Tietjens thinking about Sylvia: 'She was a thoroughbred. He had always credited her with being that. And now she was behaving as if she had every mean vice that a mare could have. Or it looked like it. Was that, then, because she had been in his stable?' In addition, in passages that he deleted from the typescript, this imagery recurs: 'If for instance a fellow kept a thoroughbred in his stable and let it develop all sorts of vices, that was about the worst thing he could do.' 'But damn it, she had always looked so perfectly fit, so perfectly clean-run, so absolutely without vice, using the word in the horsey sense.'

mistake as this was allowed to stand suggests that Ford did not read them carefully enough.[82]

A significant error on the compositor's part suggests the same thing. Ford wrote dedicatory letters by way of prefaces to the last three novels of *Parade's End*. That in *No More Parades* is addressed to William Bird. The last two paragraphs begin with the word 'So'. The published text omits the penultimate paragraph, which bears on an important point in the novel; indeed, on the very point that the letter to Bird addresses. Ford indicates in it that the thoughts and words of his characters are theirs, not his, though reviewers tended to lay both at his feet in reviews of *Some Do Not . . . .* When in *No More Parades* he has Tietjens misquote King's Regulations and General Campion misquote *Henry V*, Ford has them do so because he had never met an officer who could quote either accurately. He therefore tells Bird that 'if I represent [Campion] as saying what the Swan of Avon wrote, I might satisfy one reviewer, but, as an artist, I should never hold up my head again'. The fact that the two paragraphs begin in the same way suggests that the compositor omitted it due to 'eye-slip', rather than its being deleted by Ford or his editor. The paragraph beginning 'So it goes', which contains this sentence, has never been published in any previous edition of *No More Parades*. The significance of the omission is obvious.

As stated in the Note on this Edition, the text published here is not an edition of the typescript but a corrected text of UK, informed by a reading of the typescript, and also in this case by the variant fragment published in the *Contact Collection of Contemporary Writers*. Apart from the few exceptions described here, the typescript's significant variants from UK are not incorporated into the text, but have been recorded in the textual endnotes.

82 Janice Biala wrote to Arthur Mizener (29 May 1964) that 'Ford was the worst proof reader on earth and knew it'. Carl A. Kroch Library, Cornell University; quoted with the kind permission of the estate of Janice Biala and Cornell University.

NO MORE PARADES
A NOVEL

By
FORD MADOX FORD

For two things my heart is grieved: A man of war that suffereth from poverty and men of intelligence that are counted as refuse.

PROVERBS[1]

To WILLIAM BIRD*

MY DEAR BIRD,—

I have always held—and I hold as strongly now as ever—that a novel should have no preface. It should have no preface for aesthetico-moral reasons, and because prefatory matter takes away from the reality of, and therefore damages, a book. A dedicatory letter is a subterfuge. That subterfuge I feel forced to adopt, and must take the consequences.

The reason is this: All novels are historical, but all novels do not deal with such events as get on to the pages of history. This *No More Parades* does. It becomes, therefore, necessary to delimit what, in it, is offered as, on the author's responsibility, observed event.

State, underline and emphasize the fact how you will it is impossible to get into the heads of even intelligent public critics the fact that the opinions of a novelist's characters as stated in any novel are not of necessity the opinions of the novelist. It cannot be done. How it may be with one's public one has no means of knowing. Perhaps they read one with more generosity and care. Presumably they do, for they have either spent money on, or taken some trouble to obtain, the volume.

In this novel the events, such as it treats of, are vouched for by myself. There was in France, at the time covered by this novel, an immense base camp, unbelievably crowded with men whom we were engaged in getting up the line, working sometimes day and night in the effort. That immense army was also extremely depressed by the idea that those who controlled it overseas would—I will not use the word betray, since that implies volition—but "let us down." We were oppressed, ordered, counter-ordered, commanded, countermanded, harassed, strafed, denounced—and, above all, dreadfully worried. The never-

---

*   William Augustus Bird (1888–1963), better known as Bill Bird, founded the Three Mountains Press in Paris in 1922, published Ford's *Women and Men* in 1923, and provided him office space to edit the *transatlantic review* in 1924.

ending sense of worry, in fact, far surpassed any of the "exigencies of troops actually in contact with enemy forces," and that applied not merely to the bases, but to the whole field of military operations. Unceasing worry!

We took it out in what may or may not have been unjust suspicions of the all-powerful ones who had our lives in their hands and seemed indifferent enough to the fact. So this novel recounts what those opinions were: it does not profess to dictate whether those opinions were or were not justified. There is, I think, not one word in it which records any opinions or words of mine as being my words or opinions. I believe I may say that, as to the greater part of such public matters as are here discussed, I have no opinions at all. After seven or eight years I have been unable to form any. I present therefore only what I observed or heard.

Few writers can have engaged themselves as combatants[1] in what, please God, will yet prove to be the war that ended war, without the intention of aiding with their writings, if[2] they survived, in bringing about such a state of mind as should end wars as possibilities.

This obviously is a delicate task. If you overstate horrors you induce in your reader a state of mind such as, by reaction, causes the horrors to become matters of indifference. If you overstate heroisms you induce indifference to heroisms—of which the late war produced, Heaven knows, plenty enough, so that to be indifferent to them is villainy. Casting about, then, for a medium through which to view this spectacle, I thought of a man—by then dead—with whom I had been very intimate and with whom—as with yourself—I had at one time discussed most things under the sun. He was the English Tory.

Even then—it must have been in September, 1916, when I was in a region called the Salient,[*] and I remember the very spot where the idea came to me—I said to myself: How would all this look in the eyes of X ... —already dead, along with all English Tories? For, as a medium through which to view struggles that are after all in the end mostly emotional struggles—since as a rule for every twenty minutes of actual fighting you were alone with your

---

[*] Ford is referring to the Ypres Salient in Belgium where trench warfare started, the German advance through Belgium to France was halted, and the use of gas began.

emotions, which, being English, you did not express, for at least a month!—as a medium, what could be better than the sceptical, not ungenerous, not cold, not unconvincible eyes of an extinct frame of mind. For by the time of my relative youth when I knew X* . . . so intimately, Toryism had gone beyond the region of any practising political party. It said for a year or two: A plague on all your Houses,† and so expired.

To this determination—to use my friend's eyes as a medium—I am adhering in this series of books. *Some Do Not*—of which this one is not so much a continuation as a reinforcement—showed you the Tory at home during war-time; this shows you the Tory going up the line. If I am vouchsafed health and intelligence for long enough I propose to show you the same man in the line and in process of being re-constructed.

There is nothing more to it: I no more back the political opinions of General Campion than those of Sylvia Tietjens, who considered that the World War was just an excuse for male agape-mones;‡ I no more accept responsibility for the inaccuracies of Tietjens quoting King's Regulations§ than for the inaccuracies of the general in quoting *Henry V.*** I was roundly taken to task by the only English critic whose review of my last book I read††— after he had *horribly* misrepresented the plot of the work at a crucial point for my inaccuracy in stating that poor Roger Casement‡‡ was shot. As a matter of fact, I had been struck by the fact that a lady with whom I had been discussing Casement twice

---

* 'X' is Arthur Pierson Marwood, who founded *The English Review* with Ford in 1908. Ford said of him that 'he had the largest general, the largest encyclopaedic, knowledge that . . . it would be possible for any one man's skull to hold. . . . He had no personal ambitions, being a Yorkshire Tory Squire, a distinguished mathematician, and a fellow of some Cambridge College—Trinity, I think' (*Thus To Revisit* [London: Chapman and Hall, 1921], 59).

† Cf. Mercutio's curse in *Romeo and Juliet* III.i.91 when mortally injured: 'A plague o' both your houses'.

‡ 'An abode-of-love; esp. with unfavourable implication': *OED*.

§ King's Regulations govern the conduct and discipline in military matters. Tietjens refers to them in III.ii.

** General Campion misquotes Shakespeare in III.ii.281

†† See Gerald Gould, 'New Fiction', *Saturday Review*, 137 (17 May 1924), 512.

‡‡ Sir Roger Casement (1864–1916), a humanitarian and Irish hero, served in the Congo Free State and then in South America, exposing European atrocities. He was knighted by the king in 1911. But he supported the Easter Rising as part of Ireland's rebellion against English rule during the Great War, and was captured after leaving a German submarine and hanged.

deliberately referred to the shooting of Casement, and stated that she did so because she could not bear to think that we had hanged him. In making therefore a lady—who had loved Casement—refer to his execution in the book in question, I let her say that Casement was shot.... Indeed, I should prefer to think that he had been shot, myself.... Or still more to think that we had allowed him to escape, or commit suicide, or be imprisoned during His Majesty's pleasure.... The critic preferred to rub in the hanging. It is a matter of relative patriotism.

Whilst we are chipping, I may as well say that I have been informed that a lively controversy has raged over the same work in the United States, a New York critic having stated that I was a disappointed man intent on giving a lurid picture of present-day matrimonial conditions in England.* I hope I am no rabid patriot, but I pray to be preserved from the aspiration of painting any nation's lurid matrimonial conditions. The peculiar ones adumbrated in *Some Do Not* were suggested by the fate of a poor fellow living in a place in the South of France in which I happened to be stopping when I began the book. His misfortunes were much those of my central character, but he drank himself to death, it was said deliberately, after he had taken his wife back. He came from Philadelphia.†

So it goes. But the reader may take it that few persons ever quote correctly even when they quote verse. When it comes to prose ... No officer ever quoted King's Regs. with any assimilation to the text; and as for Shakespeare's prose ... I have heard eleven generals, ten English and one American—or to be exact nine Imperial, one Australian and one American—attempt to quote Shakespeare.... I hesitate to adumbrate the results of the attempts.... But if I represented them as saying what the Swan of Avon wrote, I might satisfy one reviewer, but, as an artist, I should never hold up my head again.[3]

So, in remembrance of our joint labours and conspiracies, and

---

* The reviewer was Joseph W. Krutch in the *Saturday Review of Literature*, 1 (18 Oct. 1924), 197.
† Ford elaborated this story in *It Was the Nightingale* (1933), ed. John Coyle (Manchester: Carcanet, 2007), 200–1. See the introduction to *Some Do Not ...* in this edition.

in token of my admiration for your beautiful achievements in
another art,

    I subscribe myself, my dear Bird,

        Your humble, obedient and obliged

F. M. F.

PARIS, 31 *October*, '24 —
    GUERMANTES 25 *May*, '25.[4]

PART I

I

WHEN you came in the space was desultory, rectangular, warm after the drip of the winter night, and transfused with a brown-orange dust that was light. It was shaped like the house a child draws.* Three groups of brown limbs spotted with brass took dim high-lights from shafts that came from a bucket pierced with holes, filled with incandescent coke and covered in with a sheet of iron in the shape of a tunnel. Two men, as if hierarchically smaller, crouched on the floor beside the brazier; four, two at each end of the hut, drooped over tables in attitudes of extreme indifference. From the eaves above the parallelogram of black that was the doorway fell intermittent drippings of collected moisture, persistent, with glass-like intervals of musical sound. The two men squatting on their heels over the brazier—they had been miners—began to talk in a low sing-song of dialect, hardly audible. It went on and on, monotonously, without animation. It was as if one told the other long, long stories to which his companion manifested his comprehension or sympathy with animal grunts. . . .

An immense tea-tray, august, its voice filling the black circle of the horizon, thundered to the ground. Numerous pieces of sheet-iron said, "Pack. Pack. Pack." In a minute the clay floor of the hut shook, the drums of ears were pressed inwards, solid noise showered about the universe, enormous echoes pushed these men—to the right, to the left, or down towards the tables, and

---

* The house in Ford's poem 'A House' is imagined saying: 'I am the House! / I resemble / The drawing of a child / That draws "just a house"': Ford Madox Hueffer, 'A House (Modern Morality Play)', *The Chapbook*, No. 21, March 1921 (London: The Poetry Bookshop, 1921), 3.

crackling like that of flames among vast underwood became the
settled condition of the night.* Catching the light from the
brazier as the head leaned over, the lips of one of the two men on
the floor were incredibly red and full and went on talking and
talking. . . .

The two men on the floor were Welsh miners, of whom the
one came from the Rhondda Valley and was unmarried; the
other, from Pontardulais, had a wife who kept a laundry, he
having given up going underground just before the war. The two
men at the table to the right of the door were sergeants-major;
the one came from Suffolk and was a time-serving man of sixteen
years seniority as a sergeant in a line regiment. The other was
Canadian of English origin. The two officers at the other end of
the hut were captains, the one a young regular officer born in
Scotland but educated at Oxford; the other, nearly middle-aged
and heavy, came from Yorkshire, and was in a militia† battalion.
The one runner on the floor was filled with a passionate rage
because the elder officer had refused him leave to go home and
see why his wife, who had sold their laundry, had not yet received
the purchase money from the buyer; the other was thinking about
a cow. His girl, who worked on a mountainy farm above Caerphilly, had written to him about a queer cow: a black-and-white
Holstein—surely to goodness a queer cow. The English sergeant-
major was almost tearfully worried about the enforced lateness of
the draft. It would be twelve midnight before they could march
them off. It was not right to keep men hanging about like that.
The men did not like to be kept waiting, hanging about. It made
them discontented. They did not like it. He could not see why
the depot quartermaster could not keep up his stock of candles

---

* When Robert Graves was interviewed about the war he explained how 'the idea of
being and staying at home was awful because you were with people who didn't understand what all this was about'. The interviewer, Leslie Smith, asked if he did not want
to tell them, and Graves replied: 'You couldn't: you can't communicate noise. Noise
never stopped for one moment – ever' (quoted in Paul Fussell, *The Great War and
Modern Memory* [New York and London: Oxford University Press, 1975], 170). Yet in
Parade's End Ford finds innovative ways to express the effects of the noises of war.
While he was in the Ypres Salient in September 1916 he had written letters to Conrad
containing what he called 'my notes upon sounds', detailing the noises made by
different artillery on different targets, and the contrast between bombardments and a
thunderstorm: *Letters* 71–4 (73).

† 'A "citizen" army as distinguished from a body of mercenaries or professional soldiers':
OED.

for the hooded lamps. The men had no call to be kept waiting, hanging about. Soon they would have to be having some supper. Quarter would not like that. He would grumble fair. Having to indent for suppers. Put his account out, fair, it would. Two thousand nine hundred and thirty-four suppers at a penny half-penny. But it was not right to keep the men hanging about till midnight and no suppers. It made them discontented and them going up the line for the first time, poor devils.

The Canadian sergeant-major was worried about a pig-skin leather pocket-book. He had bought it at the ordnance depot in the town. He imagined himself bringing it out on parade, to read out some return or other to the adjutant. Very smart it would look on parade, himself standing up straight and tall. But he could not remember whether he had put it in his kit-bag. On himself it was not. He felt in his right and left breast pockets, his right and left skirt pockets, in all the pockets of his overcoat that hung from a nail within reach of his chair. He did not feel at all certain that the man who acted as his batman had packed that pocket-book with his kit, though he declared he had. It was very annoying. His present wallet, bought in Ontario, was bulging and split. He did not like to bring it out when Imperial officers asked for something out of a return. It gave them a false idea of Canadian troops. Very annoying. He was an auctioneer. He agreed that at this rate it would be half-past one before they had the draft down to the station and entrained. But it was very annoying to be uncertain whether that pocket-book was packed or not. He had imagined himself making a good impression on parade, standing up straight and tall, taking out that pocket-book when the adjutant asked for a figure from one return or the other. He understood their adjutants were to be Imperial officers now they were in France. It was very annoying.

An enormous crashing sound said things of an intolerable intimacy to each of those men, and to all of them as a body. After its mortal vomiting all the other sounds appeared a rushing silence, painful to ears in which the blood audibly coursed. The young officer stood violently up on his feet and caught at the complications of his belt hung from a nail. The elder, across the table, lounging sideways, stretched out one hand with a downwards movement. He was aware that the younger man, who was the senior officer, was just upon out of his mind. The younger man, intolerably fatigued,[1] spoke sharp, injurious, inaudible words to his companion. The elder spoke sharp, short words, inaudible too, and continued to motion downwards with his hand over the table. The old English sergeant-major said to his junior that Captain Mackenzie had one of his mad fits again, but what he said was inaudible and he knew it. He felt arising in his motherly heart that yearned at the moment over his two thousand nine hundred and thirty-four nurslings a necessity, like a fatigue, to extend the motherliness of his functions to the orfcer. He said to the Canadian that Captain Mackenzie[2] there going temporary off his nut was the best orfcer in His Majesty's army. And going to make a bleedin' fool of hisself. The best orfcer in His Majesty's army. Not a better. Careful, smart, brave as a 'ero. And considerate of his men in the line. You wouldn't believe.... He felt vaguely that it was a fatigue to have to mother an officer. To a lance-corporal, or a young sergeant, beginning to go wrong you could mutter wheezy suggestions through your moustache. But to an officer you had to say things slantways. Difficult it was. Thank God they had a trustworthy, cool hand in the other captain. Old and good, the proverb said.

Dead silence fell.

"Lost the buggers, they 'ave," the runner from the Rhondda made his voice startlingly heard. Brilliant illuminations flickered on hut-gables visible through the doorway.

"No reason," his mate from Pontardulais rather whined in his native sing-song, "why the bleedin' searchlights, surely to goodness, should light us up for all the fuckin 'Un planes to see. I want to see my bleedin' little 'ut on the bleedin' Mumbles* again, if they don't."

"Not so much swear words, O Nine Morgan,"† the sergeant-major said.

"Now, Dai Morgan, I'm telling you," 09 Morgan's mate continued. "A queer cow it must have been whatever. Black-and-

---

* The Mumbles is a village on the western edge of Swansea Bay, south Wales. It takes its name from two islands just off the headland.

† 'O Nine' is a way of distinguishing one Morgan from another, given that this is a common Welsh name. Later we hear of 'One Seven Thomas', another widely shared Welsh name.

white Holstein it wass. . . ."

It was as if the younger captain gave up listening to the conversation. He leant both hands on the blanket that covered the table. He exclaimed:

"Who the hell are you to give me orders? I'm your senior. Who the hell . . . Oh, by God, who the hell . . . Nobody gives me orders . . ." His voice collapsed weakly in his chest. He felt his nostrils to be inordinately dilated so that the air pouring into them was cold. He felt that there was an entangled conspiracy against him, and all round him. He exclaimed: "You and your bloody pimp of a general. . . !" He desired to cut certain throats with a sharp trench-knife that he had. That would take the weight off his chest. The "Sit *down*" of the heavy figure lumping opposite him paralysed his limbs. He felt an unbelievable hatred. If he could move his hand to get at his trench-knife . . .

09 Morgan said:

"The bugger's name who's bought my bleedin' laundry is Williams . . . If I thought it was Evans Williams of Castell Goch, I'd desert."

"Took a hatred for its cawve," the Rhondda man said. "And look you, before you could say . . ." The conversation of orfcers was a thing to which they neither listened. Officers talked of things that had no interest. Whatever could possess a cow to take a hatred of its calf? Up behind Caerphilly on the mountains? On an autumny morning the whole hillside was covered with spiderwebs. They shone down the sun like spun glass. Overlooked the cow must be.

The young captain leaning over the table began a long argument as to relative seniority. He argued with himself, taking both sides in an extraordinarily rapid gabble. He himself had been gazetted* after Gheluvelt.† The other not till a year later. It was true the other was in permanent command of that depot, and he himself attached to the unit only for rations and discipline. But

---

*   Named in a news-sheet (a gazette) as having been transferred to another unit of the army.

†   A town in Flanders on the direct route to Ypres. The Germans attacked it on 29 October 1914; British forces counterattacked on the 31st. This slowed the German advance, preventing the French from being surrounded and defeated. The loss of life on both sides was extensive.

that did not include orders to sit down. What the hell, he wanted
to know, did the other mean by it? He began to talk, faster than
ever, about a circle. When its circumference came whole by the
disintegration of the atom the world would come to an end. In
the millennium there would be no giving or taking orders. Of
course he obeyed orders till then.

To the elder officer, burdened with the command of a unit of
unreasonable size, with a scratch headquarters of useless subalterns who were continually being changed, with N.C.O.'s all
unwilling to work, with rank and file nearly all colonials and
unused to doing without things, and with a depot to draw on that,
being old established, felt that it belonged exclusively to a regular
British unit and resented his drawing anything at all, the prac-
tical difficulties of his everyday life were already sufficient, and
he had troublesome private affairs. He was lately out of hospital;
the sackcloth hut in which he lived, borrowed from the Depot
medical officer who had gone to England on leave, was suffocat-
ingly hot with the paraffin heater going, and intolerably cold and
damp without it; the batman whom the M.O. had left in charge
of the hut appeared to be half-witted. These German air-raids had
lately become continuous. The Base was packed with men,
tighter than sardines. Down in the town you could not move in
the streets. Draft-finding units were commanded to keep their
men out of sight as much as possible. Drafts were to be sent off
only at night. But how could you send off a draft at night when
every ten minutes you had two hours of lights out for an air-raid?
Every man had nine sets of papers and tags that had to be signed
by an officer. It was quite proper that the poor devils should be
properly documented. But how was it to be done? He had two
thousand nine hundred and ninety-four* men to send off that
night and nine times two thousand nine hundred and ninety-four
is twenty-six thousand nine hundred and forty-six. They would
not or could not let him have a disc-punching machine of his
own, but how was the Depot armourer to be expected to punch
five thousand nine hundred and eighty-eight extra identity discs
in addition to his regular jobs?

The other captain rambled on in front of him. Tietjens did not

---

* Sergeant-Major Cowley gives the number as 2,934 earlier in the chapter.

like his talk of the circle and the millennium. You get alarmed, if
you have any sense, when you hear that. It may prove the beginnings of definite, dangerous lunacy. . . . But he knew nothing
about the fellow. He was too dark and good-looking, too
passionate, probably, to be a good regular officer on the face of
him. But he *must* be a good officer: he had the D.S.O. with a clasp,
the M.C., and some foreign ribbon up. And the general said he
was: with the additional odd piece of information that he was a
Vice-Chancellor's Latin Prize* man. . . . He wondered if General
Campion knew what a Vice-Chancellor's Latin Prize man was.
Probably he did not, but had just stuck the piece of information
into his note as a barbaric ornament is used by a savage chief.
Wanted to show that he, General Lord Edward Campion, was a
man of culture. There was no knowing where vanity would not
break out.

So this fellow was too dark and good-looking to be a good
officer: yet he *was* a good officer. That explained it. The repres-
sions of the passionate drive them mad. He must have been being
sober, disciplined, patient, absolutely repressed ever since 1914—
against a background of hell-fire, row, blood, mud, old tins. . . .
And indeed the elder officer had a vision of the younger as if in
a design for a full-length portrait—for some reason with his legs
astride, against a background of tapestry scarlet with fire and
more scarlet with blood. . . . He sighed a little; that was the life
of all those several millions. . . .

He seemed to see his draft: two thousand nine hundred and
ninety-four men he had had command of for over a couple of
months—a long space of time as that life went—men he and
Sergeant-Major Cowley had looked after with a great deal of
tenderness, looking after their morale, their morals, their feet,
their digestions, their impatiences, their desires for women. . . .
He seemed to see them winding away over a great stretch of
country, the head slowly settling down, as in the Zoo you will see
an enormous serpent slowly sliding into its water-tank. . . .
Settling down out there, a long way away, up against that impass-

---

* This University prize undoubtedly required McKechnie (the correct name of
'Mackenzie'/ 'McKenzie' as will soon be seen) to write poetry in Latin; thus his willingness later on to translate a sonnet by Tietjens into Latin.

able barrier that stretched from the depths of the ground to the peak of heaven. . . .

Intense dejection: endless muddles: endless follies: endless villainies. All these men given into the hands of the most cynically care-free intriguers in long corridors who made plots that harrowed the hearts of the world. All these men toys: all these agonies mere occasions for picturesque phrases to be put into politicians' speeches without heart or even intelligence. Hundreds of thousands of men tossed here and there in that sordid and gigantic mud-brownness of mid-winter . . . by God, exactly as if they were nuts wilfully picked up and thrown over the shoulder by one magpie. . . . But men. Not just populations. Men you worried over there. Each man a man with a backbone, knees, breeches, braces, a rifle, a home, passions, fornications, drunks, pals, some scheme of the universe, corns, inherited diseases, a greengrocer's business, a milk walk, a paper stall, brats, a slut of a wife. . . . The Men: the Other Ranks! And the poor bloody little officers. God help them. Vice-Chancellor's Latin Prize men. . . .

This particular poor bloody Prize man seemed to object to noise. They ought to keep the place quiet for him. . . .

By God, he was perfectly right. That place was meant for the quiet and orderly preparation of meat for the shambles. Drafts! A Base is a place where you meditate: perhaps you should pray: a place where in peace the Tommies should write their last letters home and describe 'ow the guns are 'owling 'orribly.

But to pack a million and a half of men into and round that small town was like baiting a trap for rats with a great chunk of rotten meat. The Hun planes could smell them from a hundred miles away. They could do more harm there than if they bombed a quarter of London to pieces. And the air defences there were a joke: a mad joke. They pooped[3] off, thousands of rounds, from any sort of pieces of ordnance, like schoolboys bombarding swimming rats with stones. Obviously your best-trained air-defence men would be round your metropolis. But this was no joke for the sufferers.

Heavy depression settled down more heavily upon him. The distrust of the home Cabinet, felt[4] by then by the greater part of that army, became like physical pain. These immense sacrifices, this ocean of mental sufferings, were all undergone to further the private vanities of men who[5] amidst these hugenesses of landscapes and forces appeared pygmies! It was the worries of all these wet millions in mud-brown that worried him. They could die, they could be massacred, by the quarter million, in shambles. But that they should be massacred without jauntiness, without confidence, with depressed brows: without parade. . . .

He knew really nothing about the officer in front of him. Apparently the fellow had stopped for an answer to some question. What question? Tietjens had no idea. He had not been listening. Heavy silence settled down on the hut. They just waited. The fellow said with an intonation of hatred:

"Well, what about it? That's what I want to know!"

Tietjens went on reflecting. . . . There were a great many kinds of madness. What kind was this? The fellow was not drunk. He talked like a drunkard, but he was not drunk. In ordering him to sit down Tietjens had just chanced it. There are madmen whose momentarily subconscious selves will respond to a military command as if it were magic. Tietjens remembered having barked: "About . . . turn," to a poor little lunatic fellow in some camp at home and the fellow who had been galloping hotfoot past his tent, waving a naked bayonet with his pursuers fifty yards behind, had stopped dead and faced about with a military stamp like a guardsman. He had tried it on this lunatic for want of any better expedient. It had apparently functioned intermittently. He risked saying:

"What about what?"

The man said as if ironically:

"It seems as if I were not worth listening to by your high and mightiness. I said: 'What about my foul squit of an uncle?' Your filthy, best friend."

Tietjens said:

"The general's your uncle? General Campion? What's he done to you?"

The general had sent this fellow down to him with a note asking him, Tietjens, to keep an eye in his unit on a very good fellow and an admirable officer. The chit was in the general's own writing, and contained the additional information as to Captain Mackenzie's scholastic prowess. . . . It had struck Tietjens as

queer that the general should take so much trouble about a casual
infantry company commander. How could the fellow have been
brought markedly to his notice? Of course, Campion was good-
natured, like another man. If a fellow, half dotty, whose record
showed that he was a very good man, was brought to his notice
Campion would do what he could for him. And Tietjens knew
that the general regarded himself, Tietjens, as a heavy, bookish
fellow, able reliably to look after one of his protégés. . . . Probably
Campion imagined that they had no work to do in that unit: they
might become an acting lunatic ward. But if Mackenzie was
Campion's nephew the thing was explained.

The lunatic exclaimed:

"Campion, *my* uncle? Why, he's *yours!*"

Tietjens said:

"Oh, no, he isn't." The general was not even a connection of
his, but he did happen to be Tietjens' godfather and his father's
oldest friend.[6]

The other fellow answered:

"Then it's damn funny. *Damn* suspicious. . . . Why should he
be so interested in you if he's not your filthy uncle? You're no
soldier. . . . You're no sort of a soldier. . . . A mealsack, that's what
you look like. . . ." He paused and then went on very quickly:
"They say up at H.Q. that your wife has got hold of the disgusting
general. I didn't believe it was true. I didn't believe you were that
sort of fellow. I've heard a lot about you!"[7*]

---

*   Sylvia is certainly close to General Campion (indeed, close enough to consider
    marrying him in *Last Post*), and has manipulated him both before and after her arrival
    in Rouen. But malicious rumour has twisted that into a slander hinted at here that
    Tietjens is conniving in an affair between them (and it is implied, in a deleted passage,
    that he is doing it for money: see endnote). This scenario perhaps owes something to
    a notorious contemporary case in which Dorothy Dennistoun sued her former
    husband, Lt-Colonel Ian Dennistoun, for maintenance after their divorce. (He had
    later married Almina, the widow of the Lord Carnarvon involved in the excavation
    of Tutankhamun's tomb.) The court case scandalised London society, and destroyed
    the reputation of the war hero and General Sir John Cowans (described as 'the finest
    quartermaster since Moses'), revealing that sexual favours had been given in return
    for military promotions. It ran in March 1925, while Ford was finishing *No More
    Parades*, so too late for the court reports to have influenced him. But Ian Dennistoun
    was living in Paris (where he and his wife had divorced in 1921) in the early 1920s,
    and selling wine. Ford may have heard of his story then and there; perhaps from gossip
    about Dorothy living with Cowans while still married to Ian. Cowans had died in
    1921. It is also possible that his death, or the imminent court case, revived memories
    of an earlier scandal in which Cowans had also figured and been reprimanded: the
    1916 case of Patsy Cornwallis-West, who had used undue influence (she moved in

Tietjens laughed at this madness. Then, in the dark brownness, an intolerable pang went all through his heavy frame—the intolerable pang of home news to these desperately occupied men, the pain caused by disasters happening in the darkness and at a distance. You could do nothing to mitigate them! ... The extraordinary beauty of the wife from whom he was separated— for she was extraordinarily beautiful!—might well have caused scandals about her to have penetrated to the general's headquarters, which was a sort of family party! Hitherto there had, by the grace of God, been no scandals. Sylvia Tietjens had been excruciatingly unfaithful, in the most painful manner. He could not be certain that the child he adored was his own. . . . That was not unusual with extraordinarily beautiful—and cruel!—women. But she had been haughtily circumspect.

Nevertheless, three months ago, they had parted. . . . Or he thought they had parted. Almost complete blankness had descended upon his home life. She appeared before him so extraordinarily bright and clear in the brown darkness that he shuddered: very tall, very fair, extraordinarily fit and clean run.[8] Thoroughbred! In a sheath gown of gold tissue, all illuminated, and her mass of hair, like gold tissue too, coiled round and round in plaits over her ears.* The features very clean-cut and thinnish; the teeth white and small; the breasts small; the arms thin, long and at attention at her sides. . . . His eyes, when they were tired, had that trick of reproducing images on their retinas with that extreme clearness, images sometimes of things he thought of, sometimes of things merely at the back of the mind. Well,[9] tonight his eyes were very tired! She was looking straight before her, with a little inimical disturbance of the corners of her lips. She had just thought of a way to hurt terribly his silent personality. . . . The semi-clearness became a luminous blue, like a tiny

Royal circles and had been a mistress of the future Edward VII) to advance the career of Lt Patrick Barrett in the Welsh Fusiliers (note the appearance of a 'Major Cornwallis' in I.ii). While the influence of these particular cases on the novel is conjectural, they show that Sylvia's shameless antics are more realistic than they might otherwise seem. See Tim Coates, *Patsy: The Story of Mary Cornwallis West* (London: Bloomsbury, 2003). I'm grateful to Will Cross for information about both cases.

*   Talking about the origin of his characters, Ford says that Sylvia came to him 'suddenly, in Amiens station': 'She was in a golden sheath-gown and her golden hair was done in bandeaux, extraordinarily brilliant in the dimness. . . . I exclaimed: "Sylvia!" So I didn't have to cast about for a name': *Nightingale* 191.

gothic arch, and passed out of his vision to the right. . . .

He knew nothing of where Sylvia was. He had given up looking at the illustrated papers. She had said she was going into a convent at Birkenhead—but twice he had seen photographs of her. The first showed her merely with Lady Fiona Grant, daughter of the Earl and Countess of Ulleswater—and a Lord Swindon, talked of as next minister for International Finance—a new Business Peer. . . . All three walking straight into the camera in the courtyard of Lord Swindon's castle . . . all three smiling! . . . It announced Mrs. Christopher Tietjens as having a husband at the front.

The sting had, however, been in the second picture—in the description of it supplied by the journal! It showed Sylvia standing in front of a bench in the park. On the bench in profile there extended himself in a guffaw of laughter, a young man in a top hat jammed well on to his head, which was thrown back, his prognathous jaw pointing upwards. The description stated that the picture showed Mrs. Christopher Tietjens, whose husband was in hospital at the Front, telling a good story to the son and heir of Lord Brigham! . . . Another of these pestilential, crooked newspaper-owning financial peers . . .

It had struck him for a painful moment whilst looking at the picture in a dilapidated mess anteroom after he had come out of hospital—that, considering the description, the journal had got its knife into Sylvia. . . . But the illustrated papers do not get their knives into society beauties. They are too precious to the photographers. . . . Then Sylvia must have supplied the information; she desired to cause comment by the contrast of her hilarious companions and the statement that her husband was in hospital at the Front. . . . It had occurred to him that she was on the warpath. But he had put it out of his mind. . . . Nevertheless, brilliant mixture as she was, of the perfectly straight, perfectly fearless, perfectly reckless, of the generous, the kind even—and the atrociously cruel, nothing might suit her better than positively to show contempt—no, not contempt! cynical hatred—for her husband, for the war, for public opinion . . . even for the interest of their child! . . . Yet, it came to him, the image of her that he had just seen had been the image of Sylvia, standing at attention, her mouth working a little, whilst she read out the

figures beside the bright filament of mercury in a thermometer.... The child had had, with measles, a temperature
that, even then, he did not dare think of. And—it was at his
sister's in Yorkshire, and the local doctor hadn't cared to take the
responsibility—he could still feel the warmth of the little
mummy-like body; he had covered the head and face with a
flannel, for he didn't care for the sight, and lowered the warm,
terrible, fragile weight into a shining surface of crushed ice in
water .... She had stood at attention, the corners of her mouth
moving a little: the thermometer going down as you watched
it.... So that she mightn't want, in damaging the father, atrociously to damage the child.... For there could not be anything
worse for a child than to have a mother known as a whore....

Sergeant-Major Cowley was standing beside the table. He said:
"Wouldn't it be a good thing, sir, to send a runner to the depot
sergeant cook and tell him we're going to indent for suppers for
the draft? We could send the other with the 128's to Quarter.
They're neither wanted here for the moment."

The other captain went on incessantly talking—but about his
fabulous uncle, not about Sylvia.[10] It was difficult for Tietjens to
get what he wanted said. He wanted the second runner sent to
the depot quartermaster with a message to the effect that if G.S.
candles for hooded lamps were not provided for the use of his
orderly room by return of bearer he, Captain Tietjens,
commanding Number XVI Casual Battalion, would bring the
whole matter of supplies for his battalion that same night before
Base Headquarters. They were all three talking at once: heavy
fatalism overwhelmed Tietjens at the thought of the stubborn-
ness showed by the depot quartermaster. The big unit beside his
camp was a weary obstinacy of obstruction. You would have
thought they would have displayed some eagerness to get his men
up into the line. Let alone that the men were urgently needed,
the more of his men went the more of *them* stayed behind. Yet
they tried to stop his meat, his groceries, his braces, his identification discs, his soldiers' small books.... Every imaginable
hindrance, and not even self-interested common sense! ... He
managed also to convey to Sergeant-Major Cowley that, as everything seemed to have quieted down, the Canadian
sergeant-major had better go and see if everything was ready for

falling his draft in.... If things remained quiet for another ten minutes, the "All Clear" might then be expected.... He knew that Sergeant-Major Cowley wanted to get the Other Ranks out of the hut with that captain carrying on like that, and he did not see why the old N.C.O. should not have what he wanted.

It was as if a tender and masculine butler withdrew himself. Cowley's grey walrus moustache and scarlet cheeks showed for a moment beside the brazier, whispering at the ears of the runners, a hand kindly on each of their shoulders. The runners went; the Canadian went. Sergeant-Major Cowley, his form blocking the doorway, surveyed the stars. He found it difficult to realize that the same pinpricks of light through black manifolding paper* as he looked at, looked down also on his villa and his elderly wife at Isleworth beside the Thames above London. He knew it to be the fact, yet it was difficult to realize. He imagined the trams going along the High Street, his missus in one of them with her supper in a string bag on her stout knees. The trams lit up and shining. He imagined her having kippers for supper: ten to one it would be kippers. Her favourites. His daughter was in the W.A.A.C.'s by now. She had been cashier to Parks's, the big butchers in Brentford, and pretty she had used to look in the glass case. Like as if it might have been the British Museum where they had Pharaohs and others in glass cases.... There were threshing machines droning away all over the night. He always said they were like threshing machines.... Crikey, if only they were! ... But they might be our own planes, of course. A good welsh rarebit he had had for tea.

In the hut, the light from the brazier having fewer limbs on which to fall, a sort of intimacy seemed to descend, and Tietjens felt himself gain in ability to deal with his mad friend. Captain Mackenzie—Tietjens was not sure that the name was Mackenzie: it had looked something like it in the general's hand—Captain Mackenzie[11] was going on about the wrongs he had suffered at the hands of some fabulous uncle. Apparently at some important juncture the uncle had refused to acknowledge acquaintanceship with the nephew. From that all the misfortunes of the nephew had arisen.... Suddenly Tietjens said:

---

* 'Carbonized paper used in making several copies of a writing at one time': *OED*.

"Look here, pull yourself together. Are you mad? Stark, staring? ... Or only just play-acting?"

The man suddenly sank down on to the bully-beef case that served for a chair. He stammered[12] a question as to what—what—what Tietjens meant.

"If you let yourself go," Tietjens said, "you may let yourself go a tidy sight farther than you want to."[13]

"You're not a mad doctor," the other said. "It's no good your trying to come it over me. I know all about you.[14] I've got an uncle who's done the dirty on me—the dirtiest dirty ever was done on a man. If it hadn't been for him I shouldn't be here now."

"You talk as if the fellow had sold you into slavery," Tietjens said.[15]

"He's your closest friend," Mackenzie seemed to advance as a motive for revenge on Tietjens. "He's a friend of the general's, too. Of your wife's as well. He's in with every one."

A few desultory, pleasurable "pop-op-ops" sounded from far overhead to the left.

"They imagine they've found the Hun again," Tietjens said. "That's all right; you concentrate on your uncle. Only don't exaggerate his importance to the world. I assure you you are mistaken if you call him a friend of mine. I have not got a friend in the world." He added: "Are you going to mind the noise? If it is going to get on your nerves you can walk in a dignified manner to a dugout, now, before it gets bad. . . . "[16] He called out to Cowley to go and tell the Canadian sergeant-major to get his men back into their shelters if they had come out. Until the "All Clear" went.

Captain Mackenzie sat himself gloomily down at table.

"Damn it all," he said, "don't think I'm afraid of a little shrapnel. I've had two periods solid of fourteen and nine months in the line. I could have got out on to the rotten staff. . . . It's damn it: it's the beastly row. . . . Why[17] isn't one a beastly girl and privileged to shriek? By God, I'll get even with some of them one of these days. . . . "

"Why not shriek?" Tietjens asked. "You[18] can, for me. No one's going to doubt your courage here."[19]

Loud drops of rain spattered down all round the hut; there was a familiar thud on the ground a yard or so away, a sharp tearing sound above, a sharper knock on the table between them.

Mackenzie took the shrapnel bullet that had fallen and turned it round and round between finger and thumb.

"You think you caught me on the hop just now," he said injuriously. "You're damn clever."[20]

Two stories down below someone let two hundred-pound dumb-bells drop on the drawing-room carpet; all the windows of the house slammed in a race to get it over; the "pop-op-ops" of the shrapnel went in wafts all over the air. There was again sudden silence that was painful, after you had braced yourself up to bear noise. The runner from the Rhondda came in with a light step bearing two fat candles. He took the hooded lamps from Tietjens and began to press the candles up against the inner springs, snorting sedulously through his nostrils. . . .

"Nearly got me, one of those candlesticks did," he said. "Touched my foot as it fell, it did. I did run. Surely to goodness I did run, cahptn."

Inside the shrapnel shell was an iron bar with a flattened, broad nose. When the shell burst in the air this iron object fell to the ground and, since it came often from a great height, its fall was dangerous. The men called these candlesticks, which they much resembled.

A little ring of light now existed on the puce colour of the blanket-covered table. Tietjens showed, silver-headed, fresh-coloured, and bulky; Mackenzie, dark, revengeful eyes above a prognathous jaw. A very thin man, thirtyish.

"You can go into the shelter with the Colonial troops, if you like," Tietjens said to the runner. The man answered after a pause, being very slow thinking, that he preferred to wait for his mate, 09 Morgan whatever.

"They ought to let my orderly room have tin hats," Tietjens said to Mackenzie. "I'm damned if they didn't take these fellows' tin hats into store again when they attached to me for service, and I'm equally damned if they did not tell me that, if I wanted tin hats for my own headquarters, I had to write to H.Q. Canadians, Aldershot,* or some such place in order to get the issue sanctioned."

"Our headquarters are full of Huns doing the Huns' work,"

* Aldershot Military Town, Hampshire, is known as 'The Home of the British Army'.

Mackenzie said hatefully. "I'd like to get among them one of these days."

Tietjens looked with some attention at that young man with the Rembrandt shadows over his dark face. He said:

"Do you believe that tripe?"

The young man said:

"No ... I don't know that I do.... I don't know what to think.... The world's rotten...."

"Oh, the world's pretty rotten, all right," Tietjens answered. And,[21] in his fatigue of mind caused by having to attend to innumerable concrete facts like the providing of households for a thousand men every few days, arranging parade states for an extraordinarily mixed set of troops of all arms with very mixed drills, and fighting the Assistant Provost Marshal to keep his own men out of the clutches of the beastly Garrison Military Police who had got a down on all Canadians, he felt he had not any curiosity at all left.... Yet he felt vaguely that, at the back of his mind, there was some reason for trying to cure this young member of the lower middle classes.

He repeated:

"Yes, the world's certainly pretty rotten. But that's not its particular line of rottenness as far as we are concerned.... We're tangled up, not because we've got Huns in our orderly rooms, but just because we've got English. That's the bat in our belfry.... That Hun plane is presumably coming back. Half a dozen of them...."

The young man, his mind eased by having got off his chest a confounded lot of semi-nonsensical ravings, considered the return of the Hun planes with gloomy indifference. His problem really was: could he stand the bloody noise that would probably accompany their return? He had to get really into his head that this was an open space to all intents and purposes. There would not be splinters of stone flying about. He was ready to be hit by iron, steel, lead, copper, or brass shell rims, but not by beastly splinters of stone knocked off house fronts. That consideration had come to him during his beastly, his beastly, his infernal, damnable leave in London, when just such a filthy row had been going on.... Divorce leave! ... Captain McKechnie second attached ninth Glamorganshires is granted leave from the 14/11 to the 29/11 for the purpose of obtaining a divorce.... The memory seemed to burst inside him with the noise of one of those beastly enormous tin-pot crashes—and it always came when guns made that particular kind of tin-pot crash: the two came together, the internal one and the crash outside. He felt that chimney-pots were going to crash on to his head. You protected yourself by shouting at damned infernal idiots; if you could out-shout the row you were safe.... That was not sensible but you got ease that way! ...

"In matters of Information they're not a patch on us." Tietjens[22] tried the speech on cautiously and concluded:[23] "We know what the Enemy rulers read in the sealed envelopes beside their breakfast bacon-and-egg plates."

It had occurred to him that it was a military duty to bother himself about the mental equilibrium of this member of the lower classes. So he talked ... *any* old talk, wearisomely, to keep his mind employed![24] Captain Mackenzie was an officer of His Majesty the King: the property, body and soul, of His Majesty and His Majesty's War Office. It was Tietjens' duty to preserve this fellow as it was his duty to prevent deterioration in any other piece of the King's property. That was implicit in the oath of allegiance.[25] He went on talking:

The curse of the army, as far as the organization is concerned, was our imbecile national belief that the game is more than the player. That was our ruin, mentally, as a nation. We were taught that cricket is more than clearness of mind, so the blasted quartermaster, O.C. Depot Ordnance Stores next door, thought he had taken a wicket if he refused to serve out tin hats to their crowd. That's the Game! And if any of his, Tietjens', men were killed, he grinned and said the game was more than the players of the game.... And of course if he got his bowling average down low enough he got promotion. There was a quartermaster in Shrewsbury[26] who'd got more D.S.O.'s and combatant medals than anyone on active service in France, from the sea to Péronne,[27] or wherever our lines ended. His achievement was to have robbed almost every wretched Tommie in the Western Command of several weeks' separation allowance ... for the good of the taxpayer, of course. The poor bloody Tommies' kids went without proper food and clothing, and the Tommies themselves had been in a state of exasperation and resentment. And nothing in the world was worse for discipline and the army as a fighting machine. But there that quartermaster sat in his office, playing the romantic game over his A.F.B.'s till the broad buff sheets fairly glowed in the light of the incandescent gas. "And," Tietjens concluded, "for every quarter of a million sterling for which he bowls out the wretched fighting men he gets a new clasp on his fourth D.S.O. ribbon. . . . The game, in short, is more than the players of the game."

"Oh, damn it!" Captain Mackenzie said. "That's what's made us what we are, isn't it?"

"It is," Tietjens answered. "It's got us into the hole and it keeps us there."

Mackenzie[28] remained dispiritedly looking down at his fingers.

"You may be wrong or you may be right," he said.[29] "It's contrary to everything that I ever heard. But I see what you mean."[30]

 "At the beginning of the war," Tietjens said, "I had to look in on the War Office, and in a room I found a fellow. . . .[31] What do you think he was doing . . . what the hell do you think he was doing? He was devising the ceremonial for the disbanding of a Kitchener battalion. You can't say we were not prepared in one matter at least. . . . Well, the end of the show was to be: the adjutant would stand the battalion at ease: the band would play *Land of Hope and Glory*,* and then the adjutant would say: *There will be no more parades*. . . . Don't you see how symbolical it was: the band playing *Land of Hope and Glory*, and then the adjutant saying *There will be no more parades?* . . . For there won't. There won't, there damn well won't. . . . No more Hope, no more Glory, no more parades for you and me any more. Nor for the country . . . Nor for the world, I dare say . . . None . . . Gone . . . Na poo, finny!† No . . . more . . . parades!"

"I dare say you're right," the other said slowly. "But, all the same, what am I doing in this show? I hate soldiering. I hate this

---

* Patriotic song based on Edward Elgar's *Pomp and Circumstance March No. 1*; the first four lines of the second stanza are the best known: 'Land of Hope and Glory, / Mother of the Free, / How shall we extol thee / Who are born of thee?'
† A corruption of the French *n'a plus . . . fini*; the correct form of which is *Il n'y en a plus . . . fini*: 'There is no more . . . finished.'

whole beastly business...."

"Then why didn't you go on the gaudy Staff?" Tietjens asked. "The gaudy Staff apparently was yearning to have you. I bet God intended you for Intelligence: not for the footslogging department."[32]

The other said wearily:

"I don't know. I was with the battalion. I wanted to stop with the battalion. I was intended for the Foreign Office. My miserable uncle got me hoofed out of that. I was with the battalion. The C.O. wasn't up to much. *Someone* had to stay with the battalion. I was not going to do the dirty on it, taking any soft job...."

"I suppose you speak seven languages and all?" Tietjens asked.

"Five," the other said patiently, "and read two more. And Latin and Greek, of course."[33]

A man, brown, stiff, with a haughty parade step, burst into the light. He said with a high wooden voice:

"'Ere's another bloomin' casualty."* In the shadow he appeared to have draped half his face and the right side of his breast with crape. He gave a high, rattling laugh. He bent, as if in a stiff bow, woodenly at his thighs. He pitched, still bent, on to the iron sheet that covered the brazier, rolled off that and lay on his back across the legs of the other runner, who had been crouched beside the brazier. In the bright light it was as if a whole pail of scarlet paint had been dashed across the man's face on the left and his chest. It glistened in the firelight—just like fresh paint, moving! The runner from the Rhondda, pinned down by the body across his knees, sat with his jaw fallen, resembling one girl that should be combing the hair of another recumbent before her. The red viscousness welled across the floor; you sometimes so see fresh water bubbling up in sand.† It astonished Tietjens to see that a

---

* In *The Marsden Case* (London: Duckworth, 1923), when George Heimann responds to the implication of bastardy, his voice is 'still gay, but it had in it an assured note of pain. One day, afterwards, I heard a man, half of whose chest had just been blown away, say: "'Ere's another bloomin' casualty!" – and the effect was much the same' (12).

† Cf. *Some Do Not* ... II.vi, when Tietjens says, during an oblique love-scene with Valentine: 'And I ... from the first moment I ... I'll tell you ... If I looked out of a door ... It was all like sand.... But to the half left a little bubbling up of water. That could be trusted. To keep on for ever.... You, perhaps, won't understand.'

human body could be so lavish of blood. He was thinking it was a queer mania that that fellow should have, that his uncle was a friend of his, Tietjens. He had no friend in trade, uncle of a fellow who in ordinary times would probably bring you pairs of boots on approval. . . . He felt as he did when you patch up a horse that has been badly hurt. He remembered a horse from a cut on whose chest the blood had streamed down over the off foreleg like a stocking. A girl had lent him her petticoat to bandage it.* Nevertheless his legs moved slowly and heavily across the floor.

The heat from the brazier was overpowering on his bent face. He hoped he would not get his hands all over blood, because blood is very sticky. It makes your fingers stick together impotently. But there might not be any blood in the darkness under the fellow's back where he was putting his hand. There was, however: it was very wet.

The voice of Sergeant-Major Cowley said from outside:

"Bugler, call two sanitary lance-corporals and four men. Two sanitary corporals and four men." A prolonged wailing with interruptions transfused the night, mournful, resigned, and prolonged.

Tietjens thought that, thank God, someone would come and relieve him of that job. It was a breathless affair holding up the corpse with the fire burning his face. He said to the other runner:

"Get out from under him, damn you! Are you hurt?" Mackenzie could not get at the body from the other side because of the brazier. The runner from under the corpse moved with short sitting shuffles as if he were getting his legs out from under a sofa. He was saying:

"Poor bloody O Nine Morgan! Surely to goodness I did not recognice the pore bugger. . . Surely to goodness I did not recognice the pore bugger."

Tietjens let the trunk of the body sink slowly to the floor. He was more gentle than if the man had been alive. All hell in the way of noise burst about the world. Tietjens' thoughts seemed to have to shout to him between earthquake shocks. He was thinking it was absurd of that fellow Mackenzie to imagine that he could know any uncle of his. He saw very vividly also the face

---

*   A reference to Tietjens' using Valentine Wannop's petticoat to bandage a horse hit by General Campion's car at the end of *Some Do Not . . .* I.vii.

of his girl who was a pacifist. It worried him not to know what
expression her face would have if she heard of his occupation,
now. Disgust? . . . He was standing with his greasy, sticky hands
held out from the flaps of his tunic. . . . Perhaps disgust! . . . It was
impossible to think in this row. . . . His very thick soles moved
gluily and came up after suction. . . . He remembered he had not
sent a runner along to I.B.D. Orderly Room to see how many of
his crowd would be wanted for garrison fatigue next day, and this
annoyed him acutely. He would have no end of a job warning the
officers he detailed. They would all be in brothels down in the
town by now. . . . He could not work out what the girl's expression would be. He was never to see her again, so what the hell did
it matter? . . . Disgust, probably! . . . He remembered that he had
not looked to see how Mackenzie was getting on in the noise. He
did not want to see Mackenzie. He was a bore. . . . How would
her face express disgust? He had never seen her express disgust.
She had a perfectly undistinguished face. Fair . . . O God, how
suddenly his bowels turned over! . . . Thinking of the girl . . . The
face below him grinned at the roof—the half face! The nose was
there, half the mouth with the teeth showing in the firelight. . . .
It was extraordinary how defined the peaked nose and the
serrated teeth were in that mess. . . . The eye looked jauntily at
the peak of the canvas hut-roof. . . . Gone with a grin. Singular
the fellow should have spoken! After he was dead. He must have
been dead when he spoke. It had been done with the last air automatically going out of the lungs. A reflex action, probably, in the
dead. . . . If he, Tietjens, had given the fellow the leave he wanted
he would be alive now! . . . Well, he was quite right not to have
given the poor devil his leave. He was, anyhow, better where he
was. And so was he, Tietjens. He had not had a single letter from
home since he had been out this time! Not a single letter. Not
even gossip. Not a bill. Some circulars of old furniture dealers.
They never neglected him![34] They had got beyond the sentimental stage at home. Obviously so. . . . He wondered if his
bowels would turn over again if he thought of the girl. He was
gratified that they had. It showed that he had strong feelings. . . .
He thought about her deliberately. Hard. Nothing happened. He
thought of her fair, undistinguished, fresh face that made your
heart miss a beat when you thought about it. His heart missed a

beat. Obedient heart! Like the first primrose. Not *any* primrose.
The *first* primrose. Under a bank with the hounds breaking
through the underwood. . . . It was sentimental to say *Du bist wie
eine blume*. . . .* Damn the German language! But that fellow was
a Jew. . . . One should not say that one's young woman was like
a flower, *any* flower. Not even to oneself. That was sentimental.
But one might say one special flower. A *man* could say that. A
man's job. She smelt like a primrose when you kissed her. But,
damn it, he had never kissed her. So how did he know how she
smelt! She was a little tranquil, golden spot. He himself must be
a bloody eunuch. By temperament. That dead fellow down there
must be one, physically. It was probably indecent to think of a
corpse as impotent. But he was, very likely. That would be why
his wife had taken up with the prize-fighter Red Evans Williams
of Castell Goch. If he had given the fellow leave the prize-fighter
would have smashed him to bits. The police of Pontardulais had
asked that he should not be let come home—because of the prize-
fighter. So he was better dead. Or perhaps not. Is death better
than discovering that your wife is a whore and being done in by
her cully? *Gwell angau na gwillth*, their own regimental badge bore
the words.† *"Death is better than dishonour"*. . . No, not death,
angau means pain. Anguish! Anguish is better than dishonour.
The devil it is! Well, that fellow would have got both. Anguish
and dishonour. Dishonour from his wife and anguish when the
prize-fighter hit him. . . . That was no doubt why his half-face
grinned at the roof. The gory side of it had turned brown.
Already! Like a mummy of a Pharaoh, *that* half looked. . . . He
was born to be a blooming casualty. Either by shell-fire or by the
fist of the prize-fighter. . . . Pontardulais! Somewhere in Mid-
Wales. He had been through it once in a car, on duty. A long,
dull village. Why should anyone want to go back to it? . . .
     A tender butler's voice said beside him: "This isn't your job,

---

*   A poem by Heinrich Heine from *Buch der Lieder* (1825), the first line of which Ford
    quotes in his essay, 'Herr Arthur Schnitzler and *Bertha Garlan'*, *Outlook*, 32 (25 Oct.
    1913), 571; he quotes the first two lines in *The March of Literature from Confucius' Day
    to Our Own* (London: Allen and Unwin, 1938): 'Du bist wie eine Blume / So hold und
    schoen und rein . . .' (723): 'You are like a flower / So sweet and fair and pure . . .'
†   In 'Pon . . . ti . . . pri . . . ith', Ford recalled the Welsh soldiers inserting the words of
    the Welch Regimental motto into the Welsh national anthem. The motto is normally
    spelt *Gwell angau na Chywilydd*. See *War Prose* 33.

sir. Sorry you had to do it.... Lucky it wasn't you, sir.... This was what done it, I should say."

Sergeant-Major Cowley was standing beside him holding a bit of metal that was heavy in his hand and like a candlestick. He was aware that a moment before he had seen the fellow, Mackenzie, bending over the brazier, putting the sheet of iron back. Careful officer, Mackenzie. The Huns must not be allowed to see the light from the brazier. The edge of the sheet had gone down on the dead man's tunic, nipping a bit by the shoulder. The face had disappeared in shadow. There were several men's faces in the doorway.

Tietjens said: "No: I don't believe that did it. Something bigger.... Say a prize-fighter's fist...."[35]

Sergeant-Major Cowley said:

"No, no prize-fighter's fist would have done that, sir.... And then he added,

"Oh, I take your meaning, sir.... O Nine Morgan's wife, sir...."

Tietjens moved, his feet sticking, towards the sergeant-major's table. The other runner had placed a tin basin with water on it. There was a hooded candle there now, alight; the water shone innocently, a half-moon of translucence wavering over the white bottom of the basin. The runner from Pontardulais said:

"Wash your hands first, sir!"

He said:

"Move a little out of it, cahptn." He had a rag in his black hands. Tietjens moved out of the blood that had run in a thin stream under the table. The man was on his knees, his hands rubbing Tietjens' boot welts heavily, with the rags. Tietjens placed his hands in the innocent water and watched light purple-scarlet mist diffuse itself over the pale half-moon. The man below him breathed heavily, sniffing. Tietjens said:

"Thomas, O Nine Morgan was your mate?"

The man's face, wrinkled, dark and ape-like, looked up.

"He was a good pal, pore old bugger," he said. "You would not like, surely to goodness, to go to mess with your shoes all bloody."

"If I had given him leave," Tietjens said, "he would not be dead now."

"No, surely not," One Seven Thomas answered. "But it is all

one. Evans of Castell Goch would surely to goodness have killed him."

"So you knew, too, about his wife!" Tietjens said.

"We thocht it wass that," One Seven Thomas answered, "or you would have given him leave, cahptn. You are a good cahptn."

A sudden sense of the publicity that that life was came over Tietjens.

"You knew that," he said. "I wonder what the hell you fellows don't know and all!" he thought. "If anything went wrong with one it would be all over the command in two days. Thank God, Sylvia can't get here!"[36]

The man had risen to his feet. He fetched a towel of the sergeant-major's, very white with a red border.

"We know," he said, "that your honour is a very goot cahptn. And Captain McKechnie is a *fery* goot cahptn, and Captain Prentiss, and Le'tennant Jonce of Merthyr . . ."[*]

Tietjens said:

"That'll do. Tell the sergeant-major to give you a pass to go with your mate to the hospital. Get someone to wash this floor."

Two men were carrying the remains of O Nine Morgan, the trunk wrapped in a ground sheet. They carried him in a bandy chair[†] out of the hut. His arms over their shoulders waved a jocular farewell. There would be an ambulance stretcher on bicycle wheels outside.

---

[*] Merthyr Tydfil, about 40 km from Cardiff, where Ford was stationed in 1916 before being sent to France.

[†] A bandy chair is formed by two men crossing their arms and linking their hands together to carry something heavy, such as a dead body.

II

THE "All Clear" went at once after that. Its suddenness was something surprising, the mournful-cheerful, long notes dying regretfully on a night that had only just gone quiet after the perfectly astonishing row. The moon had taken it into its head to rise; begumboiled, jocular and grotesque, it came from behind the shoulder of one of the hut-covered hills and sent down the lines of Tietjens'[1] huts, long, sentimental rays that converted the place into a slumbering, pastoral settlement. There was no sound that did not contribute to the silence, little dim lights shone through the celluloid casements. Of Sergeant-Major Cowley, his numerals gilded by the moon in the lines of A Company, Tietjens, who was easing his lungs of coke vapours for a minute, asked in a voice that hushed itself in tribute to the moonlight and the now keen frost:

"Where the deuce is the draft?"

The sergeant-major looked poetically down a ribbon of whitewashed stones that descended the black down-side. Over the next shoulder of hill was the blur of a hidden conflagration.

"There's a Hun plane burning down there. In Twenty-Seven's parade ground. The draft's round that, sir," he said.

Tietjens said:

"Good God!" in a voice of caustic tolerance. He added, "I did think we had drilled some discipline into these blighters in the seven weeks we have had them. . . . You remember the first time when we had them on parade and that acting lance-corporal left the ranks to heave a rock at a sea-gull . . . And called you 'Ol' Hunkey! . . . Conduct prejudicial to good order and military discipline? Where's that Canadian sergeant-major? Where's the officer in charge of the draft?"

Sergeant-Major Cowley said:

"Sergeant-Major Ledoux said it was like a cattle-stampede on the . . . some river where they come from. You *couldn't* stop them, sir. It was their first German plane. . . . And they going up the line to-night, sir."

"To-night!" Tietjens exclaimed. "Next Christmas!"

The sergeant-major said:

"Poor boys!" and continued to gaze into the distance. "I heard another good one, sir," he said. "The answer to the one about the King saluting a private soldier and he not taking any notice is: when he's dead. . . . But if you marched a company into a field through a gateway and you wanted to get it out again but you did not know any command in the drill book for change of direction, what would you do, sir? . . . You have to get that company out, but you must not use About Turn, or Right or Left Wheel. . . . There's another one, too, about saluting. . . . The officer in charge of draft is Second-Lieutenant Hotchkiss. . . .* But he's an A.S.C. officer and turned of sixty. A farrier he is, sir, in civil life. An A.S.C. major was asking me, sir, very civil, if you could not detail someone else. He says he doubts if Second-Lieutenant Hitchcock . . . Hotchkiss could walk as far as the station, let alone march the men, him not knowing anything but cavalry words of command, if he knows them. He's only been in the army a fortnight. . . ."

Tietjens turned from the idyllic scene with the words:

"I suppose the Canadian sergeant-major and Lieutenant Hotchkiss are doing what they can to get their men to come back."

He re-entered the hut.

Captain Mackenzie in the light of a fantastically brilliant hurricane lamp appeared to be bathing dejectedly in a surf of coiling papers spread on the table before him.

"There's all this bumph," he said, "just come from all the head-quarters in the bally world."

Tietjens said cheerfully:

"What's it all about?" There were, the other answered, Garrison Headquarter orders, Divisional orders, Lines of Communication orders, half a dozen A.F.W.B. two four two's. A

---

*   The name perhaps suggested by the QF Six-pounder Hotchkiss 57mm gun; originally a naval weapon, but also used variously for coastal defences or tanks. E. S. Turner, *Dear Old Blighty*, 118, writes of Commander Rawlinson's anti-aircraft defences (an Admiralty responsibility): 'He had a naval gun in Regents Park, another at Tower Bridge and a scratch lot of Hotchkiss six-pounders and pom-poms scattered about the city.'

terrific strafe from First Army forwarded from Garrison H.Q. about the draft's not having reached Hazebrouck* the day before yesterday. Tietjens said:

"Answer them politely to the effect that we had orders not to send off the draft without its complement of four hundred Canadian Railway Service men—the fellows in furred hoods. They only reached us from Etaples at five this afternoon without blankets or ring papers. Or any other papers for the matter of that."

Mackenzie was studying with increased gloom a small buff memorandum slip:

"This appears to be meant for you privately," he said. "I can't make head or tail of it otherwise. It isn't *marked* private."

He tossed the buff slip across the table.

Tietjens sank down bulkily on to his bully-beef case. He read on the buff at first the initials of the signature, "E.C. Genl.," and then: "For God's sake keep your wife off me. I *will* not have skirts round my H.Q.[2] You are more trouble to me than all the rest of my command put together."

Tietjens groaned and sank more deeply on to his beef case. It was as if an unseen and unsuspected wild beast had jumped on his neck from an overhanging branch. The sergeant-major at his side said in his most admirable butler manner:

"Colour-Sergeant Morgan and Lance-Corporal Trench are obliging us by coming from depot orderly room to help with the draft's papers. Why don't you and the other officer go and get a bit of dinner, sir? The colonel and the padre have only just come in to mess, and I've warned the mess orderlies to keep your food 'ot. . . . Both good men with papers, Morgan and Trench. We can send the soldiers' small books to you at table to sign. . . ."

His feminine solicitude enraged and overwhelmed Tietjens with blackness. He told the sergeant-major that he was to go to

---

* Ford recalled how at Hazebrouck station he was 'rendered particularly moody by the fact that on the dimmed bookstall of the dimmed station I had seen a dim copy of one of my own books', and commented: 'It seemed to me amazing that I had ever written books at all': 'Supper Reminiscences', *New York Herald Tribune Magazine* (18 Aug. 1929), 20–1, 23 (20). He had given a similar memory to the narrator of *The Marsden Case*, 302: 'I saw the back of someone's translation of one of my own books. Dusty! No human soul would ever assimilate it. And no human soul, I thought, would ever think of me again . . . .' Ford's propaganda book *Between St. Dennis and St. George* (London, New York, Toronto: Hodder and Stoughton, 1915) had been translated into French in 1916.

hell, for he himself was not going to leave that hut till the draft was moved off. Captain Mackenzie could do as he pleased. The sergeant-major told Captain Mackenzie that Captain Tietjens took as much trouble with his rag-time detachments as if he had been the Coldstream adjutant at Chelsea sending off a draft of Guards.* Captain Mackenzie said that that was why they damn well got their details off four days faster than any other I.B.D. in that camp. He *would* say that much, he added grudgingly and dropped his head over his papers again. The hut was moving slowly up and down before the eyes of Tietjens. He might have just been kicked in the stomach. That was how shocks took him. He said to himself that by God he must take himself in hand. He grabbed with his heavy hands at a piece of buff paper and wrote on it a column of fat, wet letters

a
b
b
a
a
b
b
a and so on.

He said opprobriously to Captain Mackenzie:
"Do you know what a sonnet is? Give me the rhymes for a sonnet. That's the plan of it."
Mackenzie grumbled:
"Of course I know what a sonnet is. What's your game?"
Tietjens said:
"Give me the fourteen end-rhymes of a sonnet and I'll write

---

* His Majesty's Coldstream Regiment of Foot Guards, established in 1650, is the oldest regiment in the Regular Army. Ford probably took an introductory course at the Chelsea Barracks before joining his regiment in Wales (Saunders, *Dual Life* I 486). In the 'Dedicatory Letter' to *The Good Soldier* he wrote: 'I was on parade again, being examined in drill, on the Guards' Square at Chelsea. And, since I was petrified with nervousness, having to do it before a half-dozen elderly gentlemen with red hatbands, I got my men about as hopelessly boxed as it is possible to do with the gentlemen privates of H. M. Coldstream Guards. Whilst I stood stiffly at attention one of the elderly red hatbands walked close behind my back and said distinctly in my ear, "Did you say *The* Good Soldier?"': *The Good Soldier*, 6.

the lines. In under two minutes and a half."

Mackenzie said injuriously:

"If you do I'll turn it into Latin hexameters in three. In *under* three minutes."*

They were like men uttering deadly insults the one to the other. To Tietjens it was as if an immense cat were parading, fascinated and fatal, round that hut. He had imagined himself parted from his wife.[3] He had not heard from his wife since her four-in-the-morning departure from their flat, months and eternities ago, with the dawn just showing up the chimney-pots of the Georgian roof-trees opposite. In the complete stillness of dawn he had heard her voice say very clearly "Paddington" to the chauffeur, and then all the sparrows in the inn[†] waking up in chorus.... Suddenly and appallingly it came into his head that it might not have been his wife's voice that had said "Paddington," but her maid's.... He was a man who lived very much by rules of conduct. He had a rule: *Never think on the subject of a shock at a moment of shock.* The mind was then too sensitized. Subjects of shock require to be thought all round. If your mind thinks when it is too sensitized its then conclusions will be too strong. So he exclaimed to Mackenzie:

"Haven't you got your rhymes yet? Damn it *all!*" Mackenzie grumbled offensively:

"No, I haven't. It's more difficult to get rhymes than to write sonnets.... death, moil, coil, breath...." He paused.

"Heath, soil, toil, staggereth," Tietjens said contemptuously. "That's your sort of Oxford young woman's rhyme.... Go on ... *What is it?*"

An extremely age-faded and unmilitary officer was beside the blanketed table. Tietjens regretted having spoken to him with ferocity. He had a grotesquely thin white beard. Positively, white whiskers! He must have gone through as much of the army as he had gone through with those whiskers, because no superior

---

*   Ford writes in a postscript to his Preface to *On Heaven and Poems Written on Active Service* (London: John Lane, 1918) that he and Officer Commanding the Company H. C. James did what Tietjens and McKechnie do here: 'When in a minute or two I had filled in the lines in English, in a few seconds he would supply the Latin version' (10). He includes both versions of these poems in an Appendix (111–28).

†   Gray's Inn, one of the Inns of Court, where their flat is located.

officer—not even a field-marshal—would have the heart to tell him to take them off! It was the measure of his pathos. This ghost-like object was[4] apologizing for not having been able to keep the draft in hand: he was requesting his superior to observe that these Colonial troops were[5] without any instincts of discipline. None at all. Tietjens observed that he had a blue cross on his right arm where the vaccination marks are as a rule. He imagined the Canadians talking to this hero.... The hero began to talk of Major Cornwallis of the R.A.S.C.

Tietjens said apropos of nothing:

"Is there a Major Cornwallis in the A.S.C.? Good God!"

The hero protested faintly:

"The *R*.A.S.C."

Tietjens said kindly:

"Yes. Yes. The *Royal* Army Service Corps."

Obviously his mind until now had regarded his wife's "*Paddington*" as the definite farewell between his life and hers.... He had imagined her, like Eurydice, tall, but faint and pale, sinking back into the shades.... "*Che farò senz' Euridice?*..." he hummed.* Absurd! And of course it might have been only the maid that had spoken.... She too had a remarkably clear voice. So that the mystic word "Paddington" might perfectly well be no symbol at all, and Mrs. Sylvia Tietjens, far from being faint and pale, might perfectly well be playing the very devil with half the general officers commanding in chief from Whitehall to Alaska.

Mackenzie—he *was* like a damned clerk—was transferring the rhymes that he had no doubt at last found, on to another sheet of paper. Probably he had a round, copybook hand. Positively, his tongue followed his pen round, inside his lips.† These were what His Majesty's regular officers of to-day were. Good God! A

---

*   The beginning of an aria from Christoph Gluck's opera *Orfeo ed Euridice* (1762). The question asked in Italian is 'What am I to do without Eurydice?' In Ovid's story (*Metamorphoses* 10.1) Eurydice, whom Orpheus is leading out of Hades, vanishes there forever when he turns and looks to see if his wife is following him, thereby disobeying Persephone's prohibition that he not look back to do so. Gluck nonetheless gives the story a happy ending. In comparing Sylvia to Eurydice, Tietjens hopes for Ovid's ending even as he hums Gluck's aria. Cf. Ford's story 'The Baron', *Macmillan's*, 87 (February 1903), 304–20: 'humming che farò' (314); and *Great Trade Route* (London: Allen and Unwin, 1937), 172: 'finding himself humming ché farò senz' Eurydice'.

†   So too with Lascelles in the *Fifth Queen* trilogy (London: Bodley Head, 1962), 473.

damned intelligent, dark-looking fellow. Of the type that is starved in its youth and takes all the scholarships[6] that the board schools have to offer. Eyes too big and black. Like a Malay's.... Any blasted member of any subject race.

The A.S.C. fellow had been talking positively about horses. He had offered his services in order to study the variation of pink-eye that was decimating all the service horses in the lines.* He had been a professor—positively a professor—in some farriery college or other. Tietjens said that, in that case, he ought to be in the A.V.C.—the *Royal* Army Veterinary Corps perhaps it was. The old man said he didn't know. He imagined that the R.A.S.C. had wanted his service for their own horses....

Tietjens said:

"I'll tell you what to do, Lieutenant Hitchcock.... For, damn it, you're a stout fellow...." The poor old fellow, pushing out at that age from the cloisters of some provincial university ... He certainly did not look a horsy sportsman....

The old lieutenant said:

"Hotchkiss ..." And Tietjens exclaimed:

"Of course it's Hotchkiss ... I've seen your name signing a testimonial to Pigg's Horse Embrocation.... Then if you don't want to take this draft up the line ... Though I'd advise you to ... It's merely a Cook's Tour† to Hazebrouck ... No, Bailleul ... And the sergeant-major will march the men for you ... And you will have been in the First Army Lines and able to tell all your friends you've been on active service at the real front...."

His mind said to himself while his words went on ...

"Then, good God, if Sylvia is actively paying attention to my career I shall be the laughing-stock of the whole army. I was thinking that ten minutes ago![7] ... What's to be done? What in God's name is to be done?" A black crape veil seemed to drop across his vision ... Liver ...

Lieutenant Hotchkiss said with dignity:

"I'm *going* to the front. I'm going to the real front. I was passed

---

* Pink-eye is conjunctivitis, a swelling or infection of the membrane lining the eyelids (conjunctiva).

† Thomas Cook was the first person to organise tours in England (in 1841) and, subsequently, abroad. As Thomas Cook and Son, his became a renowned worldwide travel agency until it was bought out by Companie Internationale des Wagons-Lits in 1928.

A1 this morning. I am going to study the blood reactions of the service horse under fire."

"Well, you're a damn good chap," Tietjens said. There was nothing to be done. The amazing activities of which Sylvia would be capable were just the thing to send laughter raging like fire through a cachinnating army. She could not, thank God, get into France: to that place. But she could make scandals in the papers that every Tommie read. There was no game of which she was not capable. That sort of pursuit was called "pulling the strings of shower-baths" in her circle of friends.[8]* Nothing. Nothing to be done. . . . The beastly hurricane lamp was smoking.

"I'll tell you what to do," he said to Lieutenant Hotchkiss.

Mackenzie had tossed his sheet of rhymes under his nose. Tietjens read: *Death, moil, coil, breath* ... *Saith*—"The dirty Cockney!" *Oil, soil, wraith*. . . .

"I'd be blowed," Mackenzie said with a vicious grin, "if I was going to give you rhymes you had suggested yourself . . . "

The officer said:

"I don't of course want to be a nuisance if you're busy."

"It's no nuisance," Tietjens said. "It's what we're for. But I'd suggest that now and then you say 'sir' to the officer commanding your unit. It sounds well before the men. . . . Now you go to No. XVI I.B.D. Mess ante-room . . . The place where they've got the broken bagatelle-table. . . ."†

The voice of Sergeant-Major Cowley exclaimed tranquilly from outside:

"Fall in now. Men who've got their ring papers and identity disks—three of them—on the left. Men who haven't, on the right. Any man who has not been able to draw his blankets tell Colour-Sergeant Morgan. Don't forget. You won't get any where you're going. Any man who hasn't made his will in his Soldier's Small Book or elsewhere and wants to, to consult Captain Tietjens. Any man who wants to draw money, ask Captain

---

* It was certainly a phrase Violet Hunt used in her diary. When, on 8 Sept. 1917, she heard confirmation of a rumour that Ford had failed to settle a betting debt, she sent him a cheque made out to the creditor, noting with satisfaction: 'A showerbath string pulled'. See Secor and Secor, eds, *The Return of the Good Soldier*, 11–12.

† Bagatelle is a table game related to billiards, in which small balls are struck past pins, which act as obstacles, into numbered holes; thought to be a precursor of pinball.

Mackenzie. Any R.C. who wants to go to confession after he has got his papers signed can find the R.C. padre in the fourth hut from the left in the Main Line from here.... And damn kind it is of his reverence to put himself out for a set of damn blinking mustard-faced red herrings like you who can't keep from running away to the first baby's bonfire you sees. You'll be running the other way before you're a week older, though what good they as asks for you thinks you'll be out there God knows. You *look* like a squad of infants' companions from a Wesleyan Sunday school. That's what you look like and, thank God, we've got a Navy."

Under cover of his voice Tietjens had been writing:

"Now we affront the grinning chops of *Death*," and saying to Lieutenant Hotchkiss:[9] "In the I.B.D. ante-room you'll find any number of dirty little squits of Glamorganshires drinking themselves blind over *La Vie Parisienne*.... * Ask any one of them you like...." He wrote:

"And in between our carcass and the *moil*
Of marts and cities, toil and moil and *coil*..."

"You think this difficult!" he said to Mackenzie. "Why, you've written a whole undertaker's mortuary ode in the rhymes alone," and went on to Hotchkiss: "Ask anyone you like as long as he's a P.B. officer.... Do you know what P.B. means? No, not Poor Bloody, Permanent Base. Unfit ... If he'd like to take a draft to Bailleul."

The hut was filling with devious, slow, ungainly men in yellow-brown. Their feet shuffled desultorily; they lumped dull canvas bags along the floor and held in unliterary hands small open books that they dropped from time to time. From outside came a continuing, swelling and descending chant of voices; at times it would seem to be all one laugh, at times one menace, then the motives mingled fugally, like the sea on a beach of large stones. It seemed to Tietjens suddenly extraordinary how shut in on oneself one was in this life.... He sat scribbling fast: "Old Spectre blows a cold protecting *breath* ... Vanity of vanities, the preacher *saith* ... No more parades, not any more, no *oil* ..." He

---

* A French magazine that pictured women scantily dressed and in suggestive poses.

was telling Hotchkiss, who was obviously shy of approaching the Glamorganshires in their ante-room ... "Unambergris'd our limbs in the naked *soil* ..." that he did not suppose any P.B. officer would object. They would go on a beanfeast up into the giddy line in a first-class carriage and get draft leave and command pay too probably ... "No funeral struments* cast before our wraiths ..." If any fellow does object, you just send his name to me and I will damn well shove it into extra orders....

The advanced wave of the brown tide of men was already at his feet. The extraordinary complications of even the simplest lives! ... A fellow was beside him ... Private Logan, formerly, of all queer things for a Canadian private, a trooper of the Inniskillings:[10] owner, of all queer things, of a milk-walk or a dairy farm, outside Sydney, which is in Australia ... A man of sentimental complications, jauntiness as became an Inniskilling, a Cockney accent such as ornaments the inhabitants of Sydney, and a complete distrust of lawyers. On the other hand, with the completest trust in Tietjens. Over his shoulder—he was blond, upright, with his numerals shining like gold, looked a lumpish, *café-au-lait*, eagle-nosed countenance: a half-caste member of one of the Six Nations,† who had been a doctor's errand boy in Quebec ... He had his troubles, but was difficult to understand. Behind him, very black-avised‡ with a high colour, truculent eyes and an Irish accent, was a graduate of McGill University who had been a teacher of languages in Tokio and had some sort of claim against the Japanese Government ... And faces, two and two, in a coil round the hut ... Like dust: like a cloud of dust that would approach and overwhelm a landscape: every one with preposterous troubles and anxieties, even if they did not overwhelm you personally with them ... Brown dust ...

He kept the Inniskilling waiting while he scribbled the rapid sestet to his sonnet which ought to make a little plainer what it all meant. Of course the general idea was that, when you got into

---

* Though the spelling might suggest an abbreviation of 'instruments', it is more likely a variant on 'strewment': as in 'flowers, etc. strewed on a grave' (*OED*, citing *Hamlet* V.i.256, 'Yet heere she is allowed her Virgin Rites, Her Maiden strewments [...]').

† Also known as the Iriquois Confederacy, which was composed of Mohawks, Oneidas, Onondagas, Cayugas, Senecas, and Turcaroras – tribes that inhabited north-eastern North America.

‡ *OED* glosses 'dark-a-vised' as 'Dark-complexioned'.

the line or near it, there was no room for swank: typified by expensive funerals. As you might say: No flowers by compulsion ... No more parades! ... He had also to explain, while he did it, to the heroic veterinary sexagenarian that he need not feel shy about going into the Glamorganshire Mess on a man-catching expedition. The Glamorganshires were bound to lend him, Tietjens, P.B. officers if they had not got other jobs. Lieutenant Hotchkiss could speak to Colonel Johnson, whom he would find in the mess and quite good-natured over his dinner. A pleasant and sympathetic old gentleman who would appreciate Hotchkiss's desire not to go superfluously into the line. Hotchkiss could offer to take a look at the colonel's charger: a Hun horse, captured on the Marne and called Schomburg, that was off its feed.... He added: "But don't do anything professional to Schomburg. I ride him myself!"[11]

He threw his sonnet across to Mackenzie, who with a background of huddled khaki limbs and anxious faces was himself anxiously counting out French currency notes and dubious-looking tokens ... What the deuce did men want to draw money—sometimes quite large sums of money, the Canadians being paid in dollars converted into local coins—when in an hour or so they would be going up? But they always did and their accounts were always in an incredibly entangled state. Mackenzie might well look worried. As like as not he might find himself a fiver or more down at the end of the evening for unauthorised payments. If he had only his pay and an extravagant wife to keep, that might well put the wind up him. But that was *his* funeral. He told Lieutenant Hotchkiss to come and have a chat with him in his hut, the one next the mess. About horses. He knew a little about horse-illness himself. Only empirically, of course.

Mackenzie was looking at his watch.

"You took two minutes and eleven seconds," he said. "I'll take it for granted it's a sonnet ... I have not read it because I can't turn it into Latin here ... I haven't got your knack of doing eleven things at once...."

A man with a worried face, encumbered by a bundle and a small book, was studying figures at Mackenzie's elbow. He interrupted Mackenzie in a high American voice to say that he had never drawn fourteen dollars seventy-five cents in Thrasna

Barracks, Aldershot.

Mackenzie said to Tietjens:

"You understand. I have not read your sonnet. I shall turn it into Latin in the mess: in the time stipulated. I don't want you to think I've read it and taken time to think about it."

The man beside him said:

"When I went to the Canadian Agent, Strand, London, his office was shut up . . . ."*

Mackenzie said with white fury:

"How much service have you got? Don't you know better than to interrupt an officer when he is talking? You must settle your own figures with your own confounded Colonial paymaster: I've sixteen dollars thirty cents here for you. Will you take them or leave them?"

Tietjens said:

"I know that man's case. Turn him over to me. It isn't complicated. He's got his paymaster's cheque, but doesn't know how to cash it and of course they won't give him another. . . ."

The man with slow, broad, brown features looked from one to the other officer's face and back again with a keen black-eyed scrutiny as if he were looking into a wind and dazed by the light. He began a long story of how he owed Fat-Eared Bill fifty dollars lost at House.† He was perhaps half Chinese, half Finn. He continued to talk, being in a state of great anxiety about his money. Tietjens addressed himself to the cases of the Sydney Inniskilling ex-trooper and the McGill graduate who had suffered at the hands of the Japanese Educational Ministry. It made altogether a complicated effect. "You would say," Tietjens said to himself, "that, all together, it ought to be enough to take my mind up."

The upright trooper had a very complicated sentimental history. It was difficult to advise him before his fellows. He, however, felt no diffidence. He discussed the points of the girl

---

* 'Army agents kept the accounts of army regiments, distributing pay and subsistence, dealing in supplies of clothing, claims for pensions and injury, and providing a general banking business for soldiers and their families' (RBS Heritage Online). Canada House is on Trafalgar Square, at the west end of the Strand.

† 'Lotto played (orig. in the Army) as a gambling game with special cards and checks': OED.

called Rosie whom he had followed from Sydney to British Columbia, of the girl called Gwen with whom he had taken up in Aberystwyth, of the woman called Mrs. Hosier with whom he had lived maritally, on a sleeping-out pass, at Berwick St. James, near Salisbury Plain. Through the continuing voice of the half-caste Chinaman he discussed them with a large tolerance, explaining that he wanted them all to have a bit, as a souvenir, if he happened to stop one out there. Tietjens handed him the draft of a will he had written out for him, asked him to read it attentively and copy it with his own hand into his soldier's small book. Then Tietjens would witness it for him. He said:

"Do you think this will make my old woman in Sydney part? I guess it won't. She's a sticker, sir. A regular July bur, God bless her."* The McGill graduate was beginning already to introduce a further complication into his story of complications with the Japanese Government. It appeared that in addition to his scholastic performances he had invested a little money in a mineral water spring near Kobe,† the water, bottled, being exported to San Francisco. Apparently his company had been indulging in irregularities according to Japanese law, but a pure French Canadian, who had experienced some difficulties in obtaining his baptismal certificate from a mission somewhere in the direction of the Klondyke, was allowed by Tietjens to interrupt the story of the graduate; and several men without complications, but anxious to get their papers signed so as to write last letters home before the draft moved, overflowed across Tietjens' table....

The tobacco smoke from the pipes of the N.C.O.'s at the other end of the room hung, opalescent, beneath the wire cages of the brilliant hurricane lamps hung over each table; buttons and numerals gleamed in the air that the universal khaki tinge of the limbs seemed to turn brown, as if into a gas of dust. Nasal voices, throat voices, drawling voices, melted into a rustle so that the occasional high, sing-song profanity of a Welch[12‡] N.C.O.: Why

---

* Cf. Ford's novel *The Panel: A Sheer Comedy* (London: Constable, 1912), 12–13: 'What I want you to understand [...] is that Mrs. Kerr Howe is not an awful past [*sic*]. She's just a bur. She's a sticker. That's what she is.'

† Ford's friend René Byles, the managing director of his Edwardian publisher, Alston Rivers, 'went to Japan to run a mineral water business dealing in Tan San water': *Return to Yesterday* (1931), ed. Bill Hutchings (Manchester: Carcanet, 1999), 183.

‡ Ford's Welch Regiment used this spelling.

the *hell* haffn't you got your 124? Why the bloody hell haffn't you got your 124? Don't you *know* you haff to haff your bleedin' 124's? seemed to wail tragically through a silence . . . The evening wore on and on. It astounded Tietjens, looking at one time at his watch to discover that it was only 21 hrs. 19. He seemed to have been thinking drowsily of his own affairs for ten hours. . . . For, in the end, these were his own affairs. . . . Money, women, testamentary bothers. Each of these complications from over the Atlantic and round the world were his own troubles: a world in labour: an army being moved off in the night. Shoved off. Anyhow. And over the top. A lateral section of the world. . . .

He had happened to glance at the medical history of a man beside him and noticed that he had been described as C1. . . . It was obviously a slip of the pen on the part of the Medical Board, or one of their orderlies. He had written C instead of A. The man was Pte. 197394 Thomas Johnson, a shining-faced lump of beef, an agricultural odd jobman from British Columbia where he had worked on the immense estates of Sylvia Tietjens' portentous ducal second cousin Rugeley. It was a double annoyance. Tietjens had not wanted to be reminded of his wife's second cousin, because he had not wanted to be reminded of his wife. He had determined to give his thoughts a field day on that subject when he got warm into his flea-bag in his hut that smelt of paraffin whilst the canvas walls crackled with frost and the moon shone. . . . He would think of Sylvia beneath the moon. He was determined not to now! But 197394 Pte. Johnson, Thomas, was otherwise a nuisance and Tietjens cursed himself for having glanced at the man's medical history. If this preposterous yokel was C3 he could not go on a draft . . . C1 rather! It was all the same. That would mean finding another man to make up the strength and that would drive Sergeant-Major Cowley out of his mind. He looked up towards the ingenuous, protruding, shining, liquid, bottle-blue eyes of Thomas Johnson. . . . The fellow had never had an illness. He could not have had an illness—except from a surfeit of cold, fat, boiled pork—and for that you would give him a horse's blue ball and drench which, ten to one, would not remove the cause of the belly-ache. . . .

His eyes met the non-committal glance of a dark, gentlemanly thin fellow with a strikingly scarlet hat-band, a lot of gilt about his khaki and little strips of steel chain-armour on his shoulders.... Levin ... Colonel Levin, G.S.O. II, or something, attached to General Lord Edward Campion.... How the hell did fellows get into these intimacies of commanders of units and their men? Swimming in like fishes into the brown air of a tank and there at your elbow ... Bloody spies! ... The men had all been called to attention and stood like gasping codfish. The ever-watchful Sergeant-Major Cowley had drifted to his, Tietjens', elbow. You protect your orfcers from the gawdy Staff as you protect your infant daughters in lambswool from draughts. The dark, bright, cheerful staffwallah said with a slight lisp:

"Busy, I see." He might have been standing there for a century and have a century of the battalion headquarters' time to waste like that. "What draft is this?"

Sergeant-Major Cowley, always ready in case his orfcer should not know the name of his unit or his own name, said:

"No. 16 I.B.D. Canadian First Division Casual Number Four Draft, sir."

Colonel Levin let air lispingly out between his teeth.

"No. 16 Draft not off yet ... Dear, dear! Dear, dear! ... We shall be strafed to hell by First Army...." He used the word hell as if he had first wrapped it in eau-de-cologned cotton-wadding.

Tietjens, on his feet, knew this fellow very well: a fellow who had been a very bad Society water-colour painter of good family on the mother's side: hence the cavalry gadgets on his shoulders. Would it then be good ... say good taste to explode? He let the sergeant-major do it. Sergeant-Major Cowley was of the type of N.C.O. who carried weight because he knew ten times as much about his job as any Staff officer. The sergeant-major explained that it had been impossible to get off the draft earlier. The colonel said:

"But surely, sergeant-majah ..."

The sergeant-major, now a deferential shopwalker in a lady's store, pointed out that they had had urgent instructions not to send up the draft without the four hundred Canadian Railway Service men who were to come from Etaples. These men had only arrived that evening at 5.30 ... at Rouen Station.[13] Marching them up had taken three-quarters of an hour. The colonel said:

"But surely, sergeant-majah ..."

Old Cowley[14] might as well have said "madam" as "sir" to the red hat-band.... The four hundred had come with only what they stood up in. The unit had had to wangle everything: boots, blankets, toothbrushes, braces, rifles, iron-rations, identity disks out of the depot store. And it was now only twenty-one twenty.... Cowley[15] permitted his commanding officer at this point to say:

"You must understand that we work in circumstances of extreme difficulty, sir...."

The graceful colonel was lost in an absent contemplation of his perfectly elegant knees.

"I know, of course...." he lisped. "Very difficult ..." He brightened up to add: "But you must admit you're unfortunate.... You must admit that...." The weight settled, however, again on his mind.

Tietjens said:

"Not, I suppose, sir, any more unfortunate than any other unit working under a dual control for supplies...."

The colonel said:

"What's that? Dual ... Ah, I see you're there, McKechnie.... [16] Feeling well ... feeling fit, eh?"

The whole hut stood silent. His anger at the waste of time made Tietjens say:

"If you understand, sir, we are a unit whose principal purpose is drawing things to equip drafts with...." This fellow was delaying them atrociously. He was brushing his knees with a handkerchief! "I've had," Tietjens said, "a man killed on my hands this afternoon because we have to draw tin-hats for my orderly room from Dublin on an A.F.B. Canadian from Aldershot.... Killed here ... We've only just mopped up the blood from where you're standing...."

The cavalry colonel exclaimed:

"Oh, good gracious me! ..." jumped a little and examined his beautiful shining knee-high aircraft boots. "Killed! ... Here! ... But there'll have to be a court of inquiry.... You certainly are *most* unfortunate, Captain Tietjens.... Always these mysterious ... Why wasn't your man in a dug-out? ... Most unfortunate.... We cannot have casualties among the Colonial troops.... Troops from the Dominions, I mean...."

Tietjens said grimly:

"The man was from Pontardulais ... not from any Dominion.... One of my orderly room.... We are forbidden on pain of court martial to let any but Dominion Expeditionary Force[17] men go into the dug-outs.... My Canadians were all there... It's an A.C.I. local of the eleventh of November...."

The Staff officer said:

"It makes of course, a difference! ... Only a Glamorganshire? You say ... Oh, well.... But these mysterious ..."

He exclaimed, with the force of an explosion, and the relief:

"Look here ... can you spare possibly ten ... twenty ... eh ... minutes? ... It's not exactly a service matter ... so per ..."

Tietjens exclaimed:

"You see how we're situated, colonel ..." and, like one sowing grass seed on a lawn, extended both hands over his papers and towards his men.... He was choking with rage. Colonel Levin had, under the chaperonage of an English dowager, who ran a chocolate store down on the quays in Rouen, a little French piece to whom he was quite seriously engaged. In the most naïve manner. And the young woman, fantastically jealous, managed to make endless insults to herself out of her almost too handsome colonel's barbaric French. It was an idyll, but it drove the colonel frantic. At such times Levin would consult Tietjens, who passed for a man of brains and a French scholar as to really nicely turned compliments in a difficult language.... And as to how you explained that it was necessary for a G.S.O. II, or whatever the colonel was, to be seen quite frequently in the company of very handsome V.A.D.'s and female organizers of all arms ... It was the sort of silliness as to which no gentleman ought to be consulted.... And here was Levin with the familiar feminine-agonized wrinkle on his bronzed-alabaster brow.... Like a beastly soldier-man out of a revue. Why didn't the ass burst into gesture and a throaty tenor....

Sergeant-Major Cowley naturally saved the situation. Just as Tietjens was as near saying *Go to hell* as you can be to your remarkably senior officer on parade, the sergeant-major, now a very important solicitor's most confidential clerk, began whispering to the colonel....

"The captain might as well take a spell as not.... We're

through with all the men except the Canadian Railway batch, and they can't be issued with blankets not for half an hour ... not for three-quarters. If then! It depends if our runner can find where Quarter's lance-corporal is having his supper, to issue them...." The sergeant-major had inserted that last speech deftly. The Staff officer, with a vague reminiscence of his regimental days, exclaimed:

"Damn it! ... I wonder you don't break into the depot blanket store and take what you want...."

The sergeant-major, becoming Simon Pure,* exclaimed:

"Oh, no, sir, we could never do that, sir...."

"But the confounded men are urgently needed in the line," Colonel Levin said. "Damn it, it's touch and go! ... We're rushing ..." He appreciated the fact again that he was on the gawdy Staff, and that the sergeant-major and Tietjens, playing like left backs into each other's hands, had trickily let him in.

"We can only pray, sir," the sergeant-major said, "that these 'ere bloomin' 'Uns has got quartermasters and depots and issuing departments, same as ourselves." He lowered his voice into a husky whisper. "Besides, sir, there's a rumour ... round the telephone in depot orderly room ... that there's a W.O. order at 'Edquarters ... countermanding this and other drafts...."

Colonel Levin said: "Oh, my God!" and consternation rushed upon both him and Tietjens.[18] The frozen ditches, in the night, out there; the agonized waiting for men; the weight upon the mind like a weight upon the brows; the imminent sense of approaching unthinkableness on the right or the left, according as you looked up or down the trench; the solid protecting earth of the parapet then turns into pierced mist ... and no reliefs coming from here.... The men up there thinking naïvely that they were coming, and they not coming. Why not? Good God, why not? Mackenzie said:

"Poor bloody old Bird ... His crowd had been in eleven weeks last Wednesday.... About all they could stick...."[19]

---

*   Simon Pure is a character in Susanna Centlivre's play *A Bold Stroke for a Wife* (1718): a fire-and-brimstone Quaker preacher, impersonated by Colonel Fainwell, but who then appears in person. His name has become a byword for authenticity, but also in modern usage a hypocrite, 'one who makes a great parade of virtue', as *Brewer's Dictionary of Phrase and Fable* has it.

"They'll have to stick a damn lot more," Colonel Levin said. "I'd like to get at some of the brutes...."[20] It was at that date the settled conviction of His Majesty's Expeditionary Force that the army in the field was the tool of politicians and civilians. In moments of routine that cloud dissipated itself lightly: when news of ill omen arrived it settled down again heavily like a cloud of black gas. You hung your head impotently....

"So that," the sergeant-major said cheerfully, "the captain could very well spare half an hour to get his dinner. Or for anything else...." Apart from the domestic desire that Tietjens' digestion should not suffer from irregular meals he had the professional conviction that for his captain to be in intimate private converse with a member of the gawdy Staff was good for the unit.... "I suppose, sir," he added valedictorily to Tietjens, "I'd better arrange to put this draft, and the nine hundred men that came in this afternoon to replace them, twenty in a tent.... It's lucky we didn't strike them...."

Tietjens and the colonel began to push men out of their way, going towards the door. The Inniskilling-Canadian, a small, open brown book extended deprecatingly stood, modestly obtrusive, just beside the doorpost. Catching avidly at Tietjens' "Eh?" he said:

"You'd got the names of the girls wrong in your copy, sir. It was Gwen Lewis I had a child by in Aberystwyth that I wanted to have the lease of the cottage and the ten bob a week. Mrs. Hosier that I lived with in Berwick St. James, she was only to have five guineas for a soovneer.... I've took the liberty of changing the names back again...."

Tietjens grabbed the book from him, and bending down at the sergeant-major's table scrawled his signature on the bluish page. He thrust the book back at the man and said:

"There ... fall out." The man's face shone. He exclaimed:

"Thank you, sir. Thank you kindly, captain.... I wanted to get off and go to confession. I did bad...." The McGill graduate with his arrogant black moustache put himself in the way as Tietjens struggled into his British warm.*

---

* 'British (Service) warm, a warm short overcoat worn especially by officers in the army': *OED.*

"You won't forget, sir, . . ." he began.

Tietjens said:

"Damn you, I've told you I won't forget. I never forget. You instructed the ignorant Jap in Asaki, but the educational authority is in Tokio. And your flagitious mineral-water[21] company had their headquarters at the Tan Sen spring near Kobe. . . . Is that right? Well, I'll do my best for you."

They walked in silence through the groups of men that hung round the orderly room door and gleamed in the moonlight. In the broad country street of the main line of the camp Colonel Levin began to mutter between his teeth:

"You take enough trouble with your beastly crowd . . . a whole lot of trouble. . . . Yet . . ."

"Well, what's the matter with us?" Tietjens said. "We get our drafts ready in thirty-six hours less than any other unit in this command."

"I know you do," the other conceded. "It's only all these mysterious rows. Now . . ."

Tietjens said quickly:

"Do you mind my asking: Are we still on parade? Is this a strafe from General Campion as to the way I command my unit?"[22]

The other conceded quite as quickly and much more worriedly:

"God forbid." He added more quickly still: "Old bean!" and prepared to tuck his wrist under Tietjens' elbow. Tietjens, however, continued to face the fellow. He was really in a temper.

"Then tell me," he said, "how the deuce you can manage to do without an overcoat in this weather?" If only he could get the chap off the topics of his mysterious rows they might drift to the matter that had brought him up there on that bitter night when he should be sitting over a good wood fire philandering with Mlle Nanette de Bailly. He sank his neck deeper into the sheepskin collar of his British warm. The other, slim, was with all his badges, ribands and mail, shining darkly in a cold that set all Tietjens' teeth chattering like porcelain. Levin became momentarily animated:

"You should do as I do. . . . Regular hours . . . lots of exercise . . . horse exercise. . . . I do P.T. every morning at the open window of my room . . . hardening. . . ."

"It must be very gratifying for the ladies in the rooms facing yours," Tietjens said grimly. "Is that what's the matter with Mlle Nanette, now? . . . I haven't got time for proper exercise. . . ."

"Good gracious, no," the colonel said. He now tucked his hand firmly under Tietjens' arm and began to work him towards the left hand of the road: in the direction leading out of the camp. Tietjens worked their steps as firmly towards the right and they leant one against the other. "In fact, old bean," the colonel said, "Campy is working so hard to get the command of a fighting army—though he's indispensable here—that we might pack up bag and baggage any day. . . . That is what has made Nanette see reason. . . ."

"Then what am I doing in this show?" Tietjens asked. But Colonel Levin continued blissfully:

"In fact I've got her almost practically for certain to promise that next week . . . or the week after next at latest . . . she'll . . . damn it, she'll name the happy day."

Tietjens said:

"Good hunting! . . . How splendidly Victorian!"

"That's, damn it," the colonel exclaimed manfully, "what I say myself. . . . Victorian is what it is. . . . All these marriage settlements. . . . And what is it . . . *Droits du Seigneur?** . . . And notaries . . . And the Count, having his say . . . And the Marchioness . . . And two old grand aunts . . . But . . . Hoopla! . . ." He executed with his gloved right thumb in the moonlight a rapid pirouette . . . "Next week . . . or at least the week after . . ." His voice suddenly dropped.

"At least," he wavered, "that was what it was at lunchtime. . . . Since then . . . something happened. . . ."

"You've not been caught in bed with a V.A.D.?" Tietjens asked.

The colonel mumbled:

"No . . . not in bed. . . . Not with a V.A.D . . . Oh, damn it, at the railway station. . . . With . . . The general sent me down to meet her . . . and Nanny of course was seeing off her grandmother, the Duchesse . . . The giddy cut she handed me out. . . ."

---

* 'Rights of the lord'; originally, the right of a feudal lord to have sexual relations with the bride of a vassal on their wedding night.

Tietjens became coldly furious.

"Then it *was* over one of your beastly imbecile rows with Miss de Bailly that you got me out here," he exclaimed. "Do you mind going down with me towards the I.B.D. headquarters? Your final orders may have come in there. The sappers won't let me have a telephone, so I have to look in there the last thing...." He felt a yearning towards rooms in huts, warmed by coke-stoves and electrically lit, with acting lance-corporals bending over A.F.B.'s on a background of deal pigeon-holes filled with returns on buff and blue paper. You got quiet and engrossment there. It was a queer thing: the only place where he, Christopher Tietjens of Groby, could be absently satisfied was in some orderly room or other. The only place in the world.... And why? It was a queer thing....

But not queer, really. It was a matter of inevitable selection if you came to think it out. An acting orderly-room lance-corporal was selected for his penmanship, his power of elementary figuring, his trustworthiness amongst innumerable figures and messages, his dependability. For this he differed a hair's breadth in rank from the rank and file. A hairbreadth[23] that was to him the difference between life and death. For, if he proved not to be dependable, back he went—returned to duty! As long as he was dependable he slept under a table in a warm room, his toilette arrangements and washing in a bully-beef case near his head, a billy full of tea always stewing for him on an always burning stove.... A paradise! ... No! Not a paradise: *the* paradise of the Other Ranks! ... He might be awakened at one in the morning. Miles away the enemy might be beginning a strafe.... He would roll out from among the blankets under the table amongst the legs of hurrying N.C.O.'s and officers, the telephone going like hell.... He would have to manifold innumerable short orders on buff slips on a typewriter.... A bore to be awakened at one in the morning, but not unexciting: the enemy putting up a tremendous barrage in front of the village of Dranoutre: the whole nineteenth division to be moved into support along the Bailleul-Nieppe road. In case ...

Tietjens considered the sleeping army.... That country village under the white moon, all of sackcloth sides, celluloid windows, forty men to a hut ... That slumbering Arcadia was

one of ... how many? Thirty-seven thousand five hundred, say
for a million and a half of men. ... But there were probably more
than a million and a half in that base. ... Well, round the slumbering Arcadias were the fringes of virginly glimmering tents. ...
Fourteen men to a tent. ... For a million. ... Seventy-one thousand four hundred and twenty-one tents round, say, one hundred
and fifty I.B.D.'s, C.B.D.'s, R.E.B.D.'s. ... Base depots for
infantry, cavalry, sappers, gunners, airmen, anti-airmen, tele-
phone-men, vets, chiropodists, Royal Army Service Corps men,
Pigeon Service men, Sanitary Service men, Women's Auxiliary
Army Corps women, V.A.D. women—what in the world did
V.A.D. stand for?—canteens, rest-tent attendants, barrack
damage superintendents, parsons, priests, rabbis, Mormon
bishops,[24] Brahmins, Lamas, Imams, Fanti men, no doubt, for
African troops. And all really dependent on the acting orderly-
room lance-corporals for their temporal and spiritual
salvation. ... For, if by a slip of the pen a lance-corporal sent a
Papist priest to an Ulster regiment, the Ulster men would lynch
him, and all go to hell. Or, if by a slip of the tongue at the telephone, or a slip of the typewriter, he sent a division to Westoutre
instead of to Dranoutre at one in the morning, the six or seven
thousand poor devils in front of Dranoutre might all be massacred and nothing but His Majesty's Navy could save us. ...

Yet, in the end, all this tangle was satisfactorily unravelled; the
drafts moved off, unknotting themselves like snakes, coiling out
of inextricable bunches, sliding vertebrately over the mud to dip
into their bowls—the rabbis found Jews dying to whom to admin-
ister; the vets, spavined mules; the V.A.D.'s, men without jaws
and shoulders in C.C.S.'s; the camp-cookers, frozen beef; the
chiropodists, ingrowing toe-nails; the dentists, decayed molars;
the naval howitzers, camouflaged emplacements in picturesquely
wooded dingles. ... Somehow they got there—even to the pots
of strawberry jam by the ten dozen!

For if the acting lance-corporal, whose life hung by a hair,
made a slip of the pen over a dozen pots of jam, back he went,
Returned to duty ... back to the frozen rifle, the ground-sheet on
the liquid mud, the desperate suction on the ankle as the foot was
advanced, the landscapes silhouetted with broken church towers,
the continual drone of the planes, the mazes of duckboards in vast

plains of slime, the unending Cockney humour, the great shells labelled *Love to Little Willie*....* Back to the Angel with the Flaming Sword.† The wrong side of him! ... So, on the whole, things moved satisfactorily....

He was walking Colonel Levin imperiously between the huts towards the mess quarters, their feet crunching on the freezing gravel, the colonel hanging back a little; but a mere light-weight and without nails in his elegant bootsoles, so he had no grip on the ground. He was remarkably silent. Whatever he wanted to get out he was reluctant to come to. He brought out, however:

"I wonder you don't apply to be returned to duty ... to your battalion. I jolly well should if I were you...."

Tietjens said:

"Why? Because I've had a man killed on me? ... There must have been a dozen killed to-night."

"Oh, more, very likely," the other answered. "It was one of our own planes that was brought down.... But it isn't that.... Oh, damn it! ... Would you mind walking the other way? ... I've the greatest respect ... oh, almost ... for you personally.... You're a man of intellect...."

Tietjens was reflecting on a nice point of military etiquette.

This lisping, ineffectual fellow—he was a very careful Staff officer or Campion would not have had him about the place!—was given to moulding himself exactly on his general. Physically, in costume as far as possible, in voice—for his lisp was not his own so much as an adaptation of the general's slight stutter—and above all in his uncompleted sentences and point of view....

Now, if he said:

"Look here, colonel ..." or "Look here, Colonel Levin ..." or

* The obvious reference is to Kaiser Wilhelm II (1859–1941), who was the German Commander-in-Chief during the Great War. But the 'Cockney humour' in calling him 'Willie' invokes the slang for his penis; see 'An infantile name for the penis': OED. Cf. *No Enemy*, ed. Paul Skinner (Manchester: Carcanet, 2002), 72 on 'that humour which is acrid and rather sad and which is yet the sovereign quality of the British Tommy. For to inscribe on an immense grey shell that is about to be fired at the Hun lines – to inscribe on that in huge whitewash letters "Love to Little Willie" may seem stupid and shocking to folk who were never *là-bas*. But human psychology is very complicated and it is certain that the reading of such inscriptions on the great shells by the stacks of which we pass along the highroads of France much lightens our hearts when we advance from Albert to La Boiselle.'

† i.e. Uriel, guarding the gates of the Garden of Eden.

"Look here, Stanley, my boy . . ." For the one thing an officer may not say to a superior whatever their intimacy was: "Look here, Levin . . ." If he said then:

"Look here, Stanley, you're a silly ass. It's all very well for Campion to say that I am unsound because I've some brains. He's my godfather and has been saying it to me since I was twelve, and had more brain in my left heel than he had in the whole of his beautifully barbered skull. . . . But when you say it you are just a parrot. You did not think that out for yourself. You do not even think it. You know I'm heavy, short in the wind, and self-assertive . . . but you know perfectly well that I'm as good on detail as yourself. And a damned sight more. You've never caught me tripping over a return. Your sergeant in charge of returns may have. But not you. . . ."

If Tietjens should say that to this popinjay, would that be going farther than an officer in charge of detachment should go with a member of the Staff set above him, though not on parade and in a conversation of intimacy? Off parade and in intimate conversation all His Majesty's poor bloody officers are equals . . . gentlemen having his Majesty's commission: there can be no higher rank and all that! Bilge! . . . For how off parade could this descendant of an old-clo* man from Frankfurt be the equal of him, Tietjens of Groby? He wasn't his equal in any way—let alone socially. If Tietjens hit him he would drop dead; if he addressed a little sneering remark to Levin, the fellow would melt so that you would see the old spluttering Jew swimming up through his carefully arranged Gentile features. He couldn't shoot as well as Tietjens, or ride, or play a hand at auction. Why, damn it, he, Tietjens, hadn't the least doubt that he could paint better water-colour pictures. . . . And, as for returns . . . he would undertake to tear the guts out of half a dozen new and contradictory A.C.I.'s—Army Council Instructions—and write twelve correct Command Orders founded on them, before Levin had lisped out the date and serial number of the first one. . . . He had done it several times up in the room, arranged like a French bluestocking's salon, where Levin worked at Garrison headquarters . . . He had

---

* 'Clo! Any Old Clo!' was a familiar London street-cry of rag-and-bone men collecting rags and old clothes.

written Levin's blessed command orders while Levin fussed and
fumed about their being delayed for tea with Mlle de Bailly ...
and curled his delicate moustache ... Mlle de Bailly, chaperoned
by old Lady Sachse, had tea by a clear wood fire in an eighteenth-
century octagonal room, with blue-grey tapestried walls and
powdering closets, out of priceless porcelain cups without
handles. Pale tea that tasted faintly of cinnamon!

Mlle de Bailly was a long, dark, high-coloured Provençale.[25*]
Not heavy, but precisely long, slow, and cruel; coiled in a deep
arm-chair, saying the most wounding, slow things to Levin, she
resembled a white Persian cat luxuriating, sticking out a tenta-
tive pawful of expanding claws. With eyes slanting pronouncedly
upwards and a very thin hooked nose ... Almost Japanese ...
And with a terrific cortège of relatives, swell in a French way.
One brother a chauffeur to a Marshal of France ... An aristo-
cratic way of shirking!

With all that, obviously even off parade, you might well be the
social equal of a Staff colonel: but you jolly well had to keep from
showing that you were his superior. Especially intellectually. If
you let yourself show a Staff officer that he *was* a silly ass—you
could say it as often as you liked as long as you didn't prove it!—
you could be certain that you would be for it before long. And
quite properly. It was not English to be intellectually adroit. Nay,
it was positively un-English. And the duty of field officers is to
keep messes as English as possible.... So a Staff officer would
take it out of such a regimental inferior. In a perfectly creditable
way. You would never imagine the hash headquarters warrant
officers would make of your returns. Until you were worried and
badgered and in the end either you were ejected into, or prayed
to be transferred to ... any other command in the whole
service....

And that was beastly. The process, not the effect. On the
whole Tietjens did not care where he was or what he did as long
as he kept out of England, the thought of that country, at night,
slumbering across the Channel, being sentimentally unbearable

---

* Ford and Stella Bowen had wintered in Provence in 1922–3, where Ford began
  Parade's End.

to him. . . .* Still, he was fond of old Campion, and would rather be in his command than any other. He had attached to his staff a very decent set of fellows, as decent as you could be in contact with . . . if you had to be in contact with your kind. . . . So he just said:

"Look here, Stanley, you are a silly ass," and left it at that, without demonstrating the truth of the assertion.

The colonel said:

"Why, what have I been doing now? . . . I *wish* you would walk the other way. . . ."

Tietjens said:

"No, I can't afford to go out of camp. . . . I've got to come to witness your fantastic wedding-contract to-morrow afternoon, haven't I? . . . I can't leave camp twice in one week. . . ."

"You've got to come down to the camp-guard," Levin said. "I hate to keep a woman waiting in the cold . . . though she *is* in the general's car. . . ."

Tietjens exclaimed:

"You've not been . . . oh, extraordinary enough, to bring Miss de Bailly out here? To talk to me?"

Colonel Levin mumbled, so low Tietjens almost imagined that he was not meant to hear:

"It isn't Miss de Bailly!" Then he exclaimed quite aloud: "Damn it all, Tietjens, haven't you had hints enough? . . ."

For a lunatic moment it went through Tietjens' mind that it must be Miss Wannop in the general's car, at the gate, down the hill beside the camp guard-room. But he knew folly when it presented itself to his mind. He had nevertheless turned and they were going very slowly back along the broad way between the huts. Levin was certainly in no hurry. The broad way would come to an end of the hutments; about two acres of slope would descend blackly before them, white stones to mark a sort of coastguard track glimmering out of sight beneath a moon gone dark with the frost. And, down there in the dark frost, at the end of that track,

---

* Ford, nevertheless, used 'those slumbering across the Channel' to open his poem 'A Solis Ortus Cardine . . .' of 6 September 1916, which begins: 'Oh quiet peoples sleeping bed by bed / Beneath grey roof-trees in the glimmering West, / We who can see the silver grey and red / Rise over No Man's Land—salute your rest'. *On Heaven* 37.

in a terrific Rolls-Royce, was waiting something of which Levin was certainly deucedly afraid. . . .

For a minute Tietjens' backbone stiffened. He didn't intend to interfere between Mlle de Bailly and any married woman Levin had had as a mistress. . . . Somehow he was convinced that what was in that car was a married woman. . . . He did not dare to think otherwise. If it was not a married woman it might be Miss Wannop. If it was, it couldn't be. . . . An immense waft of calm, sentimental happiness had descended upon him. Merely because he had imagined her![26] He imagined her little, fair, rather pug-nosed face: under a fur cap, he did not know why. Leaning forward she would be, on the seat of the general's illuminated car: glazed in: a regular raree show!* Peering out, shortsightedly on account of the reflections on the inside of the glass†. . . .

He was saying to Levin:

"Look here, Stanley . . . why I said you are a silly ass is because Miss de Bailly has one chief luxury. It's exhibiting jealousy. Not feeling it. Exhibiting it."

"*Ought* you," Levin asked ironically, "to discuss my fiancée before me? As an English gentleman. Tietjens of Groby and all."

"Why, of course," Tietjens said. He continued feeling happy. "As a sort of swollen best man, it's my duty to instruct you. Mothers tell their daughters things before marriage. Best men do it for the innocent Benedick. . . .[27]‡ And you're always consulting me about the young woman. . . ."

"I'm not doing it now," Levin grumbled direly.

"Then what, in God's name, are you doing? You've got a cast§

* 'A show contained or carried about in a box; a peep-show': OED.
† The image of reflections on glass figures prominently in Ford's definition of the literary techniques: 'I suppose that Impressionism exists to render those queer effects of real life that are like so many views seen through bright glass – through glass so bright that whilst you perceive through it a landscape or a backyard, you are aware that, on its surface, it reflects a face of a person behind you. For the whole of life is really like that; we are almost always in one place with our minds somewhere quite other': 'On Impressionism', *Poetry and Drama*, 2 (June and December 1914), 167–75, 323–34 (174): included in appendix to *The Good Soldier* 257–74.
‡ A reference to the professed bachelor Benedick, who marries Beatrice in Shakespeare's *Much Ado About Nothing*.
§ Rejected, cast off. The *OED* has, for one meaning of 'cast': 'Of horses, etc.: Rejected, as unfit for service, broken down', curiously connecting with *Parade's End*'s many comparisons of women – especially Sylvia – with horses. But the phrase 'cast mistress' was not uncommon in seventeenth- and eighteenth-century drama, cropping up in works by Fielding, Aphra Behn, Thomas Otway, and Sir John Vanbrugh.

mistress, haven't you, down there in old Campion's car? ..."
They were beside the alley that led down to his orderly room.
Knots of men, dim and desultory, still half filled it, a little way
down.

"I *haven't*," Levin exclaimed almost tearfully. "I never *had* a
mistress. . . ."

"And you're not married?" Tietjens asked. He used on purpose
the schoolboy's ejaculation "Lummy!" to soften the jibe. "If you'll
excuse me," he said, "I must just go and take a look at my crowd.
To see if your orders have come down."

He found no orders in a hut as full as ever of the dull mists and
odours of khaki, but he found in revenge a fine upstanding, blond,
Canadian-born lance-corporal of old Colonial lineage, with a
moving story as related by Sergeant-Major Cowley:

"This man, sir, of the Canadian Railway lot, 'is mother's just
turned up in the town, come on from Eetarpels. Come all the way
from Toronto where she was bedridden."

Tietjens said:

"Well, what about it? Get a move on."

The man wanted leave to go to his mother who was waiting in
a decent estaminet at the end of the tram-line just outside the
camp where the houses of the town began.

Tietjens said: "It's impossible. It's absolutely impossible. You
know that."

The man stood erect and expressionless; his blue eyes looked
confoundedly honest to Tietjens who was cursing himself. He
said to the man:

"You can see for yourself that it's impossible, can't you?"

The man said slowly:

"Not knowing the regulations in these circumstances I can't
say, sir. But my mother's is a very special case. . . . She's lost two
sons already."

Tietjens said:

"A great many people have. . . . Do you understand, if you
went absent off my pass I might—I quite possibly might—lose my
commission? I'm responsible for you fellows getting up the line."

The man looked down at his feet. Tietjens said to himself that
it was Valentine Wannop doing this to him. He ought to turn the
man down at once.[28] He was pervaded by a sense of her being. It

was imbecile. Yet it was so. He said to the man:

"You said good-bye to your mother, didn't you, in Toronto, before you left?"

The man said:

"No, sir." He had not seen his mother in seven years. He had been up in the Chilkoot* when war broke out and had not heard of it for ten months. Then he had at once joined up in British Columbia, and had been sent straight through for railway work, on to Aldershot where the Canadians had a camp in building. He had not known that his brothers were killed till he got there and his mother, being bedridden at the news, had not been able to get down to Toronto when his batch had passed through. She lived about sixty miles from Toronto. Now she had risen from her bed like a miracle and come all the way. A widow: sixty-two years of age. Very feeble.

It occurred to Tietjens as it occurred to him ten times a day that it was idiotic of him to figure Valentine Wannop to himself. He had not the slightest idea where she was: in what circumstances, or even in what house. He did not suppose she and her mother had stayed on in that dog-kennel of a place in Bedford Park. They would be fairly comfortable. His father had left them money.[29] "It is preposterous," he said to himself, "to persist in figuring a person to yourself when you have no idea of where they are." He said to the man:

"Wouldn't it do if you saw your mother at the camp gate, by the guard-room?"

"Not much of a leave-taking, sir," the man said; "she not allowed in the camp and I not allowed out. Talking under a sentry's nose very likely."

Tietjens said to himself:

"What a monstrous absurdity this is of seeing and talking, for a minute or so! You meet and talk. . . ." And next day at the same hour. Nothing. . . . As well not to meet or talk. . . . Yet the mere fantastic idea of seeing Valentine Wannop for a minute. . . . She not allowed in the camp and he not going out. Talking under a sentry's nose, very likely. . . . It had made him smell primroses.

---

*   In the Canadian Northwest Territory bordering Alaska; its pass was used as a route during the Klondike Gold Rush.

Primroses, like Miss Wannop. He said to the sergeant-major:

"What sort of a fellow is this?" Cowley, in open-mouthed suspense, gasped like a fish. Tietjens said:

"I suppose your mother is fairly feeble to stand in the cold?"

"A very decent man, sir," the sergeant-major got out, "one of the best. No trouble. A perfectly clean conduct sheet. Very good education. A railway engineer in civil life.... Volunteered, of course, sir."

"That's the odd thing," Tietjens said to the man, "that the percentage[30] of absentees is as great amongst the volunteers as the Derby men* or the compulsorily enlisted.... Do you understand what will happen to you if you miss the draft?"

The man said soberly:

"Yes, sir. Perfectly well."

"You understand that you will be shot? As certainly as that you stand there. And that you haven't a chance of escape."

He wondered what Valentine Wannop, hot pacifist, would think of him if she heard him. Yet it was his duty to talk like that: his human, not merely his military duty. As much his duty as that of a doctor to warn a man that if he drank of typhoid-contaminated water he would get typhoid. But people are unreasonable. Valentine too was unreasonable. She would consider it brutal to speak to a man of the possibility of his being shot by a firing party. A groan burst from him. At the thought that there was no sense in bothering about what Valentine Wannop would or would not think of him. No sense. No sense. No sense....

The man, fortunately, was assuring him that he knew, very soberly, all about the penalty for going absent off a draft. The sergeant-major, catching a sound from Tietjens, said with admirable fussiness to the man:

"There, there! Don't you hear the officer's speaking? Never interrupt an officer."

"You'll be shot," Tietjens said, "at dawn.... Literally at dawn." Why did they shoot them at dawn? To rub it in that they were

---

* The 'Derby scheme' was introduced by Lord Derby in October 1915 to counter falling rates of volunteering. Men aged 18 to 40 were told that they could continue to enlist voluntarily until 15 December 1915, or could 'attest', in which case they were sent back to their homes and jobs, but were obliged to serve when called up; meanwhile they were given a grey armband with a red crown to indicate their willingness to fight.

never going to see another sunrise. But they drugged the fellows so that they wouldn't know the sun if they saw it: all roped in a chair.... * It was really the worse for the firing party. He added to the man:

"Don't think I'm insulting you. You appear to be a very decent fellow. But very decent fellows have gone absent." He said to the sergeant-major:

"Give this man a two-hours' pass to go to the ... whatever's the name of the estaminet.... The draft won't move off for two hours, will it?" He added to the man: "If you see your draft passing the pub you run out and fall in. Like mad, you understand. You'd never get another chance."

There was a mumble like applause and envy of a mate's good luck from a packed audience that had hung on the lips of simple melodrama ... an audience that seemed to be all enlarged eyes, the khaki was so colourless.... They came as near applause as they dared, but there was no sense in worrying about whether Valentine Wannop would have applauded or not.... And there was no knowing whether the fellow would not go absent, either. As likely as not there was no mother. A girl very likely. And very likely the man would desert.... The man looked you straight in the eyes. But a strong passion, like that for escape—or a girl—will give you control over the muscles of the eyes. A little thing that, before a strong passion! One would look God in the face on the day of judgement and lie, in that case.[31]

Because what the devil did he want of Valentine Wannop? Why could he not stall off the thought of her? He could stall off the thought of his wife ... or his not-wife. But Valentine Wannop came wriggling in. At all hours of the day and night. It was an obsession. A madness.... What those fools called "a complex"! ... Due, no doubt, to something your nurse had done, or your parents said to you. At birth ... A strong passion ... or no doubt not strong enough. Otherwise he, too, would have gone absent. At any rate, from Sylvia ... Which he hadn't done. Which he hadn't done. Or hadn't he? There was no saying....

It was undoubtedly colder in the alley between the huts. A man

---

* The condemned prisoners were tied to a stake or a chair, and a piece of white cloth placed over the heart as a target. Some were drugged with morphine or alcohol.

was saying: "Hoo ... Hooo ... Hoo ..." A sound like that, and flapping his arms and hopping.... "Hand and foot, mark time!" Somebody ought to fall these poor devils in and give them that to keep their circulations going. But they might not know the command.... It was a Guards' trick, really.... What the devil were these fellows kept hanging about here for? he asked.

One or two voices said that they did not know. The majority said gutturally:

"Waiting for our mates, sir...."

"I should have thought you could have waited under cover," Tietjens said caustically. "But never mind; it's your funeral, if you like it...." This getting together ... a strong passion. There was a warmed reception-hut for waiting drafts not fifty yards away.... But they stood, teeth chattering and mumbling "Hoo ... Hooo ..." rather than miss thirty seconds of gabble.... About what the English sergeant-major said and about what the officer said and how many dollars did they give you.... And of course about what you answered back.... Or perhaps not that. These Canadian troops were husky, serious fellows, without the swank of the Cockney or the Lincolnshire Moonrakers.* They wanted, apparently, to learn the rules of war. They discussed anxiously information that they received in orderly rooms, and looked at you as if you were expounding the gospels....

But, damn it, he, he himself, would make a pact with Destiny, at that moment, willingly, to pass thirty months in the frozen circle of hell, for the chance of thirty seconds in which to tell Valentine Wannop what he had answered back ... to Destiny! ... What was the fellow in the Inferno who was buried to the neck in ice and begged Dante to clear the icicles out of his eyelids so that he could see out of them? And Dante kicked him in the face because he was a Ghibelline.... Always a bit of a swine, Dante....† Rather like ... like whom? ... Oh, Sylvia Tiet-

---

* According to a legend from Wiltshire, not Lincolnshire, locals were seen using rakes to try to catch the moon's reflection in a pond, thinking it to be a cheese. In one version they were smugglers trying to recover contraband they had hidden in the pond, and only appeared idiotic out of guile, to avoid detection.

† Tietjens' memory of *Inferno* XXXII is inaccurate. Dante accidentally kicks Bocca degli Abbati, an 'accursed traitor' to Florence, in the head; but he deliberately pulls out tufts of his hair. Given his harsh treatment of Bocca, Ford, quoting from this canto in *The March of Literature* 67, remarks that Dante 'was a man of his time'.

jens.... A good hater! ... He imagined hatred coming to him in waves from the convent in which Sylvia had immured herself.... Gone into retreat.... He imagined she had gone into retreat. She had said she was going. For the rest of the war.... For the duration of hostilities or life, whichever were the longer.... He imagined Sylvia, coiled up on a convent bed.... Hating.... Her certainly glorious hair all round her.... Hating.... Slowly and coldly.... Like the head of a snake when you examined it.... Eyes motionless: mouth closed tight.... Looking away into the distance and hating.... She was presumably in Birkenhead.... A long way to send your hatred.... Across a country and a sea in an icy night...! Over all that black land and water ... with the lights out because of air-raids and U-boats.... Well, he did not have to think of Sylvia at the moment. She was well out of it....

It was certainly getting no warmer as the night drew on.... Even that ass Levin was pacing swiftly up and down in the dusky moon-shadow of the last hutments that looked over the slope and the vanishing trail of white stones.... In spite of his boasting about not wearing an overcoat; to catch women's eyes with his pretty Staff gadgets he was carrying on like a leopard at feeding time....

Tietjens said:

"Sorry to keep you waiting, old man.... Or rather your lady.... But there were some men to see to.... And, you know ... 'The comfort and—what is it?—of the men comes before every—is it "consideration"?—except the exigencies of actual warfare'.... My memory's gone phut these days.... And you want me to slide down this hill and wheeze back again.... To see a woman! ..."

Levin screeched:

"Damn you, you ass! It's your wife who's waiting for you at the bottom there."*

---

* Sylvia Tietjens' presence at the Front might seem an implausible invention (and certainly there is no corresponding biographical evidence that Violet Hunt followed Ford into France during the war). But as E. S. Turner explains: 'It was not impossible to bluff one's way into the battle zone. One of the boldest intruders was a diplomat's wife, Lady Isabella St John, who had heard at a London tea party that her son was a casualty in France.' She was allowed to stay in the village for two days, 'during which she tried to make her way to the trenches and begged a general to let her join the Royal Army Medical Corps'. She later wrote a book about her exploit, *A Journey in Wartime*. Turner, *Dear Old Blighty* 50.

III

THE one thing that stood out sharply in Tietjens' mind when at last, with a stiff glass of rum punch, his officer's pocket-book complete with pencil because he had to draft before eleven a report as to the desirability of giving his unit special lectures on the causes of the war,[1]* and a cheap French novel on a camp chair beside him he sat in his flea-bag with six army blankets over him—the one thing that stood out as sharply as Staff tabs was that that ass Levin was rather pathetic. His unnailed bootsoles very much cramping his action on the frozen hillside, he had alternately hobbled a step or two and, reduced to inaction, had grabbed at Tietjens' elbow, while he brought out breathlessly puzzled sentences. . . .

There resulted a singular mosaic of extraordinary, bright-coloured and melodramatic statements, for Levin, who first hobbled down the hill with Tietjens and then hobbled back up, clinging to his arm, brought out monstrosities[2] of news about Sylvia's activities, without any sequence, and indeed without any apparent aim except for the great affection he had for Tietjens himself. . . . All sorts of singular things seemed to have been going on round him in the vague zone, outside all this engrossed and dust-coloured world—in the vague zone that held. . . . Oh, the civilian population, tea-parties short of butter! . . .[3]

And as Tietjens, seated on his hams, his knees up, pulled the soft woolliness of his flea-bag under his chin and damned the paraffin heater for letting out a new and singular stink, it seemed to him that this affair was like coming back after two months and trying to get the hang of battalion orders. . . . You come back to the familiar, slightly battered mess ante-room. You tell the mess orderly to bring you the last two months' orders, for it is as much as your life is worth not to know what is or is not in them. . . .

---

* In *Great Trade Route* 46, Ford recalled lecturing 'on the Ross rifle – which was a beast of a thing – or on the Causes of the War or on any other department of the rag-bag of knowledge that we had to inflict on the unfortunates committed to our charge'.

There might be an A.C.I. ordering you to wear your helmet back
to the front, or a battalion order that Mills bombs must always be
worn in the left breast pocket. Or there might be the detail for
putting on a new gas helmet! . . . The orderly hands you a dishev-
elled mass of faintly typewritten matter, thumbed out of all
chance of legibility, with the orders for November 16 fastened
inextricably into the middle of those for the 1st of December, and
those for the 10th, 15th and 29th missing altogether. . . . And all
that you gather is that headquarters has some exceedingly
insulting things to say about A Company; that a fellow called
Hartopp, whom you don't know, has been deprived of his
commission; that at a court of inquiry held to ascertain deficien-
cies in C Company Captain Wells—poor Wells!—has been
assessed at £27 11s 4d., which he is requested to pay forthwith to
the adjutant. . . .

So, on that black hillside, going and returning, what stuck out
for Tietjens was that Levin had been taught by the general to
consider that he, Tietjens, was an extraordinarily violent chap
who would certainly knock Levin down when he told him that
his wife was at the camp gates; that Levin considered himself to
be the descendant of an ancient Quaker family. . . . (Tietjens had
said *Good God!* at that); that the mysterious "rows" to which in
his fear Levin had been continually referring had been successive
letters from Sylvia to the harried general . . . and that Sylvia had
accused him, Tietjens, of stealing two pairs of her best sheets. . . .
There was a great deal more. But, having faced what he considered to be the worst of the situation, Tietjens set himself coolly
to recapitulate every aspect of his separation from his wife. He
had meant to face every aspect, not that merely social one upon
which, hitherto, he had automatically imagined their disunion to
rest. For, as he saw it, English people of good position consider
that the basis of all marital unions or disunions is the maxim: No
scenes. Obviously for the sake of the servants—who are the same
thing as the public. No scenes, then, for the sake of the public.
And indeed, with him, the instinct for privacy—as to his relationships, his passions, or even as to his most unimportant
motives—was as strong as the instinct of life itself. He would,
literally, rather be dead than an open book.

And, until that afternoon, he had imagined that his wife, too, would rather be dead than have her affairs canvassed by the other ranks.... But that assumption had to be gone over. Revised.... Of course he might say she had gone mad. But, if he said she had gone mad he would have to revise a great deal of their relationships, so it would be as broad as it was long....

The doctor's batman, from the other end of the hut, said:

"Poor bloody O Nine Morgan! ..." in a singsong,[4] mocking voice....

For though, hours before, Tietjens had appointed this moment of physical ease that usually followed on his splurging heavily down on to his creaking camp-bed in the doctor's lent hut, for the cool consideration of his relations with his wife, it was not turning out a very easy matter. The hut was unreasonably warm: he had invited Mackenzie—whose real name turned out to be McKechnie, James Grant McKechnie—to occupy the other end of it. The other end of it was divided from him by a partition of canvas and a striped Indian curtain. And McKechnie, who was unable to sleep, had elected to carry on a long—an interminable—conversation with the doctor's batman.

The doctor's batman also could not sleep and, like McKechnie, was more than a little barmy on the crumpet*—an almost non-English-speaking Welshman from God knows what up-country valley. He had shaggy hair like a Caribbean savage and two dark, resentful wall-eyes; being a miner he sat on his heels more comfortably than on a chair and his almost incomprehensible voice went on in a low sort of ululation, with an occasionally and startlingly comprehensible phrase sticking out now and then.[5]

It was troublesome, but orthodox enough. The batman had been blown literally out of most of his senses and the VIth Battalion of the Glamorganshire Regiment by some German high explosive or other, more than a year ago. But before then, it appeared, he had been in McKechnie's own company in that battalion. It was perfectly in order that an officer should gossip with[6] a private formerly of his own platoon or company, especially on first meeting him after long separation caused by a casualty to one or the other. And McKechnie had first re-met this scoundrel Jonce, or Evanns, at eleven that night—two and a half hours

---

* Partridge's *Dictionary of Slang* defines 'barmy (or dotty) in the crumpet' as 'crazy, mad'.

before.[7] So there, in the light of a single candle stuck in a stout bottle they were tranquilly at it: the batman sitting on his heels by the officer's head; the officer, in his pyjamas, sprawling half out of bed over his pillows, stretching his arms abroad, occasionally yawning, occasionally asking: "What became of Company-Sergeant-Major Hoyt?".... They might talk till half-past three.[8]

But that was troublesome to a gentleman seeking to recapture what exactly were his relations with his wife.[9]

Before the doctor's batman had interrupted him by speaking startlingly of O Nine Morgan, Tietjens had got as far as what follows with his recapitulation: The lady, Mrs. Tietjens, was certainly without mitigation a whore; he himself equally certainly and without qualification had been physically faithful to the lady and their marriage tie. In law, then, he was absolutely in the right of it. But that fact had[10] less weight than a cobweb. For after the last of her high-handed divagations from fidelity he had accorded to the lady the shelter of his roof and of his name. She had lived for years beside him, apparently on terms of hatred and miscomprehension.[11] But certainly in conditions of chastity.[12] Then, during[13] the tenuous and lugubrious small hours, before his coming out there again to France, she had given evidence of a madly vindictive passion for his person. A physical passion at any rate.

Well, those[14] were times of mad, fugitive emotions. But even in[15] the calmest times a man could not expect to have a woman live with him as the mistress of his house and mother of his heir without establishing some sort of claim upon him. They hadn't slept together. But was it not possible that a constant measuring together of your minds was as proper to give you a proprietary right as the measuring together of the limbs? It was perfectly possible. Well then ...[16]

What, in the eyes of God, severed a union? ... Certainly he had imagined—until that very afternoon—that their union had been cut, as the tendon of Achilles is cut in a hamstringing, by Sylvia's clear voice, outside his house, saying in the dawn to a cabman, "Paddington!".... He tried to go with extreme care through every detail of their last interview in his still nearly dark drawing-room at the other end of which she had seemed a mere white phosphorescence....

They had, then, parted for[17] good on that day. He was going out to France; she into retreat in a convent near Birkenhead— to which place you go from Paddington. Well then, that was one parting. That, surely, set him free for the girl![18]

He took a sip from the glass of rum and water on the canvas chair beside him. It was tepid and therefore beastly. He had ordered the batman to bring it him hot, strong and sweet, because he had been certain of an incipient cold. He had refrained from drinking it because he had remembered that he was to think cold-bloodedly of Sylvia, and he made a practice of never touching alcohol when about to engage in protracted reflection.[19] That had always been his theory: it had been immensely and empirically strengthened by his warlike experience. On the Somme, in the summer, when stand-to had been at four in the morning, you would come out of your dug-out and survey, with a complete outfit[20] of pessimistic thoughts, a dim, grey, repulsive landscape over a dull and much too thin parapet. There would be repellent posts, altogether too fragile entanglements[21] of barbed wire, broken wheels, detritus, coils[22] of mist over the positions of revolting Germans. Grey stillness; grey horrors, in front, and behind amongst the civilian populations! And clear, hard outlines to every thought.... Then your batman brought you a cup of tea with a little—quite a little—rum in it. In three or four minutes the whole world changed beneath your eyes. The wire aprons became jolly efficient protections[23] that your skill had devised and for which you might thank God; the broken wheels were convenient landmarks for raiding at night in No Man's Land. You had to confess that, when you had re-erected that parapet, after it had last been jammed in, your company had made a pretty good job of it. And, even as far as the Germans were concerned, you were there to kill the swine; but you didn't feel that the thought of them would make you sick beforehand.... You were, in fact, a changed man. With a mind of a different specific gravity.[24] You could not even tell that the roseate touches of dawn on the mists were not really the effects of rum....

Therefore he had determined not to touch his grog. But his throat had gone completely dry; so, mechanically, he had reached out for something to drink, checking himself when he had realized what he was doing. But why should his throat be dry? He hadn't been on the drink. He had not even had any dinner. And why was he in this extraordinary state? . . . For he was in an extraordinary state.[25] It was because the idea had suddenly occurred to him that his parting from his wife had set him free for his girl. . . . The idea had till then never entered his head.[26]

He said to himself: We must go methodically into this! Methodically into the history of his last day on earth. . . .

Because he swore that when he had come out to France this time he had imagined that he was cutting loose from this earth. And during the months that he had been there he had seemed to have no connection with any earthly things. He had imagined Sylvia in her convent and done with; Miss Wannop he had not been able to imagine at all. But she had seemed to be done with.

It was difficult to get his mind back to that night. You cannot force your mind to a deliberate, consecutive recollection unless you are in the mood; then it will do it whether you want it to or not. . . . He had had then, three months or so ago,[27] a very painful morning with his wife, the pain coming from a suddenly growing conviction that his wife was forcing herself into an attitude of caring for him. Only an attitude probably, because, in the end, Sylvia was a lady and would not allow herself really to care for the person in the world for whom it would be least decent of her to care. . . . But she would be perfectly capable of forcing herself to take that attitude if she thought that it would enormously inconvenience himself. . . .

But that wasn't the way, wasn't the way, wasn't the way his excited mind said to himself. He was excited because it was possible that Miss Wannop, too, might not have meant their parting to be a permanency. That opened up an immense perspective. Nevertheless, the contemplation of that immense perspective was not the way to set about a calm analysis of his relations with his wife. The facts of the story *must* be stated before the moral. He said to himself that he must put, in exact language, as if he were making a report for the use of garrison headquarters, the history of himself in his relationship to his wife. . . . And to Miss Wannop, of course. "Better put it into writing," he said.

Well then. He clutched at his pocket-book and wrote in large pencilled characters:

"When I married Miss Satterthwaite,"—he was attempting

exactly to imitate a report to General Headquarters[28]— "unknown to myself, she imagined herself to be with child by a fellow called Drake. I think she was not. The matter is debatable. I am passionately attached to the child who is my heir and the heir of a family of considerable position. The lady was subsequently, on several occasions, though I do not know how many, unfaithful to me. She left me with a fellow called Perowne, whom she had met constantly at the house of my godfather, General Lord Edward Campion, on whose staff Perowne was. That was long before the war. This intimacy was, of course, certainly unsuspected by the general.[29] Perowne is again on the staff of General Campion, who has the quality of attachment to his old subordinates, but as Perowne is an inefficient officer, he is used only for more decorative jobs. Otherwise, obviously, as he is an old regular, his seniority should make him a general, and he is only a major. I make this diversion about Perowne because his presence in this garrison causes me natural personal annoyance.[30]

"My wife, after an absence of several months with Perowne, wrote and told me that she wished to be taken back into my household. I allowed this. My principles prevent me from divorcing any woman, in particular any woman who is the mother of a child. As I had taken no steps to ensure publicity for the escapade of Mrs. Tietjens, no one, as far as I know, was aware of her absence. Mrs. Tietjens, being a Roman Catholic, is prevented from divorcing me.

"During this absence of Mrs. Tietjens with the man Perowne,[31] I made the acquaintance of a young woman, Miss Wannop, the daughter of my father's oldest friend, who was also an old friend of General Campion's. Our station in Society naturally forms rather a close ring. I was immediately aware that I had formed a sympathetic but not violent attachment[32] for Miss Wannop, and fairly confident that my feeling was returned. Neither Miss Wannop nor myself being persons to talk about the state of our feelings, we exchanged no confidences.... A disadvantage of being English of a certain station.*

* In the chapter on 'Conduct' in *The Spirit of the People* Ford discusses English suppression of the emotions, recounting the scene that provided the 'germ' for *The Good Soldier*, in which a guardian takes the ward with whom he has fallen in love to the station to leave for a trip round the world: *England and the English*, ed. Sara Haslam (Manchester: Carcanet, 2003), 313–15.

"The position continued thus for several years. Six or seven. After her return from her excursion with Perowne, Mrs. Tietjens remained, I believe, perfectly chaste. I saw Miss Wannop sometimes frequently, for a period, in her mother's house or on social occasions, sometimes not for long intervals. No expression of affection on the part of either of us ever passed. Not one. Ever.

"On the day before my second going out to France I had a very painful scene with my wife, during which, for the first time, we went into the question of the parentage of my child and other matters.[33] In the afternoon I met Miss Wannop by appointment outside the War Office. The appointment had been made by my wife, not by me. I knew nothing about it. My wife must have been more aware of my feelings for Miss Wannop than was I myself.

"In St. James's Park I invited Miss Wannop to become my mistress that evening. She consented and made an assignation. It is to be presumed that that was evidence of her affection for me. We have never exchanged words of affection. Presumably a young lady does not consent to go to bed with a married man without feeling affection for him. But I have no proof. It was, of course, only a few hours before my going out to France. Those are emotional sorts of moments for young women. No doubt they consent more easily.

"But we didn't. We were together at one-thirty in the morning, leaning over her suburban garden gate. And nothing happened. We agreed that we were the sort of persons who didn't. I do not know how we agreed. We never finished a sentence. Yet it was a passionate scene. So I touched the brim of my cap and said: *So long!** ... Or perhaps I did not even say *So long.* ... Or she.... I don't remember. I remember the thoughts I thought and the thoughts I gave her credit for thinking. But perhaps she did not think them. There is no knowing. It is no good going into them ... except that I gave her credit for thinking that we were parting for good. Perhaps she did not mean that. Perhaps I could write letters to her. And live ..."

---

* On two occasions in *The Good Soldier* the words 'So long' are used in especially trying and emotional leave-takings: when Nancy Rufford takes leave of Edward Ashburnham, and soon after goes mad: 'She said: / "So long," to Edward. / Edward answered: "So long."' (159); and when Edward takes leave of John Dowell to kill himself, his last words are: 'So long, old man, I must have a bit of a rest, you know' (162). 'So long' is, therefore, a fraught valediction in Ford's fiction.

He exclaimed:[34]

"God, what a sweat I am in! ..."

The sweat, indeed, was pouring down his temples. He became instinct with a sort of passion to let his thoughts wander into epithets and go about where they would. But he stuck at it. He was determined to get it expressed. He wrote on again:[35]

"I got home towards two in the morning and went into the dining-room in the dark. I did not need a light. I sat thinking for a long time. Then Sylvia spoke from the other end of the room. There was thus an abominable situation. I have never been spoken to with such hatred. She went, perhaps, mad. She had apparently been banking on the idea that if I had physical contact with Miss Wannop I might satisfy my affection for the girl.... And feel physical desires for *her*.... But she knew, without my speaking, that I had not had physical contact with the girl. She threatened to ruin me; to ruin me in the Army; to drag my name through the mud.... I never spoke. I am damn good at not speaking.[36] She struck me in the face. And went away. Afterwards she threw into the room, through the half-open doorway, a gold medallion of St. Michael, the R.C. patron of soldiers in action that she had worn between her breasts. I took it to mean the final act of parting. As if by no longer wearing it she abandoned all prayer for my safety.... It might just as well mean that she wished me to wear it myself for my personal protection.... I heard her go down the stairs with her maid. The dawn was just showing through the chimney-pots opposite. I heard her say: *Paddington.* Clear, high syllables! And a motor drove off.

"I got my things together and went to Waterloo. Mrs. Satter-thwaite, her mother, was waiting to see me off. She was very distressed that her daughter had not come, too. She was of opinion that it meant we had parted for good. I was astonished to find that Sylvia had told her mother about Miss Wannop because Sylvia had always been extremely reticent, even to her mother.... Mrs. Satterthwaite, who was *very* distressed—she likes me!—expressed the most gloomy forebodings as to what Sylvia might not be up to. I laughed at her. She began to tell me a long anecdote about what a Father Consett, Sylvia's confessor, had said about Sylvia years before. He had said that if I ever came to care for another woman Sylvia would tear the world to pieces to get at me.... Meaning, to disturb my equanimity! ... It was difficult to follow Mrs. Satterthwaite. The side of an officer's train, going off, is not a good place for confidences. So the interview ended rather untidily."

At this point Tietjens groaned so audibly that McKechnie, from the other end of the hut, asked if he had not said anything. Tietjens saved himself with:

"That candle looks from here to be too near the side of the hut. Perhaps it isn't. These buildings are very inflammable."

It was no good going on writing. He was no writer, and this writing gave no sort of psychological pointers. He wasn't himself ever much the man for psychology, but one ought[37] to be as efficient at it as at anything else.... Well then ... What was at the bottom of all the madness and cruelty that had distinguished both himself and Sylvia on his last day and night in his native country? ... For, mark! It was Sylvia who had[38] made, unknown to him, the appointment through which the girl had met him. Sylvia had wanted to force him and Miss Wannop into each other's arms.[39] Quite definitely. She had said as much. But she had only said that[40] afterwards. When the game had not come off. She had had too much knowledge of amatory manœuvres to show her hand before....

Why then had she done it? Partly, undoubtedly, out of pity for him. She had given him a rotten time; she had undoubtedly, at one moment,[41] wanted to give him the consolation of his girl's arms.... Why, damn it, she, Sylvia, and no one else, had forced out of him the invitation to the girl to become his mistress. Nothing but the infernal cruelty of their interview of the morning could have forced him to the pitch of sexual excitement that would make him make a proposal of illicit intercourse to a young lady to whom hitherto he had spoken not even one word of affection. It was an effect of a Sadic* kind. That was the only way to look at it scientifically. And without doubt Sylvia had known what she was doing. The whole morning; at intervals, like a person directing the whip lash to a cruel spot of pain, reiteratedly,[42] she had gone on and on. She had accused him of having Valentine Wannop for his mistress. She had accused him of

* 'Sadistic': OED.

having Valentine Wannop for his mistress. She had accused him of having Valentine Wannop for his mistress.... With maddening reiteration, like that. They had disposed of an estate; they had settled up a number of business matters; they had decided that his heir was to be brought up as a Papist—the mother's religion! They had gone, agonizedly enough, into their own relationships and past history. Into the very paternity of his child.... But always, at moments when his mind was like a blind octopus, squirming in an agony of knife-cuts, she would drop in that accusation. She had accused him of having Valentine Wannop for his mistress....

He swore by the living God.... He had never realized that he had a passion for the girl till that morning;* that he had a passion deep and boundless like the sea, shaking like a tremor of the whole world, an unquenchable thirst, a thing the thought of which made your bowels turn over.... But he had not been the sort of fellow who goes into his emotions.... Why, damn it, even at that moment when he thought of the girl, there, in that beastly camp, in that Rembrandt beshadowed hut, when he thought of the girl he named her to himself Miss Wannop....

It wasn't in that way that a man thought of a young woman whom he was aware of passionately loving. He wasn't aware. He hadn't been aware. Until that morning....

Then ... that let him out.... Undoubtedly that let him out.... A woman cannot throw her man, her official husband, into the arms of the first girl that comes along and consider[43] herself as having any further claims upon him. Especially if, on the same day, you part with him, he going out to France! *Did*[44] it let him out? Obviously it did.[45]

He caught with such rapidity at his glass of rum and water that a little of it ran over on to his thumb. He swallowed the lot, being instantly warmed....[46]

What in the world was he doing? Now? With all this introspection? ... Hang it all, he was not justifying himself....[47†] He

---

*   Cf. *The Good Soldier* 80: 'It was as if his passion for her hadn't existed; as if the very words that he spoke, without knowing that he spoke them, created the passion as they went along. Before he spoke, there was nothing; afterwards, it was the integral fact of his life.'

†   In *Some Do Not ...* I.i, Tietjens inveighs against Rossetti to Macmaster: 'Damn it. What's the sense of all these attempts to justify fornication? England's mad about it.'

had acted perfectly correctly as far as Sylvia was concerned. Not perhaps to Miss Wannop.... Why, if he, Christopher Tietjens of Groby, had the need to justify himself, what did it stand for to be Christopher Tietjens of Groby? That was the unthinkable thought.

Obviously he was not immune from the seven deadly sins. In the way of a man. One might lie, yet not bear false witness against a neighbour; one might kill, yet not without fitting provocation or for self-interest; one might conceive of theft as reiving cattle from the false Scots which was the Yorkshireman's duty; one might fornicate, obviously, as long as you did not fuss about it unhealthily.[48] That was the right of the Seigneur in a world of Other Ranks. He hadn't personally committed any of these sins to any great extent. One reserved the right so to do and to take the consequences....[49]*

But what in the world had gone wrong with Sylvia? She was giving away her own game, and that he had never known her do. But she could not have made more certain, if she had wanted to, of returning him to his allegiance to Miss Wannop than by forcing herself there into his private life, and doing it with such blatant vulgarity. For what she had done had been to make scenes before the servants! All the while he had been in France she had been working up to it. Now she had done it. Before the Tommies of his own unit. But Sylvia did not make mistakes like that. It was a game. What game? He didn't even attempt to conjecture! She could not expect that he would in the future even extend to her the shelter of his roof.... What then was the game? He could not believe that she could be capable of vulgarity except with a purpose....[50]

She was a thoroughbred. He had always credited her with being that. And now she was behaving as if she had every mean vice that a mare could have. Or it looked like it. Was that, then, because she had been in his stable? But[51] how in the world other-

---

* In the same discussion in *Some Do Not . . .* I.i Tietjens says: 'Of course, if a man who's a man wants to have a woman he has her.' The idea of doing what you want and taking what you get for it recurs in the later volumes of *Parade's End* and elsewhere in Ford's work, most notably in *A Call* (London: Chatto & Windus, 1910), which accentuates acting responsibly, when Robert Grimshaw says, 'Do what you want and take what you get for it' (216); also see *The English Novel* (1929) (Manchester: Carcanet, 1997), 93.

wise could he have run their lives? She had been unfaithful to him. She had never been anything but unfaithful[52] to him, before or after marriage. In a high-handed way so that he could not condemn her, though it was disagreeable enough to himself. He took her back into his house after she had been off with the fellow Perowne. What more could she ask? . . . He could find no answer. And it was not his business![53]

But even if he did not bother about the motives[54] of the poor beast of a woman, she was the mother of his heir. And now she was running about the world declaiming about her wrongs. What sort of a thing was that for a boy to have happen to him? A mother who made scenes before the servants! That was enough to ruin any boy's life. . . .

There was no getting away from it that that was what Sylvia had been doing. She had deluged the general with letters for the last two months or so, at first merely contenting herself with asking where he, Tietjens, was and in what state of health, conditions of danger, and the like. Very decently, for some time, the old fellow had said nothing about the matter to him. He had probably taken the letters to be the naturally anxious inquiries of a wife with a husband at the front; he had considered that Tietjens' letters to her must have been insufficiently communicative, or concealed what she imagined to be wounds or a position of desperate danger. That would not have been very pleasant in any case; women[55] should not worry superior officers about the vicissitudes of their menfolk. It was not done. Still, Sylvia was very intimate with Campion and his family—more intimate than he himself was, though Campion was his godfather. But[56] quite obviously her letters had got worse and worse.

It was difficult for Tietjens to make out exactly what she had said. His channel of information had been Levin, who was too gentlemanly ever to say anything direct at all. Too gentlemanly, too implicitly trustful of Tietjens' honour . . . and too bewildered by the charms of Sylvia, who had obviously laid herself out to bewilder the poor Staff-wallah. . . . But she had gone pretty far, either in her letters or in her conversation since she had been in that city, to which—it was characteristic—she had come without any sort of passports or papers, just walking past gentlemen in their wooden boxes at pierheads and the like, in conversation with—of all people in the world!—with Perowne, who had been returning from leave with King's dispatches, or something glorified of the Staff sort! In a special train very likely. That was Sylvia all over.

Levin said that Campion had given Perowne the most frightful dressing down he had ever heard mortal man receive. And it really was *damn* hard on the poor general, who, after happenings to one of his predecessors, had been perfectly rabid to keep skirts out of his headquarters. Indeed it was one of the crosses of Levin's worried life that the general had absolutely refused him, Levin, leave to marry Miss de Bailly if he would not undertake that that young woman should leave France by the first boat after the ceremony. Levin, of course, was to go with her, but the young woman was not to return to France for the duration of hostilities. And a fine row all her noble relatives had raised over that. It had cost Levin another hundred and fifty thousand francs in the marriage settlements. The married wives of officers in any case were not allowed in France, though you could not keep out their unmarried ones. . . .

Campion, anyhow, had dispatched his furious note to Tietjens after receiving, firstly, in the early morning, a letter from Sylvia in which she said that her ducal second-cousin, the lugubrious Rugeley, highly disapproved of the fact that Tietjens was in France at all, and after later receiving, towards four in the afternoon, a telegram, dispatched by Sylvia herself from Havre, to say that she would be arriving by a noon train. The general had been almost as much upset at the thought that his car would not be there to meet Sylvia as by the thought that she was coming at all. But a strike of French railway civilians had delayed Sylvia's arrival.[57] Campion had dispatched, within five minutes, his snorter to Tietjens, who he was convinced knew all about Sylvia's coming, and his car to Rouen Station with Levin in it.

The general, in fact, was in a fine confusion. He was convinced that Tietjens, as Man of Intellect, had treated Sylvia badly, even to the extent of stealing two pair of her best sheets, and he was also convinced that Tietjens was in close collusion with Sylvia. As Man of Intellect, Campion was convinced, Tietjens was dissatisfied with his lowly job of draft-forwarding officer, and wanted a place of an extravagantly cooshy kind in the general's

own entourage. . . . And Levin had said that it made it all the
worse that Campion in his bothered heart thought that Tietjens
really ought to have more exalted employment. He had said to
Levin:

"Damn it all, the fellow ought to be in command of my Intelligence instead of you. But he's unsound. That's what he is:
unsound. He's too brilliant. . . . And he'd talk both the hind legs
off Sweedlepumpkins." Sweedlepumpkins was the general's
favourite charger. The general was afraid of talk. He practically
never talked with anyone except about his job—certainly never
with Tietjens—without being proved to be in the wrong, and
that undermined his belief in himself.

So that altogether he was in a fine fume. And confusion. He
was almost ready to believe that Tietjens was at the bottom of
every trouble that occurred in his immense command.[58]

But, when all that was gathered, Tietjens was not much farther
forward in knowing what his wife's errand in France was.

"She[59] complains," Levin had bleated painfully at some point
on the slippery coastguard path, "about your taking her sheets.
And about a Miss . . . a Miss Wanostrocht, is it? . . . The general
is not inclined to attach much importance to the sheets. . . ."

It appeared that a sort of conference on Tietjens' case had
taken place in the immense tapestried salon in which Campion
lived with the more intimate members of his headquarters, and
which was, for the moment, presided over by Sylvia, who had
exposed various wrongs to the general and Levin. Major Perowne
had excused himself on the ground that he was hardly competent
to express an opinion. Really, Levin said, he was sulking, because
Campion had accused him of running the risk of getting himself
and Mrs. Tietjens "talked about." Levin thought it was a bit thick
of the general. Were none of the members of his staff ever to
escort a lady anywhere? As if they were sixth-form schoolboys. . . .

"But you . . . you . . . you . . ." he stuttered and shivered
together, "certainly *do* seem to have been remiss in not writing
to Mrs. Tietjens. The poor lady—excuse me!—really appears to
have been out of her mind with anxiety. . . ." That was why she
had been waiting in the general's car at the bottom of the hill.
To get a glimpse of Tietjens' living body. For they had been
utterly unable, up at H.Q., to convince her that Tietjens was even

alive, much less in that town.

She hadn't in fact waited even so long. Having apparently convinced herself by conversation with the sentries outside the guard-room that Tietjens actually still existed, she had told the chauffeur-orderly to drive her back to the Hotel de la Poste, leaving the wretched Levin to make his way back into the town by tram, or as best he might. They had seen the lights of the car below them, turning, with its gaily lit interior, and disappearing among the trees along the road farther down.... The sentry, rather monosyllabically and gruffly—you can tell all right when a Tommie has something at the back of his mind!—informed them that the sergeant had turned out the guard so that all his men together could assure the lady that the captain was alive and well. The obliging sergeant said that he had adopted that manœuvre which generally should attend only the visits of general officers and, once a day, for the C.O., because the lady had seemed so distressed at having received no letters from the captain. The guard-room itself, which was unprovided with cells,[60] was decorated by the presence of two drunks who, having taken it into their heads to destroy their clothing, were in a state of complete nudity. The sergeant hoped, therefore, that he had done no wrong. Rightly the Garrison Military Police ought to take drunks picked up outside camp to the A.P.M.'s guard-room, but seeing the state of undress and the violent behaviour of these two, the sergeant had thought right to oblige the Red Caps. The voices of the drunks, singing the martial anthem of the "Men of Harlech," could be heard corroborating the sergeant's opinion as to their states. He added that he would not have turned out the guard if it had not been for its being the captain's lady.

"A damn smart fellow, that sergeant," Colonel Levin had said. "There couldn't have been any better way of convincing Mrs. Tietjens."

Tietjens had said—and even whilst he was saying it he tremendously wished he hadn't:

"Oh, a *damned* smart fellow," for the bitter irony of his tone had given Levin the chance to remonstrate with him as to his attitude towards Sylvia. Not at all as to his actions—for Levin conscientiously stuck to his thesis that Tietjens was the soul of honour—but just as to his tone of voice in talking of the sergeant

who had been kind to Sylvia, and, just precisely, because Tietjens' not writing to his wife had given rise to the incident.
Tietjens had thought of saying that, considering the terms on
which they had parted, he would have considered himself as
molesting the lady if he had addressed to her any letter at all. But
he said nothing and, for a quarter of an hour, the incident
resolved itself into a soliloquy on the slippery hillside, delivered
by Levin on the subject of matrimony. It was a matter which,
naturally, at that moment very much occupied his thoughts. He
considered that a man should so live with his wife that she should
be able to open all his letters. That was his idea of the idyllic. And
when Tietjens remarked with irony that he had never in his life
either written or received a letter that his wife might not have
read, Levin exclaimed with such enthusiasm as almost to lose his
balance in the mist:

"I was sure of it, old fellow. But it enormously cheers me up to
hear you say so." He added that he desired as far as possible to
model his ideas of life and his behaviour on those of this his
friend. For, naturally, about as he was to unite his fortunes with
those of Miss de Bailly, that could be considered a turning point
of his career.

IV

THEY had gone back up the hill so that Levin might telephone to headquarters for his own car in case the general's chauffeur should not have the sense to return for him. But that was as far as Tietjens got in uninterrupted reminiscences of that scene. . . . He was sitting in his flea-bag, digging idly with his pencil into the squared page of his note-book which had remained open on his knees, his eyes going over and over again over the words with which his report on his own case had concluded—the words: *So the interview ended rather untidily.* Over the words went the image of the dark hillside with the lights of the town, now that the air-raid was finished, spreading high up into the sky below them. . . .

But at that point the doctor's batman had uttered, as if with a jocular, hoarse irony, the name:

"Poor bloody O Nine Morgan! . . ." and over the whitish sheet of paper on a level with his nose Tietjens perceived thin films of reddish purple to be wavering, then a glutinous surface of gummy scarlet pigment. Moving! It was once more an effect[1] of fatigue, operating on the retina, that was perfectly familiar to Tietjens. But it filled him with indignation against his own weakness. He said to himself: Wasn't the name of the wretched O Nine Morgan to be mentioned in his hearing without his retina presenting him with the glowing image of the fellow's blood? He watched the phenomenon, growing fainter, moving to the right-hand top corner of the paper and turning a faintly luminous green. He watched it with a grim irony.

Was he, he said to himself, to regard himself as responsible for the fellow's death? Was his inner mentality going to present that claim upon him? That[2] would be absurd. The end of the earth! The absurd end of the earth. . . . Yet that insignificant ass Levin had that evening asserted the claim to go into his, Tietjens of Groby's, relations with his wife. That was an end of the earth as absurd! It was the unthinkable thing, as unthinkable as the theory that the officer can be responsible for the death of the man.... But the idea had certainly presented itself to him. How could he be responsible for the death? In fact—in literalness—he was. It had depended absolutely upon his discretion whether the man should go home or not. The man's life or death had been in his hands. He had followed the perfectly correct course. He had written to the police of the man's home town, and the police had urged him not to let the man come home.... Extraordinary morality on the part of a police force! The man, they begged, should not be sent home because a prize-fighter was occupying his bed and laundry.... Extraordinary common sense, very likely.... They probably did not want to get drawn into a scrap with Red Evans of the Red Castle....

For a moment he seemed to see ... he actually saw ... O Nine Morgan's eyes, looking at him with a sort of wonder, as they had looked when he had refused the fellow his leave.... A sort of wonder! Without resentment, but with incredulity. As you might look at God, you being very small and ten feet or so below His throne when He pronounced some inscrutable judgment! ... The Lord giveth home-leave, and the Lord refuseth.... Probably not blessed, but queer, be the name of God-Tietjens!

And at the thought of the man as he was alive and of him now, dead, an immense blackness descended all over Tietjens. He said to himself: *I am very tired*. Yet he was not ashamed.... It was the blackness that descends on you when you think of your dead.... It comes, at any time, over the brightness of sunlight, in the grey of evening, in the grey of the dawn, at mess, on parade; it comes at the thought of one man or at the thought of half a battalion that you have seen, stretched out, under sheeting, the noses making little pimples: or not stretched out, lying face downwards, half buried. Or at the thought of dead that you have never seen dead at all.... Suddenly the light goes out.... In this case it was because of one fellow, a dirty enough man, not even very willing, not in the least endearing, certainly contemplating desertion.... But your dead.... *Yours* ... Your own. As if joined to your own identity by a black cord....

In the darkness[3] outside, the brushing, swift, rhythmic pacing of an immense number of men went past, as if they had been phantoms. A great number of men in fours, carried forward, irresistibly, by the overwhelming will of mankind in ruled motion.

The sides of the hut were so thin that it was[4] peopled by an innumerable throng. A sodden voice, just at Tietjens' head, chuckled:

"For God's sake, sergeant-major, stop these buggers. I'm too bloody drunk to halt them. . . ."

It made for the moment no impression on Tietjens' conscious mind. Men were going past. Cries went up in the camp. Not orders, the men were still marching. Cries.

Tietjens' lips—his mind was still with the dead—said:

"That obscene Pitkins! . . . I'll have him cashiered for this. . . ." He saw an obscene subaltern, small, with one eyelid that drooped.

He came awake at that. Pitkins was the subaltern he had detailed to march the draft to the station and go on to Bailleul under a boozy field officer of sorts.

McKechnie said from the other bed:

"That's the draft back."

Tietjens said:

"Good God! . . ."

McKechnie said to the batman:

"For God's sake go and see if it is. Come back at once. . . ."

The intolerable vision of the line, starving beneath the moon, of grey crowds murderously elbowing back a thin crowd in brown, zigzagged across the bronze light in the hut. The intolerable depression that, in those days, we felt—that all those millions were the play-things of ants busy in the miles of corridors beneath the domes and spires that rise up over the central heart of our comity, that intolerable weight upon the brain and the limbs, descended once more on those two men lying upon their elbows. As they listened their jaws fell open. The long, polyphonic babble, rushing in from an extended line of men stood easy, alone rewarded their ears.

Tietjens said:

"That fellow won't come back. . . . He can never do an errand and come back. . . ." He thrust one of his legs cumbrously out of the top of his flea-bag. He said:

"By God, the Germans will be all over here in a week's time!"

He said to himself:

"If they so betray us from Whitehall that fellow Levin has no right to pry into my matrimonial affairs. It is proper that one's individual feelings should be sacrificed to the necessities of a collective entity. But not if that entity is to be betrayed from above. Not if it hasn't the ten-millionth of a chance...." He regarded Levin's late incursion on his privacy[5] as inquiries set afoot by the general.... Incredibly painful to him: like a medical examination into nudities, but perfectly proper. Old Campion had to assure himself that the other ranks were not demoralized by the spectacle of officers' matrimonial infidelities.... But such inquiries were not to be submitted to if the whole show were one gigantic demoralization![6]

McKechnie said, in reference to Tietjens' protruded foot:

"There's no good your going out.... Cowley will get the men into their lines. He was prepared." He added: "If the fellows in Whitehall are determined to do old Puffles in,[7] why don't they recall him?"

The legend was that an eminent personage in the Government had a great personal dislike for the general in command of one army—the general being nicknamed Puffles.[8] The Government, therefore, were said to be starving his command of men so that disaster should fall upon his command.

"They can recall generals easy enough," McKechnie went on, "or anyone else!"

A heavy dislike that this member of the lower middle classes should[9] have opinions on public affairs overcame Tietjens. He exclaimed: "Oh, that's all tripe!"

He was himself outside all contact with affairs by now. But the other rumour in that troubled host had it that, as a political manœuvre, the heads round Whitehall—the civilian heads— were starving the army of troops in order to hold over the allies of Great Britain the threat of abandoning altogether the Western Front. They were credited with threatening a strategic manœuvre on an immense scale in the Near East, perhaps really intending it, or perhaps to force the hands of their allies over some political intrigue. These atrocious rumours reverberated backwards and forwards in the ears of all those millions under the black vault of heaven. All their comrades in the line were to be sacrificed as a rearguard to their departing host. That whole land was to be annihilated as a sacrifice to one vanity.[10] Now the draft had been called back. That seemed proof that the Government meant to starve the line! McKechnie groaned:

"Poor bloody old Bird! . . . He's booked. Eleven months in the front line, he's been. . . . Eleven *months!* . . . I was nine, this stretch. With him."

He added:

"Get back into bed, old bean. . . . I'll go and look after the men if it's necessary. . . . "

Tietjens said:

"You don't so much as know where their lines are. . . . " And sat listening. Nothing but the long roll of tongues came to him. He said:

"Damn it! The men ought not to be kept standing in the cold like that. . . . " Fury filled him beneath despair. His eyes filled with tears. "God," he said to himself, "the fellow Levin presumes to interfere in my private affairs. . . . Damn it," he said again, "it's like doing a little impertinence in a world that's foundering. . . . "

The world was foundering.

"I'd go out," he said, "but I don't want to have to put that filthy little Pitkins under arrest. He only drinks because he's shell-shocked. He's not man enough else, the unclean little Nonconformist. . . . "

McKechnie said:

"Hold on! . . . I'm a Presbyterian myself. . . . "

Tietjens answered:

"You would be! . . . " He said: "I beg your pardon. . . . There will be no more parades. . . . The British Army is dishonoured for ever. . . . "

McKechnie said:

"That's all right, old bean. . . . "

Tietjens exclaimed with sudden violence:

"What the hell are you doing in the officers' lines? . . . Don't you know it's a court-martial offence?"

He was confronted with the broad, mealy face of his regimental quartermaster-sergeant, the sort of fellow who wore an officer's cap against the regulations, with a Tommie's silver-plated badge. A man determined to get Sergeant-Major Cowley's job. The man had come in unheard under the roll of voices outside. He said:

"Excuse me, sir, I took the liberty of knocking. . . . The sergeant-major is in an epileptic fit. . . . I wanted your directions before putting the draft into the tents with the other men. . . . "

Having said that tentatively he hazarded cautiously: "The sergeant-major throws these fits, sir, if he is suddenly woke up.... And Second-Lieutenant Pitkins woke him very suddenly...."

Tietjens said:

"So you took on you the job of a beastly informer against both of them.... I shan't forget it." He said to himself:

"I'll get this fellow one day ..." and he seemed to hear with pleasure the clicking and tearing of the scissors as, inside three parts of a hollow square, they cut off his stripes and badges.

McKechnie exclaimed:

"Good God, man, you aren't going out in nothing but your pyjamas. Put your slacks on under your British warm...."

Tietjens said:

"Send the Canadian sergeant-major to me at the double...." to the quarter. "My slacks are at the tailor's, being pressed." His slacks were being pressed for the ceremony of the signing of the marriage contract of Levin, the fellow who had interfered in his private affairs. He continued into the mealy broad face and vague eyes of the quartermaster: "You know as well as I do that it was the Canadian sergeant-major's job to report to me.... I'll let you off this time, but, by God, if I catch you spying round the officers' lines again you are for a D.C.M...."

He wrapped a coarse, Red Cross, grey-wool muffler under the turned-up collar of his British warm.

"That swine," he said to McKechnie, "spies on the officers' lines in the hope of getting a commission by catching out bloody little squits like Pitkins, when they're drunk....[11] I'm seven hundred braces down. Morgan does not know that I know that I'm that much down. But you can bet he knows where they have gone...."

McKechnie said:

"I wish you would not go out like that.... I'll make you some cocoa...."

Tietjens said:

"I can't keep the men waiting while I dress.... I'm as strong as a horse...."

He was out amongst the bitterness, the mist, and the moon-gleams on three thousand rifle barrels, and the voices.... He was seeing the Germans pour through a thin line, and his heart was leaden.... A tall, graceful man swam up against him and said, through his nose, like an American:

"There has been a railway accident, due to the French strikers. The draft is put back till three pip emma the day after to-morrow, sir."

Tietjens exclaimed:

"It isn't countermanded?" breathlessly.

The Canadian sergeant-major said:

"No, sir.... A railway accident.... Sabotage by the French, they say.... Four Glamorganshire sergeants, all nineteen-fourteen men, killed, sir, going home on leave. But the draft is not cancelled...."

Tietjens said:

"Thank God!"

The slim Canadian with his educated voice said:

"You're thanking God, sir, for what's very much to our detriment. Our draft was ordered for Salonika till this morning. The sergeant in charge of draft returns showed me the name *Salonika* scored off in his draft roster. Sergeant-Major Cowley had got hold of the wrong story. Now it's going up the line. The other would have been a full two months' more life for us."

The man's rather slow voice seemed to continue for a long time. As it went on Tietjens felt the sunlight dwelling on his nearly coverless limbs, and the tide of youth returning to his veins. It was like champagne. He said:

"You sergeants get a great deal too much information. The sergeant in charge of returns had no business to show you his roster. It's not your fault, of course. But you are an intelligent man. You can see how useful that news might be to certain people: people that it's not to your own interest should know these things...." He said to himself: "A landmark in history...." And then: "Where the devil did my mind get hold of that expression at this moment?" They were walking in mist, down an immense lane, one hedge of which was topped by the serrated heads and irregularly held rifles that showed here and there. He said to the sergeant-major: "Call 'em to attention. Never mind their dressing, we've got to get 'em into bed. Roll-call will be at nine to-morrow."

His mind said:

"If this means the single command. . . . And it's bound to mean the single command, it's the turning point. . . . Why the hell am I so extraordinarily glad? What's it to me?"

He was shouting in a round voice:

"Now then, men, you've got to go six extra in a tent. See if you can fall out six at a time at each tent. It's not in the drill book, but see if you can do it for yourselves. You're smart men: use your intelligences. The sooner you get to bed the sooner you'll be warm. I wish I was. Don't disturb the men who're already in the tents. They've got to be up for fatigues tomorrow at five, poor devils. You can lie soft till three hours after that. . . . The draft will move to the left in fours. . . . Form fours . . . Left . . ." Whilst the voices of the sergeants in charge of companies yelped varyingly to a distance in the quick march order he said to himself:

"Extraordinarily glad. . . . A strong passion. . . . How damn well these fellows move! . . . Cannon fodder. . . . Cannon fodder. . . . That's what their steps say. . . ." His whole body shook in the grip of the cold that beneath his loose overcoat gnawed his pyjamaed limbs. He could not leave the men, but cantered beside them with the sergeant-major till he came to the head of the column in the open in time to wheel the first double company into a line of ghosts that were tents, silent and austere in the moon's very shadowy light. . . . It appeared to him a magic spectacle. He said to the sergeant-major: "Move the second company to B line, and so on," and stood at the side of the men as they wheeled, stamping, like a wall in motion. He thrust his stick halfway down between the second and third files. "Now then, a four and half a four to the right; remaining half-four and next four to the left. Fall out into first tents to right and left. . . ." He continued saying "First four and half, this four to the right. . . . Damn you, by the left! How can you tell which beastly four you belong to if you don't march by the left. . . . Remember you're soldiers, not new-chum* lumbermen. . . ."

It was sheer exhilaration to freeze there on the down-side of the extraordinarily pure air with the extraordinarily fine men. They came round, marking time with the stamp of guardsmen. He said, with tears in his voice:

---

* 'In Australia: new chum, a fresh immigrant, a greenhorn': *OED*.

"Damn it all, I gave them that extra bit of smartness.... Damn it all, there's something I've done...." Getting cattle into condition for the slaughter-house.... They were as eager as bullocks running down by Camden Town to Smithfield Market.... Seventy per cent. of them would never come back.... But it's better to go to heaven with[12] your skin shining and master of your limbs than as a hulking lout.... The Almighty's orderly room will welcome you better in all probability.... He continued exclaiming monotonously ... "Remaining half-four and next four to the left.... Hold your beastly tongues when you fall out. I can't hear myself give orders...." It lasted a long time. Then they were all swallowed up.[13]

He staggered, his knees wooden-stiff with the cold, and the cold more intense now the wall of men no longer sheltered him from the wind, out along the brink of the plateau to the other lines. It gave him satisfaction to observe that he had got his men into their lines seventy-five per cent. quicker than the best of the N.C.O.'s who had had charge of the other lines. Nevertheless, he swore bitingly at the sergeants: their men were in knots round the entrance to the alleys of ghost-pyramids.... Then there were no more, and he drifted with regret across the plain towards his country street of huts. One of them had a coarse evergreen rose growing over it. He picked a leaf, pressed it to his lips and threw it up into the wind.... "That's for Valentine," he said meditatively. "Why did I do that? ... Or perhaps it's for England...." He said: "Damn it all, this is patriotism! ... *This* is patriotism...." It wasn't what you took patriotism as a rule to be. There were supposed to be more parades about that job! ... But this was just a broke to the wide,* wheezy, half-frozen Yorkshireman, who despised every one in England not a Yorkshireman, or from more to the North, at two in the morning picking a leaf from a rose-tree and slobbering over it, without knowing what he was doing. And then discovering that it was half for a pug-nosed girl whom he presumed, but didn't know, to smell like a primrose; and half for ... England! ... At two in the morning with the thermometer ten degrees below zero....

---

* 'To the extreme; entirely, utterly. Used in various slang phrs., as blind (broke, dead, out, etc.) to the wide': OED.

Damn, it was cold! ...

And why these emotions? ... Because England, not before it was time, had been allowed to decide not to do the dirty on her associates! ... He said to himself: "It is probably because a hundred thousand sentimentalists like myself commit similar excesses of the subconscious that we persevere in this glorious but atrocious undertaking. All the same,[14] I didn't know I had it in me!" A strong passion! ... For his girl and his country! ... Nevertheless, his girl was a pro-German.... It was a queer mix-up! ... Not of course a pro-German, but disapproving of the preparation of men, like bullocks, with sleek healthy skins for the abattoirs in Smithfield.... Agreeing presumably with the squits who had been hitherto starving the B.E.F. of men.... A queer mix-up....

At half-past one the next day, in chastened winter sunlight, he mounted Schomburg, a coffin-headed, bright chestnut, captured from the Germans on the Marne by the second battalion of the Glamorganshires. He had not been on the back of the animal two minutes before he remembered that he had forgotten to look it over. It was the first time in his life that he had ever forgotten to look at an animal's hoofs, fetlocks, knees, nostrils and eyes, and to take a pull at the girth before climbing into the saddle. But he had ordered the horse for a quarter to one and, even though he had bolted his cold lunch like a cannibal in haste, there he was three-quarters of an hour late, and with his head still full of teasing problems. He had meant to clear his head by a long canter over the be-hutted downs, dropping down into the city by a bypath.[15]

But the ride did not clear his head—rather, the sleeplessness of the night began for the first time then to tell on him after a morning of fatigues, during which he had managed to keep the thought of Sylvia at arm's length. He had to wait to see Sylvia before he could see what Sylvia wanted. And morning had brought the common-sense idea that probably she wanted to do nothing more than pull the string of the showerbath—which meant committing herself to the first extravagant action that came into her head—and exulting in the consequences.[16]

He had not managed to get to bed at all the night before.

Captain McKechnie, who had had some cocoa—a beverage Tietjens had never before tasted—hot and ready for him on his return
from the lines, had kept him till past half-past four, relating with
a male fury his really very painful story. It appeared that he had
obtained leave to go home and divorce his wife, who, during his
absence in France, had been living with an Egyptologist in
Government service. Then, acting under conscientious scruples
of the younger school of the day, he had refrained from divorcing
her. Campion had in consequence threatened to deprive him of
his commission.... The poor devil—who had actually
consented to contribute to the costs of the household of his wife
and the Egyptologist—had gone raving mad and had showered
an extraordinary torrent of abuse at the decent old fellow that
Campion was.... A decent old fellow, really. For the interview,
being delicate, had taken place in the general's bedroom and the
general had not felt it necessary, there being no orderlies or junior
officers present, to take any official notice of McKechnie's
outburst. McKechnie was a fellow with an excellent military
record; you could in fact hardly have found a regimental officer
with a better record. So Campion had decided to deal with the
man as suffering from a temporary brain-storm and had sent him
to Tietjens' unit for rest and recuperation. It was an irregularity,
but the general was of a rank to risk what irregularities he considered to be of use to the service.

It had turned out that McKechnie was actually the nephew of
Tietjens' very old intimate, Sir Vincent Macmaster, of the
Department of Statistics, being the son of his sister who had
married the assistant to the elder Macmaster, a small grocer in
the Port of Leith in Scotland....[17] That indeed had been why
Campion had been interested in him. Determined as he was to
show his godson no unreasonable military favours, the general
was perfectly ready to do a kindness that he thought would please
Tietjens. All these pieces of information Tietjens had packed
away in his mind for future consideration and, it being after four-
thirty before McKechnie had calmed himself down, Tietjens had
taken the opportunity to inspect the breakfasts of the various
fatigues ordered for duty in the town, these being detailed for
various hours from a quarter to five to seven. It was a matter of
satisfaction to Tietjens to have seen to the breakfasts, and

inspected his cook-houses,[18] since he did not often manage to make the opportunity and he could by no means trust his orderly officers.

At breakfast in the depot mess-hut he was detained by the colonel in command of the depot, the Anglican padre and McKechnie; the colonel, very old, so frail that you would have thought that a shudder or a cough would have shaken his bones one from another, had yet a passionate belief that the Greek Church should exchange communicants with the Anglican: the padre, a stout, militant Churchman, had a gloomy contempt for Orthodox theology.* McKechnie from time to time essayed to define the communion according to the Presbyterian rite. They all listened to Tietjens whilst he dilated on the historic aspects of the various schisms of Christianity and accepted his rough definition to the effect that, in transubstantiation, the host actually became the divine presence, whereas in consubstantiation the substance of the host, as if miraculously become porous, was suffused with the presence as a sponge is with water.... They all agreed that the breakfast bacon supplied from store was uneatable and agreed to put up half a crown a week apiece to get better for their table.

Tietjens had[19] walked in the sunlight down the lines, past the hut with the evergreen climbing rose, in the sunlight, thinking in an interval, good humouredly about his official religion: about the Almighty as, on a colossal scale, a great English Landowner, benevolently awful, a colossal duke who never left his study and was thus invisible, but knowing all about the estate down to the last hind at the home farm and the last oak: Christ, an almost too benevolent Land-Steward, son of the Owner, knowing all about the estate down to the last child at the porter's lodge, apt to be got round by the more detrimental tenants: the Third Person of the Trinity, the spirit of the estate, the Game as it were, as distinct from the players of the game: the atmosphere of the estate, that of the interior of Winchester Cathedral just after a Handel anthem has been finished, a perpetual Sunday, with, probably, a little cricket for the young men. Like Yorkshire of a Saturday

---

* The central characters of Ford's 1910 novel *A Call* have Greek ancestry, and an Orthodox priest features in one crucial scene with Robert Grimshaw.

afternoon; if you looked down on the whole broad county you would not see a single village green without its white flannels. That was why Yorkshire always leads the averages.... Probably by the time you got to heaven you would be so worn out by work on this planet that you would accept the English Sunday, for ever, with extreme relief!

With his belief that all that was good in English literature ended with the seventeenth century, his imaginations of heaven must be materialist—like Bunyan's.* He laughed good-humouredly at his projection of a hereafter. It was probably done with. Along with cricket. There would be no more parades of that sort. Probably they would play some beastly yelping game.... Like baseball or Association football.... And heaven? ... Oh, it would be a revival meeting on a Welsh hillside. Or Chau-tauqua,† wherever that was.... And God? A Real Estate Agent, with Marxist views.... He hoped to be out of it before the cessa-tion of hostilities, in which case he might be just in time for the last train to the old heaven....‡

In his orderly hut he found an immense number of papers. On the top an envelope marked *Urgent. Private* with a huge rubber stamp. From Levin. Levin, too, must have been up pretty late. It was not about Mrs. Tietjens, or even Miss de Bailly.[20] It was a private warning that Tietjens would probably have his draft on his hands another week or ten days, and very likely another couple of thousand men extra as well. He warned Tietjens to draw

---

* In the 'Preface' to *On Heaven* 5–6, Ford says of the title-poem: 'If it is a materialist's Heaven I can't help it. I suppose I am a materialist.' *Return* 313 tells an improbable story about the *Fortnightly Review* planning to publish the poem in England, but deciding against publication after Masterman asked the advice of the Home Secre-tary, who said he would have to authorise a prosecution for blasphemy because 'It gave a materialist picture of heaven.' *The English Novel* includes an extended discussion of Bunyan.

† A town on the shore of Lake Chautaqua in extreme north-western New York state known for outdoor lectures, concerts, and dramatic performances in the summer months. 'Chautauquas' later became widespread in the United States.

‡ *No Enemy* 54 describes a child whom the protagonist, Gringoire, meets in a hotel and thinks of as Henry James's character Maisie: 'She was bothered because she could not find the tram to Heaven. Because they said her mother had gone to Heaven.' In a 1911 essay on Rossetti (a significant presence in *Some Do Not...*) Ford tells of 'a great writer who always lost his ticket when he travelled'; and decides that this unidentified man's absent-mindedness came about because he was so engrossed in his work. Similarly, thinks Ford, 'Rossetti lost quite a number of railway tickets of one kind or another [...] perhaps he even lost his ticket to Heaven': *Critical Essays*, ed. Max Saunders and Richard Stang (Manchester: Carcanet, 2002), 95–6.

all the tents he could get hold of as soon as possible. . . . Tietjens called to a subaltern with pimples who was picking his teeth with a pen-nib at the other end of the hut: "Here, you! . . . Take two companies of the Canadians to the depot store and draw all the tents you can get up to two hundred and fifty. . . . Have 'em put alongside my D lines. . . . Do you know how to look after putting up tents? . . . Well then, get Thompson . . . no, Pitkins, to help you. . . ." The subaltern drifted out sulkily. Levin said that the French railway strikers, for some political reason, had sabotaged a mile of railway, the accident of the night before had completely blocked up all the lines, and the French civilians would not let their own breakdown gangs make any repairs. German prisoners had been detailed for that fatigue, but probably Tietjens' Canadian railway corps would be wanted. He had better hold them in readiness. The strike was said to be a manœuvre for forcing our hands—to get us to take over more of the line. In that case they had jolly well dished themselves, for how could we take over more of the line without more men, and how could we send up more men without the railway to send them by? We had half a dozen army corps all ready to go. Now they were all jammed. Fortunately the weather at the front was so beastly that the Germans could not move. He finished up "Four in the morning,* old bean, *à tantôt!*"† the last phrase having been learned from Mlle de Bailly. Tietjens grumbled that if they went on piling up the work on him like this he would never get down to the signing of that marriage contract.

He called the Canadian sergeant-major to him.

"See," he said, "that you keep the Railway Service Corps in camp with their arms ready, whatever their arms are. Tools, I suppose. Are their tools all complete? And their muster roll?"

"Girtin has gone absent, sir," the slim dark fellow said, with an air of destiny. Girtin was the respectable man with the mother to whom Tietjens had given the two hours' leave the night before.

Tietjens answered:

* The time implies daybreak, courage, and leave-taking. Ford's poem 'Four in the Morning Courage', *Collected Poems*, intro. William Rose Benét (New York: Oxford University Press, 1936), 136, is set at dawn. Sylvia Tietjens' leaving her husband for a convent near Birkenhead and telling the taxi driver to take her to Paddington Station was a 'four-in-the-morning departure'.

† Till very soon, indeed.

"He would have!" with a sour grin. It enhanced his views of strictly respectable humanity. They blackmailed you with lamentable and pathetic tales and then did the dirty on you. He said to the sergeant-major:

"You will be here for another week or ten days. See that you get your tents up all right and the men comfortable. I will inspect them as soon as I have taken my orderly room. Full marching order. Captain McKechnie will inspect their kits at two."

The sergeant-major, stiff but graceful, had something at the back of his mind. It came out:

"I have my marching orders for two-thirty this afternoon. The notice for inserting my commission in depot orders is on your table. I leave for the O.T.C. by the three train. . . ."

Tietjens said:

"Your commission! . . ." It was a confounded nuisance.

The sergeant-major said:

"Sergeant-Major Cowley and I applied for our commissions three months ago. The communications granting them are both on your table together. . . ."

Tietjens said:

"Sergeant-Major Cowley. . . . Good God! Who recommended you?"

The whole organization of his confounded battalion fell to pieces. It appeared that a circular had come round three months before—before Tietjens had been given command of that unit—asking for experienced first-class warrant officers capable of serving as instructors in Officers' Training Corps, with commissions. Sergeant-Major Cowley had been recommended by the colonel of the depot, Sergeant-Major Ledoux by his own colonel. Tietjens felt as if he had been let down—but of course he had not been. It was just the way of the army, all the time. You got a platoon, or a battalion, or, for the matter of that, a dug-out or a tent, by herculean labours into good fettle. It ran all right for a day or two, then it all fell to pieces, the personnel scattered to the four winds by what appeared merely wanton orders, coming from the most unexpected headquarters, or the premises were smashed up by a chance shell that might just as well have fallen somewhere else. . . . The finger of Fate! . . .

But it put a confounded lot more work on him. . . . He said to

Sergeant-Major Cowley, whom he found in the next hut where all the paper work of the unit was done:

"I should have thought you would have been enormously better off as regimental sergeant-major than with a commission. I know I would rather have the job." Cowley answered—he was very pallid and shaken—that with his unfortunate infirmity, coming on at any moment of shock, he would be better in a job where he could slack off, like an O.T.C. He had always been subject to small fits, over in a minute, or couple of seconds even.... But getting too near a H.E. shell—after Noircourt which had knocked out Tietjens himself[21]—had brought them on, violent. There was also, he finished, the gentility to be considered. Tietjens said:

"Oh, the gentility! ... That's not worth a flea's jump.... There won't be any more parades after this war. There aren't any now. Look at who your companions will be in an officer's quarters; you'd be in a great deal better society in any self-respecting sergeants' mess." Cowley answered that he knew the service had gone to the dogs. All the same his missis liked it. And there was his daughter Winnie to be considered. She had always been a bit wild, and his missis wrote that she had gone wilder than ever, all due to the war. Cowley thought that the bad boys would be a little more careful how they monkeyed with her if she was an officer's daughter.... There was probably something in that!

Coming out into the open, confidentially with Tietjens, Cowley dropped his voice huskily to say:

"Take Quartermaster-Sergeant Morgan for R.S.M., sir."

Tietjens said explosively:

"I'm damned if I will." Then he asked: "Why?" The wisdom of old N.C.O.'s is a thing no prudent officer neglects.

"He can do the work, sir," Cowley said. "He's out for a commission, and he'll do his best...." He dropped his husky voice to a still greater depth of mystery:

"You're over two hundred—I should say nearer three hundred—pounds down in your battalion stores. I don't suppose you want to lose a sum of money like that?"

Tietjens said:

"I'm damned if I do.... But I[22] don't see.... Oh, yes, I do.... If I make him sergeant-major he has to hand over the stores all complete.... To-day.... Can[23] he do it?"

Cowley said that Morgan could have till the day after to-morrow. He would look after things till then.[24]

"But you'll want to have a flutter before you go," Tietjens said. "Don't stop for me."

Cowley said that he would stop and see the job through. He had thought of going down into the town and having a flutter. But the girls down there were a common sort, and it was bad for his complaint.... He would stop and see what could be done with Morgan. Of course it was possible that Morgan might decide to face things out. He might prefer to stick to the money he'd got by disposing of Tietjens' stores to other battalions that were down, or to civilian contractors. And stand a court martial! But it wasn't likely. He was a Nonconformist deacon, or pew-opener, or even a minister possibly, at home in Wales.... From near Denbigh![25] And Cowley had got a very good man, a first-class man, an Oxford professor, now a lance-corporal at the depot, for Morgan's place. The colonel would lend him to Tietjens and would get him rated acting quartermaster-sergeant unpaid.... Cowley had it all arranged.... Lance-Corporal Caldicott was a first-class man, only he could not tell his right hand from his left on parade. Literally could not tell them....

So the battalion settled itself down.... Whilst Cowley and he were at the colonel's orderly room arranging for the transfer of the professor—he was really only a fellow of his college—who did not know his right hand from his left, Tietjens was engaged in the remains of the colonel's furious argument as to the union of the Anglican and Eastern rites. The colonel—he was a full colonel—sat in his lovely private office, a light, gay compartment of a tin-hutment, the walls being papered in scarlet, with, on the purplish, thick, soft baize of his table-cover, a tall glass vase from which sprayed out pale Riviera roses, the gift of young lady admirers amongst the V.A.D.'s in the town because he was a darling, and an open, very gilt and leather-bound volume of a biblical encyclopædia beneath his delicate septuagenarian features. He was confirming his opinion that a union between the Church of England and the Greek Orthodox Church was the only thing that could save civilization. The whole war turned on that. The Central Empires represented Roman Catholicism, the

Allies Protestantism and Orthodoxy. Let them unite. The papacy was a traitor to the cause of civilization. Why had the Vatican not protested with no uncertain voice about the abominations practised on the Belgian Catholics? ...

Tietjens pointed out languidly objections to this theory. The first thing our ambassador to the Vatican had found out on arriving in Rome and protesting about massacres of Catholic laymen in Belgium was that the Russians before they had been a day in Austrian Poland had hanged twelve Roman Catholic bishops in front of their palaces.

Cowley was engaged with the adjutant at another table. The colonel ended his theologico-political tirade by saying:

"I shall be very sorry to lose you, Tietjens. I don't know what we shall do without you. I never had a moment's peace with your unit until you came."

Tietjens said:

"Well, you aren't losing me, sir, as far as I know." The colonel said:

"Oh, yes, we are. You are going up the line next week...." He added: "Now, don't get angry with me.... I've protested very strongly to old Campion—General Campion—that I cannot do without you." And he made, with his delicate, thin, hairy-backed, white hands a motion as of washing.

The ground moved under Tietjens' feet. He felt himself clambering over slopes of mud with his heavy legs and labouring chest. He said:

"Damn it all! ... I'm not fit.... I'm C3.... I was ordered to live in an hotel in the town.... I only mess here to be near the battalion."

The colonel said with some eagerness:

"Then you can protest to Garrison.... I hope you will.... But I suppose you are the sort of fellow that won't." Tietjens said:

"No, sir.... Of course I cannot protest.... Though it's probably a mistake of some clerk.... I could not stand a week in the line...." The profound misery of brooding apprehension in the line was less on his mind than, precisely, the appalling labour of the lower limbs when you live in mud to the neck.... Besides, whilst he had been in hospital, practically the whole of his equipment had disappeared from his kitbag—including Sylvia's two pairs of sheets!—and he had no money with which to get more. He had not even any trench-boots. Fantastic financial troubles settled on his mind.

The colonel said to the adjutant at the other purple baize-covered table:

"Show Captain Tietjens those marching orders of his.... They're from Whitehall, aren't they?... You never know where these things come from nowadays. I call them the arrow that flieth by night!"*

The adjutant, a diminutive, a positively miniature gentleman with Coldstream badges up and a dreadfully worried brow, drifted a quarto sheet of paper out of a pile, across his tablecloth towards Tietjens. His tiny hands seemed about to fall off at the wrists; his temples shuddered with neuralgia. He said:

"For God's sake do protest to Garrison if you feel you can.... We *can't* have more work shoved on us.... Major Lawrence and Major Halkett left the whole of the work of your unit to us...."

The sumptuous paper, with the royal arms embossed at the top, informed Tietjens that he would report to his VIth battalion on the Wednesday of next week in preparation for taking up the duties of divisional transport officer to the XIXth division. The order came from Room G 14 R, at the War Office. He asked what the deuce G 14 R was, of the adjutant, who in an access of neuralgic agony, shook his head miserably, between his two hands, his elbows on the tablecloth.

Sergeant-Major Cowley, with his air of a solicitor's clerk, said the room G 14 R was the department that dealt with civilian requests for the services of officers. To the adjutant who asked what the devil a civilian request for the employment of officers could have to do with sending Captain Tietjens to the XIXth division, Sergeant-Major Cowley presumed that it was because of the activities of the Earl of Beichan. The Earl of Beichan, a Levantine financier and race-horse owner, was interesting himself in army horses, after a short visit to the lines of communication. He also owned several newspapers. So they had been waking up the army transport-animals' department to please him.

* Cf. Psalms 91:5: 'Thou shalt not be afraid for the terror by night; nor for the arrow that flieth by day'.

The adjutant would no doubt have observed a Veterinary-Lieutenant Hotchkiss or Hitchcock. He had come to them through G 14 R. At the request of Lord Beichan, who was personally interested in Lieutenant Hotchkiss's theories, he was to make experiments on the horses of the Fourth Army—in which the XIXth division was then to be found.... "So," Cowley said, "you'll be under him as far as your horse lines go. If you go up."[26] Perhaps Lord Beichan was a friend of Captain Tietjens and had asked for him, too: Captain Tietjens was known to be wonderful with horses.

Tietjens, his breath rushing through his nostrils, swore he would not go up the line at the bidding of a hog like Beichan, whose real name was Stavropolides, formerly Nathan.

He said the army was reeling to its base because of the continual interference of civilians. He said it was absolutely impossible to get through his programme of parades because of the perpetual extra drills that were forced on them at the biddings of civilians. Any fool who owned a newspaper, nay, any fool who could write to a newspaper, or any beastly little squit of a novelist could frighten the Government and the War Office into taking up one more hour of the men's parade time for patent manœuvres with jampots or fancy underclothing.[27] Now he was asked if his men wanted lecturing on the causes of the war and whether he—he, good God!—would not like to give the men cosy chats on the nature of the Enemy nations....

The colonel said:

"There, there, Tietjens! ... There, there! ... We all suffer alike. *We've* got to lecture our men on the uses of a new patent sawdust stove. If you don't want that job, you can easily get the general to take you off it. They say you can turn him round your little finger...."

"He's my godfather," Tietjens thought it wise to say. "I never asked him for a job, but I'm damned if it isn't his duty as a Christian to keep me out of the clutches of this Greek-'Ebrew pagan peer.... He's not even Orthodox, colonel ...."

The adjutant here said that Colour-Sergeant Morgan of their orderly room wanted a word with Tietjens. Tietjens said he hoped to goodness that Morgan had some money for him! The adjutant said he understood that Morgan had unearthed quite a little money that ought to have been paid to Tietjens by his agents and hadn't.[28]

Colour-Sergeant Morgan was the regimental magician with figures. Inordinately tall and thin, his body, whilst his eyes peered into distant columns of cyphers, appeared to be always parallel with the surface of his table and, as he always answered the several officers whom he benefited without raising his head, his face was very little known to his superiors. He was, however, in appearance a very ordinary, thin N.C.O. whose spidery legs, when very rarely he appeared on parade, had the air of running away with him as a race-horse might do. He told Tietjens that, pursuant to his instructions and the A.C.P. i 96 b that Tietjens had signed, he had ascertained that command pay at the rate of two guineas a day and supplementary fuel and light allowance at the rate of 6s. 8d. was being paid weekly by the Paymaster-General's Department to his, Tietjens', account at his agents'. He suggested that Tietjens should write to his agents that if they did not immediately pay to his account the sum of £194 13s. 4d., by them received from the Paymaster's Department, he would proceed against the Crown by Petition of Right.* And he strongly recommended Tietjens to draw a cheque on his own bank for the whole of the money because, if by any chance the agents had not paid the money in, he could sue them for damages and get them cast[†] in several thousand pounds. And serve the devils right. They must have a million or so in hand in unpaid command and detention allowances due to officers. He only wished he could advertise in the papers offering to recover unpaid sums due by agents. He added that he had a nice little computation as to variations in the course of Gunter's Second Comet[‡] that he would like to ask Tietjens' advice[29] about one of these days. The colour-sergeant was an impassioned amateur astronomer.

So Tietjens' morning went up and down. . . . The money at the moment, Sylvia being in Rouen,[30] was of tremendous importance

---

* The 'parliamentary declaration of the rights and liberties of the people, set forth in the form of a petition to King Charles I, which was finally assented to by the king in 1628. Although not a formal statute or ordinance, "it has ever been accepted as having the full force of law"': OED.

† 'To sum up or reckon accounts': OED.

‡ Edmund Gunter (1581–1626), an English mathematician and astronomer, devised revolutionary methods of calculation that advanced accuracy in navigation.

to him and came like an answer to prayer. It was not so agreeable, however, even in a world in which, never, never, never for ten minutes did you know whether you stood on your head or your heels, for Tietjens, on going back to the colonel's private office, to find Sergeant-Major Cowley coming out of the next room in which, on account of the adjutant's neuralgia, the telephone was kept. Cowley announced to the three of them that the general had the day before ordered his correspondence-corporal to send a very emphatic note to Colonel Gillum to the effect that he was informing the competent authority that he had no intention whatever of parting with Captain Tietjens, who was invaluable in his command. The correspondence-corporal had informed Cowley that neither he nor the general knew who was the competent authority for telling Room G 14 R at the War Office to go to hell, but the matter would be looked up and put all right before the chit was sent off. . . .

That was good as far as it went. Tietjens was really interested in his present job, and although he would have liked well enough to have the job of looking after the horses of a division, or even an army, he felt he would rather it was put off till the spring, given the weather they were having and the state of his chest. And the complication of possible troubles with Lieutenant Hotchkiss who, being a professor, had never really seen a horse—or not for ten years!—was something to be thought about very seriously.[31] But all this appeared quite another matter when Cowley announced that the civilian authority who had asked for Tietjens' transfer was the permanent secretary to the Ministry of Transport. . . .

Colonel Gillum said:

"That's your brother, Mark. . . ." And indeed the permanent secretary to the Ministry of Transport was Tietjens' brother Mark, known as the Indispensable Official. Tietjens felt a real instant of dismay. He considered that his violent protest against the job would appear rather a smack in the face for poor old wooden-featured Mark who had probably taken a good deal of trouble to get him the job. Even if Mark should never hear of it, a man should not slap his brother in the face! Moreover, when he came to think of his last day in London, he remembered that Valentine Wannop, who had exaggerated ideas as to the safety of First Line Transport, had begged Mark to get him a job as divisional officer.... And he imagined Valentine's despair if she heard that he—Tietjens—had moved heaven and earth to get out of it. He saw her lower lip quivering and the tears in her eyes.... But he probably had got that from some novel, because he had never seen her lower lip quiver. He had seen tears in her eyes![32]

He hurried back to his lines to take his orderly room. In the long hut McKechnie was taking that miniature court of drunks and defaulters for him and, just as Tietjens reached it, he was taking the case of Girtin and two other Canadian privates.... The case of Girtin interested him, and when McKechnie slid out of his seat Tietjens occupied it. The prisoners were only just being marched in by a Sergeant Davis, an admirable N.C.O. whose rifle appeared to be part of his rigid body and who executed an amazing number of stamps in seriously turning in front of the C.O.'s table. It gave the impression of an Indian war dance....

Tietjens glanced at the charge sheet, which was marked as coming from the Provost-Marshal's Office. Instead of the charge of absence from draft he read that of conduct prejudicial to good order and military discipline in that.... The charge was written in a very illiterate hand; an immense beery lance-corporal of Garrison Military Police, with a red hat-band, attended to give evidence.... It was a tenuous and disagreeable affair. Girtin had not gone absent, so Tietjens had to revise his views of the respectable. At any rate of the respectable Colonial private soldier with mother complete. For there really had been a mother, and Girtin had been seeing her into the last tram down into the town. A frail old lady. Apparently, trying to annoy the Canadian, the beery lance-corporal of the Garrison Military Police had hustled the mother. Girtin had remonstrated; very moderately, he said. The lance-corporal had shouted at him. Two other Canadians returning to camp had intervened and two more police. The police had called the Canadians bloody conscripts, which was almost more than the Canadians could stand, they being voluntarily enlisted 1914 or 1915 men. The police—it was an old trick—had kept the men talking until two minutes after the last post had sounded and then had run them in for being absent off pass—and for disrespect to their red hat-bands.

Tietjens, with a carefully measured fury, first cross-examined and then damned the police witness to hell. Then he marked the charge sheets with the words, "Case explained," and told the Canadians to go and get ready for his parade. It meant, he was aware, a frightful[33] row with the provost-marshal, who was a port-winey old general called O'Hara and loved his police as if they had been ewe-lambs.

He took his parade, the Canadian troops looking like real soldiers in the sunlight, went round his lines with the new Canadian sergeant-major, who had his appointment, thank goodness, from his own authorities; wrote a report on the extreme undesirability of lecturing his men on the causes of the war, since his men were either graduates of one or other Canadian university and thus knew twice as much about the causes of the war as any lecturer the civilian authorities could provide, or else they were half-breed Micamuc Indians,* Esquimaux, Japanese, or Alaskan Russians, none of whom could understand any English lecturer.... He was aware that he would have to re-write his report so as to make it more respectful to the newspaper proprietor peer[34] who, at that time, was urging on the home Government the necessity of lecturing all the subjects of His Majesty on the causes of the war. But he wanted to get that grouse off his chest and its disrespect would pain Levin, who would have to deal with these reports if he did not get married first. Then he lunched off army sausage-meat and potatoes, mashed with their skins complete, watered with an admirable 1906 brut champagne which they bought themselves, and an appalling Canadian cheese—at the headquarters table to which the colonel had invited all the subalterns who that day were going up the line for the first time. They had some h's in their compositions, but in revenge they must have boasted of a pint of adenoid growths between them. There was, however, a charming young half-caste Goa second-lieutenant, who afterwards proved of an heroic bravery. He gave Tietjens a lot of amusing information as to the working of the purdah in Portuguese India.

---

* Perhaps an alternatively spelled reference to the Micmacs, 'a native American people inhabiting Nova Scotia, New Brunswick, Prince Edward Island, and the Gaspé Peninsula of Quebec' (*The American Heritage Dictionary*, 3rd edn, exec. ed. Anne H. Soukhanov; Boston, New York, London: Houghton Mifflin, 1992).

So, at half-past one Tietjens sat on Schomburg, the coffin-
headed, bright chestnut from the Prussian horse-raising
establishment near Celle. Almost a pure thoroughbred, this
animal had usually the paces of a dining-room table, its legs being
fully as stiff. But to-day its legs might have been made of cotton-
wool, it lumbered over frosty ground breathing stertorously and,
at the jumping ground of the Deccan Horse,* a mile above and
behind Rouen, it did not so much refuse a very moderate jump as
come together in a lugubrious crumple. It was, in the light of a
red, jocular sun, like being mounted on a broken-hearted camel.
In addition, the fatigues of the morning beginning to tell, Tietjens was troubled by an obsession of O Nine Morgan which he
found tiresome to have to stall off.[35]

"What the hell," he asked of the orderly, a very silent private
on a roan beside him, "what the hell is the matter with this horse?
. . . Have you been keeping him warm?" He imagined that the
clumsy paces of the animal beneath him added to his gloomy
obsessions.[36]

The orderly looked straight in front of him over a valley full of
hutments. He said:

"No, sir." The 'oss 'ad been put in the 'oss-standings of G depot.
By the orders of Lieutenant 'Itchcock. 'Osses, Lieutenant 'Itchcock said, 'ad to be 'ardened.

Tietjens said:

"Did you tell him that it was my orders that Schomburg was to
be kept warm? In the stables of the farm behind No. XVI I.B.D."

"The lieutenant," the orderly explained woodenly, "said as 'ow
henny departure f'm 'is orders would be visited by the extreme
displeasure of Lord Breech'em, K.C.V.O., K.C.B., etcetera." The
orderly was quivering with rage.

"You will," Tietjens said very carefully, "when you fall out with
the horses at the Hôtel de la Poste, take Schomburg and the roan
to the stables of La Volonté Farm, behind No. XVI I.B.D."[37] The
orderly was to close all the windows of the stable, stopping up any
chinks with wadding. He would procure, if possible, a sawdust
stove, new pattern, from Colonel Gillum's store and light it in

* A regular cavalry regiment of the British Indian Army. The 20th Deccan Horse was
sent to France for service on the Western Front.

the stables. He was also to give Schomburg and the roan oatmeal and water warmed as hot as the horses would take it.... And Tietjens finished sharply, "If Lieutenant Hotchkiss makes any comments, you will refer him to me. As his C.O."

The orderly seeking information as to horse-ailments, Tietjens said:

"The school of horse-copers, to which Lord Beichan belongs, believes in the hardening of all horse-flesh other than racing cattle." They bred racing-cattle. Under six blankets apiece! Personally Tietjens did not believe in the hardening process and would not permit any animal over which he had control to be submitted to it....[38] It had been observed that if any animal was kept at a lower temperature than that of its normal climatic condition it would contract diseases to which ordinarily it was not susceptible.... If you keep a chicken for two days in a pail of water it will contract human scarlet-fever or mumps if injected with either bacillus. If you remove the chicken from the water, dry it, and restore it to its normal conditions, the scarlet-fever or the mumps will die out of the animal.... He said to the orderly: "You are an intelligent man. What deduction do you draw?"[39]

The orderly looked away over the valley of the Seine.

"I suppose, sir," he said, "that our 'osses, being kept alwise cold in their standings, 'as hillnesses they wouldn't otherwise 'ave."

"Well, then," Tietjens said, "keep the poor animals warm."

He considered that here was the makings of a very nasty row for himself if, by any means, his sayings came round to the ears of Lord Beichan. But that he had to chance. He could not let a horse for which he was responsible be martyred....[40] There was too much to think about ... so that nothing at all stood out to be thought of. The sun was glowing. The valley of the Seine was blue-grey, like a Gobelins tapestry. Over it all hung the shadow of a deceased Welsh soldier.[41] An odd skylark was declaiming over an empty field behind the incinerators' headquarters.... An odd lark. For as a rule larks do not sing in December. Larks sing only when courting, or over the nest.... The bird must be oversexed. O Nine Morgan was the other thing, that accounting for the prize-fighter![42]

They dropped down a mud lane between brick walls into the town....

PART II

I

IN the admirably appointed, white-enamelled, wickerworked, bemirrored lounge of the best hotel of that town Sylvia Tietjens sat in a wickerwork chair, not listening rather abstractedly to a staff-major who was lachrymosely and continuously begging her to leave her bedroom door unlocked that night. She said:

"I don't know.... Yes, perhaps.... I don't know...." And looked distantly into a bluish wall-mirror that, like all the rest, was framed with white-painted cork bark. She stiffened a little and said:

"There's Christopher!"

The staff-major dropped his hat, his stick and his gloves. His black hair, which was without parting and heavy with some preparation of a glutinous kind, moved agitatedly on his scalp. He had been saying that Sylvia had ruined his life. Didn't Sylvia know that she had ruined his life? But for her he might have married some pure young thing. Now he exclaimed:

"But what does he want? ... Good God! ... what does he want?"

"He wants," Sylvia said, "to play the part of Jesus Christ."[1]

Major Perowne exclaimed:

"Jesus Christ! ... But he's the most foul-mouthed officer in the general's command...."

"Well," Sylvia said, "if you had married your pure young thing she'd have... What is it? ... cuckolded you within nine months...."

Perowne shuddered a little at the word. He mumbled:

"I don't see ... It seems to be the other way ..."

"Oh, no, it isn't," Sylvia said. "Think it over.... Morally, *you're* the husband.... *Immorally*, I should say.... Because he's the man I want.... He looks ill.... Do hospital authorities always tell wives what is the matter with their husbands?"

From his angle in the chair from which he had half-emerged Sylvia seemed to him to be looking at a blank wall.

"I don't see him," Perowne said.

"I can see him in the glass," Sylvia said. "Look! From here you can see him."

Perowne shuddered a little more.

"I don't want to see him.... I have to see him sometimes in the course of duty.... I don't like to...."

Sylvia said:

"*You,*" in a tone of very deep contempt. "You only carry chocolate boxes to flappers.... How can he come across you in the course of duty? ... You're not a *soldier!*"

Perowne said:

"But what are we going to do? What will *he* do?"

"I," Sylvia answered, "shall tell the page-boy when he comes with his card to say that I'm engaged.... I don't know what *he'll* do. Hit you, very likely.... He's looking at your back now...."

Perowne became rigid, sunk into his deep chair.

"But he *couldn't!*" he exclaimed agitatedly. "You said that he was playing the part of Jesus Christ. Our Lord wouldn't hit people in an hotel lounge...."

"Our Lord!" Sylvia said contemptuously. "What do you know about our Lord? ... Our Lord was a gentleman....[*] Christopher is playing at being our Lord calling on the woman taken in adultery.... He's giving me the social backing that his being my husband seems to him to call for."

A one-armed, bearded *maitre d'hôtel* approached them through groups of arm-chairs arranged for *tête-à-tête*. He said:

"Pardon ... I did not see madame at first...." And displayed a card on a salver. Without looking at it, Sylvia said:

"*Dites à ce monsieur*[†] ... that I am occupied." The *maitre d'hôtel* moved austerely away.

"But he'll smash me to pieces ..." Perowne exclaimed. "What am I to do? ... What the deuce am I to do?" There would have

---

[*] *Return* 286 ascribes Sylvia's words here verbatim to Hilaire Belloc.
[†] 'Tell that gentleman ...'

been no way of exit for him except across Tietjens' face.

With her spine very rigid and the expression of a snake that fixes a bird, Sylvia gazed straight in front of her and said nothing until she exclaimed:

"For God's sake leave off trembling.... He would not do anything to a girl like you.... He's a man...." The wickerwork of Perowne's chair had been crepitating as if it had been in a railway car. The sound ceased with a jerk.... Suddenly she clenched both her hands and let out a hateful little breath of air between her teeth.

"By the immortal saints," she exclaimed, "I swear I'll make his wooden face wince yet."

In the bluish looking-glass, a few minutes before, she had seen the agate-blue eyes of her husband, thirty feet away, over arm-chairs and between the fans of palms. He was standing, holding a riding-whip, looking rather clumsy in the uniform that did not suit him. Rather clumsy and worn out, but completely expressionless! He had looked straight into the reflection of her eyes and then looked away. He moved so that his profile was towards her, and continued gazing motionless at an elk's head that decorated the space of wall above glazed doors giving into the interior of the hotel. The hotel servant approaching him, he had produced a card and had given it to the servant, uttering three words. She saw his lips move in the three words: Mrs. Christopher Tietjens. She said, beneath her breath:

"Damn his chivalry! ... Oh, God damn his chivalry!" She knew what was going on in his mind. He had seen her, with Perowne, so he had neither come towards her nor directed the servant to where she sat. For fear of embarrassing her! He would leave it to her to come to him if she wished.

The servant, visible in the mirror, had come and gone deviously back, Tietjens still gazing at the elk's head. He had taken the card and restored it to his pocket-book and then had spoken to the servant. The servant had shrugged his shoulders with the formal hospitality of his class and, with his shoulders still shrugged and his one hand pointing towards the inner door, had preceded Tietjens into the hotel. Not one line of Tietjens' face had moved when he had received back his card. It had been then that Sylvia had sworn that she would yet make his wooden face wince. . . .

His face was intolerable. Heavy; fixed. Not insolent, but simply gazing over the heads of all things and created beings, into a world too distant for them to enter. . . . And yet it seemed to her, since he was so clumsy and worn out, almost not sporting to persecute him. It was like whipping a dying bulldog. . . .

She sank back into her chair with a movement almost of discouragement. She said:

"He's gone into the hotel. . . ."

Perowne lurched agitatedly forward in his chair. He exclaimed that he was going. Then he sank discouragedly back again:

"No, I'm not," he said, "I'm probably much safer here. I might run against him going out."

"You've realized that my petticoats protect you," Sylvia said contemptuously. "Of course, Christopher would never hit anyone in my presence."

Major Perowne was interrupting her by asking:

"What's he going to do? What's he doing in the hotel?"

Mrs. Tietjens said:

"Guess!" She added: "What would you do in similar circumstances?"

"Go and wreck your bedroom," Perowne answered with promptitude. "It's what I did when I found you had left Yssingueux."

Sylvia said:

"Ah, that was what the place was called."

Perowne groaned:

"You're callous," he said. "There's no other word for it. Callous. That's what you are."

Sylvia asked absently why he called her callous at just that juncture. She was imagining Christopher stumping clumsily along the hotel corridor looking at bedrooms, and then giving the hotel servant a handsome tip to ensure that he should be put on the same floor as herself. She could almost hear his not disagreeable male voice that vibrated a little from the chest and made her vibrate.[2]

Perowne was grumbling on. Sylvia was callous because she had forgotten the name of the Brittany hamlet in which they had spent three blissful weeks together, though she had left it so suddenly that all her outfit remained in the hotel.

"Well, it wasn't any kind of a beanfeast for me," Sylvia went on, when she again gave him her attention. "Good heavens! ... Do you think it *would* be any kind of a beanfeast with you, *pour tout potage?** Why should I remember the name of the hateful place?"

Perowne said:

"Yssingueux-les-Pervenches, such a pretty name," reproachfully.†

"It's no good," Sylvia answered, "your trying to awaken sentimental memories in me. You will have to make me forget what you were like if you want to carry on with me.... I'm stopping here and listening to your corncrake of a voice because I want to wait until Christopher goes out of the hotel ... Then I am going to my room to tidy up for Lady Sachse's party and you will sit here and wait for me."

"I'm *not*," Perowne said, "going to Lady Sachse's. Why, *he* is going to be one of the principal witnesses to sign the marriage contract. And Old Campion and all the rest of the staff are going to be there.... You don't catch *me*.... An unexpected prior engagement is my line. No fear."

"You'll come with me, my little man," Sylvia said, "if you ever want to bask in my smile again.... I'm not going to Lady Sachse's alone, looking as if I couldn't catch a man to escort me, under the eyes of half the French house of peers.... If they've got a house of peers! ... You don't catch *me*.... No fear!" she mimicked his creaky voice. "You can go away as soon as you've shown yourself as my escort...."

"But, good God!" Perowne cried out, "that's just what I mustn't do. Campion said that if he had any more of my being seen about with you he would have me sent back to my beastly regiment. And my beastly regiment is in the trenches.... You don't see *me* in the trenches, do you?"

"I'd rather see you there than in my own room," Sylvia said. "Any day!"

---

* Exclusively.
† 'Pervenches' is French for periwinkles, as explained towards the end of this chapter.

"Ah, there you are!" Perowne exclaimed with animation. "What guarantee have I that if I do what you want I shall bask in your smile as you call it? I've got myself into a most awful hole, bringing you here without papers. You never told me you hadn't any papers. General O'Hara,[3] the P.M., has raised a most awful strafe about it.... And what have I got for it? ... Not the ghost of a smile.... And you should see old O'Hara's purple face! ... Someone woke him from his afternoon nap to report to him about your heinous case and he hasn't recovered from the indigestion yet.... Besides, he hates Tietjens ... Tietjens is always chipping away at his military police ... O'Hara's lambs...."

Sylvia was not listening, but she was smiling a slow smile at an inward thought. It maddened him.

"What's your game?" he exclaimed. "Hell and hounds, what's your game? ... You can't have come here to see ... *him.* You don't come here to see me, as far as I can see. Well then ..."

Sylvia looked round at him with all her eyes, wide open as if she had just awakened from a deep sleep.

"I didn't know I was coming," she said. "It came into my head to come suddenly. Ten minutes before I started. And I came. I didn't know papers were wanted. I suppose I could have got them if I had wanted them.... You never asked me if I had any papers. You just froze on to me and had me into your special carriage.*
... I didn't know you were coming."

That[4] seemed to Perowne the last insult. He exclaimed:

"Oh, damn it, Sylvia! you *must* have known.... You were at the Quirks' squash on Wednesday evening. And *they* knew. My best friends."

"Since you ask for it," she said, "I didn't know.... And I would not have come by that train if I had known you would be going by it. You force me to say rude things to you." She added: "Why can't you be more conciliatory?" to keep him quiet for a little. His[5] jaw dropped down.

She was wondering where Christopher had got the money to pay for a bed at the hotel. Only a very short time before she had drawn all the balance of his banking account, except for a

---

* Partridge's *Dictionary of Slang* glosses 'freeze to or freeze on to' as 'to take a powerful fancy to; cling to, hold fast'.

shilling. It was the middle of the month and he could not have drawn any more pay.... That, of course, was a try on on her part. He might be forced into remonstrating. In the same way she had tried on the accusation that he had carried off her sheets. It was sheer wilfulness, and when she looked again at his motionless features she knew that she had been rather stupid.... But she was at the end of her tether: she had before now tried making accusations against her husband, but she had never tried inconveniencing him.... Now she suddenly realized the full stupidity of which she had been guilty. He would know perfectly well that those petty frightfulnesses of hers were not in the least in her note; so he would know, too, that each of them was just a try on. He would say: "She is trying to make me squeal. I'm damned if I will!"

She would have to adopt much more formidable methods. She said: "He shall ... he shall ... he *shall* come to heel."

Major Perowne had now closed his jaw. He was reflecting. Once he mumbled: "More *conciliatory*! Holy smoke!"

She was feeling suddenly in spirits: it was the sight of Christopher had done it: the perfect assurance that they were going to live under the same roof again. She would have betted all she possessed and her immortal soul on the chance that he would not take up with the Wannop girl. And it would have been betting on a certainty! ... But she had had no idea what their relations were to be, after the war. At first she had thought that they had parted for good when she had gone off from their flat at four o'clock in the morning. It had seemed logical. But, gradually, in retreat at Birkenhead, in the still, white, nun's room, doubt had come upon her. It was one of the disadvantages of living as they did that they seldom spoke their thoughts. But that was also at times an advantage. She had certainly meant their parting to be for good. She had certainly raised her voice in giving the name of her station to the taxi-man with the pretty firm conviction that he would hear her; and she had been pretty well certain that he would take it as a sign that the breath had gone out of their union.... Pretty certain. But not quite! ...

She would have died rather than write to him; she would die, now, rather than give any inkling that she wanted them to live under the same roof again.... She said to herself:

"Is he writing to that girl?" And then: "No! . . . I'm certain that
he isn't." . . . She had had all his letters stopped at the flat, except
for a few circulars that she let dribble through to him, so that he
might imagine that all his correspondence was coming through.
From the letters to him that she did read she was pretty sure that
he had given no other address than the flat in Gray's Inn. . . . But
there had been no letters from Valentine Wannop. . . . Two from
Mrs. Wannop, two from his brother Mark, one from Port Scatho,
one or two from brother officers and some official chits. . . . She
said to herself that, if there *had* been any letters from that girl, she
would have let all his letters go through, including the girl's. . . .
Now she was not so certain that she would have.

In the glass she saw Christopher marching woodenly out of the
hotel, along the path that led from door to door behind her. . . .
It came to her with extraordinary gladness—the absolute conviction that he was not corresponding with Miss Wannop. The
absolute conviction. . . . If he had come alive enough to do that
he would have looked different. She did not know how he would
have looked. But different . . . Alive! Perhaps self-conscious:
perhaps . . . satisfied . . .

For some time the major had been grumbling about his wrongs.
He said that he followed her about all day, like a lap-dog, and got
nothing for it. Now she wanted him[6] to be conciliatory. She said
she wanted to have a man on show as escort. Well then, an escort
got something. . . . At just this moment he was beginning again
with:

"Look here . . . will you let me come to your room to-night or
will you not?"

She burst into high, loud laughter. He said:

"Damn it all, it isn't any laughing matter! . . . Look here! You
don't know what I risk. . . . There are A.P.M.'s and P.M.'s and
deputy sub-acting A.P.M.'s walking about the corridors of all the
hotels in this town, all night long. . . . It's as much as my job is
worth. . . ."

She put her handkerchief to her lips to hide a smile that she
knew would be too cruel for him not to notice. And even when
she took it away, he said:

"Hang it all, what a cruel-looking fiend you are! . . . Why the
devil do I hang around you? . . . There's a picture that my

mother's got, by Burne-Jones . . . A cruel-looking woman with a distant smile . . . Some vampire . . . La Belle[7] Dame sans Merci . . .* That's what you're like."

She looked at him suddenly with considerable seriousness. . . .

"See here, Potty . . ." she began. He groaned:

"I believe you'd like me to be sent to the beastly trenches. . . . Yet a big, distinguished-looking chap like me wouldn't have a chance. . . . At the first volley the Germans fired, they'd pick me off. . . ."

"Oh, Potty," she exclaimed, "try to be serious for a minute. . . . I tell you I'm a woman who's trying . . . who's desperately wanting . . . to be reconciled to her husband! . . . I would not tell that to another soul. . . . I would not tell it to myself. . . . But one owes something . . . a parting scene, if nothing else. . . . Well, something . . . to a man one's been in bed with. . . . I didn't give you a parting scene at . . . ah, Yssingueux-les-Pervenches . . . so I give you this tip instead. . . ."

He said:

'Will you leave your bedroom door unlocked, or won't you?'

She said:

"If that man would throw his handkerchief to me, I would follow him round the world in my shift![8] . . . Look here . . . see me shake when I think of it. . . ." She held out her hand at the end of her long arm: hand and arm trembled together, minutely, then very much. . . . "Well," she finished, "if you see that and still want to come to my room . . . your blood be on your own head. . . ." She[9] paused for a breath or two and then said:

"You can come. . . . I won't lock my door. . . . But I don't say that you'll get anything . . . or that you'll like what you get. . . . That's a fair tip. . . ." She added suddenly: "You *sale fat* . . .† take what you get and be damned to you!"

Major Perowne had suddenly taken to twirling his moustaches; he said:

---

* Perowne may be thinking of a painting such as Edward Burne-Jones's *The Beguiling of Merlin* (1872–7), in which Maria Zambaco as Nimue has the kind of distant smile that he refers to – not so distant, however, that it kept Burne-Jones from becoming her lover. Keats's 'La Belle Dame Sans Merci' (1819) was painted by other Victorian artists, such as J. W. Waterhouse, Frank Dicksee, and Walter Crane.

† French for insulting epithets like 'foul fop' or its equivalent. But Sylvia's consistent description of Perowne as an 'oaf' might do here too.

"Oh, I'll chance the A.P.M.'s...."
She suddenly coiled her legs into her chair.
"I know now what I came here for," she said.

Major Wilfrid Fosbrooke Eddicker Perowne of Perowne, the son of his mother, was one of those individuals who have no history, no strong proclivities, and no, or almost no, characteristics. He had done nothing, his knowledge seemed to be bounded by the contents of his newspaper for the immediate day; at any rate, his conversation never went any farther. He was not bold, he was not shy; he was neither markedly courageous nor markedly cowardly. His mother was immoderately wealthy, owned an immense castle that hung over crags, above a western sea, much as a bird cage hangs from a window of a high tenement building, but she received few or no visitors, her cuisine being indifferent and her wine atrocious. She had strong temperance opinions and, immediately after the death of her husband, she had emptied the contents of his cellar, which were almost as historic as his castle, into the sea, a shudder going through county-family England. But even this was not enough to make Perowne himself notorious.

His mother allowed him—after an eyeopener in early youth—the income of a junior royalty, but he did nothing with it. He lived in a great house in Palace Gardens, Kensington, and he lived all alone with rather a large staff of servants who had been selected by his mother, but they did nothing at all, for he ate all his meals, and even took his bath and dressed for dinner at the Bath Club. He was otherwise parsimonious.

He had, after the fashion of his day, passed a year or two in the army when young. He had been first gazetted to His Majesty's Forty-second Regiment, but on the Black Watch* proceeding to India he had exchanged into the Glamorganshires, at that time commanded by General Campion and recruiting in and around Lincolnshire. The general had been an old friend of Perowne's mother, and, on being promoted to brigadier, had taken Perowne on to his staff as his galloper,† for, although Perowne rode rather

---

* The Royal Highland Regiment had the nickname of Black Watch, deriving from its original task of watching over the Scottish Highlands and from the tartan its members wore.

† 'An aide-de-camp, or orderly officer': OED.

indifferently, he had a certain social knowledge and could be counted on to know how correctly to address a regimental invitation to a dowager countess who had married a viscount's third son.... As a military figure otherwise he had a very indifferent word of command, a very poor drill and next to no control of his men, but he was popular with his batmen, and in a rather stiff way was presentable in the old scarlet uniform or the blue mess jacket. He was exactly six foot, to a hairbreadth, in his stockings, had very dark eyes, and a rather grating voice; the fact that his limbs were a shade too bulky for his trunk, which was not at all corpulent, made him appear a little clumsy. If in a club you asked what sort of a fellow he was your interlocutor would tell you, most probably, that he had or was supposed to have warts on his head, this to account for his hair which all his life he had combed back, unparted from his forehead. But as a matter of fact he had no warts on his head.

He had once started out on an expedition to shoot big game in Portuguese East Africa. But on its arrival his expedition was met with the news that the natives of the interior were in revolt, so Perowne had returned to Kensington Palace Gardens. He had had several mild successes with women, but, owing to his habits of economy and fear of embroglios,* until the age of thirty-four, he had limited the field of his amours to young women of the lower social orders....

His affair with Sylvia Tietjens might have been something to boast about, but he was not boastful, and indeed he had been too hard hit when she had left him even to bear to account lyingly for the employment of the time he had spent with her in Brittany. Fortunately no one took sufficient interest in his movements to wait for his answer to their indifferent questions as to where he had spent the summer. When his mind reverted to her desertion of him moisture would come out of his eyes, undemonstratively, as water leaves the surface of a sponge....

Sylvia had left him by the simple expedient of stepping without so much as a reticule on to the little French tramway that took you to the main railway line. From there she had written to him in pencil on a closed correspondence card that she had left

---

* The *OED* glosses this, rather suggestively, as a 'bad form of imbroglio'.

him because she simply could not bear either his dullness or his craking voice. She said they would probably run up against each other in the course of the autumn season in town and, after purchase of some night things, had made straight for the German spa to which her mother had retreated.

At the later date Sylvia had no difficulty in accounting to herself for her having gone off with such an oaf: she had simply reacted in a violent fit of sexual hatred, from her husband's mind. And she could not have found a mind more utterly dissimilar than Perowne's in any decently groomed man to be found in London. She could recall, even in the French hotel lounge, years after, the almost painful emotion of joyful hatred that had visited her when she had first thought of going off with him. It was the self-applause of one who has just hit upon an excruciatingly inspiring intellectual discovery. In her previous transitory infidelities to Christopher she had discovered that, however presentable the man with whom she might have been having an affair, and however short the affair, even if it were only a matter of a week-end ... Christopher had spoilt her for the other man. It was the most damnable of his qualities that to hear any other man talk of any subject—any, any subject—from stable form to the balance of power, or from the voice of a given opera singer to the recurrence of a comet—to have to pass a week-end with any other man and hear his talk after having spent the inside of the week with Christopher, hate his ideas how you might, was the difference between listening to a grown man and, with an intense boredom, trying to entertain an inarticulate schoolboy. As beside him, other men simply did not seem ever to have grown up. . . .

Just before, with an extreme suddenness, consenting to go away with Perowne, the illuminating idea had struck her: If I did go away with him it would be the most humiliating thing I could do to Christopher. . . . And just when the idea *had* struck her, beside her chair in the conservatory at a dance given by the general's sister, Lady Claudine Sandbach, Perowne, his voice rendered more throaty and less disagreeable than usual by emotion, had been going on and on begging her to elope with him. . . . She had suddenly said:

"Very well . . . let's. . . ."

His emotion had been so unbridled in its astonishment that

she had, even at that, almost been inclined to treat her own speech as a joke and to give up the revenge.... But the idea of the humiliation that Christopher must feel proved too much for her. For, for your wife to throw you over for an attractive man is naturally humiliating, but that she should leave you publicly for a man of hardly any intelligence at all, you priding yourself on your brains, must be nearly as mortifying a thing as can happen to you.

But she had hardly set out upon her escapade before two very serious defects in her plan occurred to her with extreme force: the one that, however humiliated Christopher might feel, she would not be with him to witness his humiliation; the other that, oaf as she had taken Perowne to be in casual society, in close daily relationship he was such an oaf as to be almost insufferable. She had imagined that he would prove a person out of whom it might be possible to make *something* by a judicious course of alternated mothering and scorn: she discovered that his mother had already done for him almost all that woman could do. For, when he had been an already rather backward boy at a private school, his mother had kept him so extremely short of pocket-money that he had robbed other boys' desks of a few shillings here and there— in order to subscribe towards a birthday present for the headmaster's wife. His mother, to give him a salutary lesson, had given so much publicity to the affair that he had become afflicted with a permanent bent towards shyness that rendered him by turns very mistrustful of himself or very boastful and, although he repressed manifestations of either tendency towards the outside world, the continual repression rendered him almost incapable of any vigorous thought or action....

That discovery did not soften Sylvia towards him: it was, as she expressed it, *his* funeral and, although she would have been ready for any normal job of smartening up a roughish man, she was by no means prepared to readjust other women's hopeless maternal misfits.

So she had got no farther than Ostend, where they had proposed to spend a week or so at the tables, before she found herself explaining to some acquaintances whom she met that she was in that gay city merely for an hour or two, between trains, on the way to join her mother in a German health resort. The impulse to say that had come upon her by surprise, for, until that moment, being completely indifferent to criticism, she had intended to cast no veil at all over her proceedings. But, quite suddenly, on seeing some well-known English faces in the casino it had come over her to think that, however much she imagined Christopher to be humiliated by her going off with an oaf like Perowne, that humiliation must be as nothing compared with that which she might be expected to feel at having found no one better than an oaf like Perowne to go off with. Moreover . . . she began to miss Christopher.

These feelings did not grow any less intense in the rather stuffy but inconspicuous hotel in the Rue St. Roque in Paris to which she immediately transported the bewildered but uncomplaining Perowne, who had imagined that he was to be taken to Wiesbaden for a course of light gaieties. And Paris, when you avoid the more conspicuous resorts, and when you are unprovided with congenial companionship can prove nearly as overwhelming as is, say, Birmingham on a Sunday.

So that Sylvia waited for only just long enough to convince herself that her husband had no apparent intention of applying for an immediate divorce and had, indeed, no apparent intention of doing anything at all. She sent him, that is to say, a postcard saying that letters and other communications would reach her at her inconspicuous hotel—and it mortified her not a little to have to reveal the fact that her hotel was so inconspicuous. But, except that her own correspondence was forwarded to her with regularity, no communications at all came from Tietjens.

In an air-resort in the centre of France to which she next removed Perowne, she found herself considering rather seriously what it might be expected that Tietjens *would* do. Through indirect and unsuspecting allusions in letters from her personal friends she found that if Tietjens did not put up, he certainly did not deny, the story that she had gone to nurse or be with her mother, who was supposed to be seriously ill. . . . That is to say, her friends said how rotten it was that her mother, Mrs. Satterthwaite, should be so seriously ill; how rotten it must be for her to be shut up in a potty little German kur-ort* when the world

---

* A health resort or spa (German).

could be so otherwise amusing; and how well Christopher whom they saw from time to time seemed to be getting on considering how rotten it must be for him to be left all alone....

At about this time Perowne began to become, if possible, more irritating than ever. In their air-resort, although the guests were almost entirely French, there was a newly opened golf-course, and at the game of golf Perowne displayed an inefficiency and at the same time a morbid conceit that were surprising in one naturally lymphatic. He would sulk for a whole evening if either Sylvia or any Frenchman beat him in a round, and, though Sylvia was by then completely indifferent to his sulking, what was very much worse was that he became gloomily and loud-voicedly quarrel-some over his games with foreign opponents.

Three events, falling within ten minutes of each other, made her determined to get as far away from that air-resort as was feasible. In the first place she observed at the end of the street some English people called Thurston, whose faces she faintly knew, and the emotion she suddenly felt let her know how extremely anxious she was that she should let it remain feasible for Tietjens to take her back. Then, in the golf club-house, to which she found herself fiercely hurrying in order to pay her bill and get her clubs, she overheard the conversation of two players that left no doubt in her mind that Perowne had been detected in little meannesses of moving his ball at golf or juggling with his score.... This was almost more than she could stand. And, at the same moment, her mind, as it were, condescended to let her remember Christopher's voice as it had once uttered the haughty opinion that no man one could speak to would ever think of divorcing any woman. If he could not defend the sanctity of his hearth he must lump it unless the woman wanted to divorce him....

At the time when he had said it her mind—she had been just then hating him a good deal—had seemed to take no notice of the utterance. But now that it presented itself forcibly to her again it brought with it the thought: Supposing he wasn't really only talking through his hat!

... She dragged the wretched Perowne off his bed where he had been lost in an after-lunch slumber and told him that they must both leave that place at once, and, that as soon as they

reached Paris or some larger town where he could find waiters and
people to understand his French, she herself was going to leave
him for good. They did not, in consequence, get away from the
air-resort until the six o'clock train next morning. Perowne's
passion of rage and despair at the news that she wished to leave
him took an inconvenient form, for instead of announcing any
intention of committing suicide, as might have been expected,
he became gloomily and fantastically murderous. He[10] said that
unless Sylvia swore on a little relic of St. Anthony she carried
that she had no intention of leaving him he would incontinently
kill her. He said, as he said for the rest of his days, that she had
ruined his life and caused great moral deterioration in himself.
But for her he might have married some pure young thing. Moreover, influencing him against his mother's doctrines, she had
forced him to drink wine, by an effect of pure scorn. Thus he had
done harm, he was convinced, both to his health and to his manly
proportions.... It was indeed for Sylvia one of the most unbearable things about this man—the way he took wine. With every
glass he put to his lips he would exclaim with an unbearable titter
some such imbecility as: Here is another nail in my coffin. And
he had taken to wine, and even to stronger liquor, very well.

Sylvia had refused to swear by St. Anthony. She definitely was
not going to introduce the saint into her amorous affairs, and she
definitely was not going to take on any relic an oath that she
meant to break at an early opportunity. There was such a thing
as playing it too low down: there are dishonours to which death
is preferable.[*] So, getting hold of his revolver at a time when he
was wringing his hands, she dropped it into the water-jug and
then felt reasonably safe.

Perowne knew no French and next to nothing about France,
but he had discovered that the French did nothing to you for
killing a woman who intended to leave you. Sylvia, on the other
hand, was pretty certain that, without a weapon, he could not do
much to her. If she had had no other training at her very expensive school she had had so much drilling in calisthenics as to be
singularly mistress of her limbs, and, in the interests of her beauty

[*] Given the many parallels between the thoughts of Tietjens and Valentine, here is an
   interesting echo from Tietjens to Sylvia: Cf. I.i: "'*Gwell angau na gwillth*, their own
   regimental badge bore the words. '*Death is better than dishonour.*'"

she had always kept herself very fit. . . .

She said at last:

"Very well. We will go to Yssingueux-les-Pervenches. . . . "

A rather pleasant French couple in the hotel had spoken of this little place in the extreme west of France as a lonely paradise, they having spent their honeymoon there. . . . And Sylvia wanted a lonely paradise if there was going to be any scrapping before she got away from Perowne. . . .

She had no hesitation as to what she was going to do: the long journey across half France by miserable trains had caused her an agony of home-sickness! Nothing less! . . . It was a humiliating disease from which to suffer. But it was unavoidable, like mumps. You had to put up with it. Besides, she even found herself wanting to see her child, whom she imagined herself to hate, as having been the cause of all her misfortunes. . . .

She therefore prepared, after great thought, a letter telling Tietjens that she intended to return to him. She made the letter as nearly as possible like one she would write announcing her return from a country house to which she should have been invited for an indefinite period, and she added some rather hard instructions about her maid, these being intended to remove from the letter any possible trace of emotion. She was certain that, if she showed any emotion at all, Christopher would never take her under his roof again. . . . She was pretty certain that no gossip had been caused by her escapade. Major Thurston had been at the railway station when they had left, but they had not spoken— and Thurston was a very decentish, brown-moustached fellow, of the sort that does not gossip.[11]

It had proved a little difficult to get away, for Perowne during several weeks watched her like an attendant in a lunatic asylum. But at last the idea presented itself to him that she would never go without her frocks, and, one day, in a fit of intense somnolence after a lunch, washed down with rather a large quantity of the local and fiery cordial, he let her take a walk alone. . . .

She was by that time tired of men . . . or she imagined that she was; for she was not prepared to be certain, considering the muckers she saw women coming all round her over the most unpresentable individuals. Men, at any rate, never fulfilled expectations. They might, upon acquaintance, turn out more entertaining than they appeared; but almost always taking up with a man was like reading a book you had read when you had forgotten that you had read it. You had not been for ten minutes in any sort of intimacy with any man before you said: "But I've read all this before. . . . " You knew the opening, you were already bored by the middle, and, especially, you knew the end. . . .

She remembered, years ago, trying to shock her mother's spiritual adviser, Father Consett, whom they had lately murdered in Ireland, along with Casement. . . . The poor saint had not in the least been shocked. He had gone her one better. For when she had said something like that her idea of a divvy life—they used in those days to say divvy—would be to go off with a different man every week-end, he had told her that after a short time she would be bored already by the time the poor dear fellow was buying the railway tickets. . . .*

And, by heavens, he had been right. . . . For when she came to think of it, from the day that poor saint had said that thing in her mother's sitting-room in the little German spa—Lobscheid, it must have been called—in the candle-light, his shadow denouncing her from all over the walls, to now when she sat in the palmish wickerwork of that hotel that had been new-whitely decorated to celebrate hostilities, never once had she sat in a train with a man who had any right to look upon himself as justified in mauling her about. . . . She wondered if, from where he sat in heaven, Father Consett would be satisfied with her as he looked down into that lounge. . . . Perhaps it was really he that had pulled off that change in her. . . .

Never once till yesterday. . . . For perhaps the unfortunate Perowne might just faintly have had the right yesterday to make himself for about two minutes[12]—before she froze him into a choking, pallid snowman with goggle eyes—the perfectly loathsome thing that a man in a railway train becomes. . . . Much too bold and yet stupidly awkward with the fear of the guard looking

---

* See *Some Do Not* . . . I.ii: "'You'd find,' the priest said, 'that it whittled down until the only divvy moment was when you stood waiting in the booking-office for the young man to take the tickets. . . . And then gradually that wouldn't be divvy any more. . . . And you'd yawn and long to go back to your husband.'" The *OED* glosses 'divvy' as 'Extremely pleasant, "divine", "heavenly"'.

in at the window, the train doing over sixty, without corridors.... No, never again for *me*, father, she addressed her voice
towards the ceiling....

Why in the world couldn't you get a man to go away with you
and be just—oh, light comedy—for a whole, a whole blessed
week-end. For a whole blessed life.... Why not? ... Think of
it.... A whole blessed life with a man who was a good sort and
yet didn't go all gurgly in the voice, and cod-fish-eyed and all-
overish—to the extent of not being able to find the tickets when
asked for them.... Father, dear, she said again upwards, if I could
find men like that, that[13] would be just heaven ... where there
is no marrying.... But, of course, she went on almost resignedly,
he would not be faithful to you.... And then: one would have
to stand it....

She sat up so suddenly in her chair that beside her, too, Major
Perowne nearly jumped out of his wickerwork, and asked if *he* had
come back.... She exclaimed:

"No, I'd be damned if I would.... I'd be damned, I'd be
damned, I'd be damned if I would.... Never. Never. By the living
God!"

She asked fiercely of the agitated major:

"Has Christopher got a girl in this town? ... You'd better tell
me the truth!"

The major mumbled:

"He ... No.... He's too much of a stick.... He never even
goes to Suzette's.... Except once to fetch out some miserable
little squit of a subaltern who was smashing up Mother Hardelot's
furniture...."

He[14] grumbled:

"But you shouldn't give a man the jumps like that! ... Be
conciliatory, you said...." He went on to grumble that her
manners had not improved since she had been at Yssingueux-les-
Pervenches[15] ... and then went on to tell her that in French the
words *yeux des pervenches* meant eyes of periwinkle blue. And that
was the only French he knew, because a Frenchman he had met
in the train had told him so and he had always thought that if *her*
eyes had been periwinkle blue ... "But you're not listening....
Hardly polite, I call it," he had mumbled to a conclusion....

She was sitting forward in her chair still clenching her hand

under her chin at the thought that perhaps Christopher had
Valentine Wannop in that town. That was perhaps why he
elected to remain there. She asked:

"Why does Christopher stay on in this God-forsaken hole? . . .
The inglorious base, they call it. . . ."

"Because he's jolly well got to. . . ." Major Perowne said. "He's
got to do what he's told. . . ."

She said:

"Christopher! . . . You mean to say they'd keep a man like
Christopher anywhere he didn't want to be. . . ."

"They'd jolly well knock spots off him if he went away," Major
Perowne exclaimed. . . . "What the deuce do you think your
blessed fellow is? . . . The King of England? . . ." He added with a
sudden sombre ferocity: "They'd shoot him like anybody else if
he bolted. . . . What do *you* think?"

She said:

"But all that wouldn't prevent his having a girl in this town?"

"Well, he hasn't got one," Perowne said. "He sticks up in that
blessed old camp of his like a blessed she-chicken sitting on
addled eggs. . . . That's what they say of him. . . . I don't know
anything about the fellow. . . ."

Listening vindictively and indolently, she thought she caught
in his droning tones a touch of the homicidal lunacy that had
used to underlie his voice in the bedroom at Yssingueux. The
fellow had undoubtedly about him a touch of the dull, mad
murderer of the police-courts. With a sudden animation she
thought:

"Suppose he tried to murder Christopher. . . ." And she imagined her husband breaking the fellow's back across his knee, the
idea going across her mind as fire traverses the opal. Then, with
a dry throat, she said to herself:

"I've got to find out whether he has that girl in Rouen. . . ."
Men stuck together. The fellow Perowne might well be
protecting Tietjens. It would be unthinkable that any rules of the
service could keep Christopher in that place. They could not shut
up the upper classes. If Perowne had any sense he would know
that to shield Tietjens was the way not to get her. . . . But he had
no sense. . . . Besides, sexual solidarity was a terribly strong
thing. . . . She knew that she herself would not give a woman's

secrets away in order to get her man. Then . . . how was she to ascertain whether the girl was not in that town? How? . . . She imagined Tietjens going home every night to her. . . . But he was going to spend that night with herself. . . . She knew that. . . . Under that roof. . . . Fresh from the other. . . .

She imagined him there, now. . . In the parlour of one of the little villas you see from the tram on the top of the town. . . . They were undoubtedly, now, discussing her. . . . Her whole body writhed, muscle on muscle, in her chair. . . . She must discover. . . . But how do you discover? Against a universal conspiracy. . . . This whole war was an agapemone. . . . *You went to war when you desired to rape innumerable women. . . . It was what war was for. . . . All these men, crowded in this narrow space. . . .

She stood up:

"I'm going," she said, "to put on a little powder for Lady Sachse's feast. . . . You needn't stay if you don't want to. . . ." She was going to watch every face she saw until it gave up the secret of where in that town Christopher had the Wannop girl hidden. . . . She imagined her freckled, snub-nosed faced pressed—squashed was the word—against his cheek. . . . She was going to investigate. . . .

---

* _Agapemone_, from the Greek words for _love_ and _dwelling_; so 'an abode-of-love; esp. with unfavourable implication'. Thus, D. Hooker, _Let._ 22 Aug. in L. Huxley _Life & Lett. J. D. H._ (1918) II. 317: 'The moment you allow of "promiscuous intercourse" it is all up and the thing degenerates into an agapemone' (_OED_).

She found an early opportunity to carry on her investigations. For, at dinner that night, she found herself, Tietjens having gone to the telephone with a lance-corporal, opposite what she took to be a small tradesman, with fresh-coloured cheeks, and a great, grey, forward-sprouting moustache, in a uniform so creased that the creases resembled the veins of a leaf.... A very trustworthy small tradesman: the grocer from round the corner whom, sometimes, you allow to supply you with paraffin.... He was saying to her:

"If, ma'am, you multiply two-thousand nine hundred and something by ten you arrive at twenty-nine thousand odd...."

And she had exclaimed:

"You really mean that my husband, Captain Tietjens, spent yesterday afternoon in examining twenty-nine thousand toenails.... And two thousand nine hundred toothbrushes...."

"I told him," her interlocutor answered with deep seriousness, "that these being Colonial troops it was not so necessary to examine their toothbrushes.... Imperial troops *will* use the brush they clean their buttons with for their teeth so as to have a clean toothbrush to show the medical officer...."

"It sounds," she said with a little shudder, "as if you were all schoolboys playing a game.... And you say my husband really occupies his mind with such things...."

Second-Lieutenant Cowley, dreadfully conscious that the shoulder-strap of his Sam Browne belt, purchased that afternoon at the Ordnance, and therefore brand-new, did not match the abdominal part of the belt that he had had for nearly ten years— a splendid bit of leather, that!—answered nevertheless stoutly:

"Madam! If the brains of an army aren't, the life of an army *is* ... in its feet.... And nowadays, the medical officers say, in its teeth.... Your husband, ma'am, is an admirable officer.... He says that no draft he turns out shall...."

She said:

"He spent three hours in ... You say, foot and kit inspection...."

Second-Lieutenant Cowley said:

"Of course he had other officers to help him with the kit ... but he looked at every foot himself...."

She said:

"That took him from two till five.... Then he had tea, I suppose.... And went to ... What is it? ... The papers of the draft...."

Second-Lieutenant Cowley said, muffledly through his moustache:

"If the captain is a little remiss in writing letters ... I *have* heard ... You might, madam ... I'm a married man myself ... with a daughter.... And the army is not very good at writing letters.... You might say, in that respect, that thank God we have got a navy, ma'am...."

She let him stagger on for a sentence or two, imagining that, in his confusion, she might come upon traces of Miss Wannop in Rouen. Then she said handsomely:

"Of course you have explained everything, Mr. Cowley, and I am very much obliged.... Of course my husband would not have time to write very full letters.... He is not like the giddy young subalterns who run after ..."

He exclaimed in a great roar of laughter:

"The captain run after skirts.... Why, I can number on my hands the times he's been out of my sight since he's had the battalion!"

A deep wave of depression went over Sylvia.

"Why," Lieutenant Cowley laughed on, "if we *had* a laugh against him it was that he mothered the lot of us as if he was a hen sitting on addled eggs.... For it's only a rag-time army, as the saying is, when you've said the best for it that you can.... And look at the other commanding officers we've had before we had him.... There was Major Brooks.... Never up before noon, if then, and out of camp by two-thirty. Get your returns ready for signing before then or never get 'em signed.... And Colonel Potter ... Bless my soul ... 'e wouldn't sign any blessed papers at all.... He lived down here in this hotel, and we never saw him up at the camp at all.... But the captain ... We always say that

... if 'e was a Chelsea adjutant getting off a draft of the Second Coldstreams...."

With her indolent and gracious beauty—Sylvia knew that she was displaying indolent and gracious beauty—Sylvia leaned over the tablecloth listening for items in the terrible indictment that, presently, she was going to bring against Tietjens.... For the morality of these matters is this: ... If you have an incomparably beautiful woman on your hands you must occupy yourself solely with her.... Nature exacts that of you ... until you are unfaithful to her with a snub-nosed girl with freckles: that, of course, being a reaction, is still in a way occupying yourself with your woman! ... But to betray her with a battalion.... That is against decency, against Nature.... And for him, Christopher Tietjens, to come down to the level of the men you met here! ...

Tietjens, mooning down the room between tables, had more than his usually aloof air since he had just come out of a tele-phone box. He slipped, a weary mass, into the polished chair between her and the lieutenant. He said:

"I've got the washing arranged for ..." and Sylvia gave to herself a little hiss between the teeth, of vindictive pleasure! This was indeed betrayal to a battalion. He added: "I shall have to be up in camp before four-thirty to-morrow morning...."

Sylvia could not resist saying:

"Isn't there a poem ... *Ah me, the dawn, the dawn, it comes too soon!* ... said of course by lovers in bed? ... Who was the poet?"

Cowley went visibly red to the roots of his hair and evidently beyond. Tietjens finished his speech to Cowley, who had remon-strated against his going up to the camp so early by saying that he had not been able to get hold of an officer to march the draft. He then said in his leisurely way:

"There were a great many poems with that refrain in the Middle Ages.... You are probably thinking of an albade by Arnaut Daniel,* which someone translated lately.... An albade

---

* Arnaut Daniel was the twelfth-century Troubadour poet whom Dante called *il miglior fabbro* (*Purgatorio*, canto 26); that is, 'the better craftsman' in Ezra Pound's translation *The Spirit of Romance* (New York: New Directions, 1968), 33. Pound himself had already been awarded that very title by T. S. Eliot in his dedication of *The Waste Land* (1922). Undoubtedly, Pound was the 'someone' whom Tietjens had in mind as having translated an *albade* of Daniel's, quoting this very line in Pound's 'Philadelphian accent' – 'Ah me, the darn, the darn it comes toe sune!' (*Return* 388). Francis Hueffer

was a song to be sung at dawn when, presumably, no one but lovers would be likely to sing. . . ."

"Will there," Sylvia asked, "be anyone but you singing up in your camp to-morrow at four?"

She could not help it. . . . She knew that Tietjens had adopted his slow pomposity in order to give the grotesque object at the table with them time to recover from his confusion. She hated him for it. What right had he to make himself appear a pompous ass in order to shield the confusion of anybody?

The second-lieutenant came out of his confusion to exclaim, actually slapping his thigh:

"There you are, madam. . . . Trust the captain to know everything! . . . I don't believe there's a question under the sun you could ask him that he couldn't answer. . . . They say up at the camp . . ." He went on with long stories of all the questions Tietjens *had* answered up at the camp. . . .

Emotion was going all over Sylvia . . . at the proximity of Tietjens. She said to herself: "Is this to go on for ever?" Her hands were ice-cold. She touched the back of her left hand with the fingers of her right. It *was* ice-cold. She looked at her hands. They were bloodless. . . . She said to herself: "It's pure sexual passion . . . it's pure sexual passion. . . . God! Can't I get over this?" She said: "Father! . . . You used to be fond of Christopher. . . . *Get* our Lady to get me over this. . . . It's the ruin of him and the ruin of me. But, oh *damn*, don't! . . . For it's all I have to live for. . . ." She said: "When he came mooning back from the telephone I thought it was all right. . . . I thought what a heavy wooden-horse he looked. . . . For two minutes. . . Then it's all over me again. . . . I want to swallow my saliva and I can't. My throat won't work. . . ."

She leaned one of her white bare arms on the tablecloth towards the walrus-moustache that was still snuffling gloriously:

"They used to call him Old Sol* at school." she said. "But

distinguishes the *aubade* ('implies the lovers to be divided') from the *alba* ('they are united') as morning songs of lovers: *The Troubadours* (London: Chatto and Windus, 1878), 86.

* 'Old Sol' for Solomon, son of David and Bathsheba, who ruled Israel (c. 962–922 BCE) and brought it great prosperity; thus, he is noted for his wisdom. Proverbs 30:18–19: 'There be three things which are too wonderful for me, yea, four which I know not: The way of an eagle in the air; the way of a serpent upon a rock; the way of a ship in the midst of the sea; and the way of a man with a maid.'

there's one question of Solomon's he could not answer.... The
one about the way of a man with ... Oh, a maid! ... Ask him
what happened before the dawn ninety-six—no, ninety-eight
days ago...."

She said to herself: "I can't help it.... Oh, I *can't* help it...."

The ex-sergeant-major was exclaiming happily:

"Oh, no one ever said the captain was one of these thought-
readers.... It's real solid knowledge of men and things he has....
Wonderful how he knows the men considering he was not born
in the service.... But there, your born gentleman mixes with
men all his days and knows them. Down to the ground and inside
their puttees...."

Tietjens was looking straight in front of him, his face perfectly
expressionless.

"But I bet I got him[1] ..." she said to herself and then to the
sergeant-major:

"I suppose now an army officer—one of your born
gentlemen—when a back-from-leave train goes out from any of
the great stations—Paddington, say—to the front.... He knows
how all the men are feeling.... But not what the married women
think ... or the ... the girl...."

She said to herself: "Damn it, how clumsy I am getting! ... I
used to be able to take his hide off with a word. Now I take
sentences at a time...."

She went on with her uninterrupted sentence to Cowley: "Of
course he may never be going to see his only son again, so it makes
him sensitive.... The officer at Paddington, I mean...."

She said to herself: "By God, if that beast does not give in to
me to-night he never *shall* see Michael again.... Ah, but I got
him...." Tietjens had his eyes closed, round each of his high-
coloured nostrils a crescent of whiteness was beginning. And
increasing.... She felt a sudden alarm and held the edge of the
table with her extended arm to steady herself.... Men went
white at the nose like that when they were going to faint.... She
did not want him to faint.... But he *had* noticed the word
Paddington.... Ninety-eight days before.... She had counted
every day since.... She had got that much information.... She
had said *Paddington* outside the house at dawn and he had taken
it as a farewell. He *had* ... He had imagined himself free to do

what he liked with the girl. . . . Well, he wasn't. . . . That was why he was white about the gills. . . .

Cowley exclaimed loudly:

"Paddington! . . . It isn't from there that back-from-leave trains go. Not for the front: the B.E.F. . . . Not from Paddington. . . . The Glamorganshires go from there to the depot. . . . And the Liverpools. . . . They've got a depot at Birkenhead. . . . Or is that the Cheshires? . . ." He asked of Tietjens: "Is it the Liverpools or the Cheshires that have a depot at Birkenhead, sir? . . . You remember we recruited a draft from there when we were at Penhally. . . . At any rate, you go to Birkenhead from Paddington. . . . I was never there myself. . . . They say it's a nice place. . . ."

Sylvia said—she did not want to say it:

"It's quite a nice place . . . but I should not think of staying there for ever. . . ."

Tietjens said:

"The Cheshires have a training camp—not a depot—near Birkenhead. And of course there are R.G.A.'s there. . . ." She had been looking away from him. . . . Cowley exclaimed:

"You were nearly off, sir," hilariously. "You had your peepers shut. . . ." Lifting a champagne glass, he inclined himself towards her. "You must excuse the captain, ma'am," he said. "He had no sleep last night. . . . Largely owing to my fault. . . . Which is what makes it so kind of him. . . . I tell you, ma'am, there are few things I would not do for the captain. . . ." He drank his champagne and began an explanation: "You may not know, ma'am, this is a great day for me. . . . And you and the captain are making it the greatest day of my life. . . ." Why, at four this morning there hadn't been a[2] wretcheder man in Ruin town. . . . And now . . . He must tell her that he[3] suffered from an unfortunate—a miserable—complaint. . . . One that makes one have[4] to be careful of celebrations. . . . And to-day was a day that he had to celebrate. . . . But he dare[5] not have done it where Sergeant-Major Ledoux is along with a lot of their old[6] mates. . . . "I dare not . . . I dussn't!" he finished. . . . "So I might have been sitting, now, at this very moment, up in the cold camp. . . . But for you and the captain. . . . Up in the cold camp. . . . You'll excuse me, ma'am. . . ."

Sylvia felt that her lids were suddenly wavering:

"I might have been myself," she said, "in a cold camp, too ... if I hadn't thrown myself on the captain's mercy! ... At Birkenhead, you know ... I happened to be there till three weeks ago.... It's strange that you mentioned it.... There *are* things like signs ... but you're not a Catholic! They could hardly be coincidences...."

She was trembling.... She looked, fumblingly opening it, into the little mirror of her powder-box—of chased, very thin gold with a small blue stone, like a forget-me-not in the centre of the concentric engravings.... Drake—the possible father of Michael—had given it to her.... The first thing he had ever given her. She had brought it down to-night out of defiance. She imagined that Tietjens disliked it.... She said breathlessly to herself: "Perhaps the damn thing is an ill omen...." Drake had been the first man who had ever ... A hot-breathed brute! ... In the little glass her features were chalk-white.... She looked like ... she looked like ... She had a dress of golden tissue.... The breath was short between her white set teeth.... Her face was as white as her teeth.... And ... Yes! Nearly! Her lips.... What was her face like? ... In the chapel of the convent of Birkenhead there was a tomb all of alabaster.... She said to herself:

"He was near fainting.... I'm near fainting.... What's this beastly thing that's between us? ... If I let myself faint.... But it would not make that beast's face any less wooden! ..."

She leaned across the table and patted the ex-sergeant-major's black-haired hand:

"I'm sure," she said, "you're a very good man...." She did not try to keep the tears out of her eyes, remembering his words: "Up in the cold camp." ... "I'm glad the captain, as you call him, did not leave you in the cold camp.... You're devoted to him, aren't you? ... There are others he does leave ... up in ... the cold camp.... For punishment, you know...."

The ex-sergeant-major, the tears in his eyes too, said: "Well, there *is* men you 'as to give the C.B. to ... C.B. means confined to barracks...."

"Oh, there are!" she exclaimed. "There are! ... And women, too.... Surely there are women, too? ..."

The sergeant-major said:

"Wacks, per'aps.* ... I don't know.... They say women's discipline is much like ours.... Founded on hours!"

She said:

"Do you know what they used to say of the captain? ..." She said to herself: "I pray to God the stiff, fatuous beast likes sitting here listening to this stuff.... Blessed Virgin, mother of God, make him take me.... Before midnight. Before eleven.... As soon as we get rid of this ... this ... No, he's a decent little man ... Blessed Virgin!".... "Do you know what they used to say of the captain? ... I heard the warmest banker in England say it of him...."†

The sergeant-major, his eyes enormously opened, said: "Did you know the warmest banker in England? ... But there, we always knew the captain was well connected...." She went on:

"They said of him.... He was always helping people.".... "Holy Mary, mother of God! ... He's my *husband*.... It's not a sin.... Before midnight.... Oh, give me a sign.... Or before ... the termination of hostilities.... If you give me a sign I could wait.".... "He helped virtuous Scotch students, and broken-down gentry.... And women taken in adultery.... All of them.... Like ... You know Who.... That is his model...." She said to herself: "Curse him! ... I hope he likes it.... You'd think the only thing he thinks about is the beastly duck he's wolfing down.".... And then aloud: "They used to say: 'He saved others; himself he could not save....'"‡

The ex-sergeant-major looked at her gravely:

"Ma'am," he said, "we couldn't say exactly that of the captain.... For I fancy it was said of our Redeemer.... But we 'ave said that if ever there was a poor bloke the captain could 'elp, 'elp 'im 'e would.... Yet the unit was always getting 'ellish strafs from headquarters...."

Suddenly Sylvia began to laugh.... As she began to laugh she had remembered ... The alabaster image in the nun's chapel at

---

* Members of the W.A.A.C.

† Warm: 'Comfortably off, well to do; rich, affluent. Now chiefly *colloq*.': OED.

‡ Matthew 27:41–2: 'Likewise also the chief priests mocking *him*, with the scribes and elders, said, He saved others; himself he cannot save.' Also alluded to in *Some Do Not* ... I.i and II.v.

Birkenhead the vision of which had just presented itself to her,
had been[7] the recumbent tomb of an honourable Mrs Tremayne-
Warlock.... She was said to have sinned in her youth ... And
her husband had never forgiven her.... That was what the nuns
said.... She said aloud:

"A sign...." Then to herself: "Blessed Mary! ... You've given
it me in the neck.... Yet you could not name a father for your
child, and I can name two.... I'm going mad.... Both I and he
are going to go mad...."

She thought of dashing an enormous patch of red upon either
cheek. Then she thought it would be rather melodramatic....

She made in the smoking-room, whilst she was waiting for
both Tietjens and Cowley to come back from the telephone,
another pact.... This time with Father Consett in heaven! She
was fairly sure that Father Consett—and quite possibly other of
the heavenly powers—wanted Christopher not to be worried, so
that he could get on with the war—or because he was a good sort
of dullish man such as the heavenly authorities are apt to like....
Something like that....

She was by that time fairly calm again. You cannot keep up fits
of emotion by the hour: at any rate, with her, the fits of emotion
were periodical and unexpected, though her colder passion
remained always the same.... Thus, when Christopher had
come into Lady Sachse's that afternoon, she had been perfectly
calm. He had mooned through a number of officers, both French
and English, in a great octagonal, bluish salon where Lady Sachse
gave her teas, and had come to her side with just a nod—the
merest inflexion of the head! ... Perowne had melted away
somewhere behind the disagreeable duchess. The general, very
splendid and white-headed and scarlet-tipped and gilt, had also
borne down upon her at that.... At the sight of Perowne with
her he had been sniffing and snorting whilst he talked to the
young nobleman—a dark fellow in blue with a new belt who
seemed just a shade too theatrical, he being chauffeur to a
marshal of France and first cousin and nearest relative, except for
parents and grandparents, of the prospective bride....

The general had told her that he was running the show pretty
strong on purpose because he thought it might do something to

cement the Entente Cordiale.* But it did not seem to be doing it. The French—officers, soldiers and women—kept pretty well all on the one side of the room—the English on the other. The French were as a rule more gloomy than men and women are expected to be. A marquis of sorts—she understood that these were all Bonapartist nobility†—having been introduced to her had distinguished himself no more than by saying that, for his part, he thought the duchess was right, and by saying that to Perowne who, knowing no French, had choked exactly as if his tongue had suddenly got too big for his mouth. . . .

She had not heard what the duchess—a very disagreeable duchess who sat on a sofa and appeared savagely careworn—had been saying, so that she had inclined herself, in the courtly manner that at school she had been taught to reserve for the French legitimist nobility, but that she thought she might expend upon a rather state function even for the Bonapartists, and had replied that without the least doubt the duchess had the right of the matter. . . . The marquis had given her from dark eyes one long glance, and she had returned it with a long cold glance that certainly told him she was meat for his masters. It extinguished him. . . .

Tietjens had staged his meeting with herself remarkably well. It was the sort of lymphatic thing he *could* do, so that, for the fifth of a minute, she wondered if he had any feelings or emotions at all. But she knew that he had. . . . The general, at any rate, bearing down upon them with satisfaction, had remarked:

"Ah, I see you've seen each other before to-day. . . . I thought perhaps you wouldn't have found time before, Tietjens. . . . Your draft must be a great nuisance. . . . "

Tietjens said without expression:

"Yes, we have seen each other before. . . . I made time to call at Sylvia's hotel, sir."

It was at Tietjens' terrifying expressionlessness, at that

---

*   *Entente Cordiale*, though specifically relating to an agreement between England and France dating back to 1843, generally refers to friendly relations between the two countries, which eventually led England to support France against Germany in the First World War.

†   Since legitimist nobility lost power with the French Revolution, Bonapartist nobility were an ersatz, if wealthy and influential, later creation, deriving their status from their ancestors' support of Napoleon.

completely being up to a situation, that the first wave of emotion had come over her.... For, till that very moment, she had been merely sardonically making the constatation* that there was not a single presentable man in the room.... There was not even one that you could call a gentleman ... for you cannot size up the French ... ever! ... But, suddenly, she was despairing! ... How, she said to herself, could she ever move, put emotion into, this lump! It was like trying to move an immense mattress filled with feathers. You pulled at one end, but the whole mass sagged down and remained immobile until you seemed to have no strength at all.... Until virtue went out from you....

It was as if he had the evil eye: or some special protector. He was so appallingly competent, so appallingly always in the centre of his own picture.

The general said, rather joyfully:

"Then you can spare a minute, Tietjens, to talk to the duchess! About coal! ... For goodness' sake, man, save the situation! I'm worn out...."

Sylvia bit the inside of her lower lip—she never bit her lip itself!—to keep herself from exclaiming aloud. It was just exactly what should not happen to Tietjens at that juncture.... She heard the general explaining to her, in his courtly manner, that the duchess was holding up the whole ceremony because of the price of coal. The general loved her desperately. Her, Sylvia! In quite a proper manner for an elderly general.... But he would go to no small extremes in her interests! So would his sister!

She looked hard at the room to get her senses into order again. She said:

"It's like a Hogarth picture...."†

The undissolvable air of the eighteenth century that the French contrive to retain in all their effects kept the scene singularly together. On a sofa sat the duchess, relatives leaning over her. She was a duchess with one of those impossible names: Beauchain-Radigutz or something like it. The bluish room was octagonal and vaulted, up to a rosette in the centre of the ceiling.

---

* 'To establish as certain' (*OED*); but Ford tended to use it as a French term, with the sense of describing exactly.

† William Hogarth (1697–1764), painter and engraver, drew satiric representations of English life such as *Rake's Progress*, *Gin Lane*, and *Marriage à la Mode*.

English officers and V.A.D.'s of some evident presence opened out to the left, French military and very black-clothed women of all ages, but all apparently widows, opened out to the right, as if the duchess shone down a sea at sunset. Beside her on the sofa you did not see Lady Sachse; leaning over her you did not see the prospective bride. This stoutish, unpresentable, coldly venomous woman, in black clothes so shabby that they might have been grey tweed, extinguished other personalities as the sun conceals planets. A fattish, brilliantined personality, in mufti, with a scarlet rosette, stood sideways to the duchess's right, his hands extended forward as if in an invitation to a dance; an extremely squat lady, also apparently a widow, extended, on the left of the duchess, both her black-gloved hands, as if she too were giving an invitation to the dance. . . .

The general, with Sylvia beside him, stood glorious in the centre of the clearing that led to the open doorway of a much smaller room. Through the doorway you could see a table with a white damask cloth; a silver-gilt inkpot, fretted, like a porcupine with pens, a fat, flat leather case for the transportation of documents and two notaires: one in black, fat, and bald-headed; one in blue uniform, with a shining monocle, and a brown moustache that he continued to twirl. . . .

Looking round that scene Sylvia's humour calmed her and she heard the general say:

"She's supposed to walk on my arm to that table and sign the settlement. . . . We're supposed to be the first to sign it together. . . . But she won't. Because of the price of coal. It appears that she has hothouses in miles. And she thinks the English have put up the price of coal as if . . . damn it you'd think we did it just to keep her hothouse stoves out."

The duchess had delivered, apparently, a vindictive, cold, calm, and uninterruptible oration on the wickedness of her country's allies as people who should have allowed France to be devastated and the flower of her youth slain in order that they might put up the price of a comestible that was absolutely needed in her life. There was no arguing with her. There was no British soul there who both knew anything about economics and spoke French. And there she sat, apparently immovable. She did not refuse to sign the marriage contract. She just made no motion to

go to it and, apparently, the resulting marriage would be illegal if
that document were brought to her! ...

The general said:

"Now, what the deuce will Christopher find to say to her? He'll
find something because he could talk the hind legs off anything.
But what the deuce will it be? ... "

It almost broke Sylvia's heart to see how exactly Christopher
did the right thing. He walked up that path to the sun and made
in front of the duchess a little awkward nick with his head and
shoulders that was rather more like a curtsy than a bow. It
appeared that he knew the duchess quite well ... as he knew
everybody in the world quite well. He smiled at her and then
became just suitably grave. Then he began to speak an admirable,
very old-fashioned French with an atrocious English accent.*
Sylvia had no idea that he knew a word of the language—that
she herself knew very well indeed. She said to herself that upon
her word it was like hearing Chateaubriand[†] talk—if
Chateaubriand had been brought up in an English hunting
country.... Of course Christopher *would* cultivate an English
accent: to show that he was an English country gentleman. And
he would speak correctly—to show that an English Tory can do
anything in the world if he wants to....

The British faces in the room looked blank: the French faces
turned electrically upon him. Sylvia said:

"Who would have thought ... ?" The duchess jumped to her
feet and took Christopher's arm. She sailed with him imperiously
past the general and past Sylvia. She was saying that that was just
what she would have expected of a *milor Anglais* ... *Avec un*

---

* The old-fashioned French was Ford's too, acquired from his grandfather Madox
Brown, who 'had been born and educated and lived in France until comparatively well
on in life. He spoke always with a slightly un-English accent, and supplied missing
words and phrases in his conversation with French expressions, a little old-fashioned
because he dated from the days of Brummel in Calais': 'Nice People', *Temple Bar*, 128
(Nov. 1903), 564–78 (571–2). 'My French I had from my grandfather', Ford wrote the
year after writing *No More Parades*, 'But he insisted characteristically that although
one must know French with accuracy one must speak it with a marked English accent
to show that one is an English gentleman. I still do': *A Mirror to France* (London: Duckworth, 1926), 113.

† François-Réné de Chateaubriand (1768–1848), founder of French Romanticism, was
noted for his descriptions of nature and his intimations of passion. He is best known
for his *Génie du christianisme* (1802) and his posthumous *Mémoires d'outre-tombe*
(1848–50).

spleen tel que vous l'avez![*]

Christopher, in short, had told the duchess that as his family owned almost the largest stretch of hot-house coal-burning land in England and her family the largest stretch of hothouses in the sister-country of France, what could they do better than make an alliance? He would instruct his brother's manager to see that the duchess was supplied for the duration of hostilities and as long after as she pleased with all the coal needed for her glass at the pithead prices of the Middlesbrough-Cleveland district as the prices were on the 3rd of August, nineteen fourteen.... He repeated: "The pit-head price ... *livrable au prix de l'houille-maigre dans*[8] *l'enceinte des puits de ma campagne.*"[†] ... Much to the satisfaction of the duchess, who knew all about prices.

... A triumph for Christopher was at that moment so exactly what Sylvia thought she did not want that she decided to tell the general that Christopher was a Socialist. That might well take him down a peg or two in the general's esteem ... for the general's arm-patting admiration for Tietjens, the man who did not argue but acted over the price of coal, was as much as she could bear.... But, thinking it over in the smoking-room after dinner, by which time she was a good deal more aware of what she did want, she was not so certain that she *had* done what she wanted.... Indeed, even in the octagonal room during the economical festivities that followed the signatures, she had been far from certain that she had not done almost exactly what she did not want....

It had begun with the general's exclaiming to her:

"You know your man's the most unaccountable fellow.... He wears the damn-shabbiest uniform of any officer I ever have to talk to. He's said to be unholily hard up.... I even heard he had a cheque sent back to the club.... Then he goes and makes a princely gift like that—just to get Levin out of ten minutes'

---

[*] 'an English lord ... With a spleen like yours'; *spleen* here meaning a 'proud temper ... resolute mind': OED. Cf. *The Marsden Case* 151 ('An English Lord: "Avec un spleen!"'); *Joseph Conrad* 63–4 on the first novel Ford wrote after completing *Parade's End*, *A Little Less than Gods* (London: Duckworth, 1928), 'the central figures being Ney and an English *milor* with the spleen'; *Joseph Conrad* 121 on 'such eccentricities as go with the spleen of the milor anglais'; and *No Enemy* 71 on the nineteenth-century French caricature of 'the milord with his millions, his spleen which drove him to be suicidal'.

[†] 'deliverable at the price of hot-house coal at the pit-walls of my district.'

awkwardness.... I wish to goodness I could understand the fellow.... He's got a positive genius for getting all sorts of things out of the most beastly muddles.... Why, he's even been useful to me.... And then he's got a positive genius for getting into the most disgusting messes.... You're too young to have heard of Dreyfus....* But I always say that Christopher is a regular Dreyfus.... I shouldn't be astonished if he didn't end by being drummed out of the army ... which heaven forfend!'

It had been then that Sylvia had said:

"Hasn't it ever occurred to you that Christopher was a Socialist?"

For the first time in her life Sylvia saw her husband's godfather look grotesque.... His jaw dropped down, his white hair became disarrayed and he dropped his pretty cap with all the gold oakleaves and the scarlet. When he rose from picking it up his thin old face was purple and distorted. She wished she hadn't said it: she wished she hadn't said it. He exclaimed:

"Christopher! ... A So ..." He gasped as if he could not pronounce the word. He said: "Damn it all! ... I've loved that boy.... He's my only godson.... His father was my best friend.... I've watched over him.... I'd have married his mother if she would have had me.... Damn it all, he's down in my will as residuary legatee after a few small things left to my sister and my collection of horns to the regiment I commanded...."

Sylvia—they were sitting on the sofa the duchess had left—patted him on the forearm and said:

"But general ... godfather...."

"It explains everything," he said with a mortification that was painful. His white moustache drooped and trembled. "And what makes it all the worse—he's never had the courage to tell me his opinions." He stopped, snorted and exclaimed: "By God, I *will* have him drummed out of the service.... By God, I will. I can do that much...."

---

* Alfred Dreyfus (1859–1935) was a captain in the French army falsely convicted in 1895 of providing military secrets to the Germans, the real culprit being Major F. W. Esterhazy, who was exonerated. This led to the 'Dreyfus Affair' and to Emile Zola's defence of him in *J'Accuse* (1898), which showed that the government invented the case against Dreyfus and imprisoned him on Devil's Island because he was a Jew. Eventually he was freed, returned to the army, and attained the rank of lieutenant-colonel.

His grief so shut him in on himself that she could say nothing to him. . . .

"You tell me he seduced the little Wannop girl. . . . The last person in the world he should have seduced. . . . Ain't there millions of other women? . . . He got you sold up, didn't he? . . . Along with keeping a girl in a tobacco-shop. . . . By Jove,[9] I almost lent him . . . offered to lend him money on that occasion. . . . You can forgive a young man for going wrong with women. . . . We all do. . . . We've all set up girls in tobacco-shops in our time. . . . But, damn it all, if the fellow's a Socialist it puts a different complexion. . . . I could forgive him even for the little Wannop girl, if he wasn't . . . But . . . Good God, isn't it just the thing that a dirty-minded Socialist would do? . . . To seduce the daughter of his father's oldest friend, next to me. . . . Or perhaps Wannop was an older friend than me. . . . "

He had calmed himself a little—and he was not such a fool. He looked at her now with a certain keenness in his blue eyes that showed no sign of age. He said:

"See here, Sylvia. . . . You aren't on terms with Christopher for all the good game you put up here this afternoon. . . . I shall have to go into this. It's a serious charge to bring against one of His Majesty's officers. . . . Women do say things against their husbands when they are not on good terms with them. . . . " He went on to say that he did not say she wasn't justified. If Christopher had seduced the little Wannop girl it was enough to make her wish to harm him. He had always found her the soul of honour, straight as a die, straight as she rode to hounds. And if she wished to nag against her husband, even if in little things it wasn't quite the truth, she was perhaps within her rights as a woman. She had said, for instance, that Tietjens had taken two pairs of her best sheets. Well, his own sister, her friend, raised Cain if he took anything out of the house they lived in. She had made an atrocious row because he had taken his own shaving-glass out of his own bedroom at Mountby.[10] Women liked to have sets of things. Perhaps she, Sylvia, had sets of pairs of sheets. His sister had linen sheets with the date of the battle of Waterloo on them. . . . Naturally you would not want a set spoiled. . . . But this was another matter. He ended up very seriously:

"I have not got time to go into this now . . . I ought not to be another minute away from my office. These are very serious days...." He broke off to utter against the Prime Minister and the Cabinet at home a series of violent imprecations. He went on:

"But this will have to be gone into.... It's heartbreaking that my time should be taken up by matters like this in my own family.... But these fellows aim at sapping the heart of the army.... They say they distribute thousands of pamphlets recommending the rank and file to shoot their officers and go over to the Germans.... Do you seriously mean that Christopher belongs to an organization? What is it you are going on? What evidence have you? ..."

She said:

"Only that he is heir to one of the biggest fortunes in England, for a commoner, and he refuses to touch a penny.... His brother Mark tells me Christopher could have ... Oh, a fabulous sum a year.... But he has made over Groby to me...."

The general nodded his head as if he were ticking off ideas.

"Of course, refusing property is a sign of being one of these fellows. By Jove, I must go.... But as for his not going to live at Groby: If he is setting up house with Miss Wannop.... Well, he could not flaunt her in the face of the county.... And, of course, those sheets! ... As you put it it looked as if he'd beggared himself with his dissipations.... But of course, if he is refusing money from Mark, it's another matter.... Mark would make up a couple of hundred dozen pairs of sheets without turning a hair.... Of course there are the extraordinary things Christopher says.... I've often heard you complain of the immoral way he looks at the serious affairs of life.... You said he once talked of lethal-chambering unfit children."

He exclaimed:

"I must go. There's Thurston looking at me.... But what then is it that Christopher has said? ... Hang it all: what *is* at the bottom of that fellow's mind? ..."

"He desires," Sylvia said, and she had no idea when she said it, "to model himself upon our Lord...."

The general leant back in the sofa. He said almost indulgently:

"Who's that ... our *Lord?*"

Sylvia said:

"Upon our Lord Jesus Christ...."

He sprang to his feet as if she had stabbed him with a hatpin.

"Our..." he exclaimed. "Good God!... I always knew he had a screw loose.... But..." He said briskly: "Give all his goods to the poor!... But He wasn't a... Not a Socialist! What was it He said: Render unto Caesar... It wouldn't be necessary to drum Him out of the Army..." He said: "Good Lord!... Good Lord! ... Of course his poor dear mother was a little... But, hang it! ... The Wannop girl! ..." Extreme discomfort overcame him.... Tietjens was half-way across from the inner room, coming towards them.

He said:

"Major Thurston is looking for you, sir. Very urgently...." The general regarded him as if he had been the unicorn of the royal arms, come alive. He exclaimed:

"Major Thurston!... Yes! Yes! ..." and, Tietjens saying to him:

"I wanted to ask you, sir ..." he pushed Tietjens away as if he dreaded an assault and went off with short, agitated steps.

So sitting there, in the smoking-lounge of the hotel which was cram-jam full of officers, and no doubt perfectly respectable, but over-giggling women—the sort of place and environment which she had certainly never expected to be called upon to sit in; and waiting for the return of Tietjens and the ex-sergeant-major— who again was certainly not the sort of person that she had ever expected to be asked to wait for, though for long years she had put up with Tietjens' protégé, the odious Sir Vincent Macmaster, at all sorts of meals and all sorts of places ... but of course that was only Christopher's rights ... to have in his own house, which, in the circumstances, wasn't morally hers, any snuffling, nervous, walrus-moustached or orientally obsequious protégé that he chose to patronize.... And she quite believed that Tietjens, when he had invited the sergeant-major to celebrate his commission with himself at dinner, hadn't expected to dine with her.... It was the sort of obtuseness of which he was disconcertingly capable, though at other times he was much more disconcertingly capable of reading your thoughts to the last hairsbreadth.... And, as a matter of fact, she objected much less to dining with the absolute lower classes than with merely snuffly little official critics like Macmaster, and the sergeant-major had served her turn very well when it had come to flaying the hide off Christopher.... So, sitting there, she made a new pact, this time with Father Consett in heaven....

Father Consett was very much in her mind, for she was very much in the midst of the British military authorities who had hung him....[11] She had never seemed before to be so in the midst of these negligible, odious, unpresentable, horse-laughing school-boys. It antagonized her, and it was a weight upon her, for hitherto she had completely ignored them: in this place they seemed to have a coherence, a mass ... almost a life.... They rushed in and out of rooms occupied, as incomprehensibly, as unpresentably, with things like boots, washing, vaccination certificates.... Even with old tins! ... A man with prematurely white hair and a pasty face, with a tunic that bulged both above and below his belt, would walk into the drawing-room of a lady who superintended all the acid-drop and cigarette stalls of that city and remark to a thin-haired, deaf man with an amazingly red nose—a nose that had a perfectly definite purple and scarlet diag-onal demarcation running from the bridge to the upper side of the nostrils—that he had got his old tins off his hands at last. He would have to repeat it in a shout because the red-nosed man, his head hanging down, would have heard nothing at all. The deaf man would say Humph! Humph! Snuffle. The woman giving the tea—a Mrs. Hemmerdine,* of Tarbolton, whom you might have met at home, would be saying that at last she had got twelve reams of notepaper with forget-me-nots in the top corners when the deaf-faced man would begin, gruffly and uninterruptedly, a monologue on his urgent need for twenty thousand tons of sawdust for the new slow-burning stoves in the men's huts....[12]

It was undeniably like something moving.... All these things going in one direction.... A disagreeable force set in motion by gawky schoolboys—but schoolboys of the Sixth Form, sinister, hobbledehoy, waiting in the corners of playgrounds to torture someone, weak and unfortunate.... In one or other corner of

---

* *Nightingale* 209 tells a story about a Mrs Hemmerdine (or Hammerdine) keeping a man ('at least a Field-Marshal') waiting; though Ford adds 'The name was not Hemmer-dine.'

their world-wide playground they had come upon Father Consett and hanged him. No doubt they tortured him first. And, if he made an offering of his sufferings then and there to Heaven, no doubt he was already in paradise.... Or, if he was not yet in heaven, certain of the souls in purgatory were yet listened to in the midst of their torments....

So she said:

"Blessed and martyred father, I know that you loved Christopher and wish to save him from trouble. I will make this pact with you. Since I have been in this room I have kept my eyes in the boat—almost in my lap.* I will agree to leave off torturing Christopher and I will go into retreat in a convent of Ursuline Dames Nobles†—for I can't stand the nuns of that other convent—for the rest of my life.... And I know that will please you, too, for you were always anxious for the good of my soul...."

She was going to do that if when she raised her eyes and really looked round the room she saw in it one man that looked presentable. She did not ask that he should more than look presentable, for she wanted nothing to do with the creature.[13] He was to be a sign: not a prey!

She explained to the dead priest that she could not go all the world over to see if it contained a presentable man, but she could not bear to be in a convent for ever, and have the thought that there wasn't, for other women, one presentable man in the world.... For Christopher would be no good to them. He would be mooning for ever over the Wannop girl. Or her memory. That was all one ... He was content with LOVE.... If he knew that the Wannop girl was loving him in Bedford Park, and he in the Khyber States with the Himalayas between them, he would be quite content....‡ That would be correct in its way, but not very

---

* Partridge's *Dictionary of Slang* glosses 'eyes in the boat!' with 'Keep your eyes on the job – not on that wench over there!: nautical: late C.19–20.'

† The Ursulines are a Roman Catholic religious order founded at Brescia, Italy, by Saint Angela de Merici in 1535, with the aim of educating young ladies and caring for the sick and the poor. St Ursula is their patron saint.

‡ Cf. *The Good Soldier* 153: 'To Leonora's eternal question he answered that all he desired in life was that – that he could pick himself together again and go on with his daily occupations if – the girl, being five thousand miles away, would continue to love him. He wanted nothing more, He prayed his God for nothing more. Well, he was a sentimentalist.'

helpful for other women.... Besides, if he were the only presentable man in the world, half the women would be in love with
him.... And that would be disastrous, because he was no more
responsive than a bullock in a fatting pen.

"So, father," she said, "work a miracle.... It's not very much
of a little miracle.... Even if a presentable man doesn't exist you
could put him there.... I'll give you ten minutes before I
look...."

She thought it was pretty sporting of her, for, she said to
herself, she was perfectly in earnest. If in that long, dim, green-
lamp-shaded, and of course bepalm-leaved, badly-proportioned,
glazed, ignoble public room, there appeared one decentish man,
as decentish men went before this beanfeast began, she would go
into retreat for the rest of her life....

She fell into a sort of dim trance after she had looked at her
watch. Often she went into these dim trances ... ever since she
had been a girl at school with Father Consett for her spiritual
adviser! ... She seemed to be aware of the father moving about
the room, lifting up a book and putting it down.... Her ghostly
friend! ... Goodness, he was unpresentable enough, with his
broad, open face that always looked dirtyish, his great dark eyes,
and his great mouth.... But a saint and a martyr.... She felt him
there.... What had they murdered him for? Hung at the word of
a half-mad, half-drunk subaltern, because he had heard the
confession of some of the rebels the night before they were
taken.... He was over in the far corner of the room.... She
heard him say: they had not understood, the men that had hanged
him. That is what you would say, father ... Have mercy on them,
for they know not what they do....*

Then have mercy on me, for half the time[14] I don't know what
I'm doing! ... It was like a spell you put on me. At Lobscheid.
Where my mother was, when I came back from that place
without my clothes.... You said, didn't you, to mother, but she
told me afterwards: The real hell for that poor boy, meaning
Christopher, will come when he falls in love with some young
girl—as, mark me, he will.... For she, meaning me, will tear the

---

* Luke 23:34: 'Then Jesus said, "Father forgive them, for they know not what they do"':
  Jesus' first saying on the cross, about those who crucified him.

world down to get at him.... And when mother said she was certain I would never do anything vulgar you obstinately did not agree... You knew me....

She tried to rouse herself and said: He *knew* me.... Damn it, he knew me! ... What's vulgarity to me, Sylvia Tietjens, born Satterthwaite? I do what I want and that's good enough for anyone. Except a priest. Vulgarity! I wonder mother could be so obtuse. If I am vulgar I'm vulgar with a purpose. Then it's not vulgarity. It may be vice. Or viciousness.... But if you commit a mortal sin with your eyes open it's not vulgarity.... You chance hell fire for ever.... Good enough!

The weariness sank over her again and the sense of the father's presence.... She was back again in Lobscheid, thirty-six hours free of Perowne with the father and her mother in the dim sitting-room, all antlers, candle-lit, with the father's shadow waving over the pitchpine walls and ceilings.... It was a bewitched place, in the deep forests of Germany. The father himself said it was the last place in Europe to be Christianized. Or perhaps it was never Christianized.... That was perhaps why these people, the Germans, coming from those deep, devil-infested woods, did all these wickednesses.* Or maybe they were not wicked.... One would never know properly.... But maybe the father had put a spell on her.... His words had never been out of her mind, much.... At the back of her brain, as the saying was....

Some man drifted near her and said:

"How do you do, Mrs. Tietjens? Who would have thought of seeing you here?"

She answered:

"I have to look after Christopher now and then." He remained hanging over her with a schoolboy grin for a minute, then he drifted away as an object sinks into deep water.... Father Consett again hovered near her. She exclaimed:

"But the real point is, father.... Is it sporting? ... Sporting or whatever it is?" And Father Consett breathed: "Ah! ..." with his terrible power of arousing doubts.... She said:

"When I saw Christopher ... Last night? ... Yes, it *was* last

---

* Ford's fascinating story 'Riesenberg', *The English Review*, VIII (April 1911), 25–45, presents a mysterious account of just such 'deep' and, perhaps, 'devil-infested woods'.

night.... Turning back to go up that hill.... And I had been
talking about him to a lot of grinning private soldiers.... To
madden him.... You *mustn't* make scenes before the servants....
A heavy man, tired ... come down the hill and lumbering up
again.... There was a searchlight turned on him just as he
turned.... I remembered the white bulldog I thrashed on the
night before it died.... A tired, silent beast ... with[15] a fat white
behind.... Tired out.... You couldn't see its tail because it was
turned down, the stump.... A great, silent beast.... The vet
said it had been poisoned with red lead by burglars.... It's beastly
to die of red lead.... It eats up the liver.... And you think you're
getting better for a fortnight. And you're always cold ... freezing
in the blood-vessels....[16] And the poor beast had left its kennel
to try and be let in to the fire.... And I found it at the door when
I came in from a dance without Christopher.... And got the
rhinoceros whip and lashed into it.... There's a pleasure in
lashing into a naked white beast.... Obese and silent.... Like
Christopher.... I thought Christopher might.... That
night.... It went through my head.... It hung down its head....
A great head, room for a whole British encyclopædia of mis-
information, as Christopher used to put it.... It said: 'What a
hope!' ... As I hope to be saved, though I never shall be, the dog
said: 'What a hope!' ... Snow-white in quite black bushes....
And it went under a bush.... They found it dead there in the
morning.... You can't imagine what it looked like, with its head
over its shoulder, as it looked back and said: What a hope! to
me.... Under a dark bush. An eu ... eu ... euonymus,* isn't it?
... In thirty degrees of frost with all the blood-vessels exposed on
the naked surface of the skin.... It's the seventh circle of hell,†
isn't it? the frozen one....[17] The last stud-white bulldog of that
breed.... As Christopher is the last stud-white hope of the
Groby Tory breed.... Modelling himself on our Lord.... But
our Lord was never married. He never touched on topics of sex.
Good for Him...."[18]

---

* A kind of bush or shrub cultivated for its foliage or fruit.

† The 'frozen one' is the ninth (not the seventh) circle of hell in Dante's *Inferno*, canto
XXXII. The outermost of its four circles contains those who have done violence to
family members. Given her identification of her husband with the bulldog she has
fatally beaten, Sylvia's thoughts are in the right place.

She said: "The ten minutes is up, father..." and looked at the round, starred surface between the diamonds of her wrist watch. She said: "Good God! ... Only one minute.... I've thought all that in only one minute.... I understand how hell can be an eternity...."

Christopher, very weary, and ex-Sergeant-Major Cowley, very talkative by now, loomed down between palms. Cowley was saying: "It's infamous! ... It's past bearing.... To re-order the draft at eleven...." They sank into chairs.... Sylvia extended towards Tietjens a small packet of letters. She said: "You had better look at these.... I had your letters sent to me from the flat as there was so much uncertainty about your movements...." She found that she did not dare, under Father Consett's eyes, to look at Tietjens as she said that. She said to Cowley: "We might be quiet for a minute or two while the captain reads his letters.... Have another liqueur?..."

She then observed that Tietjens just bent open the top of the letters from Mrs. Wannop and then opened that from his brother Mark:

"Curse it," she said, "I've given him what he wants! ... He knows.... He's seen the address ... that they're still in Bedford Park.... He can think of the Wannop girl as there.... He has not been able to know, till now, where she is.... He'll be imagining himself in bed with her there...."

Father Consett, his broad, unmodelled dark face full of intelligence and with the blissful unction of the saint and martyr, was leaning over Tietjens' shoulder.... He must be breathing down Christopher's back as, her mother said, he always did when she held a hand at auction and he could not play because it was between midnight and his celebrating the holy mass....

She said:

"No, I am not going mad.... This is an effect of fatigue on the optic nerves.... Christopher has explained that to me.... He says that when his eyes have been very tired with making one of his senior wrangler's calculations he has often seen a woman in[19] eighteenth-century dress looking into a drawer in his bureau.... Thank God, I've had Christopher to explain things to me.... I'll never let him go.... Never, never, let him go...."

It was not, however, until several hours later that the signifi-

cance of the father's apparition came to her and those inter-
vening hours were extraordinarily occupied—with emotions, and
even with action. To begin with, before he had read the fewest
possible words of his brother's letter, Tietjens looked up over it
and said:

"Of course you will occupy Groby.... With Michael....
Naturally the proper business arrangements will be made...." He
went on reading the letter, sunk in his chair under the green
shade of a lamp....

The letter, Sylvia knew, began with the words: "Your bitch of[20]
a wife has been to see me with the idea of getting any allowance
I might be minded to make you transferred to herself. Of course
she can have Groby, for I shan't let it, and could not be bothered
with it myself. On the other hand, you may want to live at Groby
with that girl and chance the racket. I should if I were you. You
would probably find the place worth the ... what is it? ostracism,
if there was any.... But I'm forgetting that the girl is not your
mistress unless anything has happened since I saw you.... And
you probably would want Michael to be brought up at Groby, in
which case you couldn't keep the girl there, even if you camouflaged her as governess. At least I think that kind of arrangement
always turns out badly: there's bound to be a stink, though Crosby
of Ulick did it and nobody much minded.... But it was mucky
for the Crosby children. Of course if you want your wife to have
Groby she must have enough to run it with credit, and expenses
are rising damnably. Still, our incomings rise not a little, too,
which is not the case with some. The only thing I insist on is that
you make plain to that baggage that whatever I allow her, even
if it's no end of a hot income, not one penny of it comes out of
what I wish you[21] would allow me to allow you. I mean I want you
to make plain to that rouged piece—or perhaps it's really natural,
my eyes are not what they were—that what you have is absolutely
independent of what she sucks up as the mother of our father's
heir and to keep our father's heir in the state of life that is his
due.... I hope you feel satisfied that the boy is your son, for it's
more than I should be, looking at the party.... But even if he is
not he is our father's heir all right and must be so treated....

"But be plain about that, for the trollop came to me, if you
please, with the proposal that I should dock you of any income I

might propose to allow you—and to which of course you are absolutely entitled under our father's will, though it is no good reminding you of that!—as a token from me that I disapproved of your behaviour when, damn it, there is not an action of yours that I would not be proud to have to my credit. At any rate in this affair, for I cannot help thinking that you could be of more service to the country if you were anywhere else but where you are. But you know what your conscience demands of you better than I, and I dare say these hell-cats have so mauled you that you are glad to be able to get away into any hole. But don't let yourself die in your hole. Groby will have to be looked after, and even if you do not live there you can keep a strong hand on Sanders, or whoever you elect to have as manager. That monstrosity you honour with your name—which is also mine, thank you!— suggested that if I consented to let her live at Groby she would have her mother to live with her, in which case her mother would be good to look after the estate. I dare say she would, though she has had to let her own place. But then almost every one else has. She seems anyhow a notable woman, with her head screwed on the right way. I did not tell the discreditable daughter that she— her mother—had come to see me at breakfast immediately after seeing you off, she was so upset. And she *keawert ho down i' th' ingle and had a gradely pow.** You remember how Gobbles the gardener used to say that. A good chap, though he came from Lancasheere! . . . The mother has no illusions about the daughter and is heart and soul for you. She was dreadfully upset at your going, the more so as she believes that it's her offspring has driven you out of the country and that you purpose . . . isn't stopping one the phrase?† Don't do that.

"I saw your girl yesterday. . . . She looked peaky. But of course I have seen her several times, and she always looks peaky. I do not understand why you do not write to them. The mother is clamorous because you have not answered several letters and

---

* Lancashire dialect, meaning 'cowered herself down at the ingle and had a good chat'; an ingle being 'a fire burning upon the hearth': *OED*. Ford recalls having lunch in Fall River, Massachusetts, with a trolley conductor and his Lancashire wife, she 'speaking a dialect so broad that it was all I could do to understand her. So we cowered us down i' th' ingle and had a gradely pow while the beans were baking in the bean pot. . .': *New York Essays* (New York: Rudge, 1927), 90.

† i.e. stopping a bullet.

have not sent her military information she wants for some article she is writing for a Swiss magazine...."[*]

Sylvia knew the letter almost by heart as far as that because in the unbearable white room of the convent near Birkenhead she had twice begun to copy it out, with the idea of keeping the copies for use in some sort of publicity. But, at that point, she had twice been overcome by the idea that it was not a very sporting thing to do, if you really think about it. Besides, the letter after that— she *had* glanced through it—occupied itself almost entirely with the affairs of Mrs. Wannop. Mark, in his naïve way, was concerned that the old lady, although now enjoying the income from the legacy left her by their father, had not immediately settled down to write a deathless novel; although, as he added, he knew nothing about novels....

Christopher was reading away at his letters beneath the green-shaded lamp; the ex-quartermaster had begun several sentences and dropped into demonstrative silence at the reminder that Tietjens was reading. Christopher's face was completely without expression; he might have been reading a return from the office of statistics in the old days at breakfast. She wondered, vaguely, if he would see fit to apologize for the epithets that his brother had applied to her. Probably he would not. He would consider that she having opened the letter must take the responsibility of the contents. Something like that. Thumps and rumbles began to exist in the relative silence. Cowley said: "They're coming again then!" Several couples passed them on the way out of the room. Amongst them there was certainly no presentable man; they were all either too old or too hobbledehoy, with disproportionate noses and vacant, half-opened mouths.

Accompanying Christopher's mind, as it were, whilst he read his letter had induced in her a rather different mood. The pictures in her own mind were rather of Mark's dingy breakfast-room in which she had had her interview with him—and of the outside of the dingy house in which the Wannops lived, at Bedford

---

* As Ford had done. See 'Une Partie de Cricket', *Bibliotheque universelle et revue suisse*, 85 (Jan. 1917), 117–26. This essay appears twice in *No Enemy*: in English, as Chapter 7, entitled 'A Cricket Match'; and in the original French as the 'Envoi'. He also wrote 'Pon ... ti ... pri ... ith' for the Geneva periodical *La Revue des Idées* (Nov. 1918), 233–8; a translation is in *War Prose* 30–5.

Park.... But she was still conscious of her pact with the father and, looking at her wrist watch, saw that by now six minutes had passed.... It was astonishing that Mark, who was a millionaire at least, and probably a good deal more, should live in such a dingy apartment—it had for its chief decoration the hoofs of several deceased race-winners, mounted as ink-stands, as pen-racks, as paper-weights—and afford himself only such a lugubrious breakfast of fat slabs of ham over which bled pallid eggs.... For she too, like her mother, had looked in on Mark at breakfast-time—her mother because she had just seen Christopher off to France, and she because, after a sleepless night—the third of a series—she had been walking about St. James's Park and, passing under Mark's windows, it had occurred to her that she might do Christopher some damage by putting his brother wise about the entanglement with Miss Wannop. So, on the spur of the moment, she had invented a desire to live at Groby with the accompanying necessity for additional means. For, although she was a pretty wealthy woman, she was not wealthy enough to live at Groby and keep it up. The immense old place was not so immense because of its room-space, though, as far as she could remember, there must be anything between forty and sixty rooms, but because of the vast old grounds, the warren of stabling, wells, rose-walks and fencing.... A man's place, really, the furniture very grim and the corridors on the ground floor all slabbed with great stones. So she had looked in on Mark, reading his correspondence with his copy of *The Times* airing on a chair-back before the fire—for he was just the man to retain the eighteen-forty idea that you catch cold by reading a damp newspaper. His grim, tight, brown-wooden features that might have been carved out of an old chair, had expressed no emotion at all during the interview. He had offered to have up some more ham and eggs for her and had asked one or two questions as to how she meant to live at Groby if she went there. Otherwise he had said nothing about the information she had given him as to the Wannop girl having had a baby by Christopher—for for purposes of conversation she had adhered to that old story, at any rate till that interview. He had said nothing at all. Not one word.... At the end of the interview, when he had risen and produced from an adjoining room a bowler hat and an umbrella, saying that he must now go to his office, he had put to her without any expression pretty well what stood in the letter, as far as business was concerned. He said that she could have Groby, but she must understand that, his father being now dead and he a public official, without children and occupied in London with work that suited him, Groby was practically Christopher's property to do what he liked with as long as—which he certainly would—he kept it in proper style. So that, if she wished to live there, she must produce Christopher's authorization to that effect. And he added, with an equableness so masking the proposition that it was not until she was well out of the house and down the street that its true amazingness took her breath away:

"Of course, Christopher, if what you say is true, might want to live at Groby with Miss Wannop. In that case he would have to." And he had offered her an expressionless hand and shepherded her, rather fussily, through his dingy and awkward front passages that were lit only from ground-glass windows giving apparently on to his bathroom. . . .

It wasn't until that moment, really, that, at once with exhilaration and also with a sinking at the heart, she realized what she was up against in the way of a combination. For, when she had gone to Mark's, she had been more than half-maddened by the news that Christopher at Rouen was in hospital and, although the hospital authorities had assured her, at first by telegram and then by letter, that it was nothing more than his chest, she had not had any knowledge of to what extent Red Cross authorities did or did not mislead the relatives of casualties.

So it had seemed natural that she should want to inflict on him all the injuries that she could at the moment, the thought that he was probably in pain making her wish to add all she could to that pain. . . . Otherwise, of course, she would not have gone to Mark's. . . . For it was a mistake in strategy. But then she said, to herself: "Confound it! . . . What strategy was it a mistake in? What do I care about strategy? What am I out for? . . ." She did what she wanted to, on the spur of the moment! . . .

Now she certainly realized. How Christopher had got round Mark she did not know or much care, but there Christopher certainly was, although his father had certainly died of a broken heart at the rumours that were going round about his son—

rumours she, almost as efficiently as the man called Ruggles* and more irresponsible gossips, had set going about Christopher. They had been meant to smash Christopher: they had smashed his father instead. . . . But Christopher had got round Mark, whom he had not seen for ten years. . . . Well, he probably would. Christopher was perfectly immaculate, that was a fact, and Mark, though he appeared half-witted in a North Country way, was no fool. He could not be a fool. He was a really august public official. And, although as a rule Sylvia gave nothing at all for any public official, if a man like Mark had the position by birth amongst presentable men that he certainly ought to have and was also the head of a department and reputed absolutely indispensable—you could not ignore him. . . . He said, indeed, in the later, more gossipy parts of his letter that he had been offered a baronetcy,† but he wanted Christopher to agree with his refusing it. Christopher would not want the beastly title after his death, and for himself he would be rather struck with the pip‡ than let that harlot—meaning herself—become Lady T. by any means of his. He had added, with his queer solicitude, "Of course if you thought of divorcing—which I wish to God you would, though I agree that you are right not to—and the title would go to the girl after my decease I'd take it gladly, for a title is a bit of a help after a divorce. But as it is I propose to refuse it and ask for a knighthood, if it won't too sicken you to have me a Sir. . . . For I hold no man ought to refuse an honour in times like these, as has been

---

* Ruggles, once a friend of Mark Tietjens, gathered and invented a set of lies about Christopher Tietjens, whom he despised, and told the Tietjenses' father that his son was a seducer of women, kept his friend's wife as his mistress, was a wastrel with money, and a French agent, and that Tietjens had a daughter by Valentine Wannop (whom his father may have believed to be his own daughter); which lies, the father believing, may have led to his death, if, as Tietjens believes, it was suicide. Ruggles also relayed some slander about Sylvia: that she was pregnant when Tietjens married her, and that Tietjens hushed up her elopement with Perowne. See *Some Do Not . . .* II.iii.

† A baronetcy makes one a member of a 'titled order, the lowest that is hereditary. . . . A baronet is a commoner the principle of the order being "to give rank, precedence, and title without privilege"': *OED*. Mark does not want a baronetcy because if Tietjens were to inherit it, which he emphatically does not want to do, Sylvia would become 'Lady Tietjens', an idea that Mark abhors. A knighthood, which also honours a commoner for services to the crown or country, is not hereditary; therefore, Mark is willing to accept that.

‡ According to Brewer's *Dictionary of Phrase and Fable*, 'to have' or 'to get the pip' is to be thoroughly fed up, downhearted, and miserable. It suggests a probable connection with the poultry disease 'pip', which causes fowls to pine away.

done by certain sickening intellectuals because it is like slapping the sovereign in the face and bound to hearten the other side, which no doubt was what was meant by those fellows."

There was no doubt that Mark—with the possible addition of the Wannops—made a very strong backing for Christopher if she decided to make a public scandal about him.... As for the Wannops ... the girl was negligible. Or possibly not, if she turned nasty and twisted Christopher round her fingers. But the old mother was a formidable figure—with a bad tongue, and viewed with a certain respect in places where people talked ... both on account of her late husband's position and of the solid sort of articles she wrote.... She, Sylvia, had gone to take a look at the place where these people lived ... a dreary street in an outer suburb, the houses—she knew enough about estates to know— what is called tile-healed, the upper parts of tile, the lower flimsy brick and the tiles in bad condition. Oldish houses really, in spite of their sham artistic aspect, and very much shadowed by old trees that must have been left to add to the picturesqueness.... The rooms poky, and they must be very dark.... The residence of extreme indigence, or of absolute poverty.... She understood that the old lady's income had so fallen off during the war that they had nothing to live on but what the girl made as a school-teacher, or a teacher of athletics in a girls' school.... She had walked two or three times up and down the street with the idea that the girl might come out: then it had struck her that that was rather an ignoble proceeding, really.... It was, for the matter of that, ignoble that she should have a rival who starved in an ashbin.... But that was what men were like: she might think herself lucky that the girl did not inhabit a sweetshop.... And the man, Macmaster, said that the girl had a good head and talked well, though the woman Macmaster said that she was a shallow ignoramus.... That last probably was not true; at any rate the girl had been the Macmaster woman's most intimate friend for many years—as long as they were sponging on Christopher and until, lower middle-class snobs as they were, they began to think that they could get into Society by carneying to herself.... * Still, the girl probably was a good talker and, if little, yet physically

---

*   Carney: 'To act in a wheedling or coaxing manner': OED.

uncommonly fit.... A good homespun article.... She wished
her no ill!

What was incredible was that Christopher should let her go on
starving in such a poverty-stricken place when he had something
like the wealth of the Indies at his disposal.... But the Tietjens
were hard people! You could see that in Mark's rooms ... and
Christopher would lie on the floor as lief as in a goose-feather bed.
And probably the girl would not take his money. She was quite
right. That was the way to keep him.... She herself had no want
of comprehension of the stimulation to be got out of parsimonious living.... In retreat at her convent she lay as hard and as
cold as any anchorite, and rose to the nuns' matins at four.

It was not, in fact, their fittings or food that she objected to—
it was that the lay-sisters, and some of the nuns, were altogether
too much of the lower classes for her to like to have always about
her.... That was why it was to the Dames Nobles* that she would
go, if she had to go into retreat for the rest of her life, according
to contract....

A gun manned by exhilarated anti-aircraft fellows, and so close
that it must have been in the hotel garden, shook her physically
at almost the same moment as an immense maroon pooped[22] off
on the quay at the bottom of the street in which the hotel was.
She was filled with annoyance at these schoolboy exercises. A
tall, purple-faced, white-moustached general of the more odious
type, appeared in the doorway and said that all the lights but two
must be extinguished and, if they took his advice, they would go
somewhere else. There were good cellars in the hotel. He loafed
about the room extinguishing the lights, couples and groups
passing him on the way to the door.... Tietjens looked up from
his letter—he was now reading one of Mrs. Wannop's—but

---

* In *Some Do Not* ... I.ii Father Consett suggests to Sylvia that she should go into retreat
for a month or two at a convent of Premonstratensian nuns near Birkenhead. In the
variant ending, printed as an appendix to that novel, she tells Tietjens she will go to
the Premonstratensians in Slough. That variant ends with Tietjens overhearing her
voice saying 'Paddington' to the cab driver. Though Ford removed this scene from
Some Do Not ..., he recast the material for *No More Parades*, in which it is pieced
together from Tietjens' memories of it; it becomes clear that he understood that she
meant him to take the word 'Paddington' as an indication that their marriage was over,
though he then begins to have doubts about whether it was her voice he heard. Here
she turns her mind to a convent populated by women more nearly of her own class,
that of the Ursuline Dames Nobles.

seeing that Sylvia made no motion he remained sunk in his chair. . . .

The old general said:

"Don't get up, Tietjens. . . . Sit down, lieutenant. . . . Mrs. Tietjens, I presume. . . . But of course I know you are Mrs. Tietjens. . . . There's a portrait of you in this week's. . . I forget the name. . . ." He sat down on the arm of a great leather chair and told her of all the trouble her escapade to that city had caused him. . . . He had been awakened immediately after a good lunch by some young officer on his staff who was scared to death by her having arrived without papers. His digestion had been deranged ever since. . . . Sylvia said she was very sorry. He should drink hot water and no alcohol with his lunch. She had had very important business to discuss with Tietjens, and she had really not understood that they wanted papers of grown-up people. The general began to expatiate on the importance of his office and the number of enemy agents his perspicacity caused to be arrested every day in that city and the lines of communication. . . .

Sylvia was overwhelmed at the ingenuity of Father Consett. She looked at her watch. The ten minutes were up, but there did not appear to be a soul in the dim place. . . . The father had—and no doubt as a Sign that there could be no mistaking!—completely emptied that room. It was like his humour!

To make certain, she stood up. At the far end of the room, in the dimness of the one other reading lamp that the general had not extinguished, two figures were rather indistinguishable. She walked towards them, the general at her side extending civilities all over her. He said that she need not be under any apprehension there. He adopted that device of clearing the room in order to get rid of the beastly young subalterns who would use the place to spoon in when the lights were turned down. She said she was only going to get a timetable from the far end of the room. . . .

The stab of hope that she had that one of the two figures would turn out to be the presentable man died. . . . They were a young mournful subaltern, with an incipient moustache and practically tears in his eyes, and an elderly, violently indignant bald-headed man in evening civilian clothes that must have been made by a country tailor. He was smacking his hands together to emphasize what, with great agitation, he was saying.

The general said that it was one of the young cubs on his own staff getting a dressing down from his dad for spending too much money. The young devils would get amongst the girls—and the old ones too. There was no stopping it. The place was a hotbed of ... He left the sentence unfinished. She would not believe the trouble it gave him.... That hotel itself.... The scandals....

He said she would excuse him if he took a little nap in one of the arm-chairs too far away to interfere with their business talk. He would have to be up half the night. He seemed to Sylvia a blazingly contemptible personage—too contemptible really for Father Consett to employ as an agent, in clearing the room.... But the omen was given. She had to consider her position. It meant—or did it?—that she had to be at war with the heavenly powers ! ... She clenched her hands....

In passing by Tietjens in his chair the general boomed out the words:

"I got your chit of this morning, Tietjens.... I must say ..."

Tietjens lumbered out of his chair and stood at attention, his leg-of-mutton hands stiffly on the seams of his breeches.

"It's pretty strong," the general said, "marking a charge-sheet sent down from *my* department: *Case explained.* We don't lay charges without due thought. And Lance-Corporal Berry is a particularly reliable N.C.O. I have difficulty enough to get them. Particularly after the late riots. It takes courage, I can tell you."

"If," Tietjens said, "you would see fit, sir, to instruct the G.M.P. not to call Colonial troops damned conscripts, the trouble would be over.... We're instructed to use special discretion, as officers, in dealing with troops from the Dominions. They are said to be very susceptible of insult...."

The general suddenly became a boiling pot from which fragments of sentences came away: *damned* insolence; court of inquiry; damned conscripts they were too. He calmed enough to say:

"They *are* conscripts, your men, aren't they? They give me more trouble ... I should have thought you would have wanted...."

Tietjens said:

"No, sir. I have not a man in my unit, as far as it's Canadian or British Columbian, that is not voluntarily enlisted...."

The general exploded to the effect that he was bringing the whole matter before the G.O.C.I.C.'s department. Campion could deal with it how he wished: it was beyond himself. He began to bluster away from them; stopped; directed a frigid bow to Sylvia who was not looking at him; shrugged his shoulders and stormed off.

It was difficult for Sylvia to get hold again of her thoughts in the smoking-room, for the evening was entirely pervaded with military effects that seemed to her the pranks of schoolboys. Indeed, after Cowley, who had by now quite a good skinful of liquor, had said to Tietjens:

"By Jove, I would not like to be you and a little bit on if old Blazes caught sight of you to-night," she said to Tietjens with real wonder:

"You don't mean to say that a gaga old fool like that could have any possible influence over you . . . *You!*'

Tietjens said:

"Well, it's a troublesome business, all this. . . . "

She said that it so appeared to be, for before he could finish his sentence an orderly was at his elbow extending, along with a pencil, a number of dilapidated papers. Tietjens looked rapidly through them, signing one after the other and saying intermittently:

"It's a trying time." "We're massing troops up the line as fast as we can go." "And with an endlessly changing personnel. . . . " He gave a snort of exasperation and said to Cowley: "That horrible little Pitkins has got a job as bombing instructor. He can't march the draft. . . . Who the deuce am I to detail? Who the deuce is there? . . . You know all the little . . . " He stopped because the orderly could hear. A smart boy. Almost the only smart boy left him.

Cowley barged out of his seat and said he would telephone the mess to see who was there. . . . Tietjens said to the boy:

"Sergeant-Major Morgan made out these returns of religions in the draft?"

The boy answered: "No, sir, I did. They're all right." He pulled a slip of paper out of his tunic pocket and said shyly:

"If you would not mind signing this, sir . . . I can get a lift on an A.S.C. trolly that's going to Boulogne to-morrow at six. . . . "

Tietjens said:

"No, you can't have leave. I can't spare you. What's it for?"

The boy said almost inaudibly that he wanted to get married.

Tietjens, still signing, said: "Don't.... Ask your married pals what it's like!"

The boy, scarlet in his khaki, rubbed the sole of one foot on the instep of the other. He said that saving madam's presence it was urgent. It was expected any day now. She was a real good gel. Tietjens signed the boy's slip and handed it to him without looking up. The boy stood with his eyes on the ground. A diversion came from the telephone, which was at the far end of the room. Cowley had not been able to get on to the camp because an urgent message with regard to German espionage was coming through to the sleeping general.

Cowley began to shout: "For goodness' sake hold the line.... For goodness' sake hold the line.... I'm not the general.... I'm *not* the general...." Tietjens told the orderly to awaken the sleeping warrior. A violent scene at the mouth of the quiescent instrument took place. The general roared to know who was the officer speaking.... Captain Bubbleyjocks.... Captain Cuddlestocks ... what in hell's name! And who was he speaking for? ... Who? Himself? ... Urgent was it? ... Didn't he know the proper procedure was by writing? ... Urgent damnation! ... Did he not know where he was? ... In the First Army by the Cassell Canal.... Well then ... But the spy was in L. of C. territory, across the canal.... The French civilian authorities were very concerned.... They were, damn them! ... And damn the officer. And damn the French *maire*. And damn the horse the supposed spy rode upon.... And when the officer was damned let him write to First Army Headquarters about it and attach the horse and the bandoliers as an exhibit....

There was a great deal more of it. Tietjens,[23] reading his papers still, intermittently explained the story as it came in fragments over the telephone in the general's repetitions.... Apparently the French civilian authorities of a place called Warendonck had been alarmed by a solitary horseman in English uniform who had been wandering desultorily about their neighbourhood for several days, seeming to want to cross the canal bridges, but finding them guarded.... There was an immense artillery dump in the neighbourhood, said to be the largest in the world, and the Germans dropped bombs as thick as peas all over those parts in the hopes of hitting it. . . . Apparently the officer speaking was in charge of the canal bridgehead guards: but, as he was in First Army country, it was obviously an act of the utmost impropriety to awaken a general in charge of the spy-catching apparatus on the other side of the canal. . . . The general, returning past them to an arm-chair farther from the telephone, emphasized this point of view with great vigour.

The orderly had returned; Cowley went once more to the telephone, having consumed another liqueur brandy. Tietjens finished his papers and went through them rapidly again. He said to the boy: "Got anything saved up?" The boy said: "A fiver and a few bob." Tietjens said: "How many bob?" The boy: "Seven, sir." Tietjens, fumbling clumsily in an inner pocket and a little pocket beneath his belt, held out one leg-of-mutton fist and said: "There! That will double it. Ten pounds fourteen! But it's very improvident of you. See that you save up a deuced lot more against the next one. Accouchements are confoundedly expensive things, as you'll learn, and ring money* doesn't stretch for ever! . . ." He called out to the retreating boy: "Here, orderly, come back. . . ." He added: "Don't let it get all over camp. . . . I can't afford to subsidize all the seven-months children in the battalion. . . . I'll recommend you for paid lance-corporal when you return from leave if you go on as well as you have done." He called the boy back again to ask him why Captain McKechnie had not signed the papers. The boy stuttered and stammered that Captain McKechnie was . . . He was . . .

Tietjens muttered: "Good God!" beneath his breath. He said: "The captain has had another nervous breakdown. . . ." The orderly accepted the phrase with gratitude. That was it. A nervous breakdown. They say he had been very queer at mess. About divorce. Or the captain's uncle. A barrow-night!† Tietjens said: "Yes, yes." He half rose in his chair and looked at Sylvia. She exclaimed painfully:

"You can't go. I insist that you can't go." He sank down again

---

* 'A wife's allowance from the military': Partridge's *Dictionary of Slang*.
† A humorous phrase for 'baronet', used by Captain Marryat, whom Ford read as a child.

and muttered wearily that it was very worrying. He had been put in charge of this officer by General Campion. He ought not to have left the camp at all perhaps. But McKechnie had seemed better. A great deal of the calmness of her insolence had left her. She had expected to have the whole night in which luxuriously to torment the lump opposite her. To torment him and to allure him. She said:

"You have settlements to come to now and here that will affect your whole life. Our whole lives! You propose to abandon them because a miserable little nephew of your miserable little friend. . . . "[24] She added in French: "Even as it is you cannot pay any attention to these serious matters, because of these childish pre-occupations of yours. That is to be intolerably insulting to me!" She was breathless.

Tietjens asked the orderly where Captain McKechnie was now. The orderly said he had left the camp. The colonel of the depot had sent a couple of officers as a search-party. Tietjens told the orderly to go and find a taxi. He could have a ride himself up to camp. The orderly said taxis would not be running on account of the air-raid. Could he order the G.M.P. to requisition one on urgent military service? The exhilarated air-gun pooped off thereupon three times from the garden. For the next hour it went off every two or three minutes. Tietjens said: "Yes! Yes!" to the orderly. The noises of the air-raid became more formidable. A blue express letter of French civilian make was handed to Tietjens. It was from the duchess to inform him that coal for the use of greenhouses was forbidden by the French Government. She did not need to say that she relied on his honour to ensure her receiving her coal through the British military authorities, and she asked for an immediate reply. Tietjens expressed real annoyance while he read this. Distracted by the noise, Sylvia cried out that the letter must be from Valentine Wannop in Rouen. Did not the girl intend to let him have an hour in which to settle the whole business of his life? Tietjens moved to the chair next to hers.[25] He handed her the duchess's letter.

He began a long, slow, serious explanation with a long, slow, serious apology. He said he regretted very much that when she should have taken the trouble to come so far in order to do him the honour to consult him about a matter which she would have been perfectly at liberty to settle for herself, the extremely serious military position should render him so liable to interruption. As far as he was concerned Groby was entirely at her disposal with all that it contained. And of course a sufficient income for the upkeep.

She exclaimed in an access of sudden and complete despair:

"That means that you do not intend to live there." He said that that must settle itself later. The war would no doubt last a good deal longer. While it lasted there could be no question of his coming back. She said that that meant that he intended to get killed. She warned him that, if he got killed, she would cut down the great cedar at the south-west corner of Groby. It kept all the light out of the principal drawing-room and the bedrooms above it. . . . He winced: he certainly winced at that. She regretted that she had said it. It was along other lines that she desired to make him wince.

He said that, apart from his having no intention of getting himself killed, the matter was absolutely out of his hands. He had to go where he was ordered to go and do what he was told to do.

She exclaimed:

"You! *You!* Isn't it ignoble. That you should be at the beck and call of these ignoramuses. You!"

He went on explaining seriously that he was in no great danger—in no danger at all unless he was sent back[26] to his battalion. And he was not likely to be sent back to his battalion unless he disgraced himself or showed himself negligent where he was. That was unlikely. Besides his category was so low that he was not eligible for his battalion, which, of course, was in the line. She ought to understand that every one that she saw employed there was physically unfit for the line. She said:

"That's why they're such an awful lot. . . . It is not to this place that one should come to look for a presentable man. . . . Diogenes* with his lantern was nothing to it."

He said:

"There's that way of looking at it. . . . It is quite true that most of . . . let's say *your* friends . . . were killed off during the early

---

* Diogenes of Sinope (c. 400–325 BCE), a Cynic philosopher, went through the streets of Athens in daylight with a lamp in his hand seeking to find an honest man.

days, or if they're still going they're in more active employments."[27] What she called presentableness was very largely a
matter of physical fitness.... The horse, for instance, that he
rode was rather a crock.... But though it was German and not
thoroughbred it contrived to be up to his weight.... Her friends,
more or less, of before the war were professional soldiers or of the
type. Well, they were gone: dead or snowed under. But on the
other hand, this vast town full of crocks did keep the thing going,
if it could be made to go. It was not they that hindered the show:
if it was hindered, that was done by her much less presentable
friends, the ministry who, if they were professionals at all were
professional boodlers.

She exclaimed with bitterness:

"Then why didn't you stay at home to check them, if they *are*
boodlers?"[28] She added that the only people at home who kept
social matters going at all with any life were precisely the more
successful political professionals. When you were with them you
would not know there was any war. And wasn't that what was
wanted? Was the *whole* of life to be given up to ignoble horseplay?
... She spoke with increased rancour because of the increasing
thump and rumble of the air-raid.... Of course the politicians
were ignoble beings that, before the war, you would not have
thought of having in your house.... But whose fault was that, if
not that of the better classes, who had gone away leaving England
a dreary wilderness of fellows without consciences or traditions
or manners? And she added some details of the habits at a country
house of a member of the Government whom she disliked.
"And," she finished up, "it's your fault. Why aren't *you* Lord
Chancellor, or Chancellor of the Exchequer, instead of whoever
is, for I am sure I don't know? You could have been, with your
abilities and your interests. Then things would have been efficiently and honestly conducted. If your brother Mark, with not
a tithe of your abilities can be a permanent head of a department,
what could you not have risen to with your gifts, and your influence ... and your integrity?" And she ended up: "Oh,
Christopher!" on almost a sob.

Ex-Sergeant-Major Cowley, who had come back from the telephone, and during an interval in the thunderings, had heard some
of Sylvia's light cast on the habits of members of the home

Government, so that his jaw had really hung down, now, in
another interval, exclaimed:

"Hear, hear! Madam! . . . There is nothing the captain might
not have risen to. . . . He is doing the work of a brigadier now on
the pay of an acting captain. . . . And the treatment he gets is
scandalous. . . . Well, the treatment we all get is scandalous,
tricked and defrauded as we are all at every turn. . . . And look at
this new start with the draft. . . . " They had ordered the draft to
be ready and countermanded it, and ordered it to be ready and
countermanded it, until no one knew whether he stood on is 'ed
or is 'eels. . . . It was to have gone off last night: when they'd 'ad
it marched down to the station they 'ad it marched back and told
them all it would not be wanted for six weeks. . . . Now it was to
be got ready to go before daylight to-morrow morning in motor-
lorries to the rail Ondekoeter way, the rail here 'aving been
sabotaged! . . . Before daylight so that the enemy aeroplanes
should not see it on the road. . . . Wasn't that a thing to break the
'arts of men *and* horderly rooms? It was outrageous. Did they
suppose the 'Uns did things like that?

He broke off to say with husky enthusiasm of affection to Tietjens: "Look 'ere, old . . . I mean, sir. . . . There's *no* way of getting
hold of an officer to march the draft. Them as are eligible gets to
'ear of what drafts is going and they've all bolted into their
burries. Not a man of 'em will be back in camp before five to-
morrow morning. Not when they 'ears there's a draft to go at four
of mornings like this. . . . Now . . . " His voice became husky with
emotion as he offered to take the draft hisself to oblige Captain
Tietjens. And the captain knew he could get a draft off pretty
near as good as himself: or very near. As for the draft-conducting
major he lived in that hotel and he, Cowley, 'ad seen 'im. No four
in the morning for 'im. He was going to motor to Ondekoeter
Station about seven. So there was no sense in getting the draft
off before five, and it was still dark then: too dark for the 'Un
planes to see what was moving. He'd be glad if the captain would
be up at the camp by five to take a final look and to sign any
papers that only the commanding officer could sign. But he knew
the captain had had no sleep the night before because of his,
Cowley's, infirmity, mostly, so he couldn't do less than give up a
day and a half of his leave to taking the draft. Besides, he was

going home for the duration and he would not mind getting a look at the old places they'd seen in 'fourteen, for the last time as a Cook's tourist . . . .

Tietjens, who was looking noticeably white, said:

"Do you remember O Nine Morgan at Noircourt?"

Cowley said:

"No. . . . Was 'e there? In your company, I suppose? . . . The man you mean that was killed yesterday. Died in your arms owing to my oversight. I ought to have been there." He said to Sylvia with the gloating idea N.C.O.'s had that wives liked to hear of their husband's near escapes: "Killed within a foot of the captain, 'e was.[29] An 'orrible shock it must 'ave been for the captain." A horrible mess. . . . The captain held him in his arms while he died. . . . As if he'd been a baby. Wonderful tender, the captain was! Well, you're apt to be when it's one of your own men. . . . No rank then! "Do you know the only time the King must salute a private soldier and the private takes no notice? . . . When 'e's dead. . . ."

Both Sylvia and Tietjens were silent—and silvery white in the greenish light from the lamp. Tietjens indeed had shut his eyes. The old N.C.O. went on rejoicing to have the floor to himself. He had got on his feet preparatory to going up to camp, and he swayed a little. . . .

"No," he said and he waved his cigar gloriously, "I don't remember O Nine Morgan at Noircourt. . . . But I remember . . . "

Tietjens, with his eyes still shut, said:

"I only thought he might have been a man. . . . "

"No," the old fellow went on imperiously, "I don't remember 'im. . . . But, Lord, I remember what happened to you!" He looked down gloriously upon Sylvia: "The captain caught 'is foot in. . . . You'd never believe what 'e caught 'is foot in! Never! . . . A pretty quiet affair it was, with a bit of moonlight. . . . Nothing much in the way of artillery. . . . Perhaps we surprised the 'Uns proper, perhaps they were wanting to give up their front-line trenches for a purpose. . . . There was next to no one in 'em. . . . I know it made me nervous. . . . My heart was fair in my boots, because there was so little doing! . . . It was when there was little doing that the 'Uns could be expected to do their worst. . . . Of course there was some machine-gunning. . . . There was one in particular away to the right of us.... And the moon, it was shining in the early morning. Wonderful peaceful. And a little mist.... And frozen hard.... Hard as you wouldn't believe.... Enough to make the shells dangerous."

Sylvia said:

"It's not always mud, then?" and Tietjens, to her: "He'll stop if you don't like it." She said monotonously: "No ... I want to hear."

Cowley drew himself for his considerable effect:

"Mud!" he said. "Not then.... Not by half.... I tell you, ma'am, we trod on the frozen faces of dead Germans as we doubled.... A terrible lot of Germans we'd killed a day or so before.... That was no doubt the reason they give up the trenches so easy: difficult to attack from, they was.... Anyhow, they left the dead for us to bury, knowing probably they were going, with a better 'eart! ... But it fair put the wind up me anyhow to think of what their counter-attack was going to be.... The counter-attack is always ten times as bad as the preliminary resistance. They 'as you with the rear of their trenches—the parados, we call it—as your front to boot. So I was precious glad when the moppers-up and supports come and went through us.... Laughing, they was.... Wiltshires.... My missus comes from that county.... Mrs. Cowley, I mean.... So I'd seen the captain go down earlier on and I'd said: 'There's another of the best stopped one....'" He dropped his voice a little: he was one of the noted yarners of the regiment: "Caught 'is foot, 'e 'ad, between two 'ands.... Sticking up out of the frozen ground.... As it might be in prayer.... Like this!" He elevated his two hands, the cigar between the fingers, the wrists close together and the fingers slightly curled inwards: "Sticking up in the moon-light.... Poor devil!"

Tietjens said:

"I thought perhaps it was O Nine Morgan I saw that night.... Naturally I looked dead.... I hadn't a breath in my body.... And I saw a Tommy put his rifle to his pal's upper arm and fire.... As I lay on the ground...."

Cowley said:

"Ah, you saw that.... I heard the men talking of it.... But they naturally did not say who and where!"

Tietjens said with a negligence that did not ring true:

"The wounded man's name was Stilicho.... A queer name.... I suppose it's Cornish.... It was B Company in front of us."

"You didn't bring 'em to a court martial?"[30] Cowley asked. Tietjens said: No. He could not be quite certain. Though he *was* certain.[31] But he had been worrying about a private matter. He had been worrying about it while he lay on the ground and that rather obscured his sense of what he saw. Besides, he said faintly, an officer must use his judgement. He had judged it better in this case not to have seen the ... His voice had nearly faded away: it was clear to Sylvia that he was coming to a climax of some mental torture. Suddenly he exclaimed to Cowley:

"Supposing I let him off one life to get him killed two years after. My God! That would be too beastly!"

Cowley snuffled in Tietjens' ear something that Sylvia did not catch—consolatory and affectionate. That intimacy was more than she could bear. She adopted her most negligent tone to ask:

"I suppose the one man had been trifling with the other's girl. Or wife!"

Cowley exploded:[32] "God bless you, no! They'd agreed upon it between them. To get one of them sent 'ome and the other, at any rate, out of *that* 'ell, leading him back to the dressing-station."

She said:

"You mean to say that a man would do *that*, to get out of it? ..."

Cowley said:

"God bless you, ma'am, with the '*ell* the Tommies 'as of it.... For it's in the line that the differences between the Other Ranks' life[33] and the officers' comes in.... I tell you, ma'am, old soldier as I am, and I've been in seven wars one with another ... there were times in this war when I could have shrieked, holding my right hand down...."

He paused and said: "It was my idea.... And it's been a good many others', that if I 'eld my 'and up over the parapet with perhaps my hat on it, in two minutes there would be a German sharpshooter's bullet through it. And then me for Blighty,[*] as the

---

[*] Army slang for 'England, home', deriving from a Hindustani word, *vilāyatī* (pronounced *biayati*), meaning 'foreign, and esp. European': OED. A wound serious enough to send a soldier back to England was also called 'a Blighty'.

soldiers say.... And if that could happen to me, a regimental sergeant-major, with twenty-three years in the service ..."

The bright orderly came in, said he had found a taxi, and melted into the dimness.

"A man," the sergeant-major said, "would take the risk of being shot for wounding his pal.... They get to love their pals, passing the love of women...." Sylvia exclaimed: "Oh!" as if at a pang of toothache. "They do, ma'am," he said, "it's downright touching...."

He was by now very unsteady as he stood, but his voice was quite clear. That was the way it took him. He said to Tietjens:

"It's queer, what you say about home worries taking up your mind.... I remember in the Afghan campaign, when we were in the devil of a hot corner, I got a letter from my wife, Mrs. Cowley, to say that our Winnie had the measles.... And there was only one difference between me and Mrs. Cowley: I said that a child must have flannel next its³⁴ skin, and she said flannelette was good enough. Wiltshire doesn't hold by wool as Lincolnshire does. Long fleeces the Lincolnshire sheep have.... And dodging the Afghan bullets all day among the boulders as we was, all I could think of.... For you know, ma'am, being a mother yourself, that the great thing with measles is to keep a child warm.... I kep' saying to myself—'arf crying I was—'If she only keeps wool next Winnie's skin! If she only keeps wool next Winnie's skin!'... But you know that, being a mother yourself. I've seen your son's photo on the captain's dressing-table. Michael, 'is name is.... So you see, the captain doesn't forget you and 'im."

Sylvia said in a clear voice:

"Perhaps you would not go on!"

Distracted as she was by the anti-air-gun in the garden, though it was on the other side of the hotel and permitted you to get in a sentence or two before splitting your head with a couple of irregular explosions, she was still more distracted by a sudden vision—a remembrance of Christopher's face when their boy had had a temperature of 105°³⁵ with the measles, up at his sister's house in Yorkshire. He had taken the responsibility, which the village doctor would not face, of himself placing the child in a bath full of split ice.... She saw him bending, expressionless in the strong lamp-light, with the child in his clumsy arms over the

glittering, rubbled surface of the bath. . . . He was just as expressionless then as now. . . . He reminded her now of how he had
been then: some strain in the lines of the face perhaps that she
could not analyse. . . . Rather as if he had a cold in the head—a
little suffocating, with suppressing his emotions, of course: his
eyes looking at nothing. You would not have said that he even
saw the child—heir to Groby and all that! . . . Something had
said to her, just in between two crashes of the gun: "It's his own
child. He went as you might say down to hell to bring it back to
life. . . ."* She knew it was Father Consett saying that. She knew
it was true: Christopher had been down to hell to bring the child
back. . . . Fancy facing its pain in that dreadful bath! . . . The
thermometer had dropped, running down under their eyes. . . .
Christopher had[36] said: "A good heart, he's got! A good plucked
one!" and then held his breath, watching the thin filament of
bright mercury drop to normal. . . . She said now, between her
teeth: "The child is his property as much as the damned estate. . . .
Well, I've got them both. . . ."

But it wasn't at this juncture that she wanted him tortured over
that. So, when the second gun had done its crash, she had said to
the bibulous old man:

"I wish you would not go on!" And Christopher had been
prompt to the rescue of the *convenances*† with:

"Mrs. Tietjens does not see eye to eye with us in some matters!"

She said to herself: "Eye to eye! My God! . . ." The whole of
this affair, the more she saw of it, overwhelmed her with a sense
of hatred. . . . And of depression! . . . She saw Christopher buried
in this welter of fools, playing a schoolboy's game of make-
believe. But of a make-believe that was infinitely formidable and
infinitely sinister. . . . The crashings of the gun and of all the
instruments for making noise seemed to her so atrocious and
odious because they were, for her, the silly pomp of a schoolboy-
man's game. . . . Campion, or some similar schoolboy, said:
"Hullo! Some German airplanes about. . . . That lets us out on

---

* One of several allusions to and echoes of Euripides' *Alcestis* in the tetralogy. Ford's
   intimate familiarity with the *Alcestis* derives from his translation of it: 'This writer's
   first literary work after being demobilized at the end of the last war was the translation of the *Alcestis*': *The March of Literature* 118.
† The 'conventional proprieties of life or social intercourse': *OED*.

the air-gun! Let's have some pops!"... As they fire guns in the
park on the King's birthday. It was sheer insolence to have a gun
in the garden of an hotel where people of quality might be
sleeping or wishing to converse!

At home she had been able to sustain the conviction that it
was such a game.... Anywhere: at the house of a minister of the
Crown, at dinner, she had only to say: "Do let us leave off talking
of these odious things...." And immediately there would be ten
or a dozen voices, the minister's included, to agree with Mrs. Tietjens of Groby that they had altogether too much of it....

But here! ... She seemed to be in the very belly of the ugly
affair.... It moved and moved, under your eyes dissolving, yet
always there. As if you should try to follow one diamond of
pattern in the coil of an immense snake that was in irrevocable
motion.... It gave her a sense of despair: the engrossment[37] of
Tietjens, in common with the engrossment of this disreputable
toper. She had never seen Tietjens put his head together with any
soul before: he was the lonely buffalo.... Now! Anyone: any
fatuous staff-officer, whom at home he would never so much as
have spoken to: any trustworthy beer-sodden sergeant, any street
urchin[38] dressed up as orderly.... They had only to appear and
all his mind went into a close-headed conference over some
ignoble point in the child's game: the laundry, the chiropody, the
religions, the bastards ... of millions of the indistinguishable....[39] Or their deaths as well! But, in heaven's name what
hypocrisy, or what inconceivable chicken-heartedness was this?
They promoted this beanfeast of carnage for their own ends: they
caused the deaths of men in inconceivable holocausts of pain and
terror. Then they had crises of agony over the death of one single
man. For it was plain to her that Tietjens was in the middle of a
full nervous breakdown. Over one man's death! She had never
seen him so suffer; she had never seen him so appeal for sympathy:
him, a cold fiend of reticence! Yet he was now in an agony! *Now!*
... And she began to have a sense of the infinitely spreading
welter of pain, going away to an eternal horizon of night.... 'Ell
for the Other Ranks![40] Apparently it was hell for the officers as
well.

The real compassion in the voice of that snuffling, half-
drunken old man[41] had given her a sense of that enormous

wickedness.... These horrors, these infinities of pain, this atrocious condition of the world had been brought about in order that
men should indulge themselves in orgies of promiscuity.... That
in the end was at the bottom of male honour, of male virtue,
observance of treaties, upholding of the flag.... An immense
warlock's carnival of appetites, lusts, ebrieties....* And once set
in motion there was no stopping it.... This state of things would
never cease.... Because once they had tasted of the joy—the
blood—of this game, who would let it end? ... These men talked
of these things that occupied them there with the lust of men
telling dirty stories in smoking-rooms....† That was the only
parallel!

There was no stopping it, any more than there was any stopping the by now all but intoxicated ex-sergeant-major. He was
off! With, as might be expected, advice to a young couple with
differences of opinion! The wine had made him bold!

In the depth of her pictures of these horrors, snatches of his
wisdom penetrated to her intelligence.... Queer snatches....
She was getting it certainly in the neck! ... Someone, to add to
the noise, had started some mechanical musical instrument in an
adjacent hall.

"Corn an' lasses
Served by Ras'us!"‡

a throaty voice proclaimed,

"I'd be tickled to death to know that I could go
And stay right there ... "

---

* 'instances of intoxication': OED.
† Cf. The Good Soldier 14: 'what do I know even of the smoking-room? Fellows come in
  and tell the most extraordinarily gross stories – so gross that they will positively give
  you a pain. And yet they'd be offended if you suggested that they weren't the sort of
  person you could trust your wife alone with.'
‡ 'We'll Have A Jubilee In My Old Kentucky Home' (1915); lyrics by Coleman Goetz,
  music by Walter Donaldson. The chorus goes: 'I've got a sneaky feeling 'round my
  heart / That I want to settle down / I guess I'll pack my grip and take a trip / To a good
  old southern town. / You can have your high brow airs, / Just give me three good squares
  with the corn and 'lasses [i.e. molasses], served by Rastus; / I'll be tickled to death
  to know that I can stay right there, / And I'll never care to roam; / Come on
  along with me and have a jubilee, / In my old Kentucky Home'. See http://www.
  halcyondaysmusic.com/vintage-music-january2006.php

The ex-sergeant-major was adding to her knowledge the odd detail that when he, Sergeant-Major Cowley, went to the wars— seven of them—his missus, Mrs. Cowley, spent the first three days and nights unpicking and re-hemstitching every sheet and pillow-slip in the 'ouse. To keep 'erself f'm thinking.... This was apparently meant as a reproof or an exhortation to her, Sylvia Tietjens.... Well, he was all right! Of the same class as Father Consett, and with the same sort of wisdom.

The gramophone howled: a new note of rumbling added itself to the exterior tumult and continued through six mitigated thumps of the gun in the garden.... In the next interval, Cowley was in the midst of a valedictory address to her. He was asking her to remember that the captain had had a sleepless night the night before.

There occurred to her irreverent mind a sentence of one of the Duchess of Marlborough's letters to Queen Anne.* The duchess had visited the general during one of his campaigns in Flanders. "My Lord," she wrote, "did me the honour three times in his boots!"... The sort of thing she would remember.... She would—she *would*—have tried it on the sergeant-major, just to see Tietjens' face, for the sergeant-major would not have understood.... And who cared if he did! ... He was bibulously skirting round the same idea....

But the tumult increased to an incredible volume: even the thrillings of the near-by gramophone of two hundred horse-power, or whatever it was, became mere shimmerings of a gold thread in a drab fabric of sound. She screamed blasphemies[42] that she was hardly aware of knowing. She had to scream against the noise: she was no more responsible for the blasphemy than if she had lost her identity under an anaesthetic. She *had* lost her identity.... She was one of this crowd!

The general woke in his chair and gazed malevolently at their group as if they alone were responsible for the noise. It dropped. Dead! You only knew it, because you caught the tail end of a belated woman's scream from the hall and the general shouting:

---

* One of Queen Anne's favourites, Sarah, Duchess of Marlborough, wife of John Churchill, 1st Duke of Marlborough (1650–1722), brags to the queen that she has had sexual intercourse three times with her husband at his battlefield headquarters, which is exactly what Sylvia seeks with Tietjens.

"For God's sake don't start that damned gramophone again!" In the blessed silence, after preliminary wheezes and guitar noises, an astonishing voice burst out:

"Less than the dust ...
Before thy char ... "*

And then, stopping after a murmur of voices, began:

"Pale hands I loved ... "†

The general sprang from his chair and rushed to the hall....
He came back crestfallenly.

"It's some damned civilian big-wig.... A novelist, they say.... I can't stop *him*...." He added with disgust: "The hall's full of young beasts and harlots.... *Dancing!* ... The melody had indeed, after a buzz, changed to a languorous and interrupted variation of a waltz. "Dancing in the dark!" the general said with enhanced disgust.... "And the Germans may be here at any moment.... If they knew what I know ... "

Sylvia called across to him:

"Wouldn't it be fun to see the blue uniform with the silver buttons again and some decently set-up men? ... "

The general shouted:

"*I'd* be glad to see them.... I'm sick to death of these...."

Tietjens took up something he had been saying to Cowley:[43] what it was Sylvia did not hear, but Cowley answered, still droning on with an idea Sylvia thought they had got past:

"I remember when I was sergeant in Quetta,‡ I detailed a man—called Herring—for watering the company horses, after he begged off it because he had a fear of horses.... A horse got him down in the river and drowned 'im.... Fell with him and put its

---

*   Laurence Hope, 'Less Than the Dust', from *The Garden of Kama* (1901); it begins: 'Less than the dust, beneath thy Chariot wheel'; set by Amy Woodforde-Finden, née Ward (1860–1919): 'Less than the dust', no. 2 of *Four Indian Love Lyrics* (1903). There was a wartime film *Less Than the Dust* (1916) with Mary Pickford.

†   Another setting by Amy Woodforde-Finden, 'Kashmiri Song': 'Pale hands I loved beside the Shalimar, / Where are you now?'

‡   Now in Pakistan, Quetta is near the borders of Afghanistan and Iran. It became part of the British Empire in 1876.

foot on his face.... A fair sight he was.... It wasn't any good my saying anything about military exigencies.... Fair put me off my feed, it did.... Cost me a fortune in Epsom salts...."

Sylvia was about to scream[44] out that if Tietjens did not like men being killed it ought to sober him in his war-lust, but Cowley continued meditatively:

"Epsom salts they say is the cure for it.... For seeing your dead.... And of course you should keep off women for a fortnight.... I know I did. Kept seeing Herring's face with the hoof-mark. And ... there was a piece: a decent bit of goods in what we called the Government Compound...."[45]

He suddenly exclaimed:

"Saving your ... Ma'am, I'm ..." He stuck the stump of the cigar into his teeth and began assuring Tietjens that he could be trusted with the draft next morning, if only Tietjens would put him into the taxi.

He went away, leaning on Tietjens' arm, his legs at an angle of sixty degrees with the carpet....

"He can't...." Sylvia said to herself, "he can't, not ... If he's a gentleman.... After all that old fellow's hints.... He'd be a damn coward if he kept off.... For a fortnight.... And who else is there not a public ..." She said: "O God! ..."

The old general, lying in his chair, turned his face aside to say:

"I wouldn't, madam, not if I were you, talk about the blue uniform with silver buttons here.... *We*, of course, understand...."

She said: "You see ... even that extinct volcano ... He's undressing me with his eyes full of blood veins.... Then why can't *he*? ..."

She said aloud:

"Oh, but even you, general, said you were sick of your companions!"[46]

She said to herself:

"Hang it! ... I will have the courage of my convictions ... No man shall say I am a coward...."

She said:

"Isn't it saying the same thing as you, general, to say that I'd rather be made love to by a well-set-up man in blue and silver— or anything else!—than by most of the people one sees here! ..."

The general said:

"Of course, if you put it that way, madam...."

She said:

"What other way should a woman put it?" ... She reached to the table and filled herself a lot of brandy. The old general was leering towards her:

"Bless me," he said, "a lady who takes liquor like that...."

She said:

"You're a Papist, aren't you? With the name of O'Hara and the touch of the brogue you have ... And the devil you no doubt are with.... You know what.... Well, then ... It's with a special intention! ... As you say your Hail, Maries...."

With the liquor burning inside her she saw Tietjens loom in the dim light.

The general, to her bitter amusement, said to him:

"Your friend was more than a bit on.... Not the Society surely for madam!"

Tietjens said:

"I never expected to have the pleasure of dining with Mrs. Tietjens to-night.... That officer was celebrating his commission and I could not put him off...." The general said: "Oh, ah! Of course not.... I dare say ..." and settled himself again in his chair....

Tietjens was overwhelming her with his great bulk. She had still lost her breath.... He stooped over and said: It was the luck of the half-drunk; he said:

"They're dancing in the lounge...."

She coiled herself passionately into her wickerwork. It had dull blue cushions. She said:

"Not with anyone else.... I don't want any introductions...." Fiercely! ... He said:

"There's no one there that I could introduce you to...."

She said:

"Not if it's a charity!"

He said:

"I thought it might be rather dull.... It's six months since I danced...." She felt beauty flowing over all her limbs. She had a gown of gold tissue. Her matchless hair was coiled over her ears.... She was humming Venusberg music:* she knew music if she knew nothing else. . . .

She said: "You call the compounds where you keep the W.A.A.C.'s Venusbergs, don't you? Isn't it queer that Venus should be your own? . . . Think of poor Elisabeth!"

The room where they were dancing was very dark. . . . It was queer to be in his arms. . . . She had known better dancers. . . . He had looked ill. . . . Perhaps he was. . . . Oh, poor Valentine-Elisabeth. . . . What a funny position! . . . The good gramophone played. . . . *Destiny!* . . . You see, father! . . . In his arms! . . . Of course, dancing is not really. . . . But so near the real thing! So near! . . .[47] "Good luck to the special intention! . . ." She had almost kissed him on the lips. . . . All but! *Effleurer,*† the French call it. . . . But she was not as humble. . . . He had pressed her tighter. . . . All these months without . . . My lord did me honour . . . Good for Malbrouck *s'en va-t-en guerre.* . . .‡ He *knew* she had almost kissed him on the lips. . . . And that his lips had almost responded. . . . The civilian, the novelist, had turned out the last light. . . . Tietjens said, "Hadn't we better talk? . . ." She said: "In my room, then! I'm dog-tired. . . . I haven't slept for six nights. . . . In spite of drugs. . . ." He said: "Yes. Of course! Where else? . . ." Astonishingly. . . . Her gown[48] of gold tissue was like the colobium sindonis[49]§ the King wore at the coronation. . . . As they mounted the stairs she thought what a fat tenor Tannhäuser always was! . . . The Venusberg music was dinning in her ears. . . . She said: "Sixty-six inexpressibles!** I'm as sober as a judge . . . I need to be!"

---

*   Venusberg or the Mountain of Venus is a principal setting in Richard Wagner's *Tannhäuser* (1845) where the eponymous hero is the lover of the goddess, preferring her for the moment to his intended bride, Elisabeth. Given Sylvia's desire for Tietjens and disdain for Valentine, this music fits the occasion perfectly for her.

†   To graze or skim or touch lightly in passing over.

‡   *Marlbrough s'en va-t-en guerre* ('Marlborough has left for the war') is a popular folk song (sung to the same tune as 'For He's a Jolly Good Fellow') celebrating the Duke of Marlborough's campaign in the War of the Spanish Succession, which made him legendary as a military commander of genius. The song is another instance of Sylvia's knowledge of music that perfectly suits the present occasion.

§   A 'colobium' is 'A half-sleeved or sleeveless tunic or robe, such as was worn by the clergy of the early church, by the monks, and by kings at the ceremony of coronation' (*OED*), symbolising the divesting of the world's vanity and standing unadorned before God. 'Sindonis' means 'of sindon', 'A fine thin fabric of linen; a kind of cambric or muslin' (*OED*); 'A piece of this fabric used for various purposes: a. As a shroud, spec. that in which the body of Christ was wrapped' (*OED*).

**   *OED* gives a colloquial sense for 'inexpressibles' as a euphemism for breeches or trousers.

PART III

I

A SHADOW—the shadow of the General Officer Commanding in Chief—falling across the bar of light that the sunlight threw in at his open door seemed providentially to awaken Christopher Tietjens, who would have thought it extremely disagreeable to be found asleep by that officer. Very thin, graceful and gay with his scarlet gilt oak-leaves, and ribbons, of which he had many, the general was stepping attractively over the sill of the door, talking backwards over his shoulder, to someone outside. So, in the old days, Gods had descended![1] It was, no doubt, really the voices from without that had awakened Tietjens, but he preferred to think the matter a slight intervention of Providence, because he felt in need of a sign of some sort! Immediately[2] upon awakening he was not perfectly certain of where he was, but he had sense enough to answer with coherence the first question that the general put to him and to stand stiffly on his legs. The general had said:

"Will you be good enough to inform me, Captain Tietjens, why you have no fire-extinguishers in your unit? You are aware of the extremely disastrous consequences that would follow a conflagration in your lines?"

Tietjens said stiffly:

"It seems impossible to obtain them, sir."

The general said:

"How is this? You have indented for them in the proper quarter. Perhaps you do not know what the proper quarter is?"

Tietjens said:

"If this were a British unit, sir, the proper quarter would be the Royal Engineers." When he had sent his indent in for them to the Royal Engineers they informed him that this being a unit of troops from the Dominions, the quarter to which to apply was the Ordnance. On applying to the Ordnance, he was informed that no provision was made of fire-extinguishers for troops from the Dominions under Imperial officers, and that the proper course was to obtain them from a civilian firm in Great Britain, charging them against barrack damages. . . . He had applied to several firms of manufacturers, who all replied that they were forbidden to sell these articles to anyone but to the War Office direct. . . . "I am still applying to civilian firms," he finished.[3]

The officer accompanying the general was Colonel Levin, to whom, over his shoulder, the general said: "Make a note of that, Levin, will you? and get the matter looked into." He said again to Tietjens:

"In walking across your parade-ground I noticed that your officer in charge of your physical training knew conspicuously nothing about it. You had better put him on to cleaning out your drains. He was unreasonably dirty."

Tietjens said:

"The sergeant-instructor, sir, is quite competent. The officer is an R.A.S.C. officer. I have at the moment hardly any infantry officers in the unit. But officers have to be on these parades[4]—by A.C.I. They give no orders."

The general said dryly:

"I was aware from the officer's uniform of what arm he belonged to. I am not saying you do not do your best with the material at your command." From Campion on parade this was an extraordinary graciousness. Behind[5] the general's back Levin was making signs with his eyes which he meaningly closed and opened. The[6] general, however, remained extraordinarily dry in manner, his face having its perfectly expressionless air of studied politeness which allowed no muscle of its polished-cherry surface to move. The extreme politeness of the extremely great to the supremely unimportant!

He glanced round the hut markedly. It was Tietjens' own office and contained nothing but the blanket-covered tables and, hanging from a strut, an immense calendar on which days were roughly crossed out in red ink and blue pencil. He said:

"Go and get your belt. You will go round your cook-houses with me in a quarter of an hour. You can tell your sergeant-cook. What sort of cooking arrangements have you?"

Tietjens said:

"Very good cook-houses, sir."

The general said:

"You're extremely lucky, then. Extremely lucky! . . . Half the units like yours in this camp haven't anything but company cookers and field ovens in the open. . . ." He pointed with his crop at the open door. He repeated with extreme distinctness "Go and get your belt!" Tietjens wavered a very little on his feet. He said:

"You are aware, sir, that I am under arrest."

Campion imported a threat into his voice:

"I gave you," he said, "an order. To perform a duty!"

The terrific force of the command from above to below took Tietjens staggering through the door. He heard the general's voice say: "I'm perfectly aware he's not drunk." When he had gone four paces, Colonel Levin was beside him.

Levin was supporting him by the elbow. He whispered:

"The general wishes me to go with you if you are feeling unwell. You understand you are released from arrest!"[7] He exclaimed with a sort of rapture: "You're doing splendidly. . . . It's amazing. Everything I've ever told him about you. . . . Yours is the only draft that got off this morning. . . .

Tietjens grunted:

"Of course I understand that if I'm given an order to perform a duty, it means I am released from arrest." He[8] had next to no voice. He managed to say that he would prefer to go alone. He said: ". . . He's[9] forced my hand. . . . The last thing I want is to be released from arrest. . . ."

Levin said breathlessly:

"You *can't* refuse. . . . You can't upset him. . . . Why, you *can't*. . . . Besides, an officer cannot demand a court martial."[10]

"You look," Tietjens said, "like a slightly faded bunch of wall-flowers. . . . I'm sure I beg your pardon. . . . It came into my head!" The colonel drooped intangibly, his moustache a little ragged, his eyes a little rimmed, his shaving a little ridged. He exclaimed:

"Damn it! . . . Do you suppose I don't *care* what happens to you? . . . O'Hara came storming into my quarters at half-past three. . . . I'm not going to tell you what he said. . . ." Tietjens said gruffly:

"No, don't! I've all I can stand for the moment. . . ."

Levin[11] exclaimed desperately:

"I want you to understand. . . . It's impossible to believe anything against . . ."

Tietjens faced him, his teeth showing like a badger's. He said:

"Whom? . . . Against whom? Curse you!"

Levin said pallidly:

"Against . . . Against . . . either of you. . . ."[12]

"Then leave[13] it at that!" Tietjens said. He staggered a little until he reached the main lines. Then he marched. It was purgatory. They peeped at him from the corners of huts and withdrew. . . . But they always did peep at him from the corners of huts and withdraw! That is the habit of the Other Ranks on perceiving officers.[14] The fellow called McKechnie also looked out of a hut door. He too withdrew. . . . There was no mistaking that! He had the news. . . . On the other hand, McKechnie too was under a cloud. It might be his, Tietjens', duty, to strafe McKechnie to hell for having left camp last night. So he might be avoiding him. . . .[15] There was no knowing. . . . He lurched infinitesimally to the right. The road was rough.[16] His legs felt like detached and swollen objects that he dragged after him. He must master his legs. He mastered his legs. A batman carrying a cup of tea ran against him. Tietjens said: "Put[17] that down and fetch me the sergeant-cook at the double. Tell him the general's going round the cook-houses in a quarter of an hour." The batman ran, spilling the tea in the sunlight.

In his hut, which was dim and profusely decorated with the doctor's ideals of female beauty in every known form of pictorial reproduction, so that it might have been lined with peach-blossom, Tietjens had the greatest difficulty in getting into his belt. He had at first forgotten to remove his hat, then he put his head through the wrong opening; his fingers on the buckles operated like sausages. He inspected himself in the doctor's cracked shaving-glass; he was exceptionally well shaved.

He had shaved that morning at six-thirty: five minutes after the draft had got off. Naturally, the lorries had been an hour late. It was providential that he had shaved with extra care. An insolently calm man[18] was looking at him, the face divided in two by the crack in the glass: a naturally white-complexioned double-half of a face: a patch of high colour on each cheekbone; the pepper-and-salt hair ruffled, the white streaks extremely silver. He had gone very silver lately. But he swore he did not look worn. Not careworn. McKechnie said from behind his back:

"By Jove, what's this all about. The general's been strafing me to hell for not having my table tidy!"

Tietjens, still looking in the glass, said:

"You should keep your table tidy. It's the only strafe the battalion's had."

The general, then, must have been in the orderly room of which he had put McKechnie in charge. McKechnie went on, breathlessly:

"They say you knocked the general. . . ."

Tietjens said:

"Don't[19] you know enough to discount what they say in this town?" He said to himself: "That was all right!" He had spoken with a cool edge on a contemptuous voice.

He said to the sergeant-cook who was panting—another heavy, grey-moustached, very senior N.C.O.:

"The general's going round the cook-houses. . . . You be damn certain there's no dirty cook's clothing in the lockers!" He was fairly sure that otherwise his cook-houses would be all right. He had gone round them himself the morning of the day before yesterday. Or was it yesterday? . . .

It was the day after he had been up all night because the draft had been countermanded. . . . It didn't matter. He said:

"I wouldn't serve out white clothing to the cooks. . . . I bet you've got some hidden away, though it's against orders."

The sergeant looked away into the distance, smiled all-knowingly over his walrus moustache.

"The general likes to see 'em in white," he said, "and he won't know the white clothing has been countermanded."

Tietjens said:

"The snag is that the beastly cooks always will tuck some piece of beastly dirty clothing away in a locker rather than take the trouble to take it round to their quarters when they've changed."

Levin said with great distinctness:

"The general has sent me to you with this, Tietjens. Take a

sniff of it if you're feeling dicky. You've been up all night on end two nights running." He extended in the palm of his hand a bottle of smelling-salts in a silver section of tubing. He said the general suffered from vertigo now and then. Really he himself carried that restorative for the benefit of Miss de Bailly.

Tietjens asked himself why the devil the sight of that smelling-salts container reminded him of the brass handle of the bedroom door moving almost imperceptibly ... and incredibly. It was, of course, because Sylvia had on her illuminated dressing-table, reflected by the glass, just such another smooth, silver segment of tubing.... Was everything he saw going to remind him of the minute movement of that handle?

"You can do what you please," the sergeant-cook said, "but there will always be one piece of clothing in a locker for a G.O.C.I.C.'s inspection. And the general always walks straight up to that locker and has it opened. I've seen General Campion do it three times."

"If there's any found this time, the man it belongs to goes for a D.C.M.," Tietjens said. "See that there's a clean diet-sheet on the messing board."

"The generals really like to find dirty clothing," the sergeant-cook[20] said; "it gives them something to talk about if they don't know anything else about cook-houses.... I'll put up my own diet-sheet, sir.... I suppose you can keep the general back for twenty minutes or so? It's all I ask."

Levin said towards his rolling, departing back:

"That's a damn smart man. Fancy being as confident as that about an inspection.... Ugh! ..." and Levin shuddered in remembrance of inspections through which in his time he had passed.

"He's a damn smart man!" Tietjens said. He added to McKechnie:

"You might take a look at dinners in case the general takes it into his head to go round them."

McKechnie said darkly:

"Look here, Tietjens, are you in command of this unit or am I?"

Levin exclaimed sharply, for him:

"What's that? What the ..."

Tietjens said:

"Captain McKechnie complains that he is the senior officer and should command this unit."

Levin ejaculated:

"Of all the . . ." He addressed McKechnie with vigour: "My man, the command of these units is an appointment at disposition of headquarters. Don't let there be any mistake about that!"

McKechnie said doggedly:

"Captain Tietjens asked me to take the battalion this morning. I understood he was under. . . ."

"You," Levin said, "are attached to this unit for discipline and rations. You damn well understand that if some uncle or other of yours were not, to the general's knowledge, a protégé of Captain Tietjens', you'd be in a lunatic asylum at this moment. . . ."

McKechnie's face worked convulsively, he swallowed as men are said to swallow who suffer from hydrophobia. He lifted his fist and cried out:

"My un . . ."

Levin said:

"If you say another word you go under medical care the moment it's said. I've the order in my pocket. Now,[21] fall out. At the double!"

McKechnie wavered on the way to the door. Levin added:

"You can take your choice of going up the line to-night. Or a court of inquiry for obtaining divorce leave and then not getting a divorce. Or the other thing. And you can thank Captain Tietjens for the clemency the general has shown you!"

The hut now reeling a little, Tietjens put the opened smelling bottle to his nostrils. At the sharp pang of the odour the hut came to attention. He said:

"We can't keep the general waiting."

"He told me," Levin said, "to give you ten minutes. He's sitting in your hut. He's tired. This affair has worried him dreadfully. O'Hara is the first C.O. he ever served under. A useful man, too, at his job."

Tietjens leaned against his dressing-table of meat-cases.

"You told that fellow McKechnie off, all right," he said. "I did not know you had it in you. . . ."

"Oh," Levin said, "it's just being with *him*. . . . I get his manner and it does all right.... Of course I don't often hear him have to strafe anybody in that manner. There's nobody really to stand up to him. Naturally.... But just this morning I was in his cabinet doing private secretary, and he was talking to Pe ... Talking while he shaved. And he said exactly that: You can take your choice of going up the line to-night or a court martial! ... So naturally I said as near the same as I could to your little friend...."

Tietjens said:

"We'd better go now."

In the winter sunlight Levin tucked his arm under Tietjens', leaning towards him gaily and not hurrying. The display was insufferable to Tietjens, but he recognized that it was indispensable. The bright day seemed full of things with hard edges—a rather cruel definiteness.... Liver! ...

The little depot adjutant passed them going very fast, as if before a wind. Levin just waved his hand in acknowledgment of his salute and went on, being enraptured in Tietjens' conversation. He said:

"You and ... and Mrs. Tietjens are dining at the general's to-night. To meet the G.O.C.I.C. Western Division. And General O'Hara.... We understand that you have definitely separated from Mrs. Tietjens...." Tietjens forced his left arm to violence to restrain it from tearing itself from the colonel's grasp.

His mind had become a coffin-headed, leather-jawed charger, like Schomburg. Sitting on his mind was like sitting on Schomburg at a dull water-jump. His lips said: "Bub-bub-bub-bub!" He could not feel his hands. He said:

"I recognize the necessity. If the general sees it in that way. I saw it in another way myself." His voice was intensely weary. "No doubt," he said, "the general knows best!"

Levin's face exhibited real enthusiasm. He said:

"You decent fellow! You awfully decent fellow! We're all in the same boat.... Now, will you tell me? For *him*. Was O'Hara drunk last night or wasn't he?"

Tietjens said:

"I think he was not drunk when he burst into the room with Major Perowne.... I've been thinking about it![22] I think he became drunk.... When I first requested and then ordered him to leave the room he leant against the doorpost.... He was certainly then—in disorder![23] I then told him that I should order him under arrest, if he didn't go...."[24]

Levin said:

"Mm! Mm! Mm!"

Tietjens said:

"It was my obvious duty.... I assure you that I was perfectly collected.... I beg to assure you that I was perfectly collected...."

Levin said: "I am not questioning the correctness.... But ... we are all one family.... I admit the atrocious ... the unbearable nature.... But you understand that O'Hara had the right to enter your room.... As P.M.! ..."[25]

Tietjens said:

"I am not questioning that it was his right. I was assuring you that I was perfectly collected because the general had honoured me by asking my opinion on the condition of General O'Hara...."

They had by now walked far beyond the line leading to Tietjens' office and, close together, were looking down upon the great tapestry of the French landscape.

"*He*," Levin said, "is anxious for your opinion. It really amounts to as to whether O'Hara drinks too much to continue in his job![26] ... And he says he will take your word.... You could not have a greater testimonial...."

"He could not," Tietjens said studiedly, "do anything less. Knowing me."

Levin said:

"Good heavens, old man, you rub it in!" He added quickly: "He wishes me to dispose of this side of the matter. He will take my word and yours. You will forgive ..."

The mind of Tietjens had completely failed: the Seine below looked like an S on fire in an opal. He said: "Eh?" And then: "Oh, yes! I forgive.... It's painful.... You probably don't know what you are doing."[27]

He broke off suddenly:

"By God! ... Were the Canadian Railway Service to go with my draft? They were detailed to mend the line here to-day. Also to go ...[28] I kept them back.... Both orders were dated the same day and hour. I could not get on to headquarters either from the hotel or from here. . . ."

Levin said:

"Yes, that's all right. He'll be immensely pleased. He's going to speak to you about *that*!" Tietjens gave an immense sigh of relief.

"I remembered that my orders were conflicting just before. . . . It was a terrible shock to remember. . . . If I sent them up in the lorries, the repairs to the railway might be delayed. . . . If I didn't, you might get strafed to hell. . . . It was an intolerable worry. . . ."

Levin said:

"You remembered it just as you saw the handle of your door moving. . . ."

Tietjens said from a sort of a mist:

"Yes. You know how beastly it is when you suddenly remember you have forgotten something in orders. As if the pit of your stomach had . . ."

Levin said:

"All[29] I ever thought about if I'd forgotten anything was what would be a good excuse to put up to the adjutant. . . . When I was a regimental officer . . ."

Suddenly[30] Tietjens said insistently:

"How did you know that? . . . About the door handle? Sylvia could not have seen it. . . ." He added: "And she could not have known what I was thinking. . . . She had her back to the door. . . . And to me. . . . Looking at me in the glass. . . . She was not even aware of what had happened. . . . So she could not have seen the handle move!"

Levin hesitated:

"I . . ." he said. "Perhaps I ought not to have said that. . . . You've told us. . . . That is to say, you've told . . ." He was pale in the sunlight. He said: "Old man . . . Perhaps you don't know. . . . Didn't you perhaps ever, in your childhood? . . ."

Tietjens said:

"Well . . . what is it?"

"That you talk . . . when you're sleeping!" Levin said.

Astonishingly, Tietjens said:

"What of that? . . . It's nothing to write home about! With the overwork I've had and the sleeplessness. . . ."

Levin said, with a pathetic appeal to Tietjens' omniscience:

"But doesn't it mean ... We used to say when we were boys ... that if you talk in your sleep ... you're ... in fact a bit dotty?"

Tietjens said without passion:

"Not necessarily. It means that one has been under mental pressure, but all mental pressure does not drive you over the edge. Not by any means.... Besides, what does it matter?"

Levin said:

"You mean you don't care.... Good God!" He remained looking at the view, drooping, in intense dejection. He said: "This *beastly* war! This *beastly* war! ... Look at all that view...."

Tietjens said:

"It's an encouraging spectacle, really. The beastliness of human nature is always pretty normal. We lie and betray and are wanting in imagination and deceive ourselves, always, at about the same rate. In peace and in war! But, somewhere in that view there are enormous bodies of men.... If you got a still more extended range of view over this whole front you'd have still more enormous bodies of men.... Seven to ten million.... All moving towards places towards which they desperately don't want to go. Desperately! Every one of them is desperately afraid. But they go on. An immense blind will forces them in the effort to consummate the one decent action that humanity has to its credit in the whole of recorded history. The one we are engaged in.[31] That[32] effort is the one certain creditable fact in all their lives.... But the *other* lives of all those men are dirty, potty and discreditable little affairs.... Like yours.... Like mine...."

Levin exclaimed:

"Just heavens! *What* a pessimist you are!"

Tietjens[33] said: "Can't you see that that is optimism?"[34]

"But," Levin said, "we're being beaten out of the field.... You don't know how desperate things are."

Tietjens said:

"Oh, I know pretty well. As soon as this weather really breaks we're probably done."

"We can't," Levin said, "possibly hold them. Not possibly."

"But success or failure," Tietjens said, "have nothing to do with the credit of a story. And a consideration of the virtues of humanity does not omit the other side. If we lose they win. If success is necessary to your idea of virtue—*virtus*—they then provide the success instead of ourselves. But[35] the thing is to be able to stick to the integrity of your character, whatever earthquake sets the house tumbling over your head.... That, thank God, we're doing...."

Levin said:

"I don't know.... If you knew what is going on at home ..."

Tietjens said:

"Oh, I know.... I know[36] that ground as I know the palm of my hand. I could invent that life if I knew nothing at all about the facts."

Levin said:

"I believe you could." He added: "Of course you could.... And yet the only use we can make of you is to martyrize you because two drunken brutes break into your wife's bedroom...."

Tietjens said:

"You betray your non-Anglo-Saxon origin by being so vocal.... And by your illuminative exaggerations!"

Levin suddenly exclaimed:

"What[37] the devil were we talking about?"

Tietjens said grimly:

"I am here at the disposal of the competent military authority—You!—that is inquiring into my antecedents. I am ready to go on belching platitudes till you stop me."

Levin answered:

"For goodness' sake help me. This is horribly painful. *He*—the general—has given me the job of finding out what happened last night. He won't face it himself. He's attached to you both."

Tietjens said:

"It's asking too much to ask me to help you.... What did I say in my sleep? What has Mrs. Tietjens told the general?"

"The general," Levin said, "has not seen Mrs. Tietjens. He could not trust himself. He knew she[38] would twist him round her little finger."

Tietjens said:

"He's beginning to learn. He was sixty last July, but he's beginning."

"So that," Levin said, "what we do know we learnt in the way I have told you. And from O'Hara of course. The general would not let Pe ..., the other fellow, speak a word, while he was shaving. He just said: 'I won't hear you. I won't hear you. You can take your choice of going up the line as soon as there are trains running or being broke on my personal application to the King in Council.'"[39]*

"I didn't know," Tietjens said, "that he could talk as straight as that."

"He's dreadfully hard hit," Levin answered; "if you and Mrs. Tietjens separate—and still more if there's anything real against either of you—it's going to shatter all his illusions. And . . ." He paused: "Do you know Major Thurston? A gunner? Attached to our anti-air-gun[40] crowd? . . . The general is very thick with him. . . ."

Tietjens said:

"He's one of the Thurstons of Lobden Moorside. . . . I don't know him personally. . . ."

Levin said:

"He's upset the general a good deal. . . . With something he told him. . . ."

Tietjens said:

"Good God!" And then: "He can't have told the general anything against me. . . . Then it must be against . . ."

Levin said:

"Do you want the general always to be told things against you in contradistinction to things about . . . another person."

Tietjens said:

"We[41] shall be keeping the fellows in my cook-house a confoundedly long time waiting for inspections. . . . I'm in your hands as regards the general. . . ."

Levin said:

"The general's in your hut: thankful to goodness to be alone. He never is.[42] He said he was going to write a private memorandum for the Secretary of State, and I could keep you any time I liked as long as I got everything out of you. . . ."

Tietjens said:

"Did what Major Thurston allege take place . . . Thurston has lived most of his life in France. . . . But you had better not tell me. . . ."

---

* The king acts with the advice of his privy (or private) council on the exercise of his executive authority.

Levin said:

"He's our anti-aircraft liaison officer with the French civilian authorities. Those sort of fellows generally have lived in France a good deal. A very decentish, quiet man. He plays chess with the general and they talk over the chess. . . . But the general is going to talk about what he said[43] to you himself. . . . "

Tietjens said:

"Good God! . . . He going to talk as well as you. . . . You'd say the coils were closing in. . . . "

Levin said:

"We can't go on like this. . . . It's my own fault for not being more direct. But this can't last all day. We could neither of us stand it. . . . I'm pretty nearly done. . . . "

Tietjens said:

"Where *did* your father come from, really? Not from Frankfurt? . . . "

Levin said:

"Constantinople. . . . His father was financial agent to the Sultan; my father was his son by an Armenian presented to him by the Selamlik* along with the Order of the Medjidje, first class."†

"It accounts for your very decent manner, and for your common sense. If you had been English I should have broken your neck before now."

Levin said:

"Thank you! I hope I always behave like an English gentleman. But I am going to be brutally direct now. . . . " He went on: "The really queer thing is that you should always address Miss Wannop in the language of the Victorian *Correct Letter-Writer*. You must excuse my mentioning the name: it shortens things. You said 'Miss Wannop' every two or three half-minutes. It convinced the general more than any possible assertions that your relations were perfectly . . . "

---

* 'Selamlik', from the Turkish for 'a place of greeting', is 'A room in a Muslim house set aside for business or the reception of male friends; the part of such a house reserved for men' (as opposed to the haremlik for women, *OED*). Levin is perhaps using the word to refer to the Sultan's court.

† The Order of the Medjidie is 'a Turkish order or decoration instituted in 1851 by the Sultan Abdul-Medjid': *OED*. The order was awarded to members of the British and French armed forces fighting with the Ottoman Empire against the Russians during the Crimean War of 1854–6.

Tietjens, his eyes shut, said:

"I talked to Miss Wannop in my sleep. . . ."

Levin, who was shaking a little, said:

"It was very queer. . . . Almost ghostlike. . . . There you sat, your arms on the table. Talking away. You appeared to be writing a letter to her.[44] And the sunlight streaming in at the hut. I was going to wake you, but he stopped me. He took the view that he was on detective work, and that he might as well detect. He had got it into his mind that you were a Socialist."

"He would," Tietjens commented. "Didn't I tell you he was beginning to learn things? . . ."

Levin exclaimed:

"But you aren't a So . . ."

Tietjens said:

"Of course, if your father came from Constantinople and his mother was a Georgian, it accounts for your attractiveness. You *are* a most handsome fellow. And intelligent. . . . If the general has put you on to inquire whether I am a Socialist I will answer your questions."

Levin said:

"No. . . . That's one of the questions he's reserving for himself to ask. It appears that if you answer that you are a Socialist he intends to cut you out of his will. . . ."

Tietjens said:

"His will! . . . Oh, yes, of course, he might very well leave me something. But doesn't that supply rather a motive for me to say that I *am*? I don't want his money."[45]

Levin positively jumped a step backwards. Money, and particularly money that came by way of inheritance, being one of the sacred things of life for him, he exclaimed:

"I don't see that you *can* joke about such a subject!"

Tietjens answered good-humouredly:

"Well, you don't expect me to play up to the old gentleman in order to get his poor old shekels." He added: "Hadn't we better get it over?"

Levin said:

"You've got hold of yourself?"

Tietjens answered:

"Pretty well. . . . You'll excuse my having been emotional so far. You aren't English, so it won't have embarrassed you."

Levin exclaimed in an outraged manner:

"Hang it, I'm English to the backbone! What's the matter with me?"

Tietjens said:

"Nothing.... Nothing in the world. That's just what makes you un-English. We're all ... well, it doesn't matter what's wrong with *us*.... What did you gather about my relations with Miss Wannop?"

The question was unemotionally put and Levin was still so concerned as to his origins that he did not at first grasp what Tietjens had said. He began to protest that he had been educated at Winchester and Magdalen. Then he exclaimed, "*Oh!*" And took time for reflection.

"If," he said finally, "the general had not let out that she was young and attractive ... at least, I suppose attractive ... I should have thought that you regarded her as an old maid....[46] You know, of course, that it came to me as a shock, the thought that there was anyone.... That you had allowed yourself ... Anyhow ... I suppose I'm simple...."

Tietjens said:

"What did the general gather?"

"He ..." Levin said, "he stood over you with his head held to one side, looking rather cunning ... like a magpie listening at a hole it's dropped a nut into.... First he looked disappointed: then quite glad. A simple kind of gladness. Just glad, you know.... When we got outside the hut he said 'I suppose in *vino veritas*,' and then he asked me the Latin for 'sleep' ... But I had forgotten it too...."

Tietjens[47] said:

"What did I say?"

"It's ..." Levin hesitated, "extraordinarily difficult to say what you *did* say.... I don't profess to remember long speeches to the letter.... Naturally[48] it was a good deal broken up.... I tell you, you were talking to a young lady about matters you don't generally talk to young ladies about.... And obviously you were trying to let your ... Mrs. Tietjens, down easily.... You were trying to explain also why you had definitely decided to separate from Mrs. Tietjens.... And you took it that the young lady might be troubled ... at the separation. ... "

Tietjens said carelessly:

"This is rather painful. Perhaps you would let me tell you exactly what *did* happen last night. ... "

Levin said:

"If you only would!" He added rather diffidently:[49] "If[50] you would not mind remembering that I am a military court of inquiry. It makes it easier for me to report to the general if you say things dully and in the order they happened."

Tietjens said:

"Thank you ... " and after a short interval, "I retired to rest with my wife last night at. ... I cannot say the hour exactly. Say half-past one. I reached this camp at half-past four, taking rather over half an hour to walk. What happened, as I am about to relate, took place therefore before four."

"The hour," Levin said, "is not material. We know the incident occurred in the small hours. General O'Hara made his complaint to me at three-thirty-five. He probably took five minutes to reach my quarters."

Tietjens asked:

"The exact charge was ... "

"The complaints," Levin answered, "were very numerous indeed. ... I could not catch them all. The succinct charge was at first being drunk and striking a superior officer, then merely that of conduct prejudicial in that you struck ... There is also a subsidiary charge of conduct prejudicial in that you improperly marked a charge-sheet in your orderly room. ...[51] I did not catch what all that was about. ... You appear to have had a quarrel with him about his red-caps. ... "

"That," Tietjens said, "is what it is really all about." He asked: "The officer I was said to have struck was ... ?"

Levin said:

"Perowne ... " dryly.

Tietjens said:

"You are sure it was not himself. I am prepared to plead guilty to striking General O'Hara."

"It is not," Levin said, "a question of pleading guilty. There is no charge to that effect against you, and you are perfectly aware that you are not under arrest. ... An order to perform any duty after you have been placed under arrest in itself releases you and dissolves the arrest."

Tietjens said coolly:

"I am perfectly aware of that. And that that was General Campion's intention in ordering me to accompany him round my cook-houses.... But I doubt.... I put it to you for your serious attention whether that is the best way to hush this matter up.... I think it would be more expedient that I should plead guilty to a charge of striking General O'Hara. And naturally to being drunk. An officer does not strike a general when he is sober. That would be a quite inconspicuous affair. Subordinate officers are broken every day for being drunk."

Levin had said "Wait a minute," twice. He now exclaimed with a certain horror:

"Your mania for sacrificing yourself makes you lose all ... all sense of proportion. You forget that General Campion is a gentleman. Things cannot be done in a hole-and-corner manner in this command...."

Tietjens said:

"They're done unbearably.... It would be nothing to me to be broke for being drunk, but raking up all this is hell."   •

Levin said:

"The general is anxious to know exactly what has happened. You will kindly accept an order to relate exactly what happened."

Tietjens said:

"That is what is perfectly damnable...." He remained silent for nearly a minute, Levin slapping his leggings with his riding-crop in a nervously passionate rhythm. Tietjens stiffened himself and began:

"General O'Hara came to my wife's room and burst in the door. I was there. I took him to be drunk. But from what he exclaimed I have since imagined that he was not so much drunk as misled. There was another man lying in the corridor where I had thrown him. General O'Hara exclaimed that this was Major Perowne. I had not realized that this was Major Perowne. I do not know Major Perowne very well and he was not in uniform. I had imagined him to be a French waiter coming to call me to the telephone. I had seen only his face round the door: he was looking round the door. My wife was in a state ... bordering on nudity.

I had put my hand under his chin and thrown him through the doorway. I am physically very strong and I exercised all my strength. I am aware of that. I was excited, but not more excited than the circumstances seemed to call for...."

Levin exclaimed:

"But ... At three in the morning! The telephone!"

"I was ringing up my headquarters and yours. All through the night. The O.I.C. draft, Lieutenant Cowley, was also ringing me up. I was anxious to know what was to be done about the Canadian railway men. I had three times been called to the telephone since I had been in Mrs. Tietjens' room, and once an orderly had come down from the camp. I was also conducting a very difficult conversation with my wife as to the disposal of my family's estates, which are large, so that the details were complicated. I occupied the room next door to Mrs. Tietjens and till that moment, the communicating door between the rooms being open, I had heard when a waiter or an orderly had knocked at my own door in the corridor. The night porter of the hotel was a dark, untidy, surly sort of fellow.... Not unlike Perowne."[52]

Levin said:

"Is it necessary to go into all this? We ..."

Tietjens said:

"If I am to make a statement it seems necessary. I would prefer you to question me ..."

Levin said:

"Please go on.... We accept the statement that Major Perowne was not in uniform. He states that he was in his pyjamas and dressing-gown. Looking for the bathroom."

Tietjens said: "Ah!" and stood reflecting. He said:

"May I hear the ... purport of Major Perowne's statement?"

"He states," Levin said, "what I have just said. He was looking for the bathroom. He had not slept in the hotel before. He opened a door and looked round it, and was immediately thrown with great violence down into the passage with his head against the wall. He says that this dazed him so that, not really appreciating what had happened, he shouted various accusations against the person who had assaulted him.... General O'Hara then came out of his room...."

Tietjens said:

"What accusations did Major Perowne shout?"

"He doesn't. . . ." Levin hesitated, "eh! . . . elaborate them in his statement."

Tietjens said:

"It is, I imagine, material that I should know what they are. . . ."

Levin said:

"I don't know that. . . . If you'll forgive me . . . Major Perowne came to see me, reaching me half an hour after General O'Hara. He was very . . . extremely nervous and concerned. I am bound to say . . . for Mrs. Tietjens. And also very concerned to spare yourself! . . . It appears that he had shouted out just anything. . . . As it might be 'Thieves!' or 'Fire!'. . . But when General O'Hara came out he told him, being out of himself, that he had been invited to your wife's room, and that . . . Oh, excuse me. . . . I'm under great obligations to you . . . the very greatest . . . that you had attempted to blackmail him!"

Tietjens said:

"Well! . . ."

"You understand," Levin said, and he was pleading, "that that is what he said to[53] General O'Hara in the corridor. He even confessed it was madness. . . . He did not maintain the accusation to me. . . ."

Tietjens said:

"Not that Mrs. Tietjens had given him leave? . . ."

Levin said with tears in his eyes:

"I'll not go on with this. . . . I will rather resign my commission than go on tormenting you. . . ."

"You can't resign your commission," Tietjens said.

"I can resign my appointment," Levin answered. He went on sniffling: "This beastly war! . . . This beastly war! . . ."

Tietjens said:[54]

"If what is distressing you is having to tell me that you believe Major Perowne came with my wife's permission I know it's true. It's also true that my wife expected me to be there. She wanted some fun: not adultery.[55] But I am also aware—as Major Thurston appears to have told General Campion—that Mrs. Tietjens was with Major Perowne. In France. At a place called Yssingueux-les-Pervenches. . . ."

"That wasn't the name," Levin blubbered. "It was Saint ...
Saint ... Saint something. In the Cevennes...."

Tietjens said:

"Don't, there! ... Don't distress yourself...."

"But I'm ..." Levin went on, "under great obligations to
you...."

"I'd better," Tietjens said, "finish off this matter myself."

Levin said:

"It will break the general's heart. He believes so absolutely in
Mrs. Tietjens. Who wouldn't? ... How the devil could you guess
what Major Thurston told him?"

"He's the sort of brown, trustworthy man who always does
know that sort of thing," Tietjens answered. "As for the general's
belief in Mrs. Tietjens, he's perfectly justified.... Only there will
be no more parades. Sooner or later it has to come to that for us
all...." He added with a little bitterness: "Only not for you.
Being a Turk or a Jew you are a simple, Oriental, monogamous,
faithful soul...." He added again: "I hope to goodness the
sergeant-cook has the sense not to keep the men's dinners back
for the general's inspection.... But of course he will not...."

Levin said:

"What in the world would that matter?" fiercely. "He keeps
men waiting as much as three hours. On parade."

"Of course," Tietjens said, "if that is what Major Perowne told
General O'Hara it removes a good deal of my suspicions of the
latter's sobriety. Try to get the position. General O'Hara positively burst in the little sneck of the door that I had put down and
came in shouting: 'Where is the bloody blackmailer?' And it was
a full three minutes before I could get rid of him. I had had the
presence of mind to switch off the light and he persisted in asking
for another look at Mrs. Tietjens. You see, if you consider it, he
is a very heavy sleeper. He is suddenly awakened after, no doubt,
not a few pegs. He hears Major Perowne shouting about blackmail and thieves.... I dare say this town has its quota of
blackmailers. O'Hara might well be anxious to catch one in the
act. He hates me, anyhow, because of his Red Caps. I'm a shabby-
looking chap he doesn't know much about. Perowne passes for
being a millionaire. I daresay he is: he's said to be very stingy.
That would be how he got hold of the idea of blackmail and

hypnotized the general with it. . . ."

He went on again:

"But I wasn't to know that. . . . I had shut the door on Perowne and didn't even know he was Perowne. I really thought he was the night porter coming to call me to the telephone.[56] I only saw a roaring satyr. I mean that was what I thought O'Hara was. . . .[57] And I assure you I kept my head. . . . When he persisted in leaning against the doorpost and asking for another look at Mrs. Tietjens, he kept on saying: 'The woman' and 'The hussy.' Not 'Mrs. Tietjens.'. . . I thought then that there was something queer. I said: 'This is my wife's room,' several times. He said something to the effect of how could he know she was my wife, and . . . that she had made eyes at himself in the lounge, so it might have been himself as well as Perowne. . . .[58] I dare say he had got it into his head that I had imported some tart to blackmail someone. . . . But you know. . . . I grew exhausted after a time. . . . I saw outside in the corridor one of the little subalterns he has on his staff, and I said: 'If you do not take General O'Hara away I shall order you to put him under arrest for drunkenness.' That seemed to drive the general crazy. I had gone closer to him, being determined to push him out of the door, and he decidedly smelt of whisky. Strongly. . . . But I dare say he was thinking himself outraged, really. And perhaps also coming to his senses. As there was nothing else for it I pushed him gently out of the room. In going he shouted that I was to consider myself under arrest. I so considered myself. . . . That is to say that, as soon as I had settled certain details with Mrs. Tietjens, I walked up to the camp, which I took to be my quarters, though I am actually under the M.O.'s orders to reside in this hotel owing to the state of my lungs. I saw the draft off, that not necessitating my giving any orders. I went to my sleeping quarters, it being then about six-thirty, and towards seven awakened McKechnie, whom I asked to take my adjutant's and battalion parade and orderly-room. I had breakfast in my hut, and then went into my private office to await developments. I think I have now told you everything material. . . ."

II

GENERAL Lord Edward Campion, G.C.B., K.C.M.G. (Military), D.S.O., etc., sat, radiating glory and composing a confidential memorandum to the Secretary of State for War, on a bully-beef case, leaning forward over a military blanket that covered a deal table. He was for the moment in high good humour on the surface, though his subordinate minds were puzzled and depressed. At the end of each sentence that he wrote—and he wrote with increasing satisfaction!—a mind that he was not using said: "What the devil am I going to do with that fellow?" Or: "How the devil is that girl's name to be kept out of this mess?"

Having been asked to write a confidential memorandum for the information of the home authorities as to what, in his opinion, was the cause of the French railway strike, he had hit on the ingenious device of reporting what was the opinion of the greater part of the forces under his command. This was a dangerous line to take, for he might well come into conflict with the home Government. But he was pretty certain that any inquiries that the home Government could cause to be made amongst the local civilian population would confirm what[1] he was writing—which he was careful to state was not to be taken as a communication of his own opinion. In addition, he did not care what the Government did to him.

He was satisfied with his military career. In the early part of the war, after materially helping mobilization,[2] he had served with great distinction in the East, in command mostly of mounted infantry. He had subsequently so distinguished himself in the organizing and transporting of troops coming and going overseas that, on the part of the lines of communication where he now commanded becoming of great importance, he knew that he had seemed the only general that could be given that command. It had become of enormous importance—these were open secrets!—because, owing to divided opinions in the Cabinet, it might at any moment be decided to move the bulk of

H.M. Forces to somewhere in the East. The idea underlying
this—as General Campion saw it—[3]had at least some relation to
the necessities of the British Empire and,[4] strategy embracing
world politics as well as military movements—a fact which is
often forgotten—there was this much to be said for it: The
preponderance of British Imperial interests might be advanced as
lying in the Middle and Far Easts—to the east, that is to say, of
Constantinople. This might be denied, but it was a feasible
proposition. The present operations on the Western front,
arduous, and even creditable, as they might have been until relatively lately, were very remote from our Far-Eastern possessions
and mitigated from, rather than added to, our prestige. In addition, the unfortunate display in front of Constantinople in the
beginning of the war had almost eliminated our prestige with the
Mohammedan races.* Thus a demonstration in enormous force
in any region between European Turkey and the north-western
frontiers of India might point out to Mohammedans, Hindus, and
other Eastern races, what overwhelming forces Great Britain,
were she so minded, could put into the field. It is true that that
would mean the certain loss of the war on the Western front, with
corresponding loss of prestige in the West. But the wiping out of
the French republic would convey little to the Eastern races,
whereas we could no doubt make terms with the enemy nations,
as a price for abandoning our allies, that might well leave the
Empire, not only intact, but actually increased in colonial extent,
since it was unlikely that the enemy empires would wish to be
burdened with colonies for some time.

General Campion was not overpoweringly sentimental over
the idea of the abandonment of our allies. They had won his
respect as fighting organizations and that, to the professional
soldier, is a great deal; but still he *was* a professional soldier, and
the prospect of widening the bounds of the British Empire could
not be contemptuously dismissed at the price of rather sentimental dishonour. Such bargains had been struck before during
wars involving many nations, and doubtless such bargains would
be struck again. In addition, votes might be gained by the

---

* The Gallipoli Campaign, launched to capture Istanbul (Constantinople), began in
    April 1915 and was a disastrous failure.

Government from the small but relatively noisy and menacing part of the British population that favoured the enemy nations.

But when it came to tactics—which it should be remembered concerns itself with the movement of troops actually in contact with enemy forces—[5]General Campion had no doubt that that plan was the conception of the brain of a madman. The dishonour of such a proceeding must of course be considered—and its impracticability was hopeless. The dreadful nature of what would be our debacle did we attempt to evacuate the Western front might well be unknown to, or might be deliberately ignored by, the civilian mind. But the general could almost see the horrors as a picture—and, professional soldier as he was, his mind shuddered at the picture. They had by now in the country enormous bodies of troops who had hitherto not come into contact with the enemy forces. Did they attempt to withdraw these in the first place the native population would at once turn from a friendly into a bitterly hostile factor, and moving troops through hostile country is to the nth power a more lengthy matter than moving them through territory where the native populations lend a helping hand, or are at least not obstructive. They had in addition this enormous force to ration, and they would doubtless have to supply them with ammunition on the almost certain breaking through of the enemy forces. It would be impossible to do this without the use of the local railways—and the use of these would at once be prohibited. If, on the other hand, they attempted to begin the evacuation by shortening the front, the operation would be very difficult with troops who, by now, were almost solely men trained only in trench warfare, with officers totally unused to that keeping up of communications between units which is the life and breath of a retreating army. Training, in fact, in that element had been almost abandoned in the training camps where instruction was almost limited to bomb-throwing, the use of machine-guns, and other departments which had been forced on the War Office by eloquent civilians—to the almost complete neglect of the rifle.[6] Thus at the mere hint of a retreat the enemy forces must break through and come upon the vast, unorganized, or semi-organized bodies of troops in the rear. . . .

The temptation for the professional soldier was to regard such a state of things with equanimity. Generals have not infrequently

enormously distinguished themselves by holding up retreats from
the rear when vanguard commanders have disastrously failed. But
General Campion resisted the temptation of even hoping that
this chance of distinguishing himself might offer itself. He could
not contemplate with equanimity the slaughter of great bodies of
men under his command, and not even a successful retreating
action of that description could be carried out without horrible
slaughter. And he would have little hope of conducting necessarily delicate and very hurried movements with an army that,
except for its rough training in trench warfare, was practically
civilian in texture. So that although, naturally, he had made his
plans for such an eventuality, having indeed in his private quarters four enormous paper-covered blackboards upon which he
had changed daily the names of units according as they passed
from his hands or came into them and became available, he
prayed specifically every night before retiring to bed that the task
might not be cast upon his shoulders. He prized very much his
universal popularity in his command, and he could not bear to
think of how the eyes of the Army would regard him as he put
upon them a strain so appalling and such unbearable sufferings.
He had, moreover, put that aspect of the matter very strongly in
a memorandum that he had prepared in answer to a request from
the home Government for a scheme by which an evacuation
might be effected. But he considered that the civilian element in
the Government was so entirely indifferent to the sufferings of
the men engaged in these operations, and was so completely ignorant of what are military exigencies, that the words he had
devoted to that department of the subject were merely wasted. . . .

So everything pushed him into writing confidentially to the
Secretary of State for War a communication that he knew must
be singularly distasteful to a number of the gentlemen who would
peruse it. He chuckled indeed as he wrote, the open door behind
him and the sunlight pouring in on his radiant figure. He said:

"Sit down, Tietjens. Levin, I shall not want you for ten
minutes," without raising his head, and went on writing. It
annoyed him that, from the corner of his eye, he could see that
Tietjens was still standing, and he said rather irritably: "Sit down,
sit down. . . ."

He wrote:

"It is pretty generally held here by the native population that the present very serious derangement of traffic, if not actively promoted, is at least winked at by the Government of this country. It is, that is to say, intended to give us a taste of what would happen if I took any measures here for returning any large body of men to the home country or elsewhere, and it is said also to be a demonstration in favour of a single command—a measure which is here regarded by a great weight of instructed opinion as indispensable to the speedy and successful conclusion of hostilities. . . . "

The general paused over that sentence. It came very near the quick. For himself he was absolutely in favour of a single command, and in his opinion, too, it was indispensable to any sort of conclusion of hostilities at all. The whole of military history, in so far as it concerned allied operations of any sort— from the campaigns of Xerxes and operations during the wars of the Greeks and Romans, to the campaigns of Marlborough and Napoleon and the Prussian operations of 1866 and 1870— pointed to the conclusion that a relatively small force acting homogeneously was, to the nth power again, more effective than vastly superior forces of allies acting only imperfectly in accord or not in accord at all. Modern developments in arms had made no shade at all of difference to strategy and had made differences merely of time and numbers to tactics. To-day, as in the days of the Greek Wars of the Allies, success depended on apt timing of the arrival of forces at given points, and it made no difference whether your lethal weapons acted from a distance of thirty miles or were held and operated by hand; whether you dealt death from above or below the surface of the ground, through the air by dropped missiles or by mephitic and torturing vapours. What won combats, campaigns, and, in the end, wars, was the brain which timed the arrival of forces at given points—and that must be one brain which could command their presence at these points, not a half-dozen authorities requesting each other to perform operations which might or might not fall in with the ideas or the prejudices of any one or other of the half-dozen. . . .

Levin came in noiselessly, slid a memorandum slip on to the blanket beside the paper on which the general was writing. The general read: *T. agrees completely, sir, with your diagnosis of the*

*facts, except that he is much more ready to accept General O'H.'s acts
as reasonable. He places himself entirely in your hands.*

The general heaved an immense sigh of relief. The sunlight
streaming in became very bright. He had had a real sinking at the
heart when Tietjens had boggled for a second over putting on his
belt. An[7] officer may not demand or insist on a court martial. But
he, Campion, could not in decency have refused Tietjens his
court martial if he stood out for it. He had a right to clear his character publicly. It would have been impossible to refuse him. Then
the fat would have been in the fire. For, knowing O'Hara through
pretty nearly twenty-five years—or it must be thirty!—of service
Campion was pretty certain that O'Hara had made a drunken
beast of himself. Yet he was very attached to O'Hara—one of the
old type of rough-diamond generals who swore your head off, but
were damn capable men! . . . It was a tremendous relief.

He said sharply:

"Sit down, can't you, Tietjens! You irritate me by standing
there!" He said to himself: "An obstinate fellow. . . . Why, he's
gone!" and his mind and eyes being occupied by the sentence he
had last written, the sense of irritation remained with him. He
re-read the closing clause: ". . . a single command—a measure
which is here regarded by a great weight of instructed opinion as
indispensable to the speedy and successful termination of hostilities. . . . "

He looked at this, whistling beneath his breath. It was pretty
thick. He was not asked for his opinion as to the single command:
yet he decidedly wanted to get it in and was pretty well prepared
to stand the consequences. The consequences might be something pretty bad: he might be sent home. That was quite possible.
That, even, was better than what was happening to poor Puffles,
who was being starved of men. He had been at Sandhurst with
Puffles, and they had got their commissions on the same day to
the same regiment. A damn good soldier, but too hot-tempered.
He was making an extraordinarily good thing of it in spite of his
shortage of men, which was the talk of the army. But it must be
damn agonizing for him, and a very improper strain on his men.[8]
One day—as soon as the weather broke—the enemy *must* break
through. Then he, Puffles, would be sent home. That was what
the fellows at Westminster and in Downing Street wanted.

Puffles had been a great deal too free with his tongue. They would not send him home before he had a disaster because, unless he were in disgrace, he would be a thorn in their sides: whereas if he were disgraced no one much would listen to him. It was smart practice! ... *Sharp* practice!

He tossed the sheet on which he had been writing across the table and said to Tietjens:

"Look at that, will you?" In the centre of the hut Tietjens was sitting bulkily on a bully-beef case that had been brought in ceremoniously by a runner. "He *does* look beastly shabby," the general said. "There are three ... four grease stains on his tunic. He ought to get his hair cut!" He added: "It's a perfectly damnable business. No one but this fellow would have got into it. He's a firebrand. That's what he is. A regular firebrand!"

Tietjens' troubles[9] had really shaken the general not a little. He was left up in the air. He had lived the greater part of his life with his sister, Lady Claudine Sandbach, and the greater part of the remainder of his life at Groby, at any rate after he came home from India and during the reign of Tietjens' father. He had idolized Tietjens' mother, who was a saint! What indeed there had been of the idyllic in his life had really all passed at Groby, if he came to think of it. India was not so bad, but one had to be young to enjoy that. ...

Indeed, only the day before yesterday he had been thinking that if this letter that he was thinking out did result in his being sent back, he should propose to stand for the half of the Cleveland[10] Parliamentary Division in which Groby stood. What with the Groby influence and his nephew's in the country districts, though Castlemaine had not much land left up there, and with Sandbach's interest in the ironworking districts, he would have an admirable chance of getting in. Then he would make himself a thorn in the side of certain persons.

He had thought of quartering himself on Groby. It would have been easy to get Tietjens out of the army and they could all—he, Tietjens and Sylvia—live together. It would have been his ideal of a home and of an occupation. ...

For, of course, he was getting old for soldiering: unless he got a fighting army there was not much more to it as a career for a man of sixty. If he *did* get an army he was pretty certain of a

peerage and hefty political work could still be done in the Lords.
He would have a good claim on India and that meant dying a
Field-Marshal.

On the other hand, the only command that was at all likely to
be going—except for deaths, and the health rate amongst army
commanders was pretty high!—was poor Puffles'. And that would
be no pleasant command—with the men all hammered to pieces.
He decided to put the whole thing to Tietjens. Tietjens, like a
meal-sack, was looking at him over the draft of the letter that he
had just finished reading. The general said:

"Well?"

Tietjens said:

"It's splendid, sir, to see you putting the matter so strongly. It
must be put strongly, or we're lost."

The general said:

"You think that?"

Tietjens said:

"I'm sure of it, sir.... But unless you are prepared to throw up
your command and take to politics...."

The general exclaimed:

"You're a most extraordinary fellow.... That was exactly what
I was thinking about: this very minute."

"It's not so extraordinary," Tietjens said. "A really active
general thinking as you do is very badly needed in the House. As
your brother-in-law is to have a peerage whenever he asks for it,
West Cleveland will be vacant at any moment, and with his
influence and Lord Castlemaine's—your nephew's not got much
land, but the name is immensely respected in the country
districts.... And, of course, using Groby for your headquarters...."[11]

The general said:

"That's pretty well botched, isn't it?"

Tietjens said without moving a muscle:

"Why, no, sir. Sylvia is to have Groby and you would naturally
make it your headquarters.... You've still got your hunters
there...."

The general said:

"Sylvia is really to have Groby.... Good God!"

Tietjens said:

"So it was no great conjuring trick, sir, to see that you might not mind. . . ."

The general said:

"Upon my soul, I'd as soon give up my chance of heaven . . . no, not heaven, but India, as give up Groby."

"You've got," Tietjens said, "an admirable chance of India. . . . The point is: which way? If they give you the sixteenth section. . . ."

"I hate," the general said, "to think of waiting for poor Puffles' shoes. I was at Sandhurst with him. . . ."

"It's a question, sir," Tietjens said, "of which is the best way. For the country and yourself. I suppose if one were a general one would like to have commanded an army on the Western front. . . ."

The general said:

"I don't know. . . . It's the logical end of a career. . . . But I don't feel that my career is ending. . . . I'm as sound as a roach.* And in ten years' time what difference will it make?"

"One would like," Tietjens said, "to see you doing it. . . ."

The general said:

"No one will know whether I commanded a fighting army or this damned Whiteley's outfitting store. . . ."†

Tietjens said:

"I know that, sir. . . . But the sixteenth section will desperately need a good man if General Perry is sent home. And particularly a general who has the confidence of all ranks. . . . It will be a wonderful position. You will have every man that's now on the Western front at your back after the war. It's a certain peerage. . . . It's certainly a sounder proposition than that of a free-lance—which is what you'd be—in the House of Commons."

The general said:

"Then what am I to do with my letter? It's a damn good letter. I don't like wasting letters."[12]

Tietjens said:

"You want it to show through that you back the single

---

*   Partridge's *Dictionary of Slang* glosses 'sound as a bell, roach, trout', as 'Perfectly sound and healthy'.
†   London's first department store, located on Queensway; fashionable enough for Eliza Doolittle to be sent there by Henry Higgins 'to be attired' in Shaw's *Pygmalion* (1913).

command for all you are worth, yet you don't want them to put their finger on your definitely saying so yourself?"

The general said:

"... That's it. That's just what I do want...." He added: "I suppose you take my view of the whole matter. The Government's pretence of evacuating the Western front in favour of the Middle East is probably only a put-up job to frighten our Allies into giving up the single command. Just as this railway strike is a counter-demonstration by way of showing what would happen to us if we did begin to evacuate...."

Tietjens said:

"It looks like that.... I'm not, of course, in the confidence of the Cabinet. I'm not even in contact with them as I used to be.... But I should put it that the section of the Cabinet that is in favour of the Eastern expedition is very small. It's said to be a one-man party—with hangers-on—but arguing him out of it has caused[13] all this delay. That's how I see it."

The general exclaimed:

"But, good God! ... How is such a thing possible? That man must walk along his corridors with the blood of a million—I mean it, of a million—men round his head. He could not stand up under it.... That[14] fellow is prolonging the war indefinitely by delaying us now. And men being killed all the time![15] ... I can't...." He stood up and paced, stamping up and down the hut.... "At Bonderstrom,"* he said, "I had half a company wiped out under me.... By my own fault, I admit. I had wrong information ..." He stopped and said: "Good God! ... Good God! ... I can see it now.... And it's unbearable! After eighteen years. I was a brigadier then. It was your own regiment—the Glamorganshires.... They were crowded into a little nullah† and shelled to extinction.... I could see it going on and we could not get on to the Boer guns with ours to stop 'em.... That's hell," he said, "that's the real hell.... I never inspected the Glamorganshires after that for the whole war. I

---

* Perhaps a reference to Broederstroom, in a strategically important area some twenty miles west of Pretoria, where there was no major battle but significant guerilla activity in the Second Boer War (1899–1902).

† Anglo-Indian: 'A river or stream; a watercourse, river-bed, ravine': *OED*.

could not bear the thought of facing their eyes.... Buller* was the same.... Buller was worse than I.... He never held up his head again after...."

Tietjens said:

"If you would not mind, sir, not going on...."

The general stamped to a halt in his stride. He said:

"Eh? ... What's that? What's the matter with you?"

Tietjens said:

"I had a man killed on me last night. In this very hut; where I'm sitting is the exact spot. It makes me ... It's a sort of ... Complex, they call it now...."

The general exclaimed:

"Good God! I beg your pardon, my dear boy.... I ought not to have ... I have never behaved like that before another soul in the world.... Not to Buller.... Not to Gatacre,† and they were my closest friends.... Even after Spion Kop‡ I never...." He broke off and said: "But those old memories won't interest you...." He said: "I've such an absolute belief in your trustworthiness, I *know* you won't betray what you've seen.... What I've just said...." He paused and tried to adopt the air of the listening magpie. He said: "I was called Butcher Campion in South Africa, just as Gatacre was called Backbreaker.[16] I don't want to be called anything else because I've made an ass of myself before you.... No, damn it all, not an ass. I was immensely attached to your sainted mother...." He said: "It's the proudest tribute any commander of men can have.... To be called Butcher and have your men follow you in spite of it. It shows confidence, and it gives you, as commander, confidence! ... One has to be prepared to lose men in hundreds at the right minute in order to avoid losing them in tens of thousands at the wrong! ..." He said: "Successful military operations consist not

---

* General Sir Redvers Buller was either in command or second in command in South Africa when a number of battles were lost by British forces in the Second Boer War, including that of Spion Kop. His reputation for losing battles gave him the nickname of 'Reverse Buller'. Though in many ways an excellent and innovative officer, he was made a scapegoat for military incompetence by the government and dismissed from the army in October 1901.

† Lieutenant General Sir William Forbes Gatacre had 135 men killed and 696 captured in an ambush at the battle of Stormberg in the Second Boer War.

‡ The battle of Spion Kop (24 January 1900) was noted for its slaughter of British troops.

in taking or retaining positions, but in taking or retaining them with a minimum sacrifice of effectives.... I wish to God you civilians would get that into your heads. The men have it. They know that I will use them ruthlessly—but that I will not waste one life...." He exclaimed: "Damn it, if I had ever thought I should have such troubles, in your father's days...!" He said: "Let's get back to what we were talking about.... My memorandum to the secretary...." He burst out: "My God! ... *What can that fellow think when he reads Shakespeare's When all those heads, legs, arms, joined together on the Last Day shall* ...* How does it run? Henry V's address to his soldiers ... *Every subject's body is the king's* ... *but every subject's soul is his own....*† *And there is no king, be his cause ever so just....* My God! My God! ... *as can try it out with all unspotted soldiers....*‡ Have you ever thought of that?"[17]

Alarm overcame Tietjens. The general was certainly in disorder. But over what? There was not time to think. Campion was certainly dreadfully overworked.... He exclaimed:

"Sir, hadn't you better! ..." He said: "If we could get back to your memorandum ... I am[18] quite prepared to write a report to the effect of your sentence as to the French civilian population's attitude. That would throw the onus on me...."

The general said agitatedly:

"No! No! ... You've got quite enough on your back as it is. Your confidential report states that you are suspected of having too great common interests with the French. That's[19] what makes the whole position so impossible.... [20] I'll get Thurston to write something. He's a good man, Thurston. Reliable...." Tietjens shuddered a little. The general went on astonishingly:

---

* Michael Williams, a soldier in Henry V's army, says 'the King himself hath a heavy reckoning to make, when all those legs and arms and heads chopped off in a battle shall join together at the latter day....' (*Henry V*, IV.i.133–6).

† 'Every subject's duty is the King's, but every subject's soul is his own' (*Henry V*, IV.i.175–6).

‡ 'Besides, there is no king, be his cause never so spotless, if it come to the arbitrament of swords, can try it out with all unspotted soldiers' (*Henry V*, IV.i.157–60). *The Arbitrament of Swords* was one of the titles considered for *No Enemy* (*No Enemy* xiv). This scene also gave Ford the title and epigraph for his first wartime propaganda book, *When Blood is Their Argument* (London: Hodder & Stoughton, 1915): Tietjens recalls a further quotation from it in the final chapter of *Some Do Not* ....

"'But at my back I always hear
Time's winged chariot hurrying near:
And yonder all before me lie
Deserts of vast eternity!' . . . *

That's a general's life in this accursed war. . . . You think all generals are illiterate fools. But[21] I have spent a great deal of time in reading, though I never[22] read anything written later than the seventeenth century."

Tietjens said:

"I know, sir. . . . You made me read Clarendon's *History of the Great Rebellion* when I was twelve."

The general[23] said:

"In case we . . . I shouldn't like . . . In short . . ." He swallowed: it was singular to see him swallow. He was lamentably thin when you looked at the man and not the uniform.

Tietjens thought:

"What's he nervous about? He's been nervous all the morning."†

The general said:

"I am trying to say—it's not much in my line—that in case we never met again, I do not wish you to think me an ignoramus."

Tietjens[24] thought:

"He's not ill . . . and he can't think me so ill that I'm likely to die. . . . A fellow like that doesn't really know how to express himself. He's trying to be kind and he doesn't know how to. . . ."

The general had paused. He began to say:

"But there are finer things in Marvell than that. . . ."

Tietjens thought:

"He's trying to gain time. . . . Why on earth should he? . . . What is this all about?" His mind slipped a notch. The general was looking at his finger-nails on the blanket. He said:

"There's, for instance:

---

*   Andrew Marvell, 'To His Coy Mistress' (1681), lines 21–4. Tietjens attributes these
    lines to Edmund Waller in a deleted TS passage (see textual note 22 to this chapter),
    but corrects 'Waller' to 'Marvell' in a later deleted passage (see textual note 23).
†   A deleted TS passage (see textual note 18) shows that Tietjens already knew that
    Campion is nervous because he must tell him that he is to be sent up the line.

"'The grave's a fine and secret place
*But none I think do there embrace....'"**

At those words it came to Tietjens suddenly to think of Sylvia,
with the merest film of clothing on her long, shining limbs....
She was working a powder-puff under her armpits[25] in a brilliant
illumination from two electric lights, one on each side of her
dressing table. She[26] was looking at him in the glass with the
corners of her lips just moving. A little curled.... He said to
himself:[27]

"One is going to that fine and secret place.... Why not have?"
She had emanated a perfume founded on sandalwood. As she
worked her swansdown powder-puff over those intimate regions
he could hear her humming. Maliciously![28] It was then that he[29]
had observed the handle of the door moving minutely. She had
incredible arms, stretched out amongst a wilderness of besilvered
cosmetics. Extraordinarily lascivious! Yet clean! Her gilded
sheath gown was about her hips on the chair....

Well! She[30] had pulled the strings of one too many shower-
baths!

Shining;[31] radiating glory but still shrivelled so that he
reminded Tietjens of an old apple inside a damascened helmet;
the general had seated himself once more on the bully-beef case
before the blanketed table. He fingered his very large, golden
fountain-pen. He said:

"Captain Tietjens, I should be glad of your careful attention!"
Tietjens said:

"Sir!" His heart stopped.

The general[32] said that that afternoon Tietjens would receive
a movement order. He said stiffly that he must not[33] regard this
new movement order as a disgrace. It was promotion. He, Major-
General Campion, was requesting the colonel commanding the
depot to inscribe the highest possible testimonial in his, Tietjens',
small-book. He, Tietjens, had exhibited the most extraordinary
talent for finding solutions for difficult problems—The colonel
was to write that!—In addition he, General Campion, was

---

* Marvell, 'To His Coy Mistress', lines 31–2; 'private', not 'secret' is Marvell's word in
  the first line quoted. Ford quoted these lines correctly in *Provence from Minstrels to
  Machine*, ed. John Coyle (Manchester: Carcanet, 2007), 134.

requesting his friend, General Perry, commanding the sixteenth section . . .

Tietjens thought:

"Good God. I am being sent up the line. He's sending me to Perry's Army. . . . That's[34] certain death!"

. . . To give Tietjens the appointment of second in command of the VIth Battalion of his regiment!

Tietjens said, but he did not know where the words came from:[35]

"Colonel Partridge will not like that. He's praying for McKechnie to come back!"

To himself he said:

"I shall fight this monstrous treatment of myself to my last breath."[36]

The general suddenly called out:

"There you are. . . . There is another of your infernal worries. . . . "

He put a strong check on himself, and, dryly, like the very great speaking to the very unimportant, asked:

"What's your medical category?"

Tietjens said:

"Permanent base, sir. My chest's rotten!"

The general said:

"I should forget that, if I were you. . . . The second in command of a battalion has nothing to do but sit about in arm-chairs waiting for the colonel to be killed." He added: "It's the best I can do for you. . . . I've thought it out very carefully. It's the best I can do for you."[37]

Tietjens said:

"I shall, of course, forget my category, sir. . . . "

Of course he would never fight any treatment of himself!

There[38] it was then: the natural catastrophe! As when, under thunder, a dam breaks. His mind was battling with the waters. What would it pick out as the main terror? The mud: the noise: dread always at the back of the mind? Or the worry! The worry! Your eyebrows always had a slight tension on them. . . . Like eye-strain!

The general had begun, soberly:

"You will recognize that there is nothing else that I can do."

His answering:

"I recognize, naturally, sir, that there is nothing else that you can do...." seemed rather to irritate the general. He wanted opposition: he *wanted* Tietjens to argue the matter. He was the Roman father counselling suicide to his son: but he wanted Tietjens to expostulate. So that he, General Campion, might absolutely prove that he, Tietjens, was a disgraced individual.... It could not be done. The general said:

"You will understand that I can't—no commander could!—have such things happening in my command...."[39]

Tietjens said:

"I must accept that, if you say it, sir."

The general[40] looked at him under his eyebrows. He said:

"I have already told you[41] that this is promotion. I have been much impressed by the way you have handled this command. You are, of course, no soldier, but you will make an admirable officer for the militia, that is all that our troops now are...." He said: "I will emphasize what I am saying.... No officer could—without being militarily in the wrong—have a private life that is as incomprehensible and embarrassing as yours...."

Tietjens said:[42]

"He's hit it! ..."

The general said:

"An officer's private life and his life on parade are as strategy to tactics.... I don't want, if I can avoid it, to go into your private affairs.[43] It's extremely embarrassing.... But let me put it to you that ... I wish to be delicate. But you are a man of the world![44] ... Your wife is an extremely beautiful woman.... There has been a scandal ... I admit not of your making.... But if, on the top of that, I appeared to show favouritism to you...."

Tietjens said:

"You need not go on, sir.... I understand...." He tried to remember what the brooding and odious McKechnie had said ... only two nights ago.... He couldn't remember.... It was certainly a suggestion that Sylvia was the general's mistress. It had then, he remembered, seemed fantastic....[45] Well, what else *could* they think? He said to himself: "It absolutely blocks out my staying here!" He said aloud: "Of course, it's my own fault. If a man so handles his womenfolk that they get out of hand, he has only himself to blame."

The general was going on. He pointed out that one of his predecessors had lost that very command on account of scandals about women. He had turned the place into a damned harem! ...

He burst out, looking at Tietjens with a peculiar goggle-eyed intentness:

"If you think I'd care about losing my command over Sylvia or any other damned Society woman[46] ..." He said: "I beg your pardon ..." and continued reasoningly:

"It's the men that have to be considered. They think—and they've every right to think it if they wish to—that a man who's a wrong 'un over women isn't the man they can trust their lives in the hands of...." He added: "And they're probably right.... A man who's a real wrong 'un ... I don't mean who sets up a gal in a tea-shop.... But[47] one who sells his wife, or ... At any rate, in *our* army.... The French may be different! ... Well, a man like that usually has a yellow streak when it comes to fighting.[48] ... Mind, I'm not saying always.... Usually.... There was a fellow called ..."

He went off into an anecdote....

Tietjens recognized the pathos of his trying to get away from the agonizing present moment, back to an India where it was all real soldiering and good leather and parades that had been parades. But he did not feel called upon to follow. He could not follow. He was going up the line....

He occupied himself with his mind. What was it going to do? He cast back along his military history: what had his mind done in similar moments before? ... But there had never been a similar moment! There had been the sinister or repulsive businesses of going up, getting over, standing to—even of the casualty clearing-station![49] ... But he had always been physically keener, he had never been so depressed or overwhelmed.

He said[50] to the general:

"I recognize[51] that I cannot stop in this command. I regret it, for I have enjoyed having this unit.... But does it necessarily mean the VIth Battalion?"[52]

He wondered what was his own motive at the moment. Why had he asked the general that? ... The thing presented itself as pictures: getting down bulkily from a high French train, at dawn.

The light picked out for you the white of large hunks of bread—half-loaves—being handed out to troops themselves duskily invisible.... The ovals of light on the hats of English troops: they were mostly West Countrymen. They did not seem to want the bread much.... A long ridge of light above a wooded bank: then suddenly, pervasively, a sound! ... For all the world as, sheltering from rain in a cottager's wash-house on the moors, you hear the cottager's clothes boiling in a copper ... Bubble ... bubble ... bubbubbub ... bubble ... Not terribly loud—but terribly demanding attention! ... The Great Strafe! ...

The general[53] had said:

"If I could think of anything else to do with you, I'd do it.... But all the extraordinary rows you've got into.... They block me everywhere.... Do[54] you realize that I have requested General O'Hara to suspend his functions until now? ..."

It was amazing to Tietjens how the general mistrusted his subordinates—as well as how he trusted them! ... It was probably that that made him so successful an officer. Be worked for by men that you trust: but distrust them all the time—along certain lines of frailty: liquor, women, money! ... Well, he had long knowledge of men!

He said:

"I admit, sir, that I misjudged General O'Hara. I have said as much to Colonel Levin and explained why."

The general said with a gloating irony:

"A damn pretty pass to come to.... You put a general officer under arrest.... Then you say you had misjudged him![55] ... I am not saying you were not performing a duty...." He went on to recount the classical case of a subaltern, cited in King's Regulations,* temp. William IV,† who was court-martialled and broken for not putting under arrest his colonel who came drunk on to parade.... He was exhibiting his sensuous delight in misplaced erudition.

Tietjens heard himself say with great slowness:

"I absolutely deny, sir, that I put General O'Hara under arrest! I have[56] gone into the matter very minutely with Colonel Levin."

---

* King's Regulations: a code of conduct for members of the armed forces.
† The time of William IV's reign (1830–7).

The general burst out:

"By God! I had taken that woman to be a saint.... I swear she is a saint...."

Tietjens said:

"There is no accusation against Mrs. Tietjens, sir!"

The general said:

"By God, there is!"

Tietjens said:

"I am prepared to take all the blame, sir."

The general said:

"You shan't.... I am determined to get to the bottom of all this.... You have treated your wife damn badly.... You admit to that...."

Tietjens said:

"With great want of consideration, sir...."

The general said:

"You have been living practically on terms of separation from her for a number of years? You don't deny that that was on account of your own misbehaviour. For how many years?"

Tietjens said:

"I don't know, sir.... Six or seven!"

The general said sharply:

"Think, then.... It began when you admitted to me that you had been sold up because you kept a girl in a tobacco-shop? That was at Rye in 1912...."

Tietjens said:

"We have not been on terms since 1912, sir."

The general said:

"But why? ... She's a most beautiful woman. She's adorable. What could you want better? ... She's the mother of your child...."

Tietjens said:

"Is it necessary to go into all this, sir? ... Our differences were caused by ... by differences of temperament. She, as you say, is a beautiful and reckless woman.... Reckless in an admirable way. I, on the other hand...."

The general exclaimed:

"Yes! that's just it.... What the hell are you? ... You're not a soldier. You've got the makings of a damn good soldier. You

amaze me at times. Yet you're a disaster; you are a disaster to every
one who has to do with you. You are as conceited as a hog; you
are as obstinate as a bullock.... You drive me mad.... And you
have ruined the life of that beautiful woman.... For I maintain
she[57] once had the disposition of a saint.... Now: I'm waiting for
your explanation!"

Tietjens said:

"In civilian life, sir, I was a statistician. Second secretary to the
Department of Statistics...."

The general exclaimed convictingly:

"And they've thrown you out of that! Because of the mysterious rows you made...."

Tietjens said:

"Because, sir, I was in favour of the single command...."

The general began a long wrangle: "But why were you? What
the hell had it got to do with you?" Couldn't Tietjens have given
the Department the statistics they wanted—even if it meant
faking them? What was discipline for if subordinates were to act
on their consciences? The home Government had wanted statistics faked in order to dish the Allies.... Well ... Was Tietjens
French or English? Every damn thing Tietjens did ... Every *damn*
thing, made it more impossible to do anything for him! With his
attainments he ought to be attached to the staff of the French
Commander-in-Chief. But that was forbidden in his, Tietjens',
confidential report. There was an underlined note in it to that
effect. Where else, then, in Heaven's name, could Tietjens be
sent to? He looked at Tietjens with intent blue eyes:

"Where else, in God's name ... I am not using the Almighty's
name blasphemously ... *can* you be sent to? I *know* it's probably
death to send you up the line—in your condition of health. And
to poor Perry's Army. The Germans will be through it the minute
the weather breaks."[58]

He began again: "You understand: I'm not the War Office. I
can't send any officer anywhere. I can't send you to Malta or
India. Or to other commands in France.[59] I can send you home—
in disgrace. I can send you to your own battalion. On promotion!
... Do you understand my situation? ... I have no alternative."

Tietjens said:

"Not altogether, sir."

The general swallowed and wavered from side to side. He said:
"For God's sake, try to.... I am genuinely concerned for you.
I won't—I'm damned if I will!—let it appear that you're
disgraced.... If you were McKechnie himself I wouldn't! The
only really good jobs I've got to give away are on my own staff. I
can't have you there. Because of the men. At the same time...."

He paused and said with a ponderous shyness:

"I believe there's a God.... I believe that, though wrong may
flourish, right will triumph in the end! ... If a man is innocent,
his innocence will one day appear.... In a humble way I want to
... help Providence.... I want some one to be able one day to
say: '*General Campion, who knew the ins and outs of the affair* ...'
promoted you! In the middle of it...." He said: "It isn't much.
But it's not nepotism. I would do as much for any man in your
position."

Tietjens said:

"It's at least the act of a Christian gentleman!"

A certain lack-lustre joy appeared in the general's eyes. He
said:

"I'm not used to this sort of situation.... I hope I've always
tried to help my junior officers.... But a case like this...." He
said:

"Damn it.... The general commanding the 9th French Army
is an intimate friend of mine.... But in face of your confidential
report—I *can't* ask him to ask for you. That's blocked!"

Tietjens said:

"I do not propose, sir, at any rate in your eyes, to pass as putting
the interests of any power before those of my own country. If you
examine my confidential report you will find that the
unfavourable insertions are initialled G. D.... They are the
initials of a Major Drake...."

The general said bewilderedly:

"Drake ... Drake ... I've heard the name."[60]

Tietjens said:

"It doesn't matter, sir.... Major Drake's a gentleman who
doesn't like me...."

The general said:

"There are so many. You don't try to make yourself popular, I
must say!"

Tietjens said to himself:

"The old fellow feels it! . . . But he can hardly expect me to tell him that Sylvia thinks Drake was the father of my own son, and desires my ruin!" But of course[61] the old man *would* feel it. He, Tietjens, and his wife, Sylvia, were as near a son and daughter as the old man had. The[62] obvious answer to make to the old man's query as to where he, Tietjens, ought to be sent was to remind him that his brother Mark had had an order put through to the effect that Tietjens was to be put in command of divisional transport. . . . *Could* he remind the old man of that? Was it a thing one could do?

Yet the idea of commanding divisional transport was like a vision of Paradise to Tietjens. For two reasons: it was relatively safe, being concerned with a lot of horses . . . and the knowledge that he had that employment would put Valentine Wannop's mind at rest.

Paradise! . . .[63] But *could* one wangle out of a hard into a soft job? Some other poor devil very likely wanted it. On the other hand—think of Valentine Wannop! He imagined her torture of mind, wandering about London, thinking of him in the very worst spot of a doomed army. She would get to hear of that. Sylvia would tell her! He would bet Sylvia would ring her up and tell her. Imagine, then, writing to Mark to say that he was with the transport! Mark would pass it on to the girl within half a minute. Why . . .[64] he, Tietjens, would wire. He imagined himself scribbling the wire while the general talked and giving it to an orderly the moment the talk was over. . . . But *could* he put the idea into the old man's head! *Is* it done? . . . Would, say . . . say, an Anglican saint do it?

And then . . . Was he up to the job? What about the accursed obsession of O Nine Morgan that intermittently jumped on him? All the while he had been riding Schomburg the day before, O Nine Morgan had seemed to be just before the coffin-headed brute's off-shoulder. The animal must fall! . . . He had had the passionate impulse to pull up the horse. And all the time a dreadful depression! A weight! In the hotel last night he had nearly fainted over the thought that Morgan might have been the man whose life he had spared at Noircourt. . . . It was getting to be a serious matter! It might mean that there was a crack in his,

Tietjens', brain. A lesion! If[65] that was to go on ... O Nine Morgan, dirty as he always was, and with the mystified eyes of the subject races on his face, rising up before his horse's off-shoulder![66] But alive, not with half his head cut away.... If that was to go on he would not be fit to deal with transport, which meant a great deal of riding.

But he would chance that.... Besides, some damn fool of a literary civilian had been writing passionate letters to the papers insisting that all horses and mules must be abolished in the army.... Because of their pestilence-spreading dung! .... It might be[67] decreed by A.C.I. that no more horses were to be used! .... Imagine taking battalion supplies down by night with motor lorries, which was what that genius desired to see done! ...

He remembered once or twice—it must have been in September, '16—having had the job of taking battalion transport down from Locre to B.H.Q., which were in the château of Kemmel[68] village.... You muffled every bit of metal you could think of: bits, trace-chains, axles ... and *yet*, whilst you hardly breathed, in the thick darkness some damn thing would always chink and jolt: beef tins made a noise of old iron.... And *bang*, after the long whine, would come the German shell, registered exactly on to the corner of the road where it went down by the shoulder of the hill: where the placards were ordering you not to go more than two men together.... Imagine doing it with lorries, that could be heard five miles away![69] ... The battalion would go pretty short of rations! ... The same anti-chevaline genius had emitted the sentiment that he had rather the Allies lost the war than that cavalry should distinguish themselves in any engagement! ... A wonderful passion for the extermination of dung... ! Or perhaps this hatred of the horse was social.... Because the cavalry wear long moustaches dripping with Macassar oil and breakfast off caviare, chocolate and Pommery Greno* they must be abolished! ... Something like that.... He exclaimed: "By God! How my mind wanders! How long will it go on?" He said: "I am at the end of my tether." He had missed what the general had said for some time.

The general said:

---

* A well-known and distinguished champagne.

"Well. Has he?"

Tietjens said:

"I didn't catch, sir!"

"Are you deaf?" the general asked. "I'm sure I speak plain enough. You've just said there are no horses attached to this camp. I asked you if there is not a horse for the colonel commanding the depot.... A German horse, I understand!"

Tietjens said to himself:

"Great heavens! I've been talking to him. What in the world about?" It was as if his mind were falling off a hillside. He said:

"Yes, sir ... Schomburg. But as that's a German prisoner, captured on the Marne, it is not on our strength. It is the private property of the colonel.[70] I ride it myself...."

The general exclaimed dryly:

"You *would*...." He added more dryly still: "Are you aware that there is a hell of a strafe put in against you by a R.A.S.C. second-lieutenant called Hotchkiss? ..."

Tietjens said quickly:

"If it's over Schomburg, sir ... it's a washout. Lieutenant Hotchkiss[71] has no more right to give orders about him than as to where I shall sleep.... And I would rather die than subject any horse for which I am responsible to the damnable torture Hotchkiss and that swine Lord Beichan want to inflict on service horses...."

The general said maleficently:[72]

"It looks as if you damn well will die on that account!"

He added: "You're perfectly right to object to wrong treatment of horses. But in this case your objection blocks the only other job open to you."[73] He quietened himself a little. "You are probably not aware," he went on, "that your brother Mark ..."

Tietjens said:

"Yes, I'm aware ..."

The general[74] said:

"Do you know that the 19th Division to which your brother wants you sent is attached to Fourth Army now—and it's Fourth Army horses that Hotchkiss is to play with? ... How could I send you there to be under his orders?"

Tietjens said:

"That's perfectly correct, sir. There is nothing else that you can do...." He was finished. There was now nothing left but to find out how his mind was going to take it. He wished they could go to his cook-houses![75]

The general said:

"What was I saying? ... I'm dreadfully tired.... No one could stand this...." He drew from inside his tunic a lapis-lazuli coloured, small be-coroneted note-case and selected from it a folded paper that he first looked at and then slipped between his belt and his tunic. He said: "On top of all the responsibility I have to bear!" He asked: "Has it occurred to you that, if I'm of any service to the country, your taking up my energy—*sapping* my energy over your affairs!—is aiding your country's enemies? ... I can only afford four hours' sleep as it is.... I've got some questions to ask you.... He referred to the slip of paper from his belt, folded it again and again slipped it into his belt.

Tietjens' mind missed a notch again.... It *was* the fear of the mud that was going to obsess him. Yet, curiously, he had never been under heavy fire in mud.... You would think that that would not have obsessed him. But in his ear he had just heard uttered in a whisper of intense weariness, the words: *Es ist nicht zu ertragen; es ist das dasz uns verloren hat ...* words in German, of utter despair, meaning: It is unbearable: it is that that has ruined us.... The mud! ... He had heard those words, standing amidst volcano craters of mud, amongst ravines, monstrosities of slime, cliffs and distances, all of slime.... He had been going, for curiosity or instruction, from Verdun where he had been attached to the French—on a holiday afternoon when nothing was doing, with a guide, to visit one of the outlying forts.... Deaumont? ... No, Douaumont.... Taken from the enemy about a week before.... When would that be? He had lost all sense of chronology.... In November.... A beginning of some November....[*] With a miracle of sunshine: not a cloud: the mud towering up shut you in intimately with a sky that ached for limpidity.... And the slime had moved ... following a French bombardier who was strolling along eating nuts, disreputably, his shoulders rolling.... *Déserteurs....* The moving slime was German deserters.... You could not see them: the leader of

---

[*]   Douaumont was recaptured from the Germans on 24 October 1916.

them—an officer!—had his glasses so thick with mud that you could not see the colour of his eyes, and his half-dozen decorations were like the beginnings of swallows' nests, his beard like stalactites.... Of the other men you could only see the eyes— extraordinarily vivid: mostly blue like the sky! .... Deserters! Led by an officer![76] Of the Hamburg Regiment! As if an officer of the Buffs[77]* had gone over! ... It was incredible.... And that was what the officer had said as he passed: not shamefacedly, but without any humanity left in him.... *Done!* ... Those moving saurians compacted of slime kept on passing him afterwards, all the afternoon.... And he could not help picturing their immediate antecedents for two months.... In advanced pill-boxes.... No, they didn't have pill-boxes then.... In advanced pockets of mud, in dreadful solitude amongst those ravines.... suspended in eternity, at the last day of the world. And it had horribly shocked him to hear again the German language, a rather soft voice, a little suety.... Like an obscene whisper.... The voice obviously of the damned: hell could hold nothing curious for those poor beasts....[78] His French guide had said sardonically: *On dirait l'Inferno de Dante!*† ... Well, those Germans were getting back on him. They were now to become an obsession! A complex, they said nowadays.... The general said coolly:

"I presume you refuse to answer?"

That shook him cruelly.

He said desperately:

"I had to end what I took to be an unbearable position for both parties. In the interests of my son!" Why in the world had he said that? .... He was going to be sick. It came back to him that the general had been talking of his separation from Sylvia. Last night that had happened. He said: "I may have been right: I may have been wrong...."

The general said icily:

"If you don't choose to go into it...."

Tietjens said:

"I would prefer not to...."

---

*   The nickname of the Royal East Kent Regiment (1572–1961), formerly the 3rd Regiment of Foot, whose men first wore buff-coloured leather coats and later buff facings and waistcoats to distinguish themselves from other regiments.
†   'One could say Dante's Inferno.'

The general said:

"There is no end to this.... But there are questions it's my duty to ask.... If you do not wish to go into your marital relations, I cannot force you.... But, damn it, are you sane? Are you responsible? Do you intend to get Miss Wannop to live with you before the war is over? Is she, perhaps, here, in this town, now? Is that your reason for separating from Sylvia? Now, of all times in the world!"

Tietjens said:

"No, sir. I ask you to believe[79] that I have absolutely no relations with that young lady. None! I have no intention of having any. None! ..."

The general said:

"I believe that!"

"Circumstances last night," Tietjens said, "convinced me suddenly, there, on the spot, that I had been wronging my wife.... I had been putting a strain on the lady that was unwarrantable. It humiliates me to have to say it! I had taken a certain course for the sake of the future of our child. But it was an atrociously wrong course. We ought to have separated years ago.[80] It has led to the lady's pulling the strings of all these shower-baths...."

The general said:

"Pulling the ..."

Tietjens said:

"It expresses it, sir.... Last night was nothing but pulling the string of a shower-bath. Perfectly justifiably. I maintain that it was perfectly justifiable."

The general said:

"Then why have you given her Groby? ... You're not a little soft, are you? ... You don't imagine you've ... say, got a mission? Or that you're another person? ... That you have to ... to forgive...." He took off his pretty hat and wiped his forehead with a tiny cambric handkerchief. He said: "Your poor mother was a little...."

He said[81] suddenly:

"To-night when you are coming to my dinner ...[82] I hope you'll be decent. Why do you so neglect your personal appearance? Your tunic is a disgusting spectacle...."

Tietjens said:

"I had a better tunic, sir . . . but it has been ruined by the blood of the man who was killed here last night. . . ."

The general said:

"You don't say you have only two tunics? . . . Have you no mess clothes?"

Tietjens said:

"Yes, sir, I've my blue things. I shall be all right for to-night. . . . But almost everything else I possessed was stolen from my kit when I was in hospital. . . . Even Sylvia's two pair of sheets. . . ."

"But hang it all," the general exclaimed, "you don't mean to say you've spaffled* all your father left you?"

Tietjens said:

"I thought fit to refuse what my father left me owing to the way it was left. . . ."

The general said:

"But, good God! . . . Read that!" He tossed the small sheet of paper at which he had been looking across the table. It fell face downwards. Tietjens read, in the minute handwriting of the general's:

"Colonel's horse: Sheets: Jesus Christ: Wannop girl: Socialism?"

The general said irritably:

"The other side . . . the other side. . . ."

The other side of the paper displayed the words in large capitals: WORKERS OF THE WORLD, a wood-cut of a sickle and some other objects. Then high treason for a page.[83]

The general said:

"Have you ever seen anything like that before? Do you know what it is?"

Tietjens answered:

"Yes, sir. I sent that to you. To your Intelligence. . . ."

The general thumped both his fists violently on the army blanket:

---

* This word isn't recorded in the *OED*, nor by Brewer or Partridge. From the context it is clear it means 'spent' or 'wasted', and is also used in that sense by Walter Sickert (who had taught Stella Bowen) in a 1932 exhibition catalogue: *Walter Sickert: The Complete Writings on Art*, ed. Anna Gruetzner Robins (Oxford: Oxford University Press, 2000), 622; and also by Elizabeth Sprigge in her novel *The Old Man Dies* (Macmillan, 1933), 299.

"You ..." he said. "It's incomprehensible.... It's incredible...."

Tietjens said:

"No, sir.... You sent out an order asking commanders of units to ascertain what attempts were being made by Socialists to undermine the discipline of their other ranks.... I naturally asked my sergeant-major, and he produced this sheet, which one of the men had given to him as a curiosity. It had been handed to the man in the street in London. You can see my initials on the top of the sheet!"

The general[84] said:

"You ... you'll excuse me, but you're not a Socialist yourself? ..."

Tietjens said:

"I knew you were working round to that, sir: But I've no politics that did not disappear in the eighteenth century. You, sir, prefer the seventeenth!"

"Another shower-bath, I suppose," the general said.

"Of course," Tietjens said, "if it's Sylvia that called me a Socialist, it's not astonishing. I'm a Tory of such an extinct type that she might take me for anything. The last megatherium.* She's absolutely to be excused...."

The general was not listening. He said:

"What was wrong with the way your father left his money to you? ..."

"My father," Tietjens said—the general saw his jaw stiffen—"committed suicide because a fellow called Ruggles told him that I was ... what the French called *maquereau*....† I can't think of the English word. My father's suicide was not an act that can be condoned. A gentleman does not commit suicide when he has descendants. It might influence my boy's life very disastrously...."

The general said:

---

* 'An extinct genus of huge herbivorous edentates resembling sloths'. *Transf.* 'Something of huge or ungainly proportions': OED.

† *Maquereau* is literally French for a mackerel; slang for 'pimp'. Tietjens, later in this chapter, speaks of making 'a living out of the immoral earnings of women' and 'selling your wife or mistress' accusations against him. Cf. *When the Wicked Man* (London: Cape, 1932), 288.

"I can't . . . I *can't* get to the bottom of all this. . . . What in the world did Ruggles want to go and tell your father that for? . . . What are you going to do for a living after the war? They won't take you back into your office, will they?"

Tietjens said:

"No, sir. The Department will not take me back. Every one who has served in this war will be a marked man for a long time after it is over. That's proper enough. *We're* having our fun now."

The general said:

"You say the wildest things."

Tietjens answered:

"You generally find the things I say come true, sir. Could we get this over? Ruggles told my father what he did because it is not a good thing to belong to the seventeenth or eighteenth centuries in the twentieth. Or really, because it is not good to have taken one's public-school's ethical system seriously. I am really, sir, the English public schoolboy.[*] That's an eighteenth-century product. What[85] with the love of truth that—God help me!—they rammed into me at Clifton and the belief Arnold[†] forced upon Rugby that the vilest of sins—the vilest of all sins—is to peach to the head master! That's me, sir. Other men get over their schooling. I never have. I remain adolescent.[86] These things are obsessions with me. Complexes, sir!"

The general said:

"All this seems to be very wild. . . . What's this about peaching to a head master?"[87]

Tietjens said:

"For a swan song, it's not wild, sir. You're asking for a swan song. I am to go up into the line so that the morals of the troops in your command may not be contaminated by the contemplation of my marital infelicities."

The general[88] said:

"You don't want to go back to England, do you?"

Tietjens exclaimed:

---

[*] Cf. *When Blood is Their Argument* 301: Ford describing himself as unfortunate in the sense that all men over forty are unfortunate. 'For I came into, and took very seriously, English public-school life at a time when the English public-school spirit – in many ways the finest product of a civilisation – was already on the wane.'

[†] Thomas Arnold (1795–1842) was headmaster of Rugby School from 1828 to 1841, which he made into a model for other public schools to emulate.

"Certainly not! Very certainly not! I can never go home.[89] I have to go underground somewhere. If I went back to England there would be nothing for me but going underground by suicide."

The general[90] said:

"You see all that? I can give you testimonials. . . ."[91]

Tietjens asked:

"Who couldn't see that it's impossible?"[92]

The general said:

"But . . . suicide! You won't do that. As you said: think of your son."

Tietjens said:

"No, sir. I shan't do that. But you see how bad for one's descendants suicide is. That is why I do not forgive my father. Before he did it I should never have contemplated the idea. Now I have contemplated it. That's a weakening of the moral fibre. It's contemplating a fallacy as a possibility.[93] For suicide is no remedy for a twisted situation of a psychological kind. It is for bankruptcy. Or for military disaster. For the man of action, not for the thinker. Creditors' meetings wipe the one out. Military operations sweep on. But my problem will remain the same whether I'm here or not. For it's insoluble. It's the whole problem of the relations of the sexes."

The general[94] said:

"Good God! . . ."

Tietjens said:

"No, sir, I've not gone off my chump. That's my problem! . . . But I'm a fool to talk so much. . . . It's because I don't know what to say."[95]

The general sat staring at the tablecloth: his face was suffused with blood. He had the appearance of a man in monstrous ill-humour. He said:

"You had better say what you want to say. What[96] the devil do you mean? . . . What's this all about ? . . ."

Tietjens said:

"I'm enormously sorry, sir. It's difficult to make myself plain."

The general said:

"Neither of us do. What is language for? What the *hell* is language for? We go round and round. I suppose I'm an old fool who cannot understand your modern ways . . .[97] But you're not modern. I'll do you *that* justice. . . . That beastly little McKechnie is modern. . . . I shall ram him into your divisional-transport job, so that he won't incommode you in your battalion. . . . Do you understand what the little beast did? He got leave to go and get a divorce. And then did not get a divorce. *That's* modernism. He said he had scruples. I understand that he and his wife and . . . some dirty other fellow . . . slept three in a bed. That's modern scruples. . . ."

Tietjens said:

"No, sir, it's not really. . . .[98] But what is a man to do if his wife is unfaithful to him?"

The general said as if it were an insult:

"Divorce the harlot! Or live with her! . . ." Only a beast, he went on, would expect a woman to live all her life alone in a cockloft!* She's bound to die. Or go on the streets. . . . What sort of a fellow wouldn't see that? Was there any sort of beast who'd expect a woman to live . . . with a man beside her. . . . Why, she'd . . . she'd be bound to. . . . He'd have to take the consequences of whatever happened. The general repeated: "Whatever happened! If she pulled all the strings of all the shower-baths in the world!"

Tietjens said:

"Still, sir . . . there are . . . there used to be . . . in families of . . . position . . . a certain . . ." He stopped.

The general said:

"Well . . ."

Tietjens said:

"On the part of the man . . . a certain . . . Call it . . . parade!"

The general said:

"Then there had better be no more parades. . . ." He said: "Damn it! . . . Beside us, all women are saints. . . . Think of what child-bearing is. I know the world. . . . Who would stand that? . . . You? . . . I . . . I'd rather be the last poor devil in Perry's lines!"

He looked at Tietjens with a sort of injurious cunning:

"Why *don't* you divorce?"[99] he asked.

Panic came over Tietjens. He knew it would be his last panic

---

* 'A small upper loft; a small apartment under the very ridge of the roof to which the access is usually by a ladder': *OED.*

of that interview. No brain could stand more. Fragments of scenes of fighting, voices, names, went before his eyes and ears. Elaborate problems.... The whole map of the embattled world ran out in front of him—as large as a field. An embossed map in greenish *papier mâché*—a ten-acre field of embossed *papier mâché*: with the blood of O Nine Morgan blurring luminously over it.[100] Years before ... How many months?... Nineteen, to be exact, he had sat on some tobacco plants on the Mont de Kats.... No, the Montagne Noire.* In Belgium.... What had he been doing?... Trying to get the lie of the land.... No.... Waiting to point out positions to some fat home general who had never come. The Belgian proprietor of the tobacco plants had arrived, and had screamed his head off over the damaged plants....

But, up there you saw the whole war.... Infinite miles away, over the sullied land that the enemy forces held: into Germany proper. Presumably you could breathe in Germany proper.... Over your right shoulder you could see a stump of a tooth. The Cloth Hall at Ypres: at an angle of 50° below.... Dark lines behind it.... The German trenches before Wytschaete! ...

That was before the great mines had blown Wytschaete to hell....

But—every half-minute by his wrist-watch—white puffs of cotton-wool existed on the dark lines—the German trenches before Wytschaete.† Our artillery practice.... Good shooting. Jolly good shooting!

Miles and miles away to the left ... beneath the haze of light that, on a clouded day, the sea threw off, a shaft of sunlight fell, and was reflected in a grey blur.... It was the glass roofs of a great airplane shelter!

A great plane, the largest he had then seen, was moving over, behind his back, with four little planes as an escort....[101] Over the vast slag-heaps by Béthune.... High, purplish-blue heaps, like the steam domes of engines or the breasts of women.... Bluish purple. More blue than purple.... Like all Franco-Belgian

---

*   The Mont de Cats and Mont Noir are both near Ypres.

†   Cf. 'War and the Mind: II. The Enemy': 'And little white balls would exist, one by one, at intervals of a second or so, appearing to be an inch to the right, or an inch to the left, all the way between Messines and Wytschaete. One thought comfortingly: "Our own shells." And one said aloud: "Somebody will be ducking, out there!"': *War Prose* 42.

Gobelins tapestry.... And all quiet.... Under the vast pall of quiet cloud! ...

There were shells dropping in Poperinghe.... Five miles out, under his nose.... The shells dropped. White vapour rose and ran away in plumes.... What sort of shells? ... There were twenty different kinds of shells....

The Huns were shelling Poperinghe! A senseless cruelty.* It was five miles behind the line! Prussian brutality.... There were two girls who kept a tea-shop in Poperinghe.... High coloured.... General Plumer had liked them ... a fine old general.... The shells had killed them both.... Any man might have slept with either of them with pleasure and profit.... Six thousand of H.M. officers must have thought the same about those high-coloured girls. Good girls! ... But the Hun shells got them.... What sort of fate was that? ... To be desired by six thousand men and smashed into little gobbets of flesh by Hun shells?

It appeared to be mere Prussianism—the senseless cruelty of the Hun!—to shell Poperinghe. An innocent town with a tea-shop five miles behind Ypres.... Little noiseless plumes of smoke rising under the quiet blanketing of the pale maroon skies, with the haze from the aeroplane shelters, and the great aeroplanes over the Béthune slag-heaps.... What a dreadful name—Béthune....

Probably, however, the Germans had heard that we were massing men in Poperinghe. It was reasonable to shell a town where men were being assembled.... Or we might have been shelling one of their towns with an Army H.Q. in it. So they shelled Poperinghe in the silent grey day....

That was according to the rules of the service.... General

---

* Cf. the Preface to Violet Hunt's *Their Lives* (1916) which Ford wrote from the Ypres Salient in September 1916: 'I could see the gas shells bursting in Poperinghe; it was a very great view, but I am prohibited from descanting on it. But the gas shells that the Bosches were sending into Poperinghe set me thinking. You see, there was not much sense in gassing Poperinghe: it killed a great many Belgian civilians and that is all. It was in fact, just casual cruelty, quite systematic. And as I write now, I can hear them shelling another little town a mile away – and giving us a shell too now and then, for the love of God, I suppose?

And while I was looking at that great view, perceiving the little white mushrooms of our own shells suddenly existing in the dark line under [Wytschaete] — miles and miles away [. . .]': *War Prose* 189.

Campion, accepting with equanimity what German airplanes did
to the hospitals, camps, stables, brothels, theatres, boulevards,
chocolate stalls and hotels of his town would have been vastly
outraged if Hun planes had dropped bombs on his private lodg-
ings. . . . The rules of war! . . . You spare, mutually, each other's
headquarters and blow to pieces girls that are desired by six thousand men apiece. . . .

That had been nineteen months before! . . . Now, having lost
so much emotion, he saw the embattled world as a map. . . . An
embossed map of greenish *papier mâché*. The blood of O Nine
Morgan was blurring luminously over it. At the extreme horizon
was territory labelled *White Ruthenians*! Who the devil were *those*
poor wretches?

He exclaimed to himself: "By heavens! Is this epilepsy?" He
prayed: "Blessed saints, get me spared that!" He exclaimed: "No,
it isn't! . . . I've complete control of my mind. My uppermost
mind." He said to the general:

"I can't divorce, sir. I've no grounds."

The general said:

"Don't lie. You know what Thurston knows. Do you mean that
you have been guilty of contributory misconduct? . . . Whatever
it is? And can't divorce! I don't believe it."[102]

Tietjens said to himself:

"*Why* the devil am I so anxious to shield that whore? It's not
reasonable. It is an obsession!"

White Ruthenians are miserable peoples to the south of
Lithuania. You don't know whether they incline to the Germans
or to the Poles. The Germans don't even know. . . . The Germans
were beginning to take their people out of the line where we were
weak: they were going to give them proper infantry training. That
gave him, Tietjens, a chance. They would not come over strong
for at least two months. It meant, though, a great offensive in the
spring. Those fellows had sense. In the poor, beastly trenches the
Tommies knew nothing but how to chuck bombs. Both sides did
that. But the Germans were going to cure it![103] Stood chucking
bombs at each other from forty yards. The rifle was obsolete! Ha!
ha! Obsolete! . . . The civilian psychology!

The general said:

"No! I don't believe it. I know you did not keep any girl in any tobacco-shop. I remember every word you said at Rye in 1912. I wasn't sure then. I am now.[104] You tried to let me think it. You[105] had shut up your house because of your wife's misbehaviour. You let me believe you had been sold up. You weren't sold up at all."

... Why[106] should it be the civilian psychology to chuckle with delight, uproariously, when the imbecile idea was promulgated that the rifle was obsolete? Why should public opinion force on the War Office a training-camp course that completely cut out any thorough instruction in the rifle and communication drill? It was queer.... It was of course disastrous. Queer. Not altogether mean. Pathetic, too....

"Love of truth!" the general said. "Doesn't that include a hatred for white lies? No; I suppose it doesn't, or your servants could not say you were not at home...."

... Pathetic! Tietjens said to himself. Naturally the civilian population wanted soldiers to be made to look like fools: and to be done in. They wanted the war won by men who would at the end be either humiliated or dead. Or both.* Except, naturally, their own cousins or fiancées' relatives. That was what it came to. That was what it meant when important gentlemen said that they had rather the war were lost than that cavalry should gain any distinction in it! ... But it was partly the simple, pathetic illusion of the day that great things could only be done by new inventions. You extinguished the Horse,[107] invented something very simple and became God! That is the real pathetic fallacy. You fill a flower-pot with gunpowder and chuck it in the other fellow's face, and heigh presto! the war is won. All the soldiers fall down dead! And You: you who forced the idea on the reluctant military, are the Man that Won the War. You deserve all the women in the world. And ... you get them! Once the cavalry are out of the way! ...

---

* Cf. Wyndham Lewis, *Blasting and Bombardiering* (London: Calder, 1982), 185, recalling Ford's prophecy of 1915–16: "'When this war's over,' he said, "nobody is going to worry, six months afterwards, what you did or didn't do in the course of it. One month after it's ended, it will be forgotten. Everybody will want to forget it – it will be bad form to mention it. Within a year disbanded 'heroes' will be selling matches in the gutter. No one likes the ex-soldier – if you've lost a leg, more fool you!"

"Do you think that?" I said, for he almost made my leg feel sorry for itself.

"Of course," he answered. "It's always been the same. After all the wars that's what's happened."

This worldly forecast was verified to the letter.'

The general was using the words:

"Head master!" It brought Tietjens completely back.

He said collectedly:

"Really, sir, why this strafe of yours is so terribly long is that it embraces the whole of life."

The general[108] said:

"You're not going to drag a red herring across the trail.... I say you regarded me as a head master in 1912. Now I am your commanding officer—which is the same thing. You must not peach to me. That's what you call the Arnold of Rugby touch.... But who was it said: *Magna est veritas et prev ... Prev** something!*"

Tietjens said:

"I don't remember, sir."

The general said:

"What was the secret grief your mother had? In 1912?[109] She died of it. She wrote to me just before her death and said she had great troubles. And begged me to look after you, very specially! Why did she do that?" He paused and meditated. He asked:[110] "How do you define Anglican sainthood? The other fellows have canonizations, all shipshape like Sandhurst examinations. But us Anglicans ... I've heard fifty persons say your mother was a saint. She was. But why?"

Tietjens said:

"It's the quality of harmony, sir. The quality of being in harmony with your own soul. God having given you your own soul you are then in harmony with Heaven."

The general said:

"Ah, that's beyond me.... I suppose you will refuse any money I leave you in my will?"

Tietjens said:

"Why, no, sir."

The general said:

"But you refused your father's money. Because he believed things against you. What's the difference?"

Tietjens said:

* The 'something' can be either *prevalebit* or *prevalet*. *Magna est veritas et prevalebit*, 'Great is the truth and it shall prevail', is attributed to the Apocryphal 3 Esdras 4:41. In the Appendix to Latin Vulgate, *prevalet*, 'it prevails', replaces *prevalebit*.

"One's friends ought to believe that one is a gentleman. Automatically. That is what makes one and them in harmony.[111] Probably your friends are your friends because they look at situations automatically as you look at them. . . . Mr. Ruggles knew that I was hard up. He envisaged the situation. If he were hard up, what would he do? Make a living out of the immoral earnings of women. . . . That translated into the Government circles in which he lives means selling your wife or mistress. Naturally he believed that I was the sort of fellow to sell my wife. So that's what he told my father. The point is, my father should not have believed him."

"But I . . ." the general said.

Tietjens said:

"You never believed anything against me, sir."

The general said:

"I know I've damn well worried myself to death over you . . ."

Tietjens was sentimentally[112] at rest, still with wet eyes. He was walking[113] near Salisbury in a grove, regarding long pastures and ploughlands running to dark, high elms from which, embowered. . . . Embowered was the word!—peeped the spire of George Herbert's church. . . . [114] One ought to be a seventeenth-century parson at the time of the renaissance of Anglican saintliness . . . who wrote, perhaps poems. No, not poems. Prose. The statelier vehicle!

That was home-sickness! . . . He himself was never to go home![115]

The general[116] said:

"Look here. . . . Your father. . . . I'm concerned about your father. . . . Didn't Sylvia perhaps tell him some of the things that distressed him?"

Tietjens said distinctly:

"No, sir. That responsibility cannot be put on to Sylvia. My father chose to believe things that were said against me by a perfect—or a nearly perfect—stranger. . . ." He added: "As[117] a matter of fact, Sylvia and my father were not on any sort of terms. I don't believe they exchanged two words for the last five years of my father's life."

The general's eyes were fixed with an extreme hardness on Tietjens'. He watched Tietjens' face, beginning with the edges round the nostrils, go chalk white.[118] He said: "He knows he's given his wife away! ... Good God!" With his face colourless, Tietjens' eyes of porcelain-blue stuck out extraordinarily. The general thought: "What an ugly fellow! His face is all crooked!"[119] They remained looking at each other.

In the silence the voices of men talking over the game of House came as a murmur to them. A rudimentary card game monstrously in favour of the dealer. When you heard voices going on like that you knew they were playing House.... So they had had their dinners.[120]

The general said:

"It isn't Sunday, is it?"

Tietjens said:

"No, sir; Thursday, the seventeenth, I think, of January...."

The general said:

"Stupid of me...."

The men's voices had reminded him of church bells on a Sunday. And of his youth.... He was sitting beside Mrs. Tietjens' hammock under the great cedar at the corner of the stone house at Groby. The wind being from the east-north-east the bells of Middlesbrough came to them faintly. Mrs. Tietjens was thirty; he himself thirty; Tietjens—the father—thirty-five or so. A most powerful, quiet man. A wonderful landowner. Like his predecessors for generations. It was not from him that this fellow got his ... his ... his what? ... Was it mysticism? ... Another word![121] He himself home on leave from India: his head full of polo. Talking for hours about points in ponies with Tietjens' father, who was a wonderful hand with a horse. But this fellow was much more wonderful! ... Well, he got that from the sire, not the dam! ... He and Tietjens continued to look at each other.[122] It was as if they were hypnotized. The men's voices went on in a mournful cadence. The general supposed that he too must be pale. He said to himself: "This fellow's mother died of a broken heart[123] in 1912. The father committed suicide five years after. He had not spoken to the son's wife for four or five years! That takes us back to 1912.... Then, when I strafed him in Rye, the wife was in France with Perowne."[124]*

---

* Campion's recollection here supports the dating of Part I of *Some Do Not ...* as taking place in 1912.

He looked down at the blanket on the table. He intended again to look up at Tietjens' eyes with ostentatious care. That was his technique with men. He was a successful general because he knew men. He knew that all men will go to hell over three things: alcohol, money ... and sex. This fellow apparently hadn't. Better[125] for him if he had! He thought:

"It's all gone ... mother! father! Groby! This fellow's down and out. It's a bit thick."

He thought:

"But he's right to do as he is doing."

He prepared to look at Tietjens.... He stretched out a sudden, ineffectual hand. Sitting on his beef-case, his hands on his knees, Tietjens had lurched. A sudden lurch—as an old house lurches when it is hit by a H.E. shell. It stopped at that. Then he righted himself. He continued to stare direct at the general. The general looked carefully back. He said—very carefully too:

"In case I decide to contest West Cleveland, it is your wish that I should make Groby my headquarters?"

Tietjens said:

"I beg, sir, that you will!"

It was as if they both heaved an enormous sigh of relief. The general said:

"Then I need not keep you...."

Tietjens stood[126] on his feet, wanly, but with his heels together.[127]

The general also rose, settling his belt. He said:

"... You can fall out."

Tietjens said:

"My cook-houses, sir ... Sergeant-Cook Case will be very disappointed.... He[128] told me that you couldn't find anything wrong if I gave him ten minutes to prepare...."

The general said:

"Case ... Case ... Case was in the drums when we were at Delhi. He ought to be at least Quartermaster by now.... But he had a woman he called his sister...."

Tietjens said:

"He still sends money to his sister."

The general said:[129]

"... He went absent over her when he was colour-sergeant and

was reduced to the ranks.... Twenty years ago that must be! ...
Yes, I'll see your dinners!"

In[130] the cook-house, brilliantly accompanied by Colonel
Levin, the cook-house spotless with limed walls and mirrors that
were the tops of camp-cookers, the general, Tietjens at his side,
walked between[131] goggle-eyed men in white who stood to attention holding ladles. Their eyes bulged, but the corners of their lips
curved because they liked the general and his beautifully uncon-
cerned companions. The cook-house was like a cathedral's nave,
aisles being divided off by the pipes of stoves. The floor was of
coke-brise* shining under french polish and turpentine.

The building paused, as when a godhead descends. In breathless focusing of eyes the godhead, frail and shining, walked with
short steps up to a high-priest who had a walrus moustache and,
with seven medals on his Sunday tunic, gazed away into eternity.
The general tapped the sergeant's Good Conduct ribbon with the
heel of his crop. All stretched ears heard him say:

"How's your sister, Case? ..."

Gazing away, the sergeant said:

"I'm thinking of making her Mrs. Case...."

Slightly leaving him, in the direction of high, varnished pitchpine panels, the general said:

"I'll recommend you for a Quartermaster's commission any day
you wish.... Do you remember Sir Garnet† inspecting field
kitchens at Quetta?"

All the white tubular beings with global eyes resembled the
pierrots of a child's Christmas nightmare. The general said:
"Stand at ease, men ... Stand easy!" They moved as white
objects move in a childish dream. It was all childish. Their eyes
rolled.

---

* Coke brize or breeze: 'Small cinders and cinder-dust, used in burning bricks, etc.; small
  coke and coke-dust': OED. Chambers' Dictionary explains further: 'furnace refuse
  used in making breeze brick, breeze blocks, breeze concrete for building'.
† Field Marshal Garnet Joseph Wolseley, 1st Viscount Wolseley (1833–1913), served
  in Burma, the Crimean War, the Indian Mutiny, China, Canada, and widely
  throughout Africa – including his celebrated Ashanti campaign (1873–4) and the
  Nile Expedition against the Mahdi in Sudan (1884–5). His reputation for efficiency
  led to the late nineteenth-century English phrase 'everything's all Sir Garnet',
  meaning 'all is in order'.

Sergeant Case gazed away into infinite distance.

"My sister would not like it, sir," he said. "I'm better off as a first-class warrant officer!"

With his light step the shining general went swiftly to the varnished panels in the eastern aisle of the cathedral. The white figure beside them became instantly tubular, motionless and global-eyed. On the panels were painted: TEA! SUGAR! SALT! CURRY PDR! FLOUR! PEPPER!

The general tapped with the heel of his crop on the locker-panel labelled PEPPER: the top, right-hand locker-panel. He said to the tubular, global-eyed white figure beside it: "Open that, will you, my man? . . ."[132]

To Tietjens this was like the sudden bursting out of the regimental quick-step, as after a funeral with military honours the band and drums march away, back to barracks.[*]

---

[*] Cf. *Nightingale* 19–20: 'At a British military funeral, after the Dead March in *Saul*, after the rattling of the cords from under the coffin, the rifle-firing and the long wail of the Last Post suddenly the band and drums strike up "D'ye ken John Peel?" or the "Lincolnshire Poacher" – the unit's quickstep. It is shocking until you see how good it is as a symbol.' 'John Peel' figures in *Some Do Not . . .* I.vii, during the crucial dog-cart ride during which Tietjens and Valentine fall in love; and also in *A Man Could Stand Up* – I.ii. In *Mister Bosphorus and the Muses* (London: Duckworth, 1923), 117, various quicksteps are played slowly over Bosphorus's coffin. The theme of the Last Post becomes increasingly important in the following two novels.

TEXTUAL NOTES

Key to Textual Endnotes

UK *No More Parades*. London: Duckworth, 1925
US *No More Parades*. New York: Albert & Charles Boni, 1925
TS Typescript for *No More Parades*
CE *Contact Collection of Contemporary Writers*. Paris: Contact Editions, 1925
Ed Editor
< > Deleted passages
[ ] Conjectural reading (or editorial indication that a passage is illegible)
↑ ↓ Passage (generally handwritten) inserted above a typewritten line; often to replace a deleted passage
AR Autograph revision

Most of the textual notes compare a passage from UK with the corresponding passage from TS, and where appropriate, with other witnesses. In these notes the abbreviation for the witness is given in bold typeface. Where witnesses agree, their abbreviations are listed, separated by commas. Semi-colons are used to separate the different quotations. The first quotation is always from UK; it is followed by the corresponding segment(s) from the manuscript and/or other witness(es). With segments longer than a single word in UK, the first and last words are identical in all versions, to enable ready comparison. In the example:

UK, TS anti-air-gun; **US** anti-aircraft

the UK text follows the typescript reading 'anti-air-gun', which has been revised to 'anti-aircraft' for US.

Deletions in the manuscript are quoted within angled brackets; insertions are recorded between vertical arrows. They are followed by the abbreviation 'AR' if an autograph revision. Thus:

UK the motives of; **TS** the <mental troubles> ↑motives **AR**↓ of

indicates that in TS the original typed expression 'mental troubles' has been deleted, and replaced with the autograph word 'motives' inserted above the line.

The abbreviation **Ed** is only used where the editor adopts a reading different from all the witnesses. This is mainly used only for grammatical corrections.

Discursive notes (which don't compare versions) are differentiated by not using bold face for the witness abbreviations. In the discursive notes beginning 'AR insertion', the text given in inverted commas is an autograph insertion, usually written above the line, and incorporated into UK.

The symbol ¶ is used to indicate a paragraph break in a variant quoted in the textual endnotes. For verse quoted in the footnotes, a line break is indicated by '/'.

Textual Note for Title-Page

1 **UK** Proverbs; **TS** Prov. II vii
   Ecclesiasticus 26:28: 'There be two things that grieve my heart; and the third maketh me angry: a man of war that suffereth poverty; and men of understanding that are not set by; and one that returneth from righteousness to sin; the Lord prepareth such an one for the sword.'

Textual Notes for Dedicatory Letter

1 **UK** Few writers can have engaged themselves as combatants; **TS** I engaged myself as a combatant
2 **UK** without the intention of aiding with their writings, if; **TS** with the perfectly definite intention of aiding with my pen, if
3 This paragraph is omitted in UK. It begins with the same word as the last paragraph, 'So'. Its omission suggests a slip of the eye by the compositor.
4 **UK** 25 May, '25; **TS** 25 March, '25

Textual Notes for I.i

1 **UK** younger man, intolerably fatigued, spoke; **TS** younger man, intolerably fatigued, <with the effect of stalling off fear,> spoke; **CE** younger man spoke
2 **UK** Mackenzie; **TS** <McKenzie> Mackenzie; **CE** McKechnie
3 **UK, TS** pooped; **US** popped
4 **UK** Cabinet, felt; **TS** cabinet <and particularly of the head> felt
   AR insertion: 'felt by then by the greater part of that army'
5 **UK** vanities of men who; **TS** vanities of <one, very little, man....> who
   AR insertion: 'men who amidst these hugenesses of landscapes and forces appeared pygmies!' This and the previous revision tone down what would have been understood as *ad hominem* derogations of Lloyd George.
6 This sentence is an AR insertion.
7 **UK** fellow. I've heard a lot about you!" ¶ Tietjens; **TS** fellow. ↑I've heard a lot about you! [AR]↓ <If it is true I wish you joy. He's rotten with......"¶ Tietjens

The following passage of five paragraphs, from 'Tietjens laughed at this madness.' to 'to have a mother known as a whore. . . .' is the first substantial AR insertion in TS, numbered 12a and 12b. It falls in the middle of leaf 12, which was divided in two, the lower half being renumbered as 13, and the original leaf 13 becoming 13A.

8 **UK** clean even; **TS** clean run
Compositor misread Ford's handwriting.

9 **UK** mind. Well; **TS** mind. When they were tired! Well

10 **UK** but about his fabulous uncle, not about Sylvia; **AR** but about his fantastical uncle, not about Sylvia

11 **UK** Captain Mackenzie—Tietjens was not sure that the name was Mackenzie: it had looked something like it in the general's hand—Captain Mackenzie; **TS** Captain McKenzie—Tietjens was not sure that the name was McKenzie: it had looked something like it in the general's hand—Captain McKenzie

12 **UK** He stammered; **TS** He <¶ "If you're only just playacting to yourself . . . I damn well wouldn't," Tietgens [*sic*] went on. "It's your own affair of course. But you may make it damned unpleasant for yourself." ¶ The man> stammered

13 **UK** to." ¶ "You're; **TS** to." <¶ Have you ever thought that the most damnable sort of madness—the really miserable and tragic sort—is when you're mad and know—that you are mad." ¶ The dim figure across the table said: ¶ "Don't." ¶ "It's what", Tietjens <considered> continued remorselessly, "You're aiming for. Head down. I should say so. You must know your own case best. I'm only telling you that when you visit a lunatic asylum you see half the poor devils perfectly happy. They're Emperors of China and Mr Gladstone and Queen Victoria all right. As well be that as any other sort of poor devil outside. Better. . . . But suppose. . . . ¶ "I don't want to", the other said. ¶ "It's different with the other half", Tietjens began again. "They're the ones that have let themselves go. So they're the ones that know Hell."> ¶ "You're

14 **UK** you. I've; **TS** you. <"Well, damn it, have you got an uncle that's tried to do you in?" Tietjens asked. "No, I'm not a mad-doctor. I was a statistician once. I had to get statistics. All sorts of statistics about everything. It was a mad doctor that gave me that information. Of course I've worked out the idea a bit myself." ¶ "Yes,> I've

15 **UK** said. ¶"He's; **TS** said. <"But look here sonny <very well then> —Excuse my addressing my senior as sonny—You limit your aspirations to revenging yourself on your uncle. You stick to that idea with both hands. Don't wander away into revenging yourself on the world of the General. Or me, as it might be. That would be the way to <pay> play your injurious relative's game<"> You'd find yourself shut up so tight that you could do him no more harm than the babes in the wood could to <u>their</u> uncle after thy [*sic*] had been buried in leaves. . . . ."> "He's

16 **UK** bad. . . . " He; **TS**: bad. . . . " <They appear to have found their rat. There will be lots of shrapnel over in a minute. There's no good sitting here if you don't want to. Only don't bolt—as demonstration of disobeying orders."> He

17 **UK** row. . . . Why; **TS** row. . . <It's look here . . . It's having not to shriek like a beastly girl . . .> Why; **CE** row. . . The sheer noise. . . It's. . . Look

here… It's having not to shriek like a beastly girl… Why

18 **UK** asked, "You; **TS** asked <Very likely no one would hear you. And> You

19 **UK** here." ¶ Loud; **TS** here." <We're all too well taken up with doubting our own….."> ¶ Loud

20 **UK** clever." ¶ Two; **TS** clever. <¶ "I think I damn well did", Tietjens answered, "But I don't think I'm damn clever. If I had been sure of the effect I should have been damn clever. I had to choose between letting you go and ordering you to stop. I chose ordering you to stop, but I'd no idea of the effect. There used to be a time….."> ¶ Two

21 **UK** answered. And; **TS** answered. <He said to himself wearily that he did not see that it was any of his job to probe into the mental state of a young man whose accent was not quite all right… a young man whom in other circumstances one would not know except possibly as bringing round several pairs of boots on approval. Something like that. He could not blindingly and immediately see that it was any of his job. There were institutions for taking care of the young men who brought round pairs of boots on approval…. > And

22 **UK** us." Tietjens; **TS** us." <We've got an infinite number of inemy [sic] nationals in our pay from Austrian Generals down to Polish riveters in their beastly navy yards…"> Tietjens

23 **UK** concluded: "We; **TS** concluded: <"It's about the one department in which we are efficient. It makes us the admiration of the civilised world.> "We

24 **AR** insertion: 'So he talked … <u>any</u> old talk, wearisomely, to keep his mind employed!'

25 **UK** allegiance. He; **TS** allegiance. <But still he was aware that that wasn't why he had been probing this fellow's mind, for his good, he said:> He

26 **UK** west country cathedral city; **TS** Shrewsbury

27 **UK, TS, US** Peronne; **Ed** Péronne

28 **UK** there." ¶ Mackenzie; **TS** there." <He felt a satisfaction that astonished him. The fellow had some dark woman in his life…. They had been fair. He could not remember any dark woman even…. Mrs. Duchemin? She had been dark but his relationship with her had never been such that the recollected association could make him feel sentimental. Five loud bumps came from various points of the compass and three enormous, horrible roars, breathless, one on the heels of the other. The pop-pop-popping became clear, as if the sound had acquired clean, not <wolly> wooly outlines.> ¶ Mackenzie

29 **UK** said. "It's; **TS** said <about your player and the game."> "It's

30 **UK**: mean. ¶ "At; **TS** mean. <about it's having got us into the hole we are in."> ¶ "At

31 **UK** fellow … What; **TS** fellow…. What
Emended following TS to conform to UK's general principle of using three suspension dots with a preceding space only for incomplete sentences.

32 **UK** department." ¶ The other; **TS** department." <What does the Preacher say: 'For two things my heart is grieved: a man of war that suffereth from poverty and men of intelligence that are counted as refuse' … Our Men of Intelligence are counted as refuse all right".> The other
Ford decided to use this passage as the novel's epigraph. See Introduction.

33 **UK** course." ¶ A man; **TS** course." <"And your uncle really did prevent your

going to the Foreign Office", Tietjens asked a little warmly. For however little of an infantry officer you may be by nature you do feel a little warmth—more than a little warmth—towards a regimental officer who does not put in for the soft jobs that are to be found round Headquarters—as if a woman virtuously parted from a forbidden lover! ... It used to be very like that—like deserving the V.C..... So he felt warmly against this fellow's uncle. Moreover the fellow could not really be so very mad. Dull thumps sounded from several places on the floor of the hut, a sharp small grunt from outside as if a cow had been kicked in the stomach. ¶ "He most certainly did..... He was your best friend, you...." the other was beginning. > ¶ A man

34 AR insertion: 'Some circulars of old furniture dealers. They never neglected him!'

35 AR insertion: 'Tietjens said: "No: I don't believe that did it. Something bigger.... Say a prize-fighter's fist...."'

36 AR insertion: 'He thought. "If anything went wrong with one it wd. be all over the command in two days. Thank God, Sylvia can't get here!"'

Textual Notes for I.ii

1   **UK, TS, US** Tietjen's; **Ed** Tietjens'

2   **UK** H.Q. You; **TS** H.Q. <And tell your blasted Duke that I will not have Duke's either.> You

3   AR insertion: 'He had imagined himself parted from his wife.'

4   **UK** object was; **TS** object <bleated a long tale about the draft. Apologetic and protesting. He> was

5   **UK** troops were; **TS** troops <"Ha, voice of the Mother Country!" Tietjens said to himself.> were

6   **UK** scholarships; **TS** fellowships

7   AR insertion: 'I was thinking that ten minutes ago!' (Another possible reference to one or other of the scandals involving General Cowans. See note on p. 18.)

8   AR insertion: 'She could not, thank God, get into France: to that place. But she could make scandals in the papers that every Tommie read. There was no game of which she was not capable. That sort of pursuit was called "pulling the strings of shower-baths" in her circle of friends.'

9   **UK** Hotchkiss; **TS** Hitchcock

10 **UK** Inniskillings; **TS** Inniskillens; **Ed** This variation is constant.

11 AR insertion: 'He added: "But don't do anything professional to Schomburg. I ride him myself!"'

12 **UK, TS** Welch; **US** Welsh

13 **UK** at the railway station; **TS** at Rouen Station

14 **UK** Cowley; **TS** Cosway

15 **UK** Cowley; **TS** Cosway

16 **UK** Mackenzie; **TS** McKechnie
    Levin uses the correct name in TS.

17 **UK** but Dominion Expeditionary Force; **TS** but Expeditionary Force

18 **UK** Tietjens. The frozen; **TS** Tietjens. <Even Mackenzie swore. There was in their minds an image of> The frozen

19 **UK** stick...." "They'll; **TS** stick...." <They had forgotten that he might have been listening.> "They'll
20 **UK** brutes...." It; **TS** ↑brutes...... ↓<politicians and civilians."> It
21 **UK** flagitious mineral-water; **TS** flagitious <proceedings with the> mineral-water
22 **AR** insertion: 'as to the way I command my Unit'.
23 **UK** A hairbreadth; **TS** A hair's breadth
24 **UK** mormon bishops; **TS, US** Mormon bishops
Ford had originally typed 'Bishops', but – like many of the capitals in TS – the 'B' has a line through it.
25 **UK** long, dark, high-coloured Provençale. Not; **TS** long, <fair, high-coloured Norman.> ↑dark, high coloured Provençale↓. Not
26 **AR** insertion: 'Merely because he had imagined her!'
27 **UK** Benedict; **TS** Benedick
Benedick is the correct name in Shakespeare's play.
28 **AR** insertion: 'He ought to turn the man down at once.'
29 **AR** insertion: 'His father had left them money.'
30 **UK, US** percentages; **TS** percentage
31 **UK** judgement and lie, in that case.¶ Because; **TS** judgment <.....> ↑and lie, in that case. ↓ ¶ Because

Textual Notes for I.iii

1 In TS these clauses are a typed insertion at the top of the leaf: 'his officer's pocket-book complete with pencil because he had to draft before eleven a report as to the desirability of giving his unit special lectures on the causes of the War –';
2 **UK** monstrosities of news about Sylvia's activities, without; **TS** monstrosities ↑of news about Sylvia [*sic*] activities↓ <from Tietjens' unknown career>, without
3 **UK** butter! ... ¶ And; **TS** butter! ... <The vague zone...> ¶ And
4 **UK** sing-song; **TS** singsong
Hyphenated in UK because at line-ending.
5 **UK** then. ¶ It; **TS** then <on and on and on!> ¶ It
6 **UK** gossip with; **TS** gossip <for hours and hours and hours,> with
7 **UK** before. So; **TS** before <It would be perfectly in accord with King's Regs, all the A.C.I.'s and the feudal spirit of his Majesty's Regular Forces if they talked to half-past three ac emma.> So
8 **AR** insertion on the same line at the end of the paragraph: 'They might talk till half-past three.'
9 **UK** wife. ¶ Before; **TS** wife. <Or that might be relatively easy. The point was: exactly what did he owe to the lady who had done him the honour to be at least officially the mother of his son, the heir to Groby.> ¶ Before
10 **UK** fact had; **TS** fact <you could brush away: it was less than> had
11 **UK** hatred and miscomprehension; **TS** hatred <... Till three or four months ago he would have said for certain that it had been on terms of hatred> and miscomprehension.
12 **AR** insertion: 'But certainly in conditions of chastity.'

13 **UK** Then, during; **TS** Then \<on the day, in the night\> during
14 **UK** Well, those **TS** Well \<that was a possible complication.\> Those
15 **UK** But even in; **TS** But even \<if they were not,\> in
16 **UK** then...; **TS** then....; **US, Ed** then ...
In TS the fourth dot is scored through.
17 **UK** had, then, parted for; **TS** had\<indeed parted already once,\> for
18 **UK** parting. That, surely, set him free for the girl! ¶ He; **TS** parting. ↑That, surely, set him free for the girl!↓ \<A perfectly proper parting of the English type, without so much of sentimentality as a mere: <u>So long</u>! That in itself would have justified him in considering their union out. Hamstrung, neatly and completely..... Because you do not as a rule part from a husband, however English and detached and not say as much as: <u>So long</u>, if the breach is not to be considered irrevocable, at any rate when the husband is going out to France and you, not keeping the home fires burning but going into retreat in a convent near Birkenhead..... For the expression <u>So long</u> is a defensive weapon. It is used by the English as their strong shield at once against emotion and the accusation of callousness. If you are attached to a person with all the passion in the world when you part from them you use those words to shew that you are not a Jew. If you were a Jew or a Frenchman you would say: God keep you, God guard you, God watch over you at your goings out and at your comings in from the same.... His girl, Valentine Wannop who, he was convinced, smelt like a primrose though he had no means of knowing, had indeed given him a Hebrew talisman inscribed with those words, but they had not said more than <u>So long</u> when they parted, presumably for good..... Presumably!..... Yet that was the rub. For if he were really put to answer it he could not say what Miss Wannop herself thought about the matter.... But of course it would be absurd to imagine her as thinking anything else. You do not part from a man – and avowed lover – with no more than a mere: <u>So long</u>, when he is going out to France, if you do not mean the parting to be for good. That was perfectly plain. At any rate that would be perfectly plain to any man. He was parted irrevocably from Sylvia because they had not said so much as – and from Valentine Wannop because they had said no more than: <u>So long</u>!

That was perfectly logical. His union with Sylvia, such as it was was legal; so, however much they might be disunited spiritually it remained a phenomenon of the British gentry and they use the terms of address suited to that state. When they ceased to use those terms of address the state itself might be taken to be at an end. But his union, such as it had been, with Valentine Wannop had been purely illegitimate; so, if they use to each other terms appertaining to the state of gentry it might be taken to mean that they had resumed such terms as were proper, beneath the aegis of British gentry-hood, for a young unmarried woman and a youngish married man. That was no terms at all......\> He
19 **UK** protracted reflection; **TS** protracted \<and cold-blooded\> reflection
20 **UK** a complete outfit; **TS** a ↑complete↓ \<perfectly definite\> outfit
21 **UK** posts, altogether too fragile entanglements of; **TS** posts, ↑altogether too fragile entanglements↓ \<aprons\> of
22 **UK, US** detritus, coils; **TS** detritus, repellent coils
23 **AR** insertion: 'that your skill had devised and'
24 **UK** gravity. You; **TS** gravity. \<altogether of the mind. If it were not the most

remarkable it was certainly the most spectacular example of the influence of
matter over psychology. For, in those particularly beastly circumstances of
watching and waiting for what might come when only beastlinesses from the
other side <u>could</u> come . . . your mind had nothing to do but observe itself.>
You

25 The following two sentences are an AR insertion at the foot of leaf 76 and
the top of leaf 77.

26 **UK** head. ¶ He; **TS** head. <¶ It was of course because he had been overwhelmed by the conviction that when Valentine Wannop had said: <u>So long</u>,
if indeed she had really said <<u>So long</u>> ↑that↓ in answer to his use of those
words – she had not, at least of necessity, meant that they were parting for
good. And he said to himself that he must try to remember very carefully
what had been her last words. He imagined after a time that hwat [*sic*] she
really had said was that she would not watch him out of sight because that
was unlucky. That meant that she was interested in his future. . . . But of
course she would be interested in his future to that 'extent. So that meant
nothing.> ¶ He

27 AR insertion: 'three months or so ago,'

28 AR insertion in left hand margin: 'He was attempting exactly to imitate a
report to G.H.Q.'

29 AR insertion: 'This intimacy was, of course, certainly unsuspected by the
General.'

30 **UK** garrison causes me natural personal annoyance. ¶ "My; **TS** garrison
<adds considerably to my> ↑causes me natural↓ personal <embarrassment>
↑annoyance↓. ¶ "My

31 AR insertion: 'with the man Perowne'

32 **UK** formed a sympathetic but not violent attachment; **TS** a <close>
↑sympathetic but not violent↓ attachment

33 **UK, US** other matters; **TS** other painful matters

34 AR insertion: 'He exclaimed:'

35 AR insertion: 'He wrote on again:'

36 **UK** speaking. She; **TS** speaking. <She attempted to excite my sexual
instincts, there and then. > She

37 **UK** but one ought; **TS** but <once the occasion seemed to demand it, as this
did, he was prepared to go for it baldheaded. One> ought

38 **UK** For, mark! It was Sylvia who had; **TS** For, <think only of his own cruelty
to the girl. . . It was one of the principles of every decent man that if a woman
offered herself to him he must have her. Noblesse oblige. The insult otherwise was too great . . . Oh, but even before that . . . . On the occasion of their
very first day together. . . . . But he must not wander from his last day in
Town. He must go over it all again. Psychologising. . .

But that wasn't the way wasn't the way wasn't the way his excited mind
said to himself. And he was excited because it was possible that Valentine
Wannop had not meant their parting to be a permanency. . . It opened up
an immense perspective. Nevertheless the contemplation of that immense
perspective was not the way to set about a calm analysis of his relations with
his wife. The facts of the story must be stated before the moral. . . . He had
to get down to the hard facts of his last day in London. . . .

He had had, then, a peculiarly cruel interview with Sylvia in the morning.
A long interview of bad tensions, interrupted by this and that person. At the

end, <of that> they had certainly parted. He had had after that, in St James's Park a quite unusual interview with Miss Wannop. He had invited her to become his mistress that evening and she had consented, making an assignation. Unusual. An unusual proceeding in the case of quite serious persons who were comparative strangers. It took their relations outside the state of gentryhood, exactly as he had put it to himself before... Well then... But, mark: ↑<But mark>↓ His wife> ↑It was Sylvia who↓ had

39 **UK** arms. Quite; **TS** arms. <More than that. Into bed together.> Quite

40 AR insertion: 'she had only said that'

41 AR insertion: 'at one moment'

42 **UK** pain, reiteratedly; **TS** pain, <like an agonizing note of a bell,> reiteratedly

43 **UK** conider; **TS, US** consider

44 **UK** France! *Did*; **TS** France <and don't even so much as say <u>So long</u> to him..... ¶But.... Hell.... A terrible, a terribly unwonted feeling assailed some unknown part of his anatomy. His diaphragm, perhaps. Or his bowels....> <u>Did</u>

45 AR insertion: 'Obviously it did.'

46 **UK** warmed.... ¶What; **TS** warmed.....<He remembered the day when Sylvia had announced to him her desire to return to him after having been off with the man Perowne.... That fellow was actually at that moment on old Campion's Staff..... On that day he had drunk a whole quantity of neat whisky and he had not felt warmed.... This stuff had warmed him Better stuff? No certainly not. Army rum. The other had been his father's special '65.... Specialite [*sic*] de la maison Groby... Then he wasn't in such a state of emotion now as he had been when Sylvia's letter had reached him.... ↑He had realized that it was at least a possibility that the girl still wanted him & that, now, according to his own standards he was free of her. Yet the rum warmed him. **AR**↓ His passion for the girl was not such a strong passion..... He was disappointed. He wanted his passion for the girl to be a strong passion. What in the name of hell, else, had he to identify him with the name and estate of a man? And ...> ¶What

47 **UK** himself.... He had acted perfectly correctly as far as Sylvia was concerned. Not perhaps to Miss Wannop.... Why; **TS** himself.... <Had Justifying himself! But he had never in his life, not ever once in his life done anything but ↑behave as he wanted to **AR**↓ but act in sure and certain conviction that what he did would be right ↑as men would in his day & station. **AR**↓ Never. Not ever....> ↑He had acted perfectly correctly as far as Sylvia was concerned. Not perhaps to Miss Wannop. **AR**↓.... Why

48 AR insertion: 'as long as you did not fuss about it unhealthily'

49 **UK** consequences.... ¶ But; **TS** consequences.... <But that he, he, could be in the wrong vis a vis of another person... It had not been thinkable. It was [illegible deletion] as if he had been wrong, as if he had omitted a digit in a computation as to the planets... The whole astronomic system, the whole [illegible deleted word] social system, fell to the ground.... Indeed there would be no more parades...

He said, in a sort of panic: It's the cursed rum. It has got hold of my thinking machine. But he was aware that all it had done to him had been to coarsen his language to himself. The mass and direction of his thought was bloody well what it would have been with nothing taken. . . .

He then had admitted to himself a doubt of himself. He had admitted the possibility that he had been obtuse in his dealings with another member of his world. With, say, the mother of his child. Although she wasn't herself perfectly certain that it was <u>his</u> child of which she was the mother. It was demanded of him that he should treat her in such a way as came within the four corners of their social scheme. Not necessarily with kindness or even with consideration. Their men folk might be nagging, boorish, brutal, miserly, drunken even, or unbearably eccentric. But not obtuse. If he was to be brutal or anything of the other things to his wife he had to know what he was doing and to be ready to take the consequences.

But he. . . . Look here: Sylvia was changed. That was what troubled him. For, if she were changed wasn't it perhaps his doing? For [by Heavens he] had not meant her to be. Then, if she were, he had been obtuse. And that was the sin against the Holy Ghost. . . .

It was difficult to put these things into words, even to himself, though he had a very strong sense of his meaning. . . . . If for instance a fellow kept a thoroughbred in his stable and let it develop all sorts of vices, that was about the worst thing he could do. The very worst ↑thing in the world **AR**↓, really. And he had to look at the supposition that it was what he had been doing to Sylvia. It was perhaps nonsense. . . . .

It was true> ¶ But

50 In TS this entire paragraph is an AR insertion on leaf 81a. The four sentences in the middle, from 'For what she had done' to 'Tommies of his own unit' was an additional afterthought, written below the rest of the paragraph.

51 **UK** stable? But; **TS** stable? <The thought was damnable. For> But

52 AR insertion: 'anything but un-'

53 **UK** ask? . . . He could find no answer. And it was not his business! ¶ But; **TS** ask? . . . ↑He could find no answer. And it was not his business! **AR**↓ <Apparently since that date she had lived chastely and it had been bad for her nerves. It was probably bad for a woman's nerves to live in absolute chastity for years beside a man. . . . But was it his business to think about that? Probably it was. But could he have? He didn't know how. They had lived for years without thinking speaking a word about anything that mattered. What of that? In every village and town of his native Yorkshire there were houses and cottages pointed out in which lived couples who never spoke a word at all to each other. Not a word. Grim people. His people. Husbands and wives, fathers and old maid daughters, groups of brothers. . . . Then how in the world was he to be expected to meditate upon what was a common occurrence to the humanity that he knew best. Of course the Yorkshire people led healthy lives and Sylvia had led a hot-pressed, hotly spiced existence. . . . . the difference between a hunt or and a [?] horse-show competitor. But damn it, she had always looked so perfectly fit, so perfectly clean-run, so absolutely without vice, using the word in the horsey sense. What business, then, was it of his? ↑It was not his business then . . . ↓ But of course it was his business. Even > ¶ But

54 **UK** the motives of; **TS** the <mental troubles> ↑motives **AR**↓ of

55 **UK** a woman; **TS** women

56 **UK** godfather. But; **TS** godfather. <That might just pass at a pinch.> But

57 AR insertion, left hand margin: 'But a strike of French railway civilians had
   delayed Sylvia's arrival.'
58 **UK** command. ¶ But; **TS** command. <Perhaps he was, for Sylvia Tietjens
   occupied a great deal more of <his> ↑the General's↓ mind than she ought
   to, considering the extended and worrying nature of his occupation.> ¶ But
59 **UK** was. ¶ "She; **TS** was. <and it occurred to him that she probably had not
   any errand at all. She had come on the chance of stirring things up. She
   seemed to have done that. . . .> ¶ She
60 AR insertion: 'which was unprovided with cells'

Textual Notes for I.iv

1 **UK** thin films of reddish purple to be wavering, then a glutinous surface of
   gummy scarlet pigment. Moving! It was once more an effect; **TS** thin films
   of <scarlet> ↑reddish purple **AR**↓ to be wavering, then a glutinous surface
   of gummy scarlet pigment. ↑Moving! **AR**↓ It was ↑once more **AR**↓ an effect
2 **UK, TS, US** him. That; **Ed** him? That
3 **UK** the darkness outside; **TS** the blackness outside
4 **UK** motion. The sides of the hut were so thin that that it was; **TS** motion.
   ↑The sides of the hut were so thin that **AR**↓ the blackness was
5 AR insertion: 'on his privacy'
6 **UK** demoralization! ¶ McKechnie; **TS** demoralization! <¶It suddenly
   occurred to him that he must at least call on Sylvia in her hotel during the
   next afternoon, whilst he was down in the town for the purpose of signing
   Levin's marriage-contract. The idea repelled him. It was however an obvious
   duty. He would ride Schomburg down if the horse were well enough and so
   get some exercise. . . .> ¶ McKechnie
7 **UK** do old Puffles in; **TS** do old <Swipes> ↑Puffles **AR**↓ in
8 AR insertion: '—the general being nicknamed Puffles.'
9 **UK** this member of the lower middle classes should; **TS** this <fellow>
   ↑member of the lower middle classes **AR**↓ should
10 The following two sentences are an AR insertion in TS, above the line and
   continuing at the top of the leaf.
11 AR insertion: 'when they're drunk.'
12 **UK** go to heaven with; **TS** go ↑to heaven **AR**↓ with
13 AR insertion: 'Then they were all swallowed up.'
14 AR insertion: "'It is probably because a hundred thousand sentimentalists
   like myself commit similar excesses of the subconscious that we persevere in
   this glorious but atrocious undertaking. All the same'
15 **UK** bypath. ¶ But; **TS** by-path <Now he would have to curtail his
   side. . . . .> But
16 This entire paragraph in an AR insertion in TS: the first half filling the left-
   hand margin, the second filling the top of the leaf (102).
17 The following sentence is an AR insertion in TS, above the line and continuing at the top of the leaf (103).
18 AR insertion: '(and inspected his cook-houses)'
19 **UK** ¶ Tietjens had; **TS** ¶ <The conversation had done> Tietjens <good.
   He> had

20 **UK** about Mrs. Tietjens, or even Miss de Bailly; **TS** about ↑Mrs. Tietjens, or even **AR**↓ Miss de Bailly

21 AR insertion: '—after Noircourt which had knocked out Tietjens himself—'

22 **UK** But I; **TS** But <to make that damned thief . . . > I

23 **UK** To-day. . . . Can; **TS** Today. . . <I suppose you are going to-day. . . > Can

24 AR insertion: 'He would look after things till then.'

25 AR insertion: 'From near Denbigh!'

26 AR insertion, left-hand margin and top of leaf (112): 'At the request of Lord Beichan, who was personally interested in Lieutenant Hotchkiss's theories, he was to make experiments on the horses of the Fourth Army—in which the XIXth division was then to be found. . . . "So," Cowley said, "you'll be under him as far as your horse lines go. If you go up."' The name was originally 'Buchan' here in TS, emended to 'Beichan' with four ARs on this leaf.

27 AR insertion: 'for patent manœuvres with jampots or fancy underclothing.'

28 **UK** hadn't. ¶ Colour-Sergeant; **TS** hadn't <He asked what the deuce they would all do without Morgan and told Tietjens to step into the next room.> ¶ Colour-Srgeant [*sic*]

29 **UK, TS, US** Tietjen's advice; **Ed** Tietjens' advice

30 **UK** being in that town, was; **TS** being in Rouen, was

31 AR insertion: 'And the complication of troubles with Lieut. Hotchkiss who, being a professor, had never really seen a horse—or not for ten years!—was something to be thought about very seriously.' In UK the word 'possible' was inserted before 'troubles', and 'Lieut.' expanded; presumably in proof revisions.

32 **UK** eyes! ¶ He; **TS** eyes! ¶ <There was another hasty, psychological and military knock, awaiting him when> He

33 **UK, TS** meant he was aware a frightful; **Ed** meant, he was aware, a frightful

34 **UK** the newspaper proprietor; **TS** the <Carnarvon Israelite> newspaper proprietor

35 In TS this last sentence is an AR insertion at the foot of leaf 118.

36 AR insertion, completing line at the end of the paragraph, and continuing on the line below: 'He imagined that the clumsy paces of the animal beneath him added to his gloomy obsessions.'

37 **UK** I.B.D." The orderly was to close all the windows of the stable, stopping up any chinks with wadding. He would procure, if possible, a sawdust stove, new pattern, from Colonel Gillum's store and light it in the stables. He was also to give Schomburg and the roan oatmeal and water warmed as hot as the horses would take it. . . . And Tietjens finished sharply, "If; **TS** I.B.D. <You will> ↑" The orderly was to **AR**↓ close all the windows of the stable, stopping up any chinks with wadding. <You will> ↑He would **AR**↓ procure, if possible, a sawdust stove, new pattern, from Colonel Gillum's store and light it in the stables. <You will> ↑He was also to **AR**↓ give Schomburg and the roan oatmeal and water warmed as hot as the horses would take it. . . ↑And Tietjens finished sharply **AR**↓ "If

38 **UK** to it. . . . It; **TS** to it. <You are an intelligent man: follow me carefully>. . . . It
   Deleted because, as in the passage quoted in the previous note, Ford had revised this paragraph from direct speech to narrative (which functions as a form of free indirect style, possibly reporting Tietjens' speech indirectly).

39 AR insertion: 'He said to the orderly: "You are an intelligent man. What deduction do you draw?"'

40 AR insertion: 'He could not let a horse for which he was responsible be martyred'
41 AR insertion: 'Over it all hung the shadow of the deceased Welsh soldier.' In UK 'the deceased' becomes 'a deceased'.
42 AR insertion: 'O Nine Morgan was the other thing, that accounting for the prize-fighter!'

Textual Notes for II.i

1 **UK** Christ." ¶ Major; **TS** Christ. <Calling on the woman taken in adultery...."> ¶ Major
2 **UK** vibrate. ¶ Perowne; **TS** vibrate. <She knew him so absolutely well.> ¶ Perowne
3 O'Hara's name has been emended from 'Popham' on all three occurrences in this paragraph.
4 **UK** coming." ¶ That; **TS** coming." <I don't say it would have hindered me if I had, but I didn't...." > ¶ That
5 **UK** little. His; **TS** little - <with outraged amazement>. His
6 **UK** Now she wanted him; **TS** Now ↑s↓he wanted <her> him
7 **UK, US** belle; **Ed** Belle
8 AR insertion: 'I would follow him round the world in my shift!'
9 **UK** head...." She; **TS** head... <Good God, whatever made me take up with you?.... The mothering instinct you'd say ... It is no doubt the mothering instinct that made me give you the pointer I just have...."> She
10 **UK** fantastically murderous. He; **TS** fantastically homicidal. He
11 AR insertion: 'She was pretty certain that no gossip had been caused by her escapade. Major Thurston had been at the railway station when they had left, but they had not spoken—and Thurston was a very decentish, brown-moustached fellow, of the sort that does not gossip.'
12 Typed insertion: '—before she froze him into a choking, pallid snowman with goggle eyes—'
13 **UK** that, that; **TS** that I'd go off with one a week-end and chance damnation ... But, she added, that
14 **UK** some miserable little squit of a subaltern who was smashing up Mother Hardelot's furniture...." ¶ He; **TS** some <[?]> ↑miserable↓ little squit of a subaltern who <'d got pied and> was smashing up Mother Hardelot's furniture more than she could stand...." ¶ He
15 UK and US both have a comma followed by three dots here. TS originally had 'Pervenches, and', with four dots then typed over the 'and'. If Ford had intended to replace the 'and' with the dots, it nonetheless survived. The comma, which also survived, is less equivocally an error, and has been removed here.

Textual Notes for II.ii

1 **UK, US** him, ..." she; **TS** him..." She; **Ed** him ..." she

2 **UK** there hadn't been a; **TS** there <wasn't> ↑hadn't been↓ a
3 **UK** He must tell her that he; **TS** <I> ↑He↓ must tell <you madam I> ↑her
  that he↓
4 **UK** makes one have; **TS** makes <me> ↑one↓ have
5 **UK** that he had to celebrate.... But he dare; **TS** that <I have> ↑he had↓
  to celebrate ... But <I> ↑he↓ dare
6 **UK** their old; **TS** <our> ↑their↓ old
7 **UK** Birkenhead the vision of which had just presented itself to her, had
  been; **TS** Birkenhead had been
8 **UK** *l'houille-maigre dans*; **TS** <u>L'houille dans</u>
9 **UK, US** jove; **TS** Jove
  Emended for consistency with the later instance of the name in this chapter.
10 **UK, TS, US** Mountsby; **Ed** Mountby
  In *Some Do Not ...* Ford uses both forms. 'Mountsby' has been emended to
  'Mountby' here following the editorial practice in that novel.
11 **UK** had hung him; **TS** had shot him
12 **UK** tons of sawdust for the new slow-burning stoves in the men's huts....;
  TS <iodine-dressings> ↑tons of sawdust **AR**↓ for the <inside pockets of
  tunics ... But> ↑new, slow-burning stoves in the men's huts **AR**↓..;
13 **UK** creature. He was to be a sign: not a prey! ¶ She; **TS** creature.... ¶ She
14 **UK** time I don't know what I'm doing! ... It; **TS** time..... It
15 **UK** beast ... with; **TS** beast ... Dying when I thrashed it ... With
16 Typed insertion: 'And you're always cold... freezing in the blood-vessels...'
17 Typed insertion: 'It's the seventh circle of hell, isn't it? the frozen one...'
18 **UK** Him...." ¶ She; **TS** him..." <But that's what I mean by not sporting
  ... Lashing into a dumb bull dog. You see... I swear I'd have enjoyed it
  better if it the poor beast had turned on me and torn my thigh to bits...
  ↑And I'd have gone on lashing into him... ↓ But I was thinking that
  Christopher might ... have me, if I lashed hard enough.... I've never
  forgiven myself... I never shall... It said: What a hope! As plain as could
  be... Never forgiven myself... *Never*...."> She
19 **UK, US** in a eighteenth-century dress; **TS** in eighteenth century dress; **Ed**
  in eighteenth-century dress
20 **UK** "Your — of; **TS** "Your <bitch> of;
  The TS shows that this is not Ford's deletion, but that of an editor who draws
  a line through 'bitch' and places a '2' over it to indicate to the compositor
  that he should replace the word with a dash.
21 **UK** not one penny of it comes out of what I wish you; **TS** not <one penny
  of it comes out of what I want to be> one penny
22 **UK, TS** pooped; **US** popped
23 **UK** Tietjens reading his papers still, intermittently; **TS** Tietjens as he
  <[wrote]> ↑read his papers↓, still intermittently; **US** Tietjens reading
  reading [sic] his papers still, intermittently; **Ed** Tietjens, reading his papers
  still, intermittently
24 **UK** friend...." She added in French: "Even as it is you cannot pay any attention to these serious matters, because of these childish pre-occupations of
  yours. That is to be intolerably insulting to me!" She was breathless.¶ Tietjens; **TS** friend...." ¶ Tietjens
25 **UK** hers. He; **TS** hers <and said that Miss Wannop was not in France. She
  could tell that from his brother Mark's correspondence.> He

26 **UK** he was sent back; **TS** he was returned to duty. . . sent back

27 **UK** employments." What she called presentableness was very largely a matter of physical fitness. . . . The horse, for instance, that he rode was rather a crock. . . . But though it was German and not thoroughbred it contrived to be up to his weight. . . . Her; **TS** employments. What you call presentableness is very largely a matter of physical fitness, so you won't find many splendid animals here. . . . The horse, for instance, that I ride was rather a crock. . . . <On the on the other hand we do keep the thing going somehow here> But though it's German and not thoroughbred it contrives to be up to my weight. . . ." Her;

28 **UK, US** boodlers." She; **Ed** boodlers?" She

29 **UK** was. An 'orrible shock it mus 'ave been for the captain." A horrible mess. . . . The; **TS** was. A horrible mess. . . The

30 **UK** "You didn't bring 'em to a court martial:" Cowley asked. Tietjens said: No. He **TS** "You didn't do anything?" Cowley asked. Tietjens said, No, He

31 **UK** certain. But he had been worrying about a private matter. He had been worrying about it while he lay on the ground and that rather obscured his sense of what he saw. Besides, he said faintly, an officer must use his judgment. He had judged it better in this case not to have seen the . . . His voice had nearly faded away; it was clear to Sylvia that he was coming to a climax of some mental torture. Suddenly he exclaimed to Cowley:

"Supposing I let him off one life to get him killed two years after. My God! That would be too beastly!"

Cowley snuffled in Tietjens' ear something that Sylvia did not catch—consolatory and affectionate. That intimacy was more than she could bear. She adopted her most negligent tone to ask:

I suppose

TS certain. . . . But to tell the truth, the night before, he had received some very worrying news. And to tell the truth he was thinking about that . . . Even when he lay on the ground . . . Some investments gone wrong . . . He looked at Sylvia and said: "Those Government of Kiev tramway shares, you remember." Sylvia was perfectly aware that Tietjens was heading the sergeant-major even then, off the idea that she could have caused him any anxiety . . . She asked:

"I suppose

32 **UK** exploded: God bless you, no! They'd agreed upon it between them. To get one of them sent 'ome and the other, at any rate, out of *that* 'ell, leading him back to the dressing-station. She said: ¶ "You; **TS** exploded that God bless her No! They'd agreed upon it between them. To get one of them sent 'ome and the other at any rate out of that show, leading him back to the dressing-station. She said: ¶ "You

US follows UK, except that it supplies inverted commas. However, it breaks the convention of both UK and US of starting a new paragraph when a new speaker is introduced; i.e. before 'She said'. The change from indirect to direct speech must have been made in proof and implies the need for inverted commas, which have been supplied here, together with the new paragraph that should have accompanied them.

33 **UK** between the Other Ranks' life and; **TS** between the Tommy's life and

34 **UK** it's; **TS, US** its

35 **UK** 105°; **TS** 110° 105+

36 **UK** Christopher had; **TS** Christopher—You could see he was in—had

37 **UK** despair: the engrossment; **TS** despair <at an immense task>: the evident engrossment

38 **UK** to: any trustworthy beer-sodden sergeant, any street urchin; **TS** to: any street-urchin

39 **UK** indistinguishable.... Or their deaths as well! They promoted this bean-feast of carnage for their own ends: they caused the deaths of men in inconceivable holocausts of pain and terror. Then they had crises of agony over the death of one single man. For it was plain to her that Tietjens was in the middle of a full nervous breakdown. Over one man's death! She had never seen him so suffer; she had never seen him so appeal for sympathy: him, a cold fiend of reticence! Yet he was now in agony! *Now!* ... And; **TS** indistinguishable.... And

40 **UK** the Other Ranks! Apparently it was hell for the officers as well. ¶ The; **TS** the Tommies.... ¶ The

41 **UK** voice of the snuffling, half-drunken old man; **TS** ↑voice of that↓ half-drunk man

42 **UK** screamed blasphemies that she was hardly aware of knowing. She; **TS** screamed: "Oh God! Damn! Hell! ... This B ... y row!" . . She

43 **UK** Cowley: what it was Sylvia did not hear, but Cowley answered, still droning on with an idea Sylvia thought they had got past: ¶ I remember; **TS** Cowley:

"It's absurd, of course," he said, "but I could not enjoy my ride this afternoon because I had ... the sense of <him> ↑Oh Nine Morgan↓ hanging to my snaffle. The old Schomburg coming down any minute.

Cowley said:

Ah! It takes you like that ... When you see your dead ... Of course it's nonsense ... He wasn't with the battalion at Noircourt ... I could prove it by looking up my parade states ... 'E joined after we were at Steenewerck in support ... "

Tietjens said:

"I'd be obliged if you would look it up ... I can't help thinking he looked at me very significantly when I refused him his leave ... It would be funny if I let him off one life over the shooting to get him killed by refusing him his leave ... It's not very important, but I'd be obliged ... It affects my calculations connected with the doctrine of chances. <.>"

Sylvia said:

"You ... got a man killed!"

Tietjens answered:

"Yes. The man you heard was killed yesterday I'd refused leave to the day before.... "

Sergeant-major Cowley commented:

"It does put your off your feed ... I remember

44 **UK** about to scream out that if Tietjens did not like men being killed it ought to sober him; **TS** about to say it ought to sober him

45 **AR** insertion: 'in what we called the Government Compound'

46 **UK** sick of your companions!"; **TS** sick of ... "

47 **UK** near! ... "Good; **TS** near! ... General O'Hara had said: "Good

48 **UK** Astonishingly.... Her gown; **TS** Astonishingly ... She said to herself: "My ... <.> The gown

49 **UK, TS, US** sidonis; **Ed** sindonis

Textual Notes for III.i

1 **UK** outside. So, in the old days, Gods had descended! It; **TS** outside. ↑So, in the old days, Godheads descended! **AR**↓ It
Cf. III.ii: 'The building paused, as when a godhead descends.'
2 **UK** sort! Immediately; **TS** sort! <to hearten him in a difficult but probably clearing situation.> Immediately
3 AR insertion: '"I am still applying to civilian firms," he finished.'
4 **UK** unit. But officers have to be on these parades—by A.C.I. They give no orders."; **TS** unit. But officers have to be on these parades. ↑They give no orders. **AR**↓"
5 **UK** graciousness. Behind; **TS** graciousness. <It came to Tietjens that this was indeed a providential visit.> Behind
6 **UK** making signs with his eyes which he meaningly closed and opened. The; **TS** making <extraordinary grimaces of encouragement> ↑signs with his eyes which he meaningly closed & opened. **AR**↓ The
7 AR insertion: 'You understand you are released from arrest!'
8 **UK** arrest." He; **TS** ↑arrest.↓ <That must upset him....."> He
AR insertion: '"Of course I understand that if I'm given an order to perform a duty, it means I am released from arrest."'
9 **UK** said: "... He's; **TS** said: <Damn it...> He's
10 AR insertion in left-hand margin: 'Besides, an officer cannot demand a court martial.'
11 **UK** moment...." ¶ Levin; **TS** moment ... " <I must stifle these beastly lies.... I'm going to!" ¶ Levin exclaimed: ¶ "Your wife didn't ... Mrs Tietjens wasn't...." ¶ Tietjens said: ¶ "You keep your <damn> tongue off Mrs Tietjens' name... I can bloody <well> walk to my own quarters...."> ¶ Levin
12 **UK** Against ... either of you...."; **TS** Against.... <Mrs. Tietjens> ↑Either of you! **AR**↓...."
13 **UK** "Then leave; **TS** "Then <, damn you,> leave
14 AR insertion: 'That is the habit of the Other Ranks on perceiving officers.'
15 AR insertion: 'So he might be avoiding him.'
16 The order of this and the preceding sentence has been transposed in TS.
17 **UK** said: "Put; **TS** said: <"Damn you> "Put
18 **UK** insolently calm man; **TS** <A calmly> ↑An↓ insolently ↑calm↓ man
19 **UK** said: ¶"Don't; **TS** said: <"You silly ass ... > "Don't
20 **UK** like to find dirty clothing," the sergeant-cook; **TS** like it," the sergeant-cook
21 **UK** pocket. Now; **TS** pocket. <Understand that ... Another word to me. Or any other soul. About this whole delusion of yours!> Now
22 AR insertion: 'I've been thinking about it!'
23 Typed insertion: 'He was certainly then—in disorder!'
24 AR insertion: 'if he didn't go'
25 **UK** P.M.! ...." ¶ Tietjens; **TS** P.M.!... <It causes a good deal>...."¶ Tietjens

26 AR insertion: 'It really amounts to as to whether O'Hara drinks too much to continue in his job!'

27 **UK** know what you are doing." ¶ He; **TS** know <how painful> ↑what you are doing. **AR↓**" ¶ He

28 AR insertion: 'Also to go . . . . ."

29 **UK** Levin said: ¶ "All; **TS** Levin said: ¶ <"How could you care about the damned Ragtime service.> "All

30 **UK** officer . . . " ¶ Suddenly; **TS** officer. . . . ↑<But of course you're different. **AR**>"↓ ¶ Suddenly

31 AR insertion in left-hand margin: 'in the effort to consummate the one decent action that humanity has to its credit in the whole of recorded history. The one we are engaged in!'

32 **UK** in. That effort is the; **TS** ↑in↓ <. . . Duty! . . . It's> ↑That effort↓ the

33 **UK** are! ¶ Tietjens; **TS** are! ¶ <"No, no, no, I'm not."> Tietjens

34 UK and US both indent 'Tietjens said', but neither follows their usual convention of starting a new paragraph for the speech itself, which has been inserted here. UK has a full stop after 'said', US a colon, adopted here; UK also has a full stop after 'optimism', US a question mark, adopted here. Emended because the anomalies result from the previous deletion.

35 **UK** credit of a story. And a consideration of the virtues of humanity does not omit the other side. If we lose they win. If success is necessary to your idea of virtue—*virtus*—they then provide the success instead of ourselves. But the thing; **TS** the credit of <your> ↑a **AR↓** story. ↑And a consideration of the virtues of humanity does not omit the other side. If we lose they win. If success is necessary to your idea of virtue—*virtus*—they then provide the success instead of ourselves. . . . <But it isn't necessary. **AR↓** The> ↑But the **AR↓** thing

36 **UK** know. . . . I know; **TS** know . . . <The usual discreditabilities . . . You forget> I know

37 **UK** exclaimed: ¶ "What; **TS** exclaimed: <"My head's going round . . . What in the world are we here for?> ¶ "What

38 **UK** knew she; **TS** knew <that, whatever her game was,> she

39 **UK** Council.'" "I didn't; **TS** Council'" . . . <Which of course as things are, would mean that that beast would be called up to serve as a Tommie".> ¶ "I didn't

40 **UK, TS** anti-air-gun; **US** anti-aircraft

41 **UK** said: ¶ "We; **TS** said: ¶ <"Yes, damn you. Yes!" He added:> "We

42 AR insertion: 'He never is.'

43 UK inserts a comma here, which US omits. TS has it, after the three-word phrase 'what he said', a typed insertion between the lines, which otherwise wouldn't have made sense. The comma was thus probably an error introduced while trying to correct another.

44 AR insertion: 'You appeared to be writing a letter to her.'

45 AR insertion: 'I don't want his money.'

46 AR insertion: 'thought that you regarded her as an old maid.'

47 **UK** too. . . . " ¶Tietjens said:; **TS** too . . .

Tietjens said:

<"Well, I see what the general gathered . . . What did <u>you</u> . . . If I'm to go on talking in my sleep I'd like to know what I've to face . . . I mean, what I am apt to say . . . Under anaethetics [*sic*] one is said to utter obscenities that

are rather appalling..."

Levin said:

"<u>You</u>... It's what I am trying to tell you. . You addressed Miss Wannop as if you were the Victorian Correct Letter Writer composing an epistle to an infants' school teacher. Of course the matter wasn't...."

Tietjens said:

"What was the [?] 'matter,' as you call it?"

Levin said painfully:

"My dear fellow... It was about what happened last night. . You <u>know</u> what happened. The general wants me to get your version confirmed out of your own mouth. He says that if I can assure him that you confirm what you said then, he will take your word for it as against the version of O'Hara and Pe... The other swine.">

Tietjens said:

48 **UK** letter.... Naturally it was a good deal broken up.... I; **TS** letter.... <and you wrapped it all up> ↑Naturally it was a good deal broken up. **AR**↓ ... I

49 AR insertion: 'He added rather diffidently:'

50 **UK** diffidently: "If; **TS** diffidently: <¶ "I can't" Tietjens said, "go into psychologies. That's not my line, and I don't, when I'm awake, talk like a book or throw veils over things..." ¶ Levin said: ¶ "Oh, talk as like a book as you can.> "If

In *Joseph Conrad* 196, Ford recalled: 'a body of younger men with whom the writer spent some years would say, after dinner: "Talk like a book, H.... Do talk like a book!" The writer would utter some speeches in the language that he employed when talking with Conrad: but he never could utter more than a sentence or two at a time. The whole mess would roar with laughter [...]'; Cf. *Portraits From Life* 210, on how his fellow officers would urge him: 'Speak like a book, H.... Do speak like a book for a minute or two', and he would perform with clichés like: 'After mature consideration I have arrived at the conclusion [...]'.

51 AR insertion: 'in your orderly room'

52 AR insertion: 'Not unlike <Levin> Perowne.'

53 **UK** said to General O'Hara in the corridor. He even confessed it was madness; **TS** said to <the> general <... in his temper. His> ↑O'Hara in the corridor. He even [conceded] it was **AR**↓ madness

54 **UK** said: ¶ "If; **TS** said: ¶ "<Look here. Don't distress yourself.> If

55 AR insertion in left-hand margin: 'It's also true that my wife expected me to be there. She wanted some fun: not adultery. But'

56 AR insertion: 'I really thought he was the night porter coming to call me to the telephone.'

57 AR insertion: 'I mean that was what I thought O'Hara was'

58 Typed insertion: 'so it might have been himself as well as Perowne'

Textual Notes for III.ii

1 **UK** that any inquiries that the home Government could cause to be made amongst the local civilian population would confirm what; **TS** that <any

French Civilian whom that home government might consult would agree
with> ↑any inquiries that the home government could cause to be made
amongst the local civilian population would confirm **AR**↓ what

2 AR insertion: 'after materially helping mobilization'

3 AR insertion: '—as General Campion saw it—'

4 TS has a comma here, omitted by UK and US to the detriment of the syntax.

5 AR insertion in left-hand margin: 'when it came to tactics—which it should
be remembered concerns itself with the movement of troops actually in
contact with enemy forces—'

6 AR insertion: '—to the almost complete neglect of the rifle!'

7 **UK** belt. An; **TS** belt <An officer under arrest may not wear a belt or perform
a duty. If he is ordered to do either by a competent superior that washes out
the charge against him.> An

8 AR insertion: 'for him, and a very improper strain on his men'

9 **UK** Tietjens' troubles; **TS** <It> ↑Tietjens' troubles **AR**↓

10 **UK** Cleveland Parliamentary Division in; **TS** Cleveland ↑Parliamentary
Division **AR**↓ in

11 **UK** of course, using Groby for your headquarters. . . .”; **TS** of course <the
influence of> ↑using **AR**↓ Groby ↑for your headquarters **AR**↓. . .”

12 AR insertion: 'I don't like wasting letters.'

13 **UK** expedition is very small. It's said to be a one-man party—with hangers-
on—but arguing him out of it has caused all this delay. That's how I see it.”
¶ The; **TS** expedition. <If they argue him out of that they'd probably starve
the line for a bit – as a sop in the pan for more delay.”> ↑is very small. It's
said to be a one man party—with hangers on—but arguing him out of it has
<meant delay> caused all this delay. That's how I see it.” **AR**↓ ¶ The

14 **UK** it. . . . That; **TS** it. . . . <Do you know what it is to have men die on you?
. . .> That

15 AR insertion: 'indefinitely by delaying us now. And men being killed all the
time.'

16 **UK** Backacher; **TS** Backbreaker
Clearly a compositor's misreading of TS

17 **UK** that?” ¶ Alarm overcame Tietjens. The general was certainly in
disorder. But over what? There was not time to think. Campion was certainly
dreadfully overworked. . . . He exclaimed: ¶ “Sir, hadn't; **TS** that?” ¶ <Tiet-
jens who knew very well what was coming. ↑A very C>Alarm overcame
Tietjens. The general was certainly in disorder. But over what? There was
not time to think. Campion was certainly dreadfully overworked. . . . He
AR↓ exclaimed: ¶ “<Good God>, sir, hadn't

18 **UK** memorandum . . . I am; **TS** memorandum <memorandum. . . .” He
thought: “My God, I am going to be sent up the line. . . It's a back door way
out . . .” He said: “I suggest that> If you interpolated the words: ‘I am
informed by such of my subaltern officers as frequent the society of the native
population of the better class that . . .' and then as your memorandum reads.
That will throw the onus on the subaltern officers. . . I am
The last three lines are undeleted in TS but do not appear in UK, so were
presumably deleted in proof.

19 **UK** you are suspected of having too great common interests with the French.
That's; **TS** you are a Franco-maniac. That's

20 AR insertion: 'the whole position so impossible'

21 **UK** think all generals are illiterate fools. But; **TS** think <I'm an illiterate old fool.> ↑all generals are illiterate fools **AR**↓ But

22 **UK** though I never; **TS** though <... I bet you can't tell me who wrote that ... Then there's at

       This ae neet, This ae neet
       Every neet and all
       Fire and fleet and neat to eat
       And Christ receive thy saul...'"

Tietjens, the sweat coming out all over him prayed to God to be enabled to hold his tongue. He could not. He said to himself: "By this sin fell the angels.... Pride in erudition!" He said aloud against his teeth:

"Why, sir ↑Tietjens said **AR**↓ the last is our own Groby Likewake Dirge... I am sure they sang it round my father when he lay with the three corpse candles round him and a plate of bread and salt on his chest..."

The general said:

"You think they did?"

"I am sure my old nurse saw to it," Tietjens said. "I never even asked her, I was so sure... The other quotation is from Waller's <u>To His Coy Mistress</u>..." The general said, a little coldly:

"Ah... You recognize that... What else did Waller write? ...> I never Sir Walter Scott's *Border Minstrelsy*, ed. Henderson (Edinburgh & London: William Blackwood & Sons, 1902), II.170–2 quotes Scott's version of the traditional 'Cleveland Lyke-wake Dirge':

       This ae nighte, this ae nighte,
       Every nighte and alle;
       Fire and sleete and candle lighte,
       And Christe receive thye saule.

23 **UK** twelve." ¶ The general; **TS** twelve." ¶ twelve." <It has been the greatest influence on my life.... " He added: "Waller's other most famous poem... except for Thus sang they in the English boat.... is in his <u>Horatian Ode upon Cromwell's Return from Ireland</u>...."

The general said:

"<u>Damn</u> Cromwell...."

Tietjens said:

"The famous, hackneyed quotation is about Charles I. I don't know how Marvell—of course I meant Andrew Marvell when I said Waller. I don't know how Marvell had the courage to write it into an Ode to Cromwell ... I hope I should have the same courage if it came to my last day ... before going up the line, say...."

The general looked at him beneath his brows:

"I thought I'd caught you", he said, "When you said Waller instead of Marvell: <u>Go lovely rose</u> or <u>The seas are quiet</u> is not a patch on>

The general

This deletion is replaced by the passage of 21 lines that follows, from 'The general said' to 'There's for instance', which is an AR written on a separate leaf numbered 257a.

The line 'Thus sang they in the English boat' is also Marvell, from his poem 'Bermudas'.

24 **UK** ignoramus." ¶ Tietjens; **TS** ignoramus <If I don't read your confounded modern stuff...."> ¶ Tietjens

25 **UK** her armpits; **TS** her <hairless> ↑shining↓ armpits

26 **UK** dressing-table. She; **TS** dressing-table. <The nipples of her breasts had the definition of old, carved ivory.> She

27 **UK** himself: ¶ "One is going to that fine and secret place.... Why not have?" She; **TS** himself: ¶ "<Curse it ... If> One is going to that fine and secret place.... Why not?" She

28 **UK** humming. Maliciously!; **TS** humming. <She certainly made a sound like: "Poor Valentine Elsiabeth [sic]!".... He> ↑Maliciously!↓ Sylvia had thought of 'poor Valentine-Elisabeth' at the end of II.ii.

29 **AR** insertion: 'It was then that he'

30 **UK** Well! She; **TS** Well! She had bitched her chance ... She

31 **UK** shower-baths! ¶ Shining; radiating glory but still shrivelled so that he reminded Tietjens of an old apple inside a damascened helmet; the general; **TS** showerbaths. ¶ <The door-handle had moved decisively under his eyes!>

The general had naturally recited [the whole—positively the whole of **AR**]

"He nothing common did or mean
Upon that memorable scene,
But with his keener eye
The axe's edge did try.
Nor called the Gods with vulgar spite
To vindicate his helpless right
But bowed his comely head
Down as upon a bed ...."

↑He said:

That's about the execution of Charles I." ... <He was looking a little [memorable]> ... **AR**↓

Well! No general who read a little seventeenth-century literature could miss such a chance..... Charles I ... An odious man who smelt so that none of his courtiers dared to come near him! ...

Shining; radiating a glory that the melancholy Charles had never known, ↓but still shrivelled so that he reminded Tietjens of an old apple inside a damascened helmet **AR**↑; the general

32 **UK** "Sir!" His heart stopped. ¶ The general; **TS** "Sir!" <He could not keep out of his voice a shade of irony.> ↑His heart stopped **AR**↓ ¶ The general

33 **AR** insertion in left-hand margin: 'that afternoon Tietjens would receive a movement order. He said stiffly that he must not'

34 **UK** Tietjens thought: ¶ "Good God. I am being sent up the line. He's sending me to Perry's Army.... That's; **TS** Tietjens <said to himself: "Good God:> He's sending me <up the line> ↑to Perry's section.↓ **AR**] ¶ That's

35 **AR** insertion: 'but he did not know where the words came from:'

36 **UK** back!" ¶ To himself he said: ¶ "I shall fight this monstrous treatment of myself to my last breath." ¶ The general; **TS** back. ¶ The general

37 **AR** insertion: 'He added: "It's the best I can do for you.... I've thought it out very carefully. It's the best I can do for you."'

38 **UK** sir...." ¶ Of course he would never fight any treatment of himself! ... ¶ There **TS** sir...." ¶ "I shall of course forget <it> ↑my category **AR**↓, sir.... "He was wondering how long his godfather could go on without breaking..... His godfather suddenly broke! ¶ Tietjens hardly listened: ¶

There
39 Leaf 261 was divided horizontally here, and a substantial autograph passage inserted, taking up all of 261a and the top of 261b. The following sentence was deleted where 261 was cut: 'He repeated the same sentiment in several different forms'.

The autograph insertion runs from 'Tietjens said: ¶ If you would not mind, sir' [revised in UK to read 'Tietjens said: ¶ I must accept that'] to 'He was going up the line'.

40 **UK** Tietjens said: ¶ "I must accept that, if you say it, sir." ¶ The general; **TS** Tietjens said: ¶ If you would not mind, sir . . . If it's not disagreeable or painful . . . would you tell me what <there> is alleged against me. . . In service matters ¶ The general

41 **UK** told you that; **TS** [but in autograph insertion] told you <there is nothing against you> that

42 **UK** "He's hit it! . . ." ¶ The; **TS** [but in autograph insertion] "He's hit it! . . ." <[How he knows the service!] . . ."> ¶ The

As the deletion from the TS insertion makes even clearer, Tietjens is talking to himself here, Campion's not responding in his speech exemplifying Ford's principle that 'no speech of one character should ever answer the speech that goes before it' (*Joseph Conrad* 188). If the effect is to induce a momentary confusion about whether Tietjens is speaking aloud or not, that reflects Tietjens' state of crisis, as when he says later in the chapter: 'Great heavens! I've been talking to him.'

43 **UK** affairs. It's; **TS** [but in autograph insertion] affairs. <It would be painful to both of us.> It's

44 **AR** insertion in left-hand margin [of autograph insertion]: 'But you are a man of the world!'

45 **AR** insertion in left-hand margin [of autograph insertion]: 'It had then, he remembered, seemed fantastic.'

46 **UK, US** woman; **TS** whore
Perhaps an instance of Duckworth's censoring Ford; perhaps Ford's altering the proof.

47 **UK** But one who sells his wife, or . . . At; **TS** [but in autograph insertion] But <a blackmailer who> one who sells his wife, <or, damn it [illegible] her to a general> ↑or . . . ↓ At

48 **AR** insertion [in autograph insertion]: 'when it comes to fighting'

49 Typed insertion: '—even of the casualty clearing-station!'

50 **UK** overwhelmed. ¶ He said; **TS** overwhelmed <Or bothered by an imbecile superior . . . The general insisted on replies.> ¶<Tietjens> ↑He↓ said

51 **UK** general: ¶ I recognize; **TS** general. <"You have not said, sir, to what happening you refer."> I recognize

52 **AR** insertion: "'I recognize that I cannot stop in this command. I regret it, for I have enjoyed having this unit. . . . But does it necessarily mean the VIth Battalion?'"

53 **UK** Strafe! . . . ¶ The general; **TS** Strafe! . . But he had been a good deal worried at the time by an incomprehensible letter he had had from Sylvia the night before. An incomprehensibly insulting letter! The first he had received from her, handed to him just before he had got into the train at Rouen..... ¶ The general

54 **UK** said: ¶ "If I could think of anything else to do with you, I'd do it. . . . But

all the extraordinary rows you've got into.... They block me everywhere.... Do; **TS** said: ¶ <"[Damn it. What] could I refer to but your
incredible proceedings of last night...> ["If I could think of anything else
to do with you, I'd do it.... But <you cannot go [illegible] you absolutely
cannot... And> all the extraordinary rows you've got into.... They block
me everywhere.... **AR**] Do

55 AR insertion in left-hand margin: 'Then you say you had misjudged him!'
56 **UK** arrest!" I have; **TS** arrest!" ¶ The general said very swiftly:

"It is reported to me that you did... By a subaltern on O'Hara's staff who
was there....."

Tietjens said:

"The subaltern, sir, was in the passage. He can only imperfectly have
heard what went on in the room. I should judge that he was also very
nervous. He tried to induce the general to go away. The general shouted
repeatedly: 'By God! You put me under arrest?' ↑So no doubt the subaltern
thought I had. **AR**↓ But all that I had said to the lieutenant was that if the
general did not go away I should request him to put the general under
arrest...."

He said to himself:

"Good God! Why am I making this long, fumbling explanation!"

The general said with restraint:

"You assure me, in cold blood, that the general was in the room!"

Tietjens said:

"I have

57 **UK** she once had the disposition of a saint.... Now; **TS** she <is a> ↑once
had the disposition of a **AR**↓ saint ... as <your sainted mother was...> Now
58 Leaf 266 was divided here, and the bottom two-thirds numbered 266b,
allowing for the insertion of autograph leaf 266a, which runs from 'He began
again' to 'You don't try to make yourself popular, I must say!'".
59 AR insertion in left-hand margin of autograph inserted leaf: 'I can't send you
to Malta or India. Or to other commands in France.'
60 **UK** name" ¶ Tietjens; **TS, US** name." ¶ Tietjens
61 **UK** feels it! ... But he can hardly expect me to tell him that Sylvia thinks
Drake was the father of my own son, and desires my ruin!" But of course; **TS**
feels it! . ." But of course
62 **UK** had. The; **TS** had. A solitary old man! That was reasonable. ↑It was a
new idea to Tietjens. But it was reasonable. **AR**↓ He <,Tietjens,> had then
to think about this stupid old man's feelings. It was an additional worry. The
63 **UK** rest. ¶ Paradise! ...;**TS** rest. It was like a vision of sunlight in Paradise
to him because he knew that it was like a vision of sunlight in paradise to
her... She had had a charwoman whose son had been put into the first-line
transport as a reward for gallantry over an extended and exhausting period.
The son had written a rapturous letter home describing the soft job of living
in tents in the sunlight, <far> ↑four miles↓ behind the line. The charwoman
not being able to read had had to read the letter to her. It described the divisional transport-officer as having a space of a smooth green field marked out
near his tent where he practiced casting dry flies to pass the time – and woe
betide any Tommie who led a horse across it! ...

It had occurred to Tietjens that casting dry flies would be a good occupation to try for taking the edge off thought! He had played Patience all his

life: but you could not do that in orderly room <without exciting comment> so he had substituted the writing of sonnets which was a <little> too troublesome to be good. You wanted something that would employ only half your mind. He wondered if Mckechnie had ever Latinised <that> ↑the **AR**↓ sonnet <.....> ↑he had written just before something hit oh Nine Morgan! **AR**↓

   Paradise!...

The fly-casting episode refers back to *Some Do Not* ... II.v, where it is told from Valentine's point of view. Perhaps Ford thought it repetitive, or came to feel Tietjens would have been unlikely to have heard of it from her.

64 The third dot in UK has been erroneously printed above the line.

65 **UK** weight! In the hotel last night he had nearly fainted over the thought that Morgan might have been the man whose life he had spared at Noircourt.... It was getting to be a serious matter! It might mean that there was a crack in his, Tietjens', brain. A Lesion! If; **TS** weight! If

66 AR insertion: 'rising up before his horse's off-shoulder!'

67 **UK** be decreed by A.C.I. that no more horses were to be used! .... Imagine; **TS** be <done> ↑decreed by A.C.I. that no more horses were to be used! **AR**↓ .... Imagine

68 **UK, US, TS** Kemmell; **Ed** Kemmel
The correct spelling of the village is Kemmel.

69 AR insertion: 'that could be heard five miles away.'

70 AR insertion: 'It is the private property of the colonel.'

71 **UK** washout. Lieutenant; **TS** wash-out. Schomburg, as I have told you, is not on the strength. <He is the private property of Colonel Thompson who has asked me to exercise and look after him.> Lieutenant

72 **UK** said malificently: ¶ "It looks as if you; **TS** said <limply> ↑maleficently **AR**↓: ¶ "There you are then.... ↑as you always do you wangle yourself out of the strafe. But... **AR**↓" He exclaimed with violence: "Then ↑It looks as if **AR**↓ you
US emends to 'maleficently'; the AR to TS is ambiguous, but there is no dot above what should be the first 'e' in 'maleficently'.

73 AR insertion at foot of leaf: "'You're perfectly right to object to wrong treatment of horses. But in this case your objection blocks the only other job open to you.'"

74 **UK** aware ..." ¶ The general said: "Do you know that the 19th Division to which your brother wants you sent is attached to Fourth Army now—and it's Fourth Army horses that Hotchkiss is to play with? ... How could I send you there to be under his orders?" ¶Tietjens said: ¶ "That's perfectly; **TS** aware <of that> <↑that my brother Mark asked me to be put in command of that 19th division transport **AR**↓> He must keep the general off of long speeches: his brain would not keep on to them. He <said: "they told me at the depot orderly room that the order had come through that they had protested to you that I am indispensable here"> ↑asked why shouldn't I have that job, sir? **AR**↓ ¶The general said sharply: ¶ "You're not getting at me... <For sending you>....." ¶ ↑Tietjens said: "No sir!: ¶ The general said: "Do you know that the 19th Division is attached to Fourth Army ... And it's Fourth Army horses that Hotchkiss is to play with? ... How could I send you there?" ¶ Tietjens said: ¶ "<No> ↑Well **AR**↓, sir.... <It's> ↑That's **AR**↓ perfectly

UK fails to start a new paragraph with the general's speech beginning 'Do you know [. . .], as did Ford inserting the autograph revision in the left-hand margin; emended here.

75 AR insertion: 'He was finished. There was now nothing left but to find out how his mind was going to take it. He wished they could go to his cook-houses!'

76 AR insertion: 'Led by an officer!'

77 **UK** As if an officer of the Buffs had gone; **TS** As if <the Black Watch had> ↑an officer of the Buffs had **AR**↓ gone

78 **UK, TS** beasts... His; **US** beasts.... His

79 **UK** believe that; **TS** believe <for Miss Wannop's sake> that

80 AR insertion: 'But it was an atrociously wrong course. We ought to have separated years ago.'

81 **UK** little ...." ¶ He said; **TS** little...." <His voice changed suddenly to an exquisite softness: "Do you know", he said, "that, before you were born your sainted mother had... Well, like who was it?.. the mother of some saint ... Thomas à Becket, was it ... She went through London calling: Gilbert! Gilbert! Wasn't that she?"> ¶ He said

82 **UK** dinner ... I hope you'll be decent. Why; **TS** dinner ... <Tell me, now>... ↑I hope you'll be decent. **AR**↓ Why

83 AR insertion: 'Then high treason for a page.'

84 **UK** London. You can see my initials on the top of the sheet!" ¶ The general; **TS** London. I asked Colonel Levin if many like it had been sent in because it was interesting as coming from a Russian source. Colonel Levin said it was the only one. Other subversive literature was all English and rather ordinary. I presume that that was why he called your attention to this one. You can see my initials on the top of the sheet!" ¶ The general

85 **UK** product. What; **TS** product, <I've the Christist religion that is enjoined on the Winchester boy; the belief in a divinely-privileged social ring that exists at Eton; the simple veneration for the school that you find at Blundell's; the patriotism of Harrow; the love for the past of Westminster;> What

86 AR insertion: 'Other men get over their schooling. I never have. I remain adolescent.'

87 AR insertion: 'What's this about peaching to a head master?'

88 **UK** contemplation of my marital infelicities. The general; **TS** contemplation of <me. That is perfectly correct. You> ↑my marital infelicities! I **AR**↓ cannot do anything else. There is only one thing. Is there nowhere else for me to go but to my own battalion. <It will cause a devil of a lot of awkwardness. Colonel Bird wants that little squit McKechnie for second in command. McKechnie wants the job too. The battalion is quite properly a close band of brothers by now.> I shall be an interloper..." ¶ The general

89 AR insertion: 'I can never go home.'

90 **UK** suicide." ¶ The general; **TS** suicide." <¶ The general pondered:

"If I sent you home it would be taken as a sign of your being in disgrace... Over last night! That's too appalling to contemplate! I won't have that thought of you. Something must be done..."

Tietjens said:

"You can do nothing, sir. You are my godfather... There's also the danger that I've got a very attractive wife. There's literally nothing for me but the front line...">

The general
91 AR insertion: 'I can give you testimonials. . . .'"
92 AR insertion: 'see that it's impossible?'"
93 AR insertion: 'But you see how bad for one's descendants suicide is. That is why I do not forgive my father. Before he did it I should never have contemplated the idea. Now I have contemplated it. That's a weakening of the moral fibre. It's contemplating a fallacy as a possibility. For'
94 **UK** of the relation of the sexes." ¶ The general; **TS** of whether marriage is or isn't a sacrament." ¶ The general
95 Leaf 279 has been divided at this point, and the top fragment ends with the instruction '279A-C follows'. What appears to be the lower portion of the leaf has been numbered 279b, and a leaf with half a page of additional autograph was inserted between them, and numbered 279a; its text running from 'The general sat staring at the tablecloth' to 'difficult to make myself plain'. However, much of this added autograph material was then deleted in proof, as per the following note.
96 **UK** say. What; **TS** say."
    Tietjens said:
    "Did you ever read . . . You've read the XVIIth century, sir . . . <u>A Woman Killed with Kindness</u>!"
    The general said:
    "No . . . Yes . . . I don't know. What's it got to do with it? What's it about . . ."
    Tietjens said:
    "It's the story of a woman who was false to her husband . . ." In the time of James I. The husband, a Christlike sort of fellow takes her back, but allots her separate rooms and an atmosphere of pious resignation. She, pathetically, dies.
    The general said:
    "What
    A Woman Killed with Kindness is a play by Thomas Heywood (early 1570s–1641).
97 **UK, US** modern ways . . . But; **TS** modern. . . But; **Ed** modern ways. . . . But
    In TS the sentence trails off, which accounts for the use of three dots. The addition of 'ways' has been allowed to stand, as possibly authorial; but a fourth dot would normally have been added once the sentence was complete.
98 **UK** not really. . . . But what is a man to do if his wife is unfaithful to him?" ¶ The general said as if it were an insult; **TS** not really. . . . ↑But what is a man to do if his wife is unfaithful to him?" AR↓ ¶ <The general looked at him with sudden sharp cunning:> The general said as if it were an insult
    Leaf 279C begins with these words, and runs for another half-page of autograph, to 'Why don't <u>you</u> divorce" he asked'.
99 **UK** Why *don't* you divorce; **TS** Why don't <u>you</u> divorce
100 On leaf 280, the following sentences are deleted: '<At the extreme end was territory labelled: White Ruthenians. . . Who the deuce were those poor devils?>.' After that, this leaf has been divided; at the foot of the top portion is the instruction '280a-c follows'. 280a is a full-page autograph insertion, running from 'Years before', to 'Any man might have slept with either.' Leaf 280b continues from 'of them with pleasure and profit' for three-quarters of a page, to 'Who the devil were <u>those</u> poor wretches?'

(emended from 'poor devils?' in the autograph insertion). 280c appears to be the lower portion of 280.

101　AR insertion in the left-hand margin of the inserted autograph leaf: 'with four little planes as an escort'.

102　**UK** believe it." ¶ Tietjens said to himself: ¶ "*Why*; **TS** believe it." ¶ <He resembled a good hound on the scent at last.> Tietjens said ↑to himself **AR↓**: ¶ <"At last!".... It had got him. He said: > "<u>Why</u>

103　AR insertion: 'But the Germans were going to cure it!'

104　AR insertion: 'I am now.'

105　**UK** You had shut up your house because of your wife's misbehaviour. You let me believe you had been sold up. You; **TS** You ↑had **AR↓** shut up your house ↑for a reason. You let me believe you had been sold up. **AR↓** You

106　**UK** all." ¶ *Why*; **TS** all." < <u>Why</u> do you do these things? It's deception. You say you have a love of truth."> ¶ Tietjens decided <- <u>decided</u> -> that all this being very agitating and painful he had better attend to the problems of the war. <u>Why</u>

107　AR insertion: 'extinguished the Horse, <and>'

108　**UK** life." ¶ The general; **TS** life." <Politics, strategy, sex, finance, the single command, ethics, education, heredity...."> ¶ The general

109　**UK** 1912; **TS** 19<13>↑12**AR↓**

110　**UK** meditated. He asked: "How; **TS** meditated: "Look after you! Have I done it? I don't know... I made you, as you say, read Clarendon when you were twelve.... The greatest book in the world ... That's what formed your character. The seventeenth century...."

　　Tietjens suddenly felt his eyes fill: intolerably warm and soothing. As if Valentine Wannop had spoken.

　　He said:

　　"Yes, sir.... If I had been George Herbert ..."

　　The general said:

　　"Yes. Yes. <u>Sweet day so cool, so calm, so bright</u>.... And <u>Makes that and</u> ... I forget ... <u>the action</u> ..."

　　Tietjens said:

　　"You make me very homesick, sir. They were my mother's ..."

　　The general said:

　　"Yes, yes ..." He asked: "How

111　**UK** harmony. Probably; **TS** harmony. <↑if they [illegible] **AR↓** If they believe things against you without explanation they are not created to be your friends.> Probably

112　**UK** you ..." ¶Tietjens was sentimentally; **TS** you ..."

　　Tietjens said:

　　"Yes, sir. About whether you ought to fork out your savings to save me from the consequences of my rash expenditure over a young woman in a tobacco shop – whom you didn't at bottom believe in!"

　　<"But how in the world do you propose to live?"

　　Tietjens asked absently:

　　"After the war, sir?" ... He added: "I don't know, sir. Few people do!">

　　He was sentimentally

113　**UK** walking near Salisbury in a grove, regarding long pastures and ploughlands running to dark, high; **TS** walking ↑near Salisbury **AR↓** in a grove, regarding <over the near hedge> long pastures ↑and ploughlands **AR↓**

running to ↑dark, AR↓ high

114 **UK** church.... One ought to be a seventeenth-century; **TS** church....
<A> ↑ One ought to be a **AR**↓ seventeenth-century

115 AR insertion: 'He himself was never to go home!'

116 **UK** home! ¶The general; **TS** home!
<He said:
"I, sir.... I shall make a living as an old furniture dealer ..." He continued into the general's speechlessness: "I've got a certain gift for it. I can detect fakes extraordinarily without knowing how. You needn't be alarmed sir. I know what I'm doing. Sir James Donaldson has offered to take me into partnership, he's been so impressed with my knack. It probably comes from my being in harmony with the seventeenth century to some extent. That's my period. In furniture, I mean....."
The general said: drily:
"You'll probably do what you want in spite of anything I can say. You could anticipate my decease if you liked: to a small extent, I'm not desperately poor."
Tietjens said:
"I don't want money, sir.">
The general

117 **UK** added: "As; **TS** added: <"Naturally Mr Ruggles moved in the same circles as Sylvia herself – where you might make a living by selling your wife, say, to financial cabinet minister: or at any rate where you alleged that such things are done. I daresay they aren't. But it's an atmosphere of pulling the strings of shower baths." He finished:> "As

118 AR insertion: 'He said: "He knows he's given himself away! ... Good God!"'. The word 'himself' was presumably revised to 'his wife' in proof.

119 **UK** all crooked!" They; **TS** all out of drawing!" They
The following sentence: 'They remained looking at each other' has been added by hand, and the leaf (286) divided at this point. What appears to be the remaining half is a heavily revised leaf numbered 289, and begins '<They looked at each other hard.> It was as if they had hypnotized each other' (revised in UK to 'It was as if they were hypnotized'). In between has been inserted a typed leaf (with autograph corrections) originally numbered '288', but with '287–' inserted in autograph before the typed number. All the remaining leaves have been re-numbered by hand. Leaf '287–8' begins with the deleted line '<Gidding... The seventeenth century, High Church Order...">', which is actually the continuation of leaf 290 (in the middle of the long deleted passage in note 122 below). This indicates that the final seven or eight leaves were reordered as part of the extensive revision of this conclusion.

120 AR insertion: 'They had had their dinners.'

121 AR insertion: 'Was it mysticism? ... Another word!'

122 AR insertion: 'He and Tietjens continued to look at each other.' This leaf ('287–8') has also been cut off at this point, but the bottom quarter does not appear elsewhere in TS. The following leaf, 289, begins with a deleted sentence: '<They looked at each other hard>', replaced with the AR insertion: 'It was as if they had hypnotized each other. The men's voices went on in a mournful cadence.'

123 **UK** heart in 1912. The father committed suicide five years after. He; **TS**

heart ↑in 1912 **AR**↓. The father committed suicide ↑five years after **AR**↓. He

124 **UK** France with Perowne." ¶ He; **TS** France with..." <He said: "All gone... And why? [because] ... The fellow's going up the line too.... " He said: "It's a bit thick!" ... But he's right to do what he's doing." **AR**> ¶ He

125 **UK** hadn't. Better; **TS** hadn't <Then why had the world fallen on him like a ton of bricks? There was positively <u>no</u> not sending him up the line> Better The passage from 'Better' to 'as he is doing' is an AR insertion, slightly revised.

126 **UK** you...." ¶ Tietjens stood; **TS** you..."

<Tietjens said:

"If I might sit a minute longer...." The general waved a white hand of graciousness. He said: "After all I've never told him what was his mother's idea before he was born. I shan't now..." The sentimental moment was past. He said however:

I suppose you never took a vow ... of poverty or anything? At say your mother's request. I'm not asking with any motive."

Tietjens said:

"No, sir ... But to live with my mother was like a lesson in the love of simplicity."

The general said:

"That was the ... what I was trying to get at ... the way your mother behaved. As a mother."

Tietjens said:

"It was rather like living beside one of the nuns of little Gidding!"

The general said: heartily:

"At any rate there's nothing of the saint about you... It did not rub off.... For of all the damn fellows for getting into messes ... I'm talking of the Army.... "

Tietjens said:

"Hasn't it possibly occurred to you that some of my mother's air rubbing off onto me has given me an aspect of serenity that makes ... oh, generals ... give me jobs that are. . Well, beyond my experience... I'm no soldier. No Tietjens ever was."

The general said:

"Oh, You will pass.">

Tietjens stood

127 **UK** together. ¶ The general also rose, settling his belt. He said: ¶ "... You can fall out." ¶ Tietjens; **TS** together. <He said: ¶ "Praise from...."> ¶ The general also rose, settling his belt. He said: ¶ <"It's not exactly praise. But there's one essential quality for a soldier... lying himself out of tight places. You've got that>... "You can fall out." <Find Levin for me, will you"> ¶ Tietjens

128 **UK** disappointed.... He; **TS** disappointed <broken hearted... Oh, do come and look at my cook-houses. They will be splendid. The men will have had their dinners and all cleaned up. I never asked you a favour, sir.... But Sergeant Case> He

129 **UK** said: ¶ "... He; **TS** said: ¶ "<I can't understand why he doesn't marry the doxy.> ... He

130 **UK** dinners!" ¶ In; **TS** ↑dinners'" **AR** ↓<cook-houses." I bet you I catch you out."

Tietjens said:

"I respectfully bet that if you do I find an excuse. . ."

They moved towards the door side by side. The general tapped Tietjens on the shoulder with the horn handle of his crop.

I wanted to ask you something before we go. . .", he said. "You know everything. . ." He said: "By the bye. . . With your [?] health. . . I'm bound to say it's alarmed me. . . you can be in hospital in ten days after you reach your battalion. . ."

Tietjens said:

"Oh I can last two months of it, sir. I know myself. . ."

The general said:

"I'm damned sorry. . . But . . . Damn it it sounds a callous thing to say But we must take the rough with the smooth. We're both soldiers, you and I . . ."

Tietjens said:

"I wish you would not worry, sir. ↑If one does what he likes one must take what one gets for it. **AR**↓ I've figured it out very carefully I shall last two months. The German offensive cannot begin before the 17 of March. They have to re-train their men to use the rifle. It'll be me for Blighty before then. After quite a quiet time! Besides you will ↑we shall **AR**↓ have the single command by the middle of February. . .

The general said: His jaw fallen down ↑The Germans will make their great breakthrough in March." **AR**↓

"Yes? Yes?"

"You would be able to say," Tietjens asked, "that however many women he had to do with He was the only man that never treated a woman badly." ↑It's a pity he never married. That's perhaps why the Churches are moribund. It's a pity. . . ." **AR**↓

The general said:

"Yes. . . Yes. . . We do treat them. . . There's no way of finding out how <u>not</u> to treat them . . . not badly. . . I had. . . In Quetta. . . And think of child-birth. . . I swear I'd rather go – where you're going than. . . ."

Tietjens said:

"It's probably about an equal chance, sir, . . .">

In

131 AR insertion: 'the general, Tietjens at his side, walked between'

132 **UK** my man? . . ." ¶To Tietjens; **TS** my man? . . .

<Tietjens whispered in the ear of Colonel Levin beside him:

"Who was the ass who said: There will be no more parades?"

Levin exclaimed: "I never!" in tones so acute that the general looked back from the opening door of the locker!

Tietjens said:

"Deserts of vast eternity! . . . What do you suppose is in that damned locker?">

TS ends with this deleted passage, and omits UK's closing sentence, which (unless the final leaf is missing) must have been added in proof.

SELECT BIBLIOGRAPHY

Works by Ford (whether as 'Hueffer' or 'Ford')

Ancient Lights and Certain New Reflections: Being the Memories of a Young Man (London: Chapman and Hall, 1911); published as *Memories and Impressions* (New York: Harper, 1911)

The Benefactor (London: Brown, Langham, 1905)

Between St. Dennis and St. George (London: Hodder and Stoughton, 1915)

A Call (London: Chatto and Windus, 1910)

The Cinque Ports (Edinburgh and London: William Blackwood and Sons, 1900)

Collected Poems, ed. William Rose Benét (New York: Oxford University Press, 1936)

The Correspondence of Ford Madox Ford and Stella Bowen, ed. Sondra Stang and Karen Cochran (Bloomington and Indianapolis: Indiana University Press, 1994)

Critical Essays, ed. Max Saunders and Richard Stang (Manchester: Carcanet, 2002)

England and the English, ed. Sara Haslam (Manchester: Carcanet, 2003) (collecting Ford's trilogy on Englishness with *The Heart of the Country* and *The Spirit of the People*)

The English Novel from the Earliest Days to the Death of Joseph Conrad (London: Constable, 1930)

The Fifth Queen (London: Alston Rivers, 1906)

The Fifth Queen Crowned (Eveleigh Nash, 1908)

The Ford Madox Ford Reader, with Foreword by Graham Greene; ed. Sondra J. Stang (Manchester: Carcanet, 1986)

The Good Soldier, ed. Martin Stannard (Norton Critical Edition; New York and London: W. W. Norton & Company, 1995)

Great Trade Route (London and Toronto: Oxford University Press, 1937)

The Heart of the Country (London: Alston Rivers, 1906)

'A House (Modern Morality Play)', *The Chapbook*, 21, March 1921

(London: The Poetry Bookshop, 1921)

It Was the Nightingale (1933), ed. John Coyle (Manchester: Carcanet, 2007)

Joseph Conrad: A Personal Remembrance (London: Duckworth, 1924; Boston: Little, Brown, 1924)

Last Post (London: Duckworth, 1928) – the fourth and final novel of *Parade's End*

Letters of Ford Madox Ford, ed. Richard M. Ludwig (Princeton, NJ: Princeton University Press, 1965)

A Little Less Than Gods: A Romance (London: Duckworth, 1928)

A Man Could Stand Up – (London: Duckworth, 1926) – the third novel of *Parade's End*

The March of Literature (London: Allen and Unwin, 1939)

The Marsden Case (London: Duckworth, 1923)

Mightier Than the Sword (London: Allen and Unwin, 1938)

A Mirror to France (London: Duckworth, 1926)

Mister Bosphorus and the Muses or a Short History of Poetry in Britain. Variety Entertainment in Four Acts... with Harlequinade, Transformation Scene, Cinematograph Effects, and Many Other Novelties, as well as Old and Tried Favourites, illustrated by Paul Nash (London: Duckworth, 1923)

New York Essays (New York: William Edwin Rudge, 1927)

No More Parades (London: Duckworth, 1925) – the second novel of *Parade's End*

No Enemy (1929), ed. Paul Skinner (Manchester: Carcanet, 2002)

On Heaven and Poems Written on Active Service, The Bodley Head (London: John Lane, 1918)

The Panel: A Sheer Comedy (London: Constable, 1912)

Portraits from Life (Boston and New York: Houghton Mifflin Company, 1937)

Pound/Ford: the Story of a Literary Friendship: the Correspondence between Ezra Pound and Ford Madox Ford and Their Writings About Each Other, ed. Brita Lindberg-Seyersted (London: Faber & Faber, 1982)

Privy Seal (London: Alston Rivers, 1907)

Provence (1935), ed. John Coyle (Manchester: Carcanet, 2009)

Return to Yesterday (1931), ed. Bill Hutchings (Manchester: Carcanet, 1999)

'Riesenberg', *English Review* 8 (April 1911), 25–45

Some Do Not ... (London: Duckworth, 1924) – the first novel of *Parade's End*

The Spirit of the People (London: Alston Rivers, 1907)

Thus to Revisit (London: Chapman and Hall, 1921)

War Prose, ed. Max Saunders (Manchester: Carcanet, 1999)
When Blood is Their Argument (London: Hodder and Stoughton, 1915)
When the Wicked Man (London: Jonathan Cape, 1932)

Other Works

Angier, Carole, *Jean Rhys: Life and Work* (Boston, Toronto, London: Little, Brown, 1990)
Bowen, Stella, *Drawn from Life* (London: Collins, 1941).
Fussell, Paul, *The Great War and Modern Memory* (New York and London: Oxford University Press, 1975)
Gordon, Ambrose, Jr, *The Invisible Tent: The War Novels of Ford Madox Ford* (Austin, TX: University of Texas Press, 1964)
Harvey, David Dow, *Ford Madox Ford: 1873–1939: A Bibliography of Works and Criticism* (Princeton, NJ: Princeton University Press, 1962)
Hueffer, Francis, *The Troubadours* (London: Chatto and Windus, 1878)
Hunt, Violet, *Their Lives* (New York: Brentano's, 1916)
McAlmon, Robert, ed., *Contact Collection of Contemporary Writers* (Paris: Contact Editions, 1925)
Partridge, Eric, *Partridge's Concise Dictionary of Slang and Unconventional English* (London: Macmillan, 1989)
Pound, Ezra, *The Spirit of Romance* (New York: New Directions, 1968)
Saunders, Max, *Ford Madox Ford: A Dual Life*, 2 vols (Oxford: Oxford University Press, 1996)
Secor, Robert, and Secor, Marie, *The Return of the Good Soldier: Ford Madox Ford and Violet Hunt's 1917 Diary*, English Literary Studies No. 30 (University of Victoria, 1983)
Stang, Sondra J., ed., *The Presence of Ford Madox Ford* (Philadelphia: University of Pennsylvania Press, 1981)
Wiesenfarth, Joseph, *Ford Madox Ford and the Regiment of Women: Violet Hunt, Jean Rhys, Stella Bowen, Janice Biala* (Madison, WI: University of Wisconsin Press, 2005)

Further Critical Reading on *Parade's End*

Armstrong, Paul, *The Challenge of Bewilderment: Understanding and Representation in James, Conrad, and Ford* (Ithaca, NY, and London: Cornell University Press, 1987)

Attridge, John, '"I Don't Read Novels ... I Know What's in 'em": Impersonality, Impressionism and Responsibility in *Parade's End*', in *Impersonality and Emotion in Twentieth-Century British Literature*, ed. Christine Reynier and Jean-Michel Ganteau (Montpellier: Université Montpellier III, 2005)

Auden, W. H., 'Il Faut Payer', *Mid-Century*, 22 (Feb. 1961), 3–10

Becquet, Alexandra, 'Modernity, Shock and Cinema: The Visual Aesthetics of Ford Madox Ford's *Parade's End*', in *Ford Madox Ford and Visual Culture*, ed. Laura Colombino, International Ford Madox Ford Studies, 8 (Amsterdam and New York: Rodopi, 2009), 191–204

Bergonzi, Bernard, *Heroes' Twilight: A Study of the Literature of the Great War* (Manchester: Carcanet, 3rd edn, 1996)

Bradbury, Malcolm, 'The Denuded Place: War and Ford in *Parade's End* and *U. S. A.*', in *The First World War in Fiction*, ed. Holger Klein (London and Basingstoke: Macmillan, rev. edn, 1978), 193–209

—'Introduction', *Parade's End* (London: Everyman's Library, 1992)

Brasme, Isabelle, 'Between Impressionism and Modernism: *Some Do Not ...*, a poetics of the *Entre-deux*', in *Ford Madox Ford: Literary Networks and Cultural Transformations*, ed. Andrzej Gasiorek and Daniel Moore, International Ford Madox Ford Studies, 7 (Amsterdam and New York: Rodopi, 2008), 189–99

Brown, Dennis, 'Remains of the Day: Tietjens the Englishman', in *Ford Madox Ford's Modernity*, ed. Robert Hampson and Max Saunders, International Ford Madox Ford Studies, 2 (Amsterdam and Atlanta, GA: Rodopi, 2003), 161–74

Brown, Nicholas, *Utopian Generations: The Political Horizon of Twentieth-Century Literature* (Princeton, NJ: Princeton University Press, 2005)

Buitenhuis, Peter, *The Great War of Words: British, American and Canadian Propaganda and Fiction, 1914–1933* (Vancouver: University of British Columbia Press, 1987)

Calderaro, Michela A., *A Silent New World: Ford Madox Ford's Parade's End* (Bologna: Editrice CLUEB [Cooperativa Libraria Universitaria, Editrice Bologna], 1993)

Caserio, Robert L., 'Ford's and Kipling's Modernist Imagination of Public Virtue', in *Ford Madox Ford's Modernity*, ed. Robert Hampson and Max Saunders, International Ford Madox Ford Studies, 2 (Amsterdam and Atlanta, GA: Rodopi, 2003), 175–90

Cassell, Richard A., *Ford Madox Ford: A Study of his Novels* (Baltimore: Johns Hopkins University Press, 1962)

—*Ford Madox Ford: Modern Judgements* (London: Macmillan, 1972)

—*Critical Essays on Ford Madox Ford* (Boston: G. K. Hall, 1987)

Colombino, Laura, *Ford Madox Ford: Vision, Visuality and Writing* (Oxford: Peter Lang, 2008)

Conroy, Mark, 'A Map of Tory Misreading in *Parade's End*', in *Ford Madox Ford and Visual Culture*, ed. Laura Colombino, International Ford Madox Ford Studies, 8 (Amsterdam and New York: Rodopi, 2009), 175–90.

Cook, Cornelia, 'Last Post', *Agenda*, 27:4–28:1, Ford Madox Ford special double issue (winter 1989–spring 1990), 23–30

Davis, Philip, 'The Saving Remnant', in *Ford Madox Ford and Englishness*, ed. Dennis Brown and Jenny Plastow, International Ford Madox Ford Studies, 5 (Amsterdam and New York: Rodopi, 2006), 21–35

Deer, Patrick, *Culture in Camouflage: War, Empire, and Modern British Literature* (Oxford: Oxford University Press, 2009)

DeKoven, Marianne, 'Valentine Wannop and Thematic Structure in Ford Madox Ford's *Parade's End*', *English Literature in Transition (1880–1920)*, 20:2 (1977), 56–68

Erskine-Hill, Howard, 'Ford's Novel Sequence: An Essay in Retrospection', *Agenda*, 27:4–28:1, Ford Madox Ford special double issue (winter 1989–spring 1990), 46–55

Frayn, Andrew, '"This Battle Was not Over": *Parade's End* as a Transitional Text in the Development of "Disenchanted" First World War Literature', in *Ford Madox Ford: Literary Networks and Cultural Transformations*, ed. Andrzej Gasiorek and Daniel Moore, International Ford Madox Ford Studies, 7 (Amsterdam and New York: Rodopi, 2008), 201–16

Gasiorek, Andrzej, 'The Politics of Cultural Nostalgia: History and Tradition in Ford Madox Ford's *Parade's End*', *Literature & History*, 11:2 (third series) (autumn 2002), 52–77

Green, Robert, *Ford Madox Ford: Prose and Politics* (Cambridge: Cambridge University Press, 1981)

Haslam, Sara, *Fragmenting Modernism: Ford Madox Ford, the Novel, and the Great War* (Manchester: Manchester University Press, 2002)

Heldman, J. M., 'The Last Victorian Novel: Technique and Theme in *Parade's End*', *Twentieth Century Literature*, 18 (Oct. 1972), 271–84

Hoffmann, Charles G., *Ford Madox Ford: Updated Edition* (Boston: Twayne Publishers, 1990)

Holton, Robert, *Jarring Witnesses: Modern Fiction and the Representation of History* (Hemel Hempstead: Harvester Wheatsheaf, 1994)

Hynes, Samuel, 'Ford Madox Ford: Three Dedicatory Letters to *Parade's End*, with Commentary and Notes', *Modern Fiction Studies*, 16:4 (1970), 515–28

—*A War Imagined: The First World War and English Culture* (London: The Bodley Head, 1990)

Judd, Alan, *Ford Madox Ford* (London: Collins, 1990)

Kashner, Rita, 'Tietjens' Education: Ford Madox Ford's Tetralogy', *Critical Quarterly*, 8 (1966), 150–63

MacShane, Frank, *The Life and Work of Ford Madox Ford* (New York: Horizon; London: Routledge & Kegan Paul, 1965)

— ed., *Ford Madox Ford: The Critical Heritage* (London: Routledge, 1972)

Meixner, John A., *Ford Madox Ford's Novels: A Critical Study* (Minneapolis: University of Minnesota Press; London: Oxford University Press, 1962)

Mizener, Arthur, *The Saddest Story: A Biography of Ford Madox Ford* (New York: World, 1971; London: The Bodley Head, 1972)

Monta, Anthony P., '*Parade's End* in the Context of National Efficiency', in *History and Representation in Ford Madox Ford's Writings*, ed. Joseph Wiesenfarth, International Ford Madox Ford Studies, 3 (Amsterdam and New York: Rodopi, 2004), 41–51

Moore, Gene, 'The Tory in a Time of Change: Social Aspects of Ford Madox Ford's *Parade's End*', *Twentieth Century Literature*, 28:1 (spring 1982), 49–68

Moser, Thomas C., *The Life in the Fiction of Ford Madox Ford* (Princeton, NJ: Princeton University Press, 1980)

Munton, Alan, 'The Insane Subject: Ford and Wyndham Lewis in the War and Post-War', in *Ford Madox Ford: Literary Networks and Cultural Transformations*, ed. Andrzej Gasiorek and Daniel Moore, International Ford Madox Ford Studies, 7 (Amsterdam and New York: Rodopi, 2008), 105–30

Parfitt, George, *Fiction of the First World War: A Study* (London: Faber & Faber, 1988)

Radford, Andrew, 'The Gentleman's Estate in Ford's *Parade's End*', *Essays in Criticism* 52:4 (Oct. 2002), 314–32

Saunders, Max, 'Ford and European Modernism: War, Time, and *Parade's End*', in *Ford Madox Ford and 'The Republic of Letters'*, ed. Vita Fortunati and Elena Lamberti (Bologna: Editrice CLUEB [Cooperativa Libraria Universitaria, Editrice Bologna], 2002), 3–21

—'Introduction', Ford Madox Ford, *Parade's End* (Harmondsworth: Penguin, 2002), vii–xvii

Seiden, Melvin, 'Persecution and Paranoia in *Parade's End*', *Criticism*, 8:3 (summer 1966), 246–62

Skinner, Paul, '"Not the Stuff to Fill Graveyards": Joseph Conrad and *Parade's End*', in *Inter-relations: Conrad, James, Ford, and Others*, ed.

Keith Carabine and Max Saunders (Lublin: Columbia University Press, 2003), 161–76

—'The Painful Processes of Reconstruction: History in *No Enemy* and *Last Post*', in *History and Representation in Ford Madox Ford's Writings*, ed. Joseph Wiesenfarth, International Ford Madox Ford Studies, 3 (Amsterdam and New York: Rodopi, 2004), 65–75

Snitow, Ann Barr, *Ford Madox Ford and the Voice of Uncertainty* (Baton Rouge: Louisiana State University Press, 1984)

Sorum, Eve, 'Mourning and Moving On: Life after War in Ford Madox Ford's *The Last Post*', in *Modernism and Mourning*, ed. Patricia Rae (Lewisburg, PA: Bucknell University Press, 2007), 154–67

Stang, Sondra J., *Ford Madox Ford* (New York: Ungar, 1977)

Tate, Trudi, 'Rumour, Propaganda, and *Parade's End*', *Essays in Criticism*, 47:4 (Oct. 1997), 332–53

—*Modernism, History and the First World War* (Manchester: Manchester University Press, 1998)

Trotter David, 'Ford Against Lewis and Joyce', in *Ford Madox Ford: Literary Networks and Cultural Transformations*, ed. Andrzej Gasiorek and Daniel Moore, International Ford Madox Ford Studies, 7 (Amsterdam and New York: Rodopi, 2008), 131–49

Weiss, Timothy, *Fairy Tale and Romance in Works of Ford Madox Ford* (Lanham, MD: University Press of America, 1984)

Wiesenfarth, Joseph, *Gothic Manners and the Classic English Novel* (Madison: University of Wisconsin Press, 1988)

Wiley, Paul L., *Novelist of Three Worlds: Ford Madox Ford* (Syracuse, NY: Syracuse University Press, 1962)

THE
FORD
MADOX
FORD
SOCIETY

Ford c. 1915   ©Alfred Cohen, 2000   Registered Charity No. 1084040

This international society was founded in 1997 to promote knowledge of and interest in Ford. Honorary Members include Julian Barnes, A. S. Byatt, Hans-Magnus Enzensberger, Samuel Hynes, Alan Judd, Bill Nighy, Ruth Rendell, Michael Schmidt, John Sutherland, and Gore Vidal. There are currently over one hundred members, from more than ten countries. Besides regular meetings in Britain, we have held conferences in Italy, Germany, the U.S.A, and France. Since 2002 we have published International Ford Madox Ford Studies; a series of substantial annual volumes distributed free to members. *Ford Madox Ford: A Reappraisal* (2002), *Ford Madox Ford's Modernity* (2003), *History and Representation in Ford Madox Ford's Writings* (2004), *Ford Madox Ford and the City* (2005), *Ford Madox Ford and Englishness* (2006), *Ford Madox Ford's Literary Contacts* (2007), *Ford Madox Ford: Literary Networks and Cultural Transformations* (2008), *Ford Madox Ford and Visual Culture* (2009), and *Ford Madox Ford, Modernist Magazines and Editing* (2010) are all still available. Future volumes are planned on Ford and France, on his pre-war work, and on *Parade's End* and the First World War. If you are an admirer, an enthusiast, a reader, a scholar, or a student of anything Fordian, then this Society would welcome your involvement.

The Ford Madox Ford Society normally organises events and publishes Newsletters each year. Future meetings are planned in Glasgow, London, the Netherlands and Germany. The Society also inaugurated a series of Ford Lectures. Speakers have included Alan Judd, Nicholas Delbanco, Zinovy Zinik, A. S. Byatt, Colm Tóibín, and Hermione Lee. To join, please see the website for details; or send your name and address (including an e-mail address if possible), and a cheque made payable to 'The Ford Madox Ford Society', to:

Dr Paul Skinner, 7 Maidstone Street, Victoria Park, Bristol BS3 4SW, UK.
Telephone: 0117 9715008; Fax: 0117 9020294 Email: p.skinner370@btinternet.com

Annual rates: **Sterling:** Individuals: £12 (by standing order; otherwise £15); Concessions £8; **Euros:** €15.00 (by standing order; otherwise €20.00); Concessions €8.50. **US Dollars:** Any category: $25

For further information, either contact Paul Skinner (Treasurer) at the above address, or Sara Haslam (Chair) by e-mail at: s.j.haslam@open.ac.uk
The Society's Website is at: **http://open.ac.uk/Arts/fordmadoxford-society**